Gregory
Heath
Iain

Hathaway House, Books 7–9

Dale Mayer

HATHAWAY HOUSE, BOOKS 7–9
Beverly Dale Mayer
Valley Publishing Ltd.

Copyright © 2019, 2020

This is a work of fiction. Names, characters, places, brands, media, and incidents are either the product of the author's imagination or are used fictitiously. Any resemblance to actual events, locales, or persons, living or dead, is entirely coincidental.

ISBN-13: 978-1-773364-31-5
Print Edition

Books in This Series:

About This Bundle

Welcome to Hathaway House, a heartwarming military romance series from USA TODAY best-selling author Dale Mayer. Here you'll meet a whole new group of friends, along with a few favorite characters from Heroes for Hire. Instead of action, you'll find emotion. Instead of suspense, you'll find healing. Instead of romance, ... oh, wait. ... There is romance—of course!

Welcome to Hathaway House. Rehab Center. Safe Haven. Second chance at life and love.

Gregory

Navy SEAL Gregory Parkins knows he's not so bad off as to need what Hathaway House offers, but he'll do anything to get in. RN Meredith Anderson is there, and Greg loves Meredith. In the time since they split up, his life has been one disaster after another, including the one that ended his career—the career that separated them in the first place.

Meredith was horrified to hear what happened to Gregory. But seeing his file was an even bigger shock. Greg thinks he's basically back to normal, but Meredith knows he has a long way to go. She doesn't know how to tell him, without running the risk of him leaving Hathaway House before his healing can really take place.

But the last thing she wants is for him to walk away from her again. Not if there is any chance that they can find their way back to each other ...

Heath

Overjoyed at his transfer to Hathaway House, Heath Jorgenson is anxious to maximize his potential and to get better from the multiple injuries that sidelined him. But rest is necessary for recovery, and Heath's body won't give him any. Even when he buckles under and accepts the need for drugs, his body rejects them. And all the determination in the world won't matter when your own body is working against you.

Just when he's about to give up, respite comes from the unlikeliest of sources. The sound of the cleaning lady slowly and methodically washing the hall floor outside his room lulls him to sleep and allows him to see some of the progress he's desperate for.

Hailee Cisco is grateful for the part-time job of washing floors at Hathaway House. Sure, it isn't glamorous, but it's honest work, and, along with her other job, it's enough to pay the bills—of which Hailee has many. When Dani, the heart of and the partial owner of Hathaway House, offers Hailee a full-time job, Hailee is delighted at the chance to cut back to just one job.

Until she realizes that her change in hours has an unintended impact on Heath's sleep patterns …

Iain

Getting accepted to Hathaway House is the new start Iain MacLeod has been waiting for. His old VA center has put him on the road to recovery, but he's nowhere near where he wants to be. Much work remains to be done, and Iain is determined to do what's necessary to get back to full power. But he has hit the limit of his current professionals' abilities.

He needs a new team. New eyes. New methods. He can only hope that Hathaway House has what he needs to keep moving forward.

Robin Carruthers works in the veterinary clinic at Hathaway House. When she connects with Iain, she's his biggest cheerleader and enjoys watching him take steps toward greater recovery. Until she realizes that, while Iain is growing in major ways, ... she isn't. When traumas from her past intrude on the present, and Robin is forced to confront issues of her own, she's afraid she and Iain won't find their way back to each other again ...

Gregory

Hathaway House, Book 7

Dale Mayer

Prologue

G REGORY PARKINS STARED at the application in his hand and wondered. He'd had this thing printed off and filled out half a dozen times in the last couple weeks, and every time he had balled it up and threw it away. Hathaway House was just one of many other rehab centers that he had thought of going to. He knew he needed to go to this one though, but it wasn't so much for himself but because of the woman he had left behind.

He wouldn't have had a clue that she was even there if not for a write-up about Hathaway House that had hit the internet and gone viral. Something about Dani and her father and what they had accomplished since they built the center. The article had piqued his interest, and he'd gone looking to see what kind of a rehab center it was. His research had led him to photographs of the staff at the center, and there, sure enough, he'd seen the photo that had sent him into a tailspin.

Meredith, the woman he had left behind the last time he had headed off on a mission. It had already been five years, but he'd never forgotten her. Gregory could only hope that she'd never forgotten him either. But the chances were, she'd moved on, was likely married and had a family by now.

But he didn't know that. Should he reach out to her or just ignore this? *Ignore?* His laugh was hollow, completely devoid of emotions. He knew he couldn't ignore her. Wasn't that evident by the number of times he'd filled out the paper applications only to crumple them up and throw them away? He and Meredith had spent three wonderful weeks together, and he thought he'd found *the one*.

When he had finally told her that he was leaving again, she'd been heartbroken. Desolate. Her brother had died overseas, and she didn't want to deal with the same kind of loss again. Gregory understood, but he'd signed up for the navy as soon as he could, right out of school. He'd been honored to join, and his career had fulfilled him every year since. No way would he walk away at that point.

As soon as he left her, he regretted his decision.

He knew he should have turned around and found a way to make this work, but instead, he'd buried himself in his work and had tried to forget her. And, for a time, he'd managed. But then he had been blown up by an IED. Now, if he went to look for her, he would feel like *he* was second-best, like he had only come back to her because he was no longer whole. No longer fit for the navy, so she was his second choice.

Again.

Just like before.

But for different reasons.

He didn't want that. Nor did he want her to feel that way.

Yet, if she was still at the rehab center and single, they had a chance to work on a whole new level of a relationship. And with so many more problems than they had originally. Even to him, that sounded harsh, but the truth was often harsh. He didn't even know why she would want him back in this state. He'd be offering her less than what he had been before, and yet, he'd walked away from her.

He snorted.

As if he were fully capable of walking away anymore. Because he no longer could. ... Not without crutches, a wheelchair or a prosthetic.

Gregory laid the paperwork off to the side. He had also filled out the online form but hadn't really worked on the last couple questions, determined to at least do that much as he knew Hathaway House could help him physically if nothing else. Maybe he could walk away from Meredith again and not regret it this time. Maybe, just maybe, he could find a whole new life. Sometimes one had to go through the pain to get to the closure, and eventually, to reach a new life at the other end.

He quickly filled out the last few questions online; then his gaze landed on Meredith's picture once more. Not giving himself much chance to rethink anything, he reviewed the online application—the same as the physical paperwork he had filled out a dozen times—and hit Send.

For better or for worse, his application was in.

Chapter 1

MEREDITH ANDERSON STOOD at the reception desk as she watched her colleague flip through the stacks of incoming patients. "How many today?"

"Three," Melissa said. "I can't believe it. We've had such a high turnover lately."

"Yes, but a good high turnover," Meredith replied. "Every patient's gone home in much better shape than they arrived. It's not a case of them leaving because they aren't happy or leaving because they, ... you know, ... passed away," she said. "They're leaving because they can go home in better shape than when they first got here."

"I know," Melissa said, a beautiful smile breaking across her face. "It's awesome. But, at the same time, that's three new people today alone. We need more nurses if this keeps up." She handed off the files for Meredith's review and said, "I think they're all coming in this afternoon."

Meredith shook her head. "And we need more doctors and therapists too, and poor Dani needs at least one full-time assistant. Plus, Stan could use another veterinarian as well. I know he's waiting on Aaron to complete his studies, but maybe they can hire a temporary vet in the meantime?"

"Dani's interviewing now for some position. Not sure for what position but you know she won't hire someone to help her until the rest of us have more help."

"So true. One of us may have to hire someone behind her back," Meredith whispered with a sly grin.

"As if Dani doesn't know everything that's going on here," Melissa said, grinning too. "But there's always the major. He could get that done." Melissa winked.

"Good idea. We should approach him on that matter the next time we see him alone—or at least not with Dani." Meredith sighed. "Back to the work at hand." She looked at the first new patient intake file and noted that this guy was fifty-seven years old, with two damaged hips and both knees gone. She winced. "Ouch, Bob." She flipped to the second new patient's file. This one was a much younger man, yet he had severe back injuries—which was not unusual here. Hathaway House worked miracles with patients thought to be permanently damaged and beyond improvement.

The third new patient's file came with an even greater shock. This one had a missing foot and half his lower leg and a forearm that had a recent surgery.

She found an unopened envelope added to the file. It contained a further typed update from the surgeon, stating how he was cautiously optimistic after the last surgical procedure, would have liked to have had the patient under his care for six more weeks, but that the patient was deter-mined to make this switch in order to take advantage of an empty bed here. The doctor's handwritten note at the bottom added that the patient's mental outlook was just as important as his physical outlook, so the doctor felt good about this patient's decision. Would love to hear from his new surgeons as to Gregory's six-week checkup. *Hmmm.*

Also, this patient was missing a couple ribs and had some steel plates inserted. She whistled when she took a look at the X-ray of the steel plates and then a few photos of his back, both pre-op and post-op. "Wow, I bet you met up with an IED and not in a good way," she whispered. She flipped through the thick file, shaking her head at the damage noted in his records and confirmed by more before and after photos of his chest and his arms and legs included too, then looked at the patient's name.

Gregory Parkins.

Her heart stalled.

She picked up the file, walked around the corner to Dani's office and asked, "Dani, do you know this guy?"

Dani looked up, saw the folder in Meredith's hand and asked, "What's the name?"

"Gregory," she said. "Gregory ... Parkins."

"No. He's one of the new patient intakes, isn't he?" Dani asked, before settling in her chair, leaning back, and instantly recognizing the look on Meredith's face. "What is it?"

"I knew him five years ago," Meredith said, rooted in place.

"Oh my," Dani said, as she bounced to her feet. "Like *knew* him?"

"The love of my life," Meredith said drily. "At least for three glorious weeks."

Dani let out a peal of laughter. "Oh my," she said again. "Well, I'm glad you had those three weeks."

"Yes. ... And no. ... I didn't want him to go back to the navy, but he went anyway." Meredith was near tears and felt so stupid. She thought she had dealt with this. Over and over and over again. She reminded herself that this was five years ago. *Five.* Why couldn't she forget Gregory? It was *only* three weeks of her life. ... She swallowed, shook her head, trying to not cry in front of Dani.

Dani frowned, walked toward her friend. "One of the hardest lessons anybody has to learn when dealing with military men," Dani said, "is to realize that these men go into the navy or the air force or whatever because they have a deep abiding passion for it. They have already made the heart-heavy decision to leave family and friends and loved ones to take on that lifestyle. And not just for one hitch or one tour. It's in their blood or deep in their soul or resident in their very DNA. They have to follow that drive, that pull, or they are never happy themselves. It's almost impossible for them to walk away from the military call."

"Oh, I realized that afterward," Meredith said. "*Immediately* afterward, ... yet I was too late.'

Dani patted her friend on the shoulder. "And," Dani continued, "it takes a special woman to pair up with these men. As a nurse, you are more qualified than most to deal with their war wounds, both physical and mental." She saw the pained look on Meredith's face. "But dealing with the long and constant separations are another matter entirely. Nursing school probably doesn't cover that issue. ... Sit down, Meredith," she said softly, leading her dumbstruck friend into a nearby chair.

"When I couldn't find *any* other man to *even begin* to replace him, I ... I realized that a little bit of him was a whole lot better than none of him."

Dani nodded in understanding. "Long-distance relationships are not for everybody. To only see your partner when they're back home every once in a while ..." She shook her head. "Some women can handle six months of single life at a time, even when married on paper. I'm dealing with being engaged, and yet, separated from my fiancé now while Aaron is in school and not living here at Hathaway House or even in town. And I'm okay with that. For the most part. *For now.* For a couple years of his hard work at school, while I suffer through those couple years of me dealing with the absence of him, then we can be together twenty-four seven for three hundred and sixty-five days of every year thereafter."

Dani laughed. "There are times I don't think I can do this, but ... but you have to understand your own tolerances for this setup. Like wives whose husbands worked on the pipeline or even now work on those Gulf Coast offshore rigs. I hear they are on one week and off the next, or some work two weeks on-site and are off two weeks. That doesn't compare to the military's tours, which are so far away and for much longer stretches of time. But regardless it's a different lifestyle, and both parties have to be okay with it for those relationships to work." Dani sat next to Meredith and rubbed her arm. "But now you get to meet Gregory again."

"Yeah," Meredith said, holding up his thick file folder. "His body has been destroyed."

"Yes," Dani said. "I remember that case. The question really is, can you handle working with him, or would you like me to assign him to somebody else?"

"I'll handle it," she said. "Just like I handle every other patient." Meredith took a deep inhale, letting it out slowly. "But to read what's happened to him ..." Meredith shook her head, words failing her. She looked at Dani and winced. "Why do I feel so guilty? Why am I ... so very mad? Why am I feeling such frustration and helplessness? ... Why am I even telling you all this right after I just said I could handle this?"

"Like what drove Gregory to serve, you have a drive within you that makes you a great nurse. You have empathy for your patients. It may be in overdrive with Gregory, but I understand. Totally. And maybe it's a good thing that you have seen this now," she said, "so that, when you do see him for the first time, you won't be shocked, and you won't let him down by crying." She noted Meredith's trembling lower lip.

"This is so hard," Meredith whispered. "I loved him so very much."

"Well, I'm a great believer in true love lasting forever," she said. "So, if you loved him, maybe that love is still there."

"Maybe. ... Maybe I still do love him even now. Maybe that's why I can't just close that chapter of my life, why I have remembered him at the most random times over these last five years," Meredith said sadly. "But he walked away from me, so what kind of love is that?"

"Was he as devastated as you were to leave you behind?"

Meredith shook her head. "He wasn't glib about it, if that's what you mean."

Dani smiled softly. "He was in pain?"

"I thought so," Meredith whined, wiping the tears in her eyes.

"So the big tough guy was hiding his feelings?"

"Probably. At least I hope so." Meredith hiccupped.

"And you never heard from him again?"

"Not one word."

"Yet you said you still thought about him, didn't you?"

Meredith nodded, her head down.

"So maybe the big tough navy guy thought about you too, over the years."

Meredith shrugged, still not making eye contact with Dani.

Dani paused, giving Meredith a moment to catch her

composure.

Meredith straightened in the chair, sniffled, raised her head to glare at Dani and repeated her question. "But he walked away from me, so what kind of love is that?"

"The kind of love that you can't argue with," Dani said. "Your love doesn't necessarily have to be the same love that anybody else has. Love is individual. It's unique to all of us and to each relationship. The trick to it is making it yours, whatever version it is."

"I wish you'd been around five years ago," Meredith said, slumping in her chair. "Because that would have helped me a lot."

"Wouldn't it?" Dani said. "But I had my own demons to deal with too. You must work your way through this. Just give it time."

"I thought I did. I thought I already had. I survived five years without him. That should have been enough. That should have been plenty. But it wasn't. I thought that was hard. And now I have to get myself together in a handful of hours before he pops into my life again. What I dealt with for five years doesn't begin to compare with *this*." She raised Gregory's heavy file in the air and shook it. "And now I can't let him know how affected I am by his physical condition?" she asked.

"Yes," Dani said. "As a medical professional—and as his friend—the biggest thing is to never show pity. Especially for these men, but all men in general, what with their egos and that protector mindset and the provider image they all seem born with. But particularly when dealing with these military types, wounded or not. Never let Gregory think that you consider him less of a man than he was before."

GREGORY SLOWLY MADE his way up the ramp on crutches, an orderly helping on either side. He knew he was being beyond stubborn, and his latest surgeon would be swearing mad to see this, and Gregory knew he was probably pushing his luck, but it seemed wrong to be wheeled over the threshold to this next stage of his life. He wanted to face it head-on. He also knew that chances were, the crutches weren't the right thing to do. It was too early yet. Too soon after the latest surgery on his arm. Which was iffy yet. Too soon after the added exertion of traveling.

As he stood in the reception area, trembling but vertical, he could see one of the orderlies motioning to somebody just out of his view. Next thing Gregory knew, a wheelchair backed up to him. The orderly leaned down and said, "Sit." Gregory recognized the order inherent in that soft word. Shaky and needing a hand, he managed to sit in the wheelchair, desperately trying not to show how relieved he was to get off his foot and relieving the stress off his back and arm.

A woman stepped from an office nearby and smiled at him. "Welcome to Hathaway House," she said. "I'm Dani, owner and manager."

He smiled and shook her hand. "I'm glad to be here," he said honestly. "I was pretty surprised when I was accepted."

"We accept a lot of people from all walks of life and with all kinds of injuries."

He nodded but didn't say anything.

She motioned to the orderly beside him and said, "Gregory's assigned to 242."

The orderly nodded, and together the three of them proceeded down one of the many hallways off the main reception area, while Dani explained the workings of Hathaway House. It looked pretty normal to Gregory, a hallway with lots of doors, people in wheelchairs and people on crutches. Nothing special at all.

She pointed to a door up ahead and said, "This one's yours." She opened it wide, and he went in.

Pleasantly surprised, he realized he had a private room with a window and almost like a balcony, if he could get out there to enjoy it. A bed and a bath. He nodded and said, "Well, this is nice."

She chuckled. "How to damn with faint praise."

He flushed at that. "Sorry," he said. "I was just thinking that, as I came down the hallway, it seemed very much like every other center I've been in."

The orderly behind him laughed. "There's nothing ordinary about this place," he said. "Yes, it looks like bedroom upon bedroom, and yes, you'll see an awful lot of similar-looking patients. But that's where the resemblance ends."

Dani dropped a stack of paperwork and a tablet on his bed. "Most of that is self-explanatory," she said. "But, because of what you just said, let's take a quick walk around, and you can see what you get to look forward to."

They wheeled him back out into the hallway and down a few more doors and turned a corner, and then everything opened up. He was surprised—again—when they kept on going into a big entertainment section. Even though it was midafternoon or so, people were gathered here, noisily playing pool and various other board games, like checkers and chess, along with maybe poker at one table and other card games at a couple more. He had to smirk when he saw a jigsaw puzzle spread nearby across a bigger table, and already a couple men were seated there, quietly immersed in the activity, ignoring the hoots and hollers from the tables next to them.

But what called to Gregory more was an outdoor deck area, with its railing providing a panoramic view of probably three sides of this property. When they got closer to another glass double-wide doorway, the entrance opened up to a large cafeteria. All the while, the orderly kept on rambling about different things, such as when mealtimes were, ... food always available anytime he was hungry, day or night, so he was to come and get something. ... Coffee always fresh, ... juices and fruits, ... water.

Gregory didn't pay much attention to it. He was keenly taking in the layout with interest. When Dani led him to the railing side so he could look down and see the horses in the fields and the pool beneath him, Gregory found himself truly smiling for the very first time since he had gotten here. "Now this is more like it," he said.

She looked at him. "You like horses?"

"Yep, used to rodeo when I was a kid."

She chuckled, making Gregory's smile widen. "Well," she said, "I do have a couple horses that we use for riding sometimes. So anytime you want to or think you're strong enough to get on the back of one again, those requests go through me. But we'll also need your therapist's and doctor's permissions. Still, it's definitely something you can look forward to," she concluded.

"Thank you. I'd like that," he said sincerely.

"But no rodeoing," she added as if on second thought. "However, I'm happy to take you on a quarter horse and go out in the pastures for an hour or two, as soon as you're strong enough."

"Great. What about the pool?"

"As soon as you're cleared, you get pool time."

"Well then, I'd like to get through the therapists, the doctors and the testing as soon as possible," he said, "because I'm half fish, and I've really, really missed the water."

"Spoken like a true Navy SEAL." The woman had a gentle smile on her lips as she spoke. It made her seem even warmer and more welcoming than before.

Gregory was watching her motion with her left hand as she kept on speaking until she stopped and walked up to a big barreled-chested man, sitting comfortably in a wheelchair—or as comfortable as one could sit with stumps where his legs should be. Both of them were bandaged, and he held something in his beefy arms so small that Gregory couldn't see what it was from where he sat. Dani reached down and scooped it up, then, coming back to him, she resumed talking.

"We have a veterinary clinic below us. They perform the normal functions of an animal clinic. However, they serve a double duty for us as we also run a lot of shelter animals through here, and we have multiple therapy animals in-house too."

At this point, Gregory realized what the man had been holding. It was the tiniest little dog he had ever seen, and Dani held it out to him.

"This is Chickie. Don't ever feed him because he's missing most of his stomach and doesn't digest food very well. But he's got a huge fan following in the place."

Gregory reached out and gently cuddled the tiniest, most broken-looking Chihuahua he'd ever seen in his life. He drew him up to his face to give him a kiss. It's huge eyes and little tongue licked at Gregory's mouth and chin and broke his heart.

"Wow, how many therapy animals are here?" Just then a very large Maine coon cat hopped up into his lap and purred, batting at his hand. He was so surprised to have the cat and Chickie in his arms that he stared in amazement, but his free hand immediately stroked the beautiful gray cat.

"That's Thomas," she said. "Helga's around here too. She's a Newfoundlander dog with three legs. You'll see Thomas there is missing a back leg too."

"Doesn't seem to affect his jumping though," Gregory noted.

"No, if anything, he uses it to get more food and cuddles out of everybody," she said in a dry tone. "A baby llama is over there"—Dani pointed out to a nearby field—"Her name is Lovely. The horse at her side—they're a bonded pair—is called Appie. They were both removed from their owner for abuse. Appie's hooves were almost curled over they were so long, and he was starved. Lovely was in the same condition, but thankfully both of them have recovered quite nicely. We have a filly here too. We also have my horses, which are my own personal mounts, and my home is adjacent to the center." She pointed again as she spoke. "We have more dogs, and we have a goat." She laughed. "If you like animals, you're in the right place."

"I love animals," Gregory said. Chickie, as if understanding, curled up ever-so-slightly into the crook of his elbow and looked to be going to sleep while Thomas curled up on his lap, prepared to stay there. He stared at them in amazement. "Seriously, I love all animals. So can they go back to my room too?"

"They can go with you back to your room, but you have to leave your door open, so they can come and go at will," she answered him. "Independence and freedom for our people and our animals is paramount here. Thomas has litter boxes throughout our center, and Chickie, while carried about mostly, has a special bed up at the front reception area. Racer, another of our therapy animals, has a set of wheels that come off and on, but they allow him to race around the hallways. So leave your door open if you have any animals, so they're never forcibly kept in your room. As soon as that happens, it's a strike against you, and you won't be allowed to keep the animals at all."

"Freedom," he said, "it's so important to everyone."

"So is independence," Dani responded with a smile. "And they have that here in spades. Don't feed *any* of the animals. Most of them are on special diets. We do have a full-time vet downstairs. You'll meet him soon enough," she said. "And, if you ever want to visit some of the animals downstairs, we have an elevator that can get you down there. There are also stairs and a ramp, depending on what skill level you're currently at. You're welcome to go down there at any time. They often have animals that just need some love. From foster animals to rescue animals that are in for surgery from all kinds of incidents, you're welcome to visit."

He could feel his heart expanding with joy just even holding little Chickie against his heart. "Wow," he whispered, lifting the little guy up again and kissing the top of his head. "These guys have got to be one of the biggest blessings to your place."

"Oh? But not the pool?" Dani laughed.

"Well, that's a big help too," Gregory said with a smile. "So, how do I get started?"

"Well, it's four p.m., so you get to start today by going over the paperwork. We have some signatures required." She led the way back to his room. "The tablet has your schedule keyed in, and it also has a list of your medical team members. You've been assigned a primary doctor and three secondary doctors, plus a primary care nurse, a therapist, and half a dozen other people in your team," she said with a wave of her hand. "All of their bios are listed, so you can see who they are and what they specialize in. They each will interview you. Once they are done with that, they will get together and create a special treatment program for you here."

"Okay, thank you."

"No problem. You won't see two of the doctors right now though. I believe one is in town doing surgery, but he'll be back later tonight. So you could have people from your team stopping by your room up to eight p.m. tonight. We do try to prevent people from going to your room after eight on any given night. ... That is, except for the night-shift nurses."

"Right. I think my medical records made it here already, didn't they?"

"They did, indeed." They were already back in his room. "You'll find a robe and some towels, so you can shower whenever you are ready. Your personal belongings are here too." She pointed to his bag. "We don't unpack for our residents. We feel that helps you acclimate quicker if you know where your personal effects are. However, if at any time you need help, please don't hesitate to ask. We especially don't want to overtax you or stress you further after your travels to get here to us today. And dinnertime is around an hour from now."

"But I can eat even though I haven't met the rest of the team?" he asked hopefully.

"Yes, that's correct. Just the more of your team you can see today and tomorrow, the better. Your rehab program can't really start until you've met everybody on your team. So make yourself available as much as you can."

"May I bring food back to my room?" he asked, wondering just how strict the rules here were.

"You are welcome to eat in your room, but I'd suggest doing that in about an hour or so, whether here or in the cafeteria. Now that you've arrived, a notice has gone out to everybody on your team, so you're likely to get inundated by them in the next hour," she replied. "Therefore, I suggest you wait until at least five-thirty p.m. to visit the cafeteria. I'll input a note, saying that you're heading in for food after that time."

"Okay, good."

Dani handed him the paperwork and the tablet and showed him that he had a call button to contact her or the nurses in case of any issues.

And then she was gone.

Chapter 2

EREDITH HATED THE fact that she was nervous. Yet she gave herself some kudos for doing as well as she was, given her seven-hour notice to deal with a pretty major surprise in her life. Shaking that thought off, she set aside her personal issues and donned her professional hat, so to speak. She knew she needed to see Gregory. She was his primary care nurse, she kept reminding herself. She'd stopped by once, but one of his doctors had already been in there with Gregory. She'd immediately taken that as an excuse to walk on by.

But she couldn't put it off for long, regardless of how many other people were on his team. They all needed to see Gregory to do their jobs properly. And, with Gregory's current extensive physical problems, they all had to meet with him immediately to get his rehab started. She sighed. She'd see him, doing her best to be there for him, but she'd rather do it before dinner and get that initial meet-and-greet behind her. Then maybe she could relax some. Put some of her fears aside. She quickly snagged her files and the tablet and walked toward his room. She could feel her heart shaking and her fingers sweating. She hated that. Absolutely hated that.

Dani's words echoed in her mind. *Don't show him pity.*

Meredith definitely wouldn't do that, but she was already having trouble dealing with his battered body because she knew how broken he was; his medical file had been quite comprehensive. When she compared that to how he'd been before and how much pain he'd been through in the interim, her heart broke every time she thought about it because she should have been there with him. There *for* him. But he hadn't let her.

No, that's not true. They hadn't even given themselves the chance to take that step. They hadn't given themselves the chance to even have that kind of an opportunity, to see if they could have had a real relationship. Once he'd said he was going back, she got angry, and that had been it.

She knocked on his door. It was open a couple inches, but she wasn't sure if he was alone.

"Come in."

Taking a deep breath, she pushed open the door and walked in as if nothing was different. She smiled up at him and said, "Hi, welcome to Hathaway House." She had to stop herself from instinctively hugging Gregory.

Gregory looked at her and muttered, "Hi," but he didn't show any signs of recognition.

She tilted her head to the side and introduced herself. "I'm Meredith."

He nodded slowly. "I remember," he said, but his tone was indifferent, like he was talking about the weather or something.

Meredith's heart sank, but she schooled her expression. At least she hoped she did. *So no hugs needed or wanted by this Gregory.* Giving a polite nod, she replied, "Good, I hope the time we had together has been forgotten."

He tilted his head ever-so-slightly. "Meaning?"

She took a deep breath and said, "Just that we were

friends once, and I don't want our prior relationship to hold back your healing."

Instantly, he dropped his gaze, and then he smiled and said, "Thank you for that. I have no intention of letting that happen."

Not quite the response that she wanted but okay. *I'm his primary care nurse.* She returned his smile. "I'll be your primary care nurse, as I was assigned to your medical team. I don't know if you've seen everybody else yet on your team," she said, "but obviously I have a little more history with you than probably the other members."

"You might have known me before," he said with a curt nod, "but the last five years have seen a lot of changes."

"Obviously, and not for the better, and for that I'm sorry," she said sincerely. "Sometimes life can be a bear."

He gave a hard laugh at that. "That's one way to call it."

She motioned toward the door. "It's almost five-thirty, and we have a notation here that you wanted to eat then. Do you want to come with me so I can show you the ropes?"

Gregory hesitated.

Immediately she backed up and said, "Got it. If you need me for anything, just hit the Call button." And, with that, she disappeared.

"OUCH," GREGORY MUTTERED. "Couldn't have made that any worse if I'd tried."

He should have called her back, and he probably still could, but it would be a bit awkward now. He should have just done it, so why hadn't he?

He stared at the tablet in front of him and realized he

could call her back. Once again forcing himself to do what didn't come naturally, he pushed the button and then sat here and waited. When she came around the doorway, a puzzled frown on her face, he just stared at her.

She shook her head, looked at him and asked, "What's up?"

"If you hadn't run away quite so fast," he said, "I could have explained. I would like to go to the cafeteria. … Yes, I would like you to show me the ropes. But I need to make a trip to the washroom first, and that can take me a little time." He watched as a smile bloomed across her face.

"Well then, why don't you do that now? I have to step into my office anyway, and I'll be back in a few minutes." And then, just like the first time, she disappeared.

Gregory took a deep breath and slowly let it out. He just needed to process a little faster. Everything in his life seemed to have slowed down since sustaining his injuries. It's not that he'd had a brain trauma, but he didn't seem to have the lightning-quick mentality that he'd had before. He didn't know if it was something from the initial injury itself or just another side effect due to these big changes in his life's circumstances.

Regardless, she had given him a second chance, and, if he could at least put them on a friendly basis, then she was right. It wouldn't slow down his healing. Meredith had had a lovely personality before—hopefully she still did. It was that in particular which had attracted him to her, her fresh openness to everything and to everyone.

He'd always admired her, her bubbliness, her offer of friendship that had been so welcome back then. He didn't want to lose it now if she was offering it a second time. Whether it would come to anything more, he didn't know, but he didn't want to take the chance of it being here and him being too proud to pick up what was offered. He had a lot of issues, and pride was one of them. So was stubbornness. But the biggest issue right now was to see if anything still remained between them.

She was lovely as always. Inside and out.

Unlike him. He stared down at his broken body and shook his head, then maneuvered himself to the edge of the bed, and, with his crutches, he slowly made his way to the bathroom, albeit very shakily. When he was done, he was done in more ways than one. As much as he wanted to go to the cafeteria under his own steam, he would have to use the wheelchair tonight. Back out of the bathroom again, he slowly made his way to the wheelchair, clumsily collapsing into it.

Catching his breath, he carefully laid the crutches across the bed. One of the biggest challenges was having what he needed available when he wanted it. Like his crutches. He needed to have them on hand, and invariably they were just out of reach. He would see about getting a sling to carry them on the back of his wheelchair or whatever was the current update for that. He wouldn't need either for long. At least not full-time. He had high hopes for a prosthetic and knew that was possible here at Hathaway House.

Finally, he wheeled his way slowly to the doorway of his room and looked around the corner, and there she was, walking toward him.

A smile lit up her face. "Hungry?"

Gregory didn't answer immediately. He sank back into his chair, realizing that, for the first time in a very long time, he might actually get through this. Meaning, reconnecting with her and getting his body as healed as was possible. He smiled back at her. "Absolutely. I'm starved."

With that, he slowly turned the wheelchair down the hallway, hoping she wouldn't offer him any assistance. There were only so many dents to his pride that a man could take. But she walked at his side quite comfortably as he slowly maneuvered his chair. He appreciated her slower pace, so that he wasn't pushed into rushing. He didn't think he could handle that right now. Then again, she was probably used to being around people like him. She dealt with broken men all the time.

Chapter 3

A S FAR AS Meredith was concerned, this was one of the strangest feelings she'd had. It was as if not only had time had disappeared so that they were once again walking together but also had disappeared in a way that neither was acknowledging.

They hadn't left on the best of circumstances, and yet, they were also not meeting in the best of circumstances, and they were both ignoring the great big span of time between those two emotion-filled points. Inside, she didn't quite know what to say or how to act, so, as donning the mantle of professionalism, she gave him information regarding the Hathaway House cafeteria as they walked along. "If ever you're hungry outside of normal mealtimes," she said, "you can contact Dennis at any time. There's also always coffee and muffins and tea and hot water. ... Things like that are available all hours too. And there's a big refrigerator full of juices and dairy products, if you can eat dairy."

"Good to know," he said, his tone noncommittal.

She slid a glance his way, but his gaze busily darted around in all directions but hers. When she noted that, she sighed. "You should be very comfortable here," she said suddenly. "A lot of people are here for similar conditions, a lot of people at various stages of rehab, ... various stages of healing. Most of them have quite the story, but they're all here with one thought in mind, and that's to get better and to go home."

He nodded but didn't add to that.

Sensing the same yawning uncomfortableness between them, Meredith didn't want to walk any faster because he was in his wheelchair. Still, the doors to the cafeteria couldn't come fast enough. "These doors are almost always open. If you see them closed, they are automatic. So, as soon as you put pressure on this"—she stood on the sensor—"they will open."

"That's convenient," he responded.

"When you consider we have people in all states of mobility, it's pretty necessary." When they got to the large area, she said, "There's seating inside and outside. Where would you like to go?"

He pointed to the far back corner, out on the deck. "Depending on how hot the sun is, I wouldn't mind some sunlight," Gregory said. "After being in rehab for so long, that's in short supply. I'm probably completely vitamin D deficient," he joked.

"That sounds good then. Do you need a hand at the cafeteria end?" She tapped his shoulder to point to the other side, and he immediately changed direction.

"I think I can manage. It's similar to what I've had to maneuver through before," he said.

Meredith smiled.

"But hopefully the food here is much better."

She didn't make a comment on that, but she knew that was often a complaint about various centers from the people who transferred in to Hathaway House.

As soon as he got up to the front of the line and saw the food selections, his eyebrows shot up. "Well, it looks good."

He breathed in deeply. "And it smells wonderful."

She got him a tray off the stack and then smiled at Dennis behind the counter. "Dennis, this is Gregory," she said. "He's a new arrival."

"One of several, I hear." Dennis gave a big smile to Gregory and said, "Welcome to Hathaway House. What kind of food do you like?"

"Well, meat and potatoes would work nicely," Gregory joked, smiling up at the big face behind the buffet-style offerings from the kitchen.

Dennis returned his smile. "We've got lots of that here. Chicken, roast beef, fish. ... What's your choice?"

"Roast beef," he said. "Does it come with gravy and mashed potatoes?"

"It certainly can," Dennis said. "Do you want green vegetables of any kind?"

Meredith saw Gregory scrunching his nose, like he was obviously contemplating saying no, so she nudged him gently. "Remember. You're here to heal."

Gregory shot her a half-sulky, half-annoyed look, making Dennis laugh heartily.

"How about a side salad?" Dennis offered.

"Not a whole lot of nutrients in a small side salad," Meredith chipped in, totally unfazed by Gregory's look.

VERY QUICKLY GREGORY had a large plate of food in front of him—and, yes, he had steamed green vegetables too. Meredith came behind him, holding her dinner tray. He could see that she had chicken with steamed vegetables and a salad on the side. As they made their way to the other side of the room, Meredith spoke. "You can have coffee now, or you can come back for it later."

"How busy does it get?" he asked, looking around.

"At the wrong time, very busy." She laughed. "We have hundreds of patients and staff here. It's a pretty busy corner of our world. There are lots and lots of seating, but still, the seats will fill rather quickly if we come at rush time."

He nodded. "It doesn't look too bad right now, so maybe I'll risk the coffee a little bit later." With the tray on his lap, he wheeled outside ever-so-slowly, trying to navigate through the tables full of people. He didn't recognize anybody; they all seemed to be seated with friends or staff. Lots of laughter and conversations floated around him.

He made his way to the far side of the deck, where he found an empty table out in the sun. He sat here for a moment with his face up and then realized that he hadn't really asked her if she was eating with him. He turned around, searching for her, and, not seeing her, his heart sank before he saw that she'd stopped to talk to somebody. And, with a wave goodbye, she looked up, saw him waiting for her, nodded and walked toward him.

His own anxiety had brought on that sense of rejection. She should reject him. It would be the right thing to do. After all, he'd rejected her and everything she stood for.

Then she'd done the same thing to him.

He busied himself moving chairs and getting his wheelchair up to the table and then removed everything from his tray. There was just something about cafeteria-style dining that he hated. He always took his food off the tray, even if it was more work to clean up afterward. It seemed more like a real dining room and not an institutionalized cafeteria if he did it this way.

He sat here, unrolling his cutlery from his cloth napkin, and realized he should have got some water. Glancing back, he noticed it was by the coffee, large glasses poured already. He frowned, considering whether he should make the trip, when Meredith arrived, placed her tray down and said, "I'm going to get water. Do you want a glass?"

"I was just wondering if it was worth making the trip for."

"I'll grab you one," she said and disappeared again.

He should have sat on the other side of the table, so he could look at the people, but he would much rather sit on this side by the railing, where he could look at the acres of green grass and the animals dotting the landscape.

It was a stunning location, plus having the vet down below was beyond interesting. From what Gregory had seen, the animals were a lovely addition, and he knew his own myriad emotions and his heartbeat had calmed considerably when he had met Chickie. And he'd met Thomas the cat but had yet to see Helga—he thought that was her name, but he wasn't sure. A Newfoundlander dog would be hard to miss.

As he stared out across the meadow, waiting for Meredith before he dug in, he saw something black wandering along the fence line. When Meredith returned, giving him a glass of water, he motioned to the fence and said, "Would that be Helga?"

She looked over the rail, nodded and said, "Yes, indeed, it is."

"Do they get to run around on their own like that?"

"They do. The grounds are fenced, so, once they're on that side of it, they can't leave the property, but there are miles of open fields for them to run in and romp around," she admitted. "Still, they're all very attached to their people."

Gregory laughed at that. "I'd love to make a trip down-stairs and see the rest of the clinic."

"You will. You just arrived, so give it time."

"Do I need permission to go down there?"

"No," she said. "Not really. We just need to allow for a little bit of time to make it happen. Overtaxing yourself at the outset is the worst thing you can do. And it happens all too often with new arrivals."

"Right," he said. "I've been told that before."

"Still as stubborn as ever, I presume," she said in a teasing voice.

He shrugged and gave her a lopsided grin. "Guilty as charged."

"Well, your team will work on that. Stubbornness is good sometimes. … It's just not good all the time."

"It's what got me here," he said quietly. "I didn't think I'd ever make it this far."

"Well, I'm glad you were wrong," she said with a gentle smile. "We've seen many success stories here. Some conditions get completely turned around in the end. Just because a doctor says something will happen doesn't mean that's what ends up happening. Miracles can and do happen all the time."

"I'm starting to realize that." Gregory stared at her long enough to make her feel uncomfortable, then looked at his food and said, "If this tastes as good as it looks, that's a miracle right here."

At that, she laughed out loud. "Our kitchen's one of the best. We all enjoy the food here. We are constantly complaining about getting fat."

He looked at her and raised an eyebrow. "I haven't seen anybody fat yet."

"No, it's not exactly something we encourage, among the staff or the patients," she said. "We do tailor an exercise program when needed, and, if we have to, we can curtail a patient's diet, but we try not to."

"Of course. Most of the people who you have here were active servicemen at some time, weren't they?"

"Yes," she said, "but, on occasion, exceptions have been made to accept civilians as well. Dani has a wide network, and sometimes people call in favors to see if they can get friends and family in, and almost always she does what she can to accommodate them."

"How do you stay active?"

"I like to jog," she admitted. "And I spend a fair bit of time in the pool, usually in the evenings though."

"Does it get busy?" Gregory stared around the railing, down at the far side below, where the pool was, but he couldn't quite see it from where he sat.

"No," she replied. "To accommodate the number of people we can have here at any given time, it is a big pool, but not very many people around the place seem to have an interest in it. Or at least not at any one time, a fact I've always appreciated."

"Of course," Gregory agreed as he tackled his dinner with gusto, stopping about one-third of the way through before speaking again. "Wow, this is really good food."

"It is, isn't it?"

He nodded and then, knowing that he was still dancing around their own issues, asked, "How long have you been here?"

"A few years," she said noncommittally.

He nodded. "So what did you do when I left?"

She took her time answering. "I went back to work at

the same job, but I was struggling, and I desperately wanted a change of scenery, something to help me heal."

Just then Dani walked up to them and interrupted the conversation. She smiled down at Gregory. "Looks like you're settling in just fine." She motioned at his very full plate.

"Dennis was very generous," Gregory said, smiling.

"Dennis runs a tight ship. And he's been here since forever and thoroughly enjoys his work and the people."

"It shows," Gregory admitted. "It's nice to see someone who truly enjoys his work."

"Well, the potatoes are real," she said, laughing, "and the desserts are really made from scratch, so, whenever you're done with round one, feel free to go get round two." She winked at Meredith and left.

Chapter 4

MEREDITH APPRECIATED THE break in the conversation. She wasn't ready to get into their history, and she was in no way ready to get into their future. She motioned at his plate. "Are you likely to eat more?"

"I don't know," he said. "Hard to say. ... I've got rather a lot here. But that's not the same thing as dessert."

"Right, dessert is a back-tummy thing."

He chuckled. "Absolutely. Besides, you know I've always had a sweet tooth."

At that, she stopped and then shrugged. "Well, the person I knew a few years ago is different from the person I'm with right now," she said. "Honestly, I don't remember that you had a sweet tooth." Immediately after she said that, the conversation froze again. When somebody called her name from the far side, she looked over to see Stan walking toward her.

"Here comes the vet," she said, "so, if you want to ask any questions about downstairs, this is your opportunity." She looked at Gregory to see the frustration on his face. Good, that's how she felt inside too. She didn't know if he felt that way because they were always being interrupted or because they weren't ready to have a conversation on their history. She didn't really know that she wanted to have that conversation either.

Everything about his reappearance in her life was just so much out of the blue that she found it confusing. He had arrived in her world years ago and had taken up every moment of her time, and then she'd ended up losing him almost as fast. Now she was stuck wondering if she even wanted to open any doors again.

But she needed to be friendly. Professionally speaking. For his sake and her own. It was also very important for his healing, and, although she had a hard time with his decision back then, she was as much to blame as he was, and she supposed they did need to clear the air. Otherwise, it would be hard for both of them to move on.

But it was all happening so fast that she wasn't having any chance to reassess or to consider the implications of his presence now.

He was a good person, ... a really good person, but, if he wasn't for her, she would be fine with that. At least she had been fine all these years in his absence. Professionally, she wanted to make sure he got back on his feet, but personally, she wanted to see him move forward as a happy, healthy, well-adjusted male, entering a new stage of his life.

Then maybe she could too.

She wanted to think that she had nothing to still deal with in regard to their relationship, but she knew that there was. As it stood, she was determined to be as much of a pro as she could possibly be, to do what she needed to do to help him heal and to stay friendly but to not get involved.

Now, if only she could trust her heart to follow through with her plan.

"What's with the serious thoughts?" Stan asked as he arrived, a big smile on his face.

She looked up at him, gave him a half a smile and said,

"Stan, meet Gregory. He's a new arrival."

Gregory reached up to shake his hand only to see that he had something small and rust-colored in his arms. "And who is that?" he asked in delight.

Stan chuckled. "This is Morgan. He's got some long ridiculous pedigree name." Stan smiled. "But this little guy has abandonment issues right now. His mom was supposed to be here to pick him up a couple hours ago, and she got a flat tire and is delayed, so, if he's in his cage, he hollers and whines and breaks my heart. Therefore, I'm wandering around, introducing him to everybody."

Immediately Gregory reached out to pet the little rust-colored Maltese. "He's adorable."

"And not really appropriate to bring around food, what with all his long hair," Stan said. "I came to grab a coffee, and I was going to take him outside for a bit, but then I saw lovely Meredith here, and I know how much she loves puppies."

"I don't think there's anything that wears fur that I don't love," Meredith confessed, pushing her empty plate back and adjusting her chair slightly. "May I hold him?"

Stan gently passed the little dog over, who immediately licked Meredith's neck and chin. She chuckled. "He's lovely."

"If you can hang on to him for a sec, I'll grab a coffee." And, just like that, Stan disappeared.

She laughed and scratched the little guy as he woofed slightly and snuggled in closer. She looked over at Gregory, a big grin on her face. "See? There are huge advantages to being here," she said.

"For patients *and* staff apparently," he said. "I half want to cuddle him myself, but I'm still eating."

"And that's the disadvantage of taking so much food," Meredith teased. "I was done in half the time."

"You just ate too fast," he said. "I, on the other hand, am enjoying my meal."

"That's one way to look at it." She snickered. "I often visit the clinic, spending some time with the foster animals. They all need love."

"It's great that this option is here," Gregory said. "For the patients, it's got to be a huge factor in their healing."

"A lot of the animals need rehabilitation too because they're petrified of people or are a little aggressive," she said. "We integrate them slowly with our human patients, giving these abused animals time to get to know each other and then to get adjusted to being around the people here." She kept on snuggling the dog while she spoke. "Most of our human patients are a whole lot slower at dealing with the animals, so the animals already sense that they're injured and that they're not as dangerous as some two-legged people." She spoke softly, her tone holding no judgment or pity. "And, like this little guy here, he's just lonely and wants to be loved."

"I think that describes the ongoing state for a lot of us," Gregory said in a cryptic remark.

She wondered at it but kept her voice low as she replied simply, "True enough." Meredith avoided his gaze the entire time, instead focusing on wrapping both arms around the puppy and hugging him affectionately. Seeing Stan coming toward her, Meredith stood. "Can you carry him and your coffee, or do you want me to come with you?"

He laughed in delight. "You just want to come and spend time with this little guy."

"That's true." She didn't deny it. Glancing down at

Gregory, Meredith bade him goodbye as she picked up her tray with her free hand, then filled it with her empty dishes and disappeared.

Sure, it was running away. But sometimes taking the closest exit was the smartest thing. Gregory would be here for months, and there would be an awful lot of stress and tough times ahead for him. And for her. They had time to talk. And she wouldn't push it right now.

She smiled at Stan as they took the back door down one level.

Stan looked at her and said, "Something in that exit of yours looked like you were escaping."

"Absolutely," she said. "We had a thing five years ago. I didn't want him to go back into the navy, and he went."

"Ouch," he said. "Yeah, definitely going to be some fun times ahead."

"No," she responded. "Not really. He made a new life for himself, and I've made a new life for myself too."

"I don't believe that. From just those thirty seconds I spent around you two, I can feel the pent-up emotions. You've both got something to say to the other one. Maybe you and Gregory have been putting in the time to make it through the last five years, but circumstances have thrown you back together again," he said with a gentle smile. "There's a reason for that."

"Sure," she said. "It's called closure."

WELL, GREGORY GOT to spend some time with her. Obviously a lot of the people here were her friends, maybe even her family, in a loose way for her.

It had been nice to have her company over dinner. Yet she wouldn't stick around just because of him. Maybe if things had gone differently five years ago, but they hadn't. So, once again, he was the odd man out. A state Gregory should be used to but wasn't.

Ever since he'd walked away from her, he'd found it difficult to adjust. His buddies had joked and had bugged him about it, and he had definitely been a good friend and a well-respected and revered part of their SEALs team, but he had felt differently after he and Meredith broke up. As if he'd left a part of himself behind. A part of himself that he knew he could never reclaim because of their circumstances. Because of their professional passions. Which unfortunately had been at odds with their personal passions.

Now here he was with her, and it was just a little too stunning to believe. He'd been shocked when he'd been accepted, then overjoyed, followed by complete panic. On the other hand, the food at this one-of-a-kind rehab center was delicious, and that filled a gaping appetite within him. Looking at Meredith revived another kind of appetite. But she was out of bounds to him now. By the time he finished eating and pushed his plate back, he was stuffed.

Dennis walked over with a big smirk on his face. "Well?"

"Delicious," Gregory stated. "I was looking forward to trying out your desserts, but I'm too full."

"You can take something back to your room," Dennis said. "The one thing we do ask is that you not waste food. You're welcome to all you can eat, but, if you're not going to eat it, don't take it."

"That makes sense," he said. "Keeps costs down too."

"It's the only way to keep costs down and to keep the quality of the food up. So it's all good. You're welcome to anything and everything you want, just make sure that you try to eat it."

"I've got no problem with that," Gregory said. "I'm going to make my way over there and grab a cup of coffee."

"No need," he said. "I'll grab you one. Do you want cream or sugar?"

"Black," Gregory said with a smirk. "Always pure black and strong."

"I'll see what I can do."

Gregory watched as Dennis walked over, disposed of the tray of dishes on a big shelf that slipped through to the kitchen side and then poured a cup of coffee. As he returned, he said, "I've got fresh cinnamon buns coming out of the oven. They're actually out now. We just iced them. … Do you want one?"

It was beyond him to say no, so he nodded and said, "I'll sit here outside and try to recover from my trip, while I wait for room to show up in my stomach to eat that dessert. I presume tomorrow will start with a bang for me, and I guess this might be the last night I'll enjoy myself for a while." Gregory said it with a laugh, but he knew that some rehab sessions were brutally painful.

Dennis nodded. "I'm glad to see you know what's coming," he said. "It's always so sad when I see somebody new, and they have no clue what to expect. I don't know where they get the idea that a pill will fix them or an hour in a hot tub, like this is some spa or retreat. I guess it's our general drive-through mentality coupled with our dependence on convenience. But that first day of PT will knock any misconceptions right out of them. It usually takes about six weeks before I see them again looking anything but agonized."

"Are the therapists good here?" Gregory hated the note of anxiety in his voice and the nagging little voice in his head that slammed him for being more focused on Meredith than on the level of care Gregory might find here. Not that he hadn't checked out some credentials here. But he would admit his main focus had been elsewhere. Besides, as far as his previous rehab center had been concerned, Gregory didn't need to come here at all. But he had disagreed because he certainly wasn't back to fit form, even for his new reality, and what Gregory wanted was to be as strong and as capable as he could be. In the present, given these new circumstances for him.

"They're very good," Dennis said, turning around to face him. "They'll get you into shape, but you may not like their methods."

"I've been beaten up by a lot of therapists before," he replied with a crooked grin. "I'm hoping for a helping hand that will unlock the secrets to getting my strength back. I have so many injuries that my body is still in shock."

Dennis pondered that for a while before speaking. "Then you need to cut back on the meat and triple your vegetable intake to load up your body with the most nutrients possible from a variety of colorful foods that are easily digestible, saving your body's energy for the more important healing matters," he suggested. "Also the carbs can be eased back into your body slowly. After all, your body has enough healing to deal with right now. It needs its energy to be directed to that healing. Yes, these carbs are good for almost instant energy, but, if you flood your system with too much insulin, it'll make you tired, and your body won't give you the best performance of your life."

At that, Gregory laughed. "Well, I certainly agree with

some of that. I'm guessing you have a dietitian on staff, right?"

Dennis nodded. "I think we've got every medical-related profession covered in here. As soon as you think there's a problem in any one direction, make sure you talk to somebody. Somebody here can give you a hand. Be right back." Dennis returned a few moments later with a huge cinnamon bun slathered in cream cheese icing. Handing him a fork, he spoke, "It's still pretty hot. You might want to use that." He disappeared into the crowd again.

Gregory looked around to see the groups at the various tables had shifted and reformed with new groups, new people and new conversations. Several were out on the deck with him as the sun was still high. It was hot out here, but he didn't want to go inside yet. He had felt smothered in the hospital environment. And not much less so in his previous rehab location. He still craved fresh air. But he also felt the fatigue, probably from the large dinner as Dennis had mentioned.

Not to mention the excitement and the stress of traveling and knowing he would meet Meredith again. And then, of course, meeting her, actually having dinner with her, and yet, searching for that same connection that they'd shared before, and not finding it had been draining. He could handle the physical stressors much easier than the emotional ones.

He didn't know if their connection was gone because too much time had passed or because she had deliberately detached from him. He wouldn't blame her if she had.

He'd had such high hopes when he'd realized he was coming here, and, right now, it looked like all of them were dashed.

Chapter 5

MEREDITH DIDN'T TRY to avoid Gregory for the next few days, but she did not go out of her way to stop in and say hi either. She did her job and carried on.

As it was, the staffing was a little challenging as one of the nurses went down sick, and another one was off on holiday, so routines got shuffled around, and job duties got shuffled around with them. On Gregory's third day here, she ended up going to his room, back on his schedule as his day nurse. As she walked into his room, he looked up and smiled in surprise.

"Hey, I haven't seen you in a while. Figured maybe you were avoiding me."

"Of course not," she said with a frown. "I've got no reason to. It's just been crazy busy."

He nodded, but it was a small nod. His gaze seemed searching.

She smiled reassuringly at him. "One of the nurses is on holiday, and one's sick, so we all have to pitch in to cover these absences. We don't have enough staff as it is, but Dani is interviewing. It takes time to find qualified people," she explained. Then wondered if giving that many details made her seem defensive. She mentally shook her head. *You're his primary care nurse.*

He settled back ever-so-slightly.

"How are you settling in?" she asked.

"Good," he said. "It's been pretty easy so far. … Almost like a holiday here." He had a big grin on his face.

She smirked. "Well, it is, until it isn't."

He grimaced at that. "I hear you, but, so far, there's been nothing I haven't handled easily."

"But you're still in the testing stage, aren't you?"

"Yes," he said, "it seems like it. Every day they run me through another gamut of tests, whether its blood work, lab work, physio work, mental work, emotional work or something else." He shook his head in disgust.

She laughed at that. "Well, what we ultimately want, when you get out of here, is a whole, healthy, strong person, and, if you're lacking development in any of those areas," she said, "then you're in trouble all around."

"I get the theory of that, but waiting to get started isn't much fun."

"Gotcha." She finished checking him over. "Maybe this afternoon you will begin the real work."

"I hope so. I'm starting to feel a little guilty even being here and taking up a bed as I'm not as bad as the rest of these guys."

"You mean, the ones who wince and groan as they get up and get a cup of coffee and head back at a turtle's pace and walk like they're old men?" she asked, withholding her grin.

"Exactly, then I find out some of them have been here for a long time, and I realize how good I'm actually doing."

"Well, I wouldn't worry about it," she said. "Once you start your PT, you might find you're a little more related to those older-looking men than you think."

He shook his head. "Not likely. I've already done lots of

months of rehab."

She didn't say anything at that, just smiled gently. "Let's hope in a couple days you feel the same way."

Meredith knew that Gregory was following the pattern of a lot of the young men who came into this rehab center; coming in strong, a little bit arrogant and some of them cocky, they thought they could handle whatever was thrown at them. Once the staff started them on their custom programs, they broke down very quickly. She didn't want to see Gregory at that stage, but she also knew how important it was for the therapists to get rid of that ego and to start digging in deep and finding out who the patients were and what they really wanted in their life and from their bodies.

Everyone needed to find out whether Gregory was prepared to work for the intended results or not.

Physiotherapy wasn't for sissies, and, when they had multiple injuries—like Gregory, who'd come to a certain point and hadn't progressed further—then it was time for a change, and, in this case, it would be a big disruptive change because nobody here did things quite the same way as they did at other rehab places.

She'd heard it time and time again. It started as a holiday but then almost turned into a prison camp by the time they got started because the rehab work required was intense and a lot was demanded of the patients. Now the good news was that, on the other end all that hard work, it paid off in spades, and the patients were overjoyed to be who they became.

The journey was not easy—or fast—nor was it something that they could take lightly. A lot of soul-searching went on. A lot of getting to the bottom of what was holding them back. They did have a psychologist on staff, and every patient had sessions with him. It was very important to make sure that the mental and emotional state of these patients was as healthy as their physical state, and, most of the time, these internal states were often in worse shape.

Some of these men had PTSD, and some had survived incredible traumas and losses: friends dying in front of them, commanders walking away, and sometimes whole teams being blown up, their lives with them.

She hadn't attended any of those sessions because, of course, they were personal and private for the patients, but she'd heard from some of the men afterward about just how eye-opening those sessions were. But only after the men had reached a turning point, where they would actually discuss what they'd been through. And some of the men took months and months and months to get to that point. Some of them were much more open, in touch with who they were before they got here.

But she didn't think Gregory would fit that category. But then, she could be wrong. It had been five years. Five very long years, and she, for one, had changed a lot. But now that she looked at him, she wondered if the changes she had gone through were all that good or if she'd changed all that much. She hadn't been stressed physically as much as he had; she hadn't been as challenged emotionally as he had; she hadn't even had to walk away from her career as he had. And, in many ways, she wondered if she'd changed at all.

GREGORY WATCHED HER leave with a thoughtful expression on his face. He had worried that she was avoiding him. That wasn't what he wanted between them; to at least be friends would be nice. But, he had to admit, to be more than that would be better.

A hard knock came on the door, and he looked up to see Shane—his assigned therapist. He came into Gregory's room, rubbing his hands together, gleefully saying, "You ready?"

Gregory nodded. "I am."

"Well, you'll know for sure pretty soon," Shane said. He was a huge, six foot four, strappingly muscled man, but it was lean muscle, and he always carried a bright cheerfulness that Gregory envied.

Shane motioned at the wheelchair and said, "Come on in that. We'll head over to the first room."

"Why the wheelchair?" Gregory asked. He'd been to a lot of different therapy sessions, and he highly doubted it would be anything much. He'd done very well before, and his former therapists had always been positive and cheerful, giving Gregory lots of praise. He didn't see how it would be any different here. Matter of fact, he was back to feeling guilty that he was even wasting their time.

Shane looked at him and said, "Trust me. The wheelchair might look easy now, but you'll want it when you come back."

Frowning at that and hoping Shane was wrong, Gregory made his way to the wheelchair, sat down and slowly wheeled his way behind Shane.

Shane walked in a steady line to one of the rooms Gregory had been in earlier for some testing. Shane motioned to him. "Wheel over to the side and stand up, then hop over here to this mat," he said.

"What are we starting with?" Gregory asked as he followed the instructions.

Once he sat on the mat, Shane said, "We'll start with floor work, and I'm telling you right now, anytime that we get to a point where you need to stop, you must say so. There's no shame in telling me to stop. I'm the only one who will hear you say it. When we hit a pain level of six out of ten, I want to hear about it. You'll do your body more harm than good if you overstress it."

Gregory just waved his hand at him. "I'll be fine. What do you want me to do?"

Shane sighed gently, as if he had seen and heard that many, many times, but then he launched into a three-hour session that started off easy. But, by the time he was done, Gregory lay on the mat on his back, his body completely filmed in sweat, visible tremors racking up and down his spine.

He didn't know what had just happened, but it was something completely different than what he had expected. And he realized just how useless all his previous therapy sessions had been.

Maybe his previous therapists had given him too much positive reinforcement and hadn't bothered to make him work. But no way would Shane let Gregory off the hook on anything. Shane wanted results, and, according to him, he would get them. It made things very difficult for Gregory when he lay here in shock on the floor, wanting to cry like a baby.

Shane squatted beside him. "How are you doing?"

"I'm fine," he gasped out.

"Well, you're not fine," Shane said. "And you didn't tell me to stop either."

Gregory winced at that.

Shane saw that and nodded. "You can't let your pride or

your ego come between you and a therapy session," he said. "That's never a good thing."

"How would I know?" he asked.

"Know what? That I would put you through the paces? Well, if you must know, I took it easy on you today," he said. "I was watching to see at what point you would say something and realized you just wouldn't. Because, for you, it's still all about saving face and still all about being the best, and it's still all about giving a presentation instead of actually being true and honest to the broken body that you're currently living with. And you have to get rid of all that.

"If you want to get back to where you were, if you want to be that strong, capable, vibrant man that you see yourself as in your head, then you must let go of all that facade. Now you've got about forty-five minutes until dinnertime. I suggest you head back to your room and get a shower, and we'll start again tomorrow." He got up, seemingly unconcerned, and walked over to make some notes on his tablet.

Gregory lay on the floor, his body so damn weak that he doubted he could make it to his wheelchair, but he'd be damned if he'd ask for help. He rolled over, got up and swayed.

Instantly Shane was there, gripping his forearm. "Remember that thing about pride?" he scolded.

And Gregory, for once, almost felt shame. "Now that you're here," he gasped, "can you get me to my wheelchair?"

"The easiest way is to bring the wheelchair to you," Shane replied. He shifted his position, reached out, snagged it, twirled it around and brought it up right behind Gregory so he could sit down.

Once he'd collapsed, Gregory slowly turned his wheelchair toward the door without saying another word to Shane and headed out.

With all his training, Gregory had always expected to be the best, and somehow he thought he was still. Somehow he thought he had been giving his all and doing everything exactly as he needed to.

Yet always a little bit of him wondered if he had been fooling himself, but he had ignored that nudging.

Slowly, moving as carefully as he could, he made his way to his room, and, as soon as he had the door closed, he leaned back, closed his eyes and cried.

Chapter 6

MEREDITH CAME AROUND the corner to see Gregory on his way to his bedroom … and caught sight of his face. He'd found out the reality of being here. She knew Gregory had Shane on his team. Shane was many, many things, and some would say he was a taskmaster, but he was also a good guy, and he wouldn't push Gregory farther than he had to go, but Shane would push Gregory right up to that level. And obviously, Gregory's introduction was a little more than he'd expected.

She walked a few steps, wondering if she should knock on his door—when she heard him sob. Immediately her hand went to her mouth, and her heart broke. She hustled away before anybody else realized what was going on and then ran to sit in the privacy of her on-site living quarters, wondering what she should do.

Her shift had ended an hour ago. She had planned to go for an early dinner, but realizing he was as hurt as he was, … should she check in on him? Would he even answer her? Would he answer anybody today?

Obviously today had been hard—physically and mentally and emotionally—and, if he knew he wasn't alone, maybe it would help. Then again, right now he probably only wanted to be alone. Still warring with herself, she quickly changed, checked the time and realized he'd had a good half hour to shower and potentially pull himself together again. Maybe she'd go by his room again and just knock.

Walking past his room, she stopped, hesitated, then rapped hard. There was no answer. She frowned because she'd seen him go inside. It was possible he'd already headed to dinner; the only other option was he was possibly asleep. She knocked again and thought she heard something on the other side.

"Gregory, it's Meredith." She waited and then said in a more authoritative voice, "Let me in."

"The door is unlocked," he said, bristling.

She reached for the handle to check, and it was, indeed, unlocked. She opened the door. The patient's room doors all had locks, but the medical staff had keys if they needed to open any. It was a patient's right to have privacy, but it wasn't right to lock everybody out, not in a medical facility like this one.

She stepped inside and took one look at him. He sat on his bed, just a towel around his waist, his body stiff, as if putting on a casual, *Hey, I'm fine, good enough* show. Meredith may have been fooled if she hadn't heard him crying earlier.

"I was wondering if you felt up for dinner." She saw the whisper of pain across his face. "I know you had your first session today with Shane. He's a really good guy," she said, knowing she was rambling on but unable to stop herself. "And he's fair, but he's also tough. I know he would have worked you hard today. So, if you want to crash on your bed, maybe I can bring you something." He looked at her, and she could see him warring with the idea. "Remember. It's not a weakness to accept help," she said gently. She watched as his shoulders sagged, and then his chest deflated.

"Honestly," he finally spoke, "I'm not sure I could make it out there."

Meredith nodded briskly, her compassionate understanding written all over her face. "What would you like for dinner?"

"I'm not … I'm not even hungry."

"And that's one of the reasons I wanted to check on you. To get you some food. You need to keep fueling that body. You need good healthy food, and you need to keep those nutrients flowing to heal properly," she said.

"In that case, just bring me whatever you think I need." He waved a hand at her. "I'm so damn tired, I don't think I can even get pants on."

Meredith walked over to his chest of drawers and pulled open the top one. "How about a pair of boxers or just a pair of sleep pants?" She held them both up as she walked over to him. He frowned at them and chose the boxers.

She gave him the boxers, folded the others and laid them on the small table. "If you want to put these pants on, then fine, you can do that too," she said. "If they're still here when I come back, I'll put them back in the drawer." With that, Meredith turned and headed to the door.

"Meredith …"

She spun and looked at him, raising an eyebrow. "Yes, Gregory. What's up?"

He hesitated, and she could see how hard this was for him. Finally, he managed to say, "Thanks."

She beamed at him and quickly left his room. It was either that or cry. To see a strong man come to the point of crying was very heartbreaking, but it was also heartwarming. He had a long way to go, but it sounded like he was on his way. And that was worth so much.

She didn't know who he was right now, but she liked the man she saw. Maybe even more than the Gregory she'd met five years ago. This one had something about him that just endeared him to her. It wasn't like she collected lame ducks or broken bits of humanity, but to see the strength and to see that humanity inside Gregory now come out in full force? ... Well, it was worth everything to her.

KNOWING HIS ENERGY was quickly fading, Gregory managed to get the boxers on and laid the towel over the small table. Standing up just long enough to pull down the bedcovers, he collapsed on the bed, already tilted upward. That way he could rest—or eat—in a seated position, and he closed his eyes.

Meredith's offer had come at a perfect time. Gregory was grateful he didn't have to go to the cafeteria for dinner. He was also a little worried about her seeing him like this, but it was obvious that she had seen how he felt regardless, so his act of looking strong and not in crappy shape hadn't worked. He hadn't really expected to have a real hope for a relationship with her, but there was always a chance. Still ... it wasn't looking so good to date.

He reached for the sleep pants, struggled to get them on, and then, panting, he collapsed back on the bed. He knew it would take time for his heart rate to calm down and for his sense of complete exhaustion to disappear.

It was early, ... only like five-thirty p.m., but hopefully, with any luck, he'd feel better after dinner. Right now he knew he wasn't leaving his bed for the rest of the evening. He'd been warned, but he'd just been so sure that he knew what to expect ...

Something that gave him both hope and trepidation was the thought that tomorrow was another day, and he would face Shane again. Now the good news was that he knew—if he could keep up with Shane's onslaught of physical rehab— that, in six weeks, Gregory would be incredibly improved. Getting to that point though ... was tenuous at best.

Gregory had never turned his back on a challenge before.

He just hadn't thought he would face this kind of challenge. He'd thought this would be minor.

Maybe it had been his way of dealing with the fact that so little was going on in his world that he thought this would be nothing, when, in truth, this was incredible. He dozed off, and then woke up when he heard someone call him. He opened his eyes to see Meredith handing something to him.

"You ready for food?"

"Sure," he murmured, shifting. "Sorry. I'm exhausted."

"I know," she said. "I can hear it in your voice. Do you want help to sit up?"

He shook his head. "I'm trying to figure out how these beds work."

"This is one of the new ones, so everything is adjustable." She quickly showed him the remote and how it worked. With a couple adjustments, he sat almost upright. She brought the small table closer to the side of the bed and placed his tray on it.

As he looked around, she had also brought in a small trolley, and a ton of food was there. "Are you eating too?"

She hesitated and then asked, "Is that okay?"

"Of course," he said. "I'm delighted to have the company."

"I didn't want you to eat alone," she said. "But if you'd

prefer to or to eat later, that's fine."

"Please," he said, "join me." He turned to look at the tray in front of him. "Wow, how did you know that I absolutely love meat pies?"

"I didn't know, but it is one of Dennis's favorite dishes, and he does an incredible job on these. So, when I saw them, I figured you might like one."

"They're homemade?"

"Well, if you're asking if Dennis made them, yes, he did."

Gregory bent to cut into the crust and watched as the steam rose from the center. "You're really lucky to have him."

"Absolutely," Meredith said. "But, at the same time, I think he loves being here. So, if anything, it's a mutual admiration."

He chuckled at that. "There's a lot worse things in life." The trolley was in front of her, like a table. "Can you eat like that?" he asked.

"I was going to put the tray on my lap," she said as she moved her tray off the trolley and sat down on the visitor's chair with her legs lifted on the balls of her feet.

"As long as you're comfortable," he said.

"I've never been better. Now eat."

"I notice an awful lot of green on my plate," he groaned, studying the food choices.

"Yes, you need the vegetables."

"It'll take weeks of inhaling vegetables to notice a difference in my body."

"Were you planning on doing anything in those weeks other than to be here and to try to heal?"

He stopped, frowned, looked at her and said, "Okay,

that was mean."

She laughed. "Not really. If you don't give your body what it needs, it has to take it from your stores. And you don't have any stores to give it, so buck up, and start eating properly."

"But I like my potatoes," he complained.

"And you have a couple," she said, "but you have a lot more veggies. And, when you're done with all those veggies, I brought you a salad."

He stared at her in horror.

She laughed out loud. "But you like salad."

"But I'd rather have the meat pies," he said.

"We're back to the fact that you told me to get whatever you need, so I did."

He looked at her plate and said, "You have mostly green."

"I love vegetables," she said with a smile. "I know how important they are for me too."

"And what if I don't quite like vegetables so much?" He stabbed a fork into the broccoli and picked up a piece, studied it for a long moment, then popped it into his mouth. He lifted his eyebrows. "Okay, so this broccoli is really good."

"All broccoli is really good," she corrected.

He shook his head but found himself craving the vegetables, and, before long, they were all gone. He stared at his empty plate in amazement. "Dennis has a swift hand with vegetables too," he said.

"Absolutely," she said. "And, if you eat the salad and everything else, you get dessert."

"What if, instead of dessert, I want another meat pie?" he asked craftily.

"If you think you can still eat it, then you can have it." She laughed. "I'll cheerfully go down and get it for you. We just ask that, whatever you take, you eat."

"And that's a good rule. I wish the entire world would follow it. I've seen too many starving children the world over, and yet, back here, we're so overfed that we're dumping food on a daily basis. It's criminal!"

"Not until they change the laws, it isn't." She sighed. "But it's one of the things that we're strict about here. In order to keep the food quality up, we have to keep the costs down, and that means less waste." She laughed suddenly. "Now I sound like Dennis."

"Well, those meat pies are never going to waste." But suddenly Gregory came to the bottom of his salad bowl and realized he was really stuffed. "I don't think I can even eat another meat pie, and that just breaks my heart."

"If you want, I can ask him to save you one for lunch tomorrow."

He turned and looked at her in surprise. "Would he do that?" he asked hopefully.

She laughed. "He has no problem doing that."

"If there are any left …"

She nodded. "When I go get us coffee, I'll ask him. Doesn't mean there are many left, but, if there are, I'm sure he'd be happy to put away a couple for you."

Gregory smiled. "And I would love that. Thank you."

He watched as she ate at a much slower pace than him. She still had a whole bowl of salad to get through. But she worked away, quite happily enjoying every bite. That had been one of the things he'd always remembered about her. She'd lived life to the fullest, enjoying everything. Whether it was a glass of water, the sunshine, or the sound of a bird, it had always amazed him. He'd been much more of a go-getter type, while she had been happy to sit and relax.

Gregory had never really found a way to relax back then, but, ever since his hospitalization, he'd had more than enough time to sit still and to think about life. He hadn't yet found the art of enjoying stillness, but even here—having her eat her meal like she was—it's like she didn't want to be anywhere else. And he couldn't be happier with that thought.

Chapter 7

MEREDITH WOKE UP the next morning feeling a little sick. Maybe she was just tired; maybe she caught the flu that was going around. Or maybe it was the excitement of finally having Gregory here. So much worrying, so much waiting, and now he was here. She had a flashback of his first couple days, and they had survived. Some sort of camaraderie existed between them. Not exactly a friendship—she felt more professional toward him than anything—but, on the inside, she still had that little bit of anxiety. She wasn't sure what that meant.

He'd looked so beaten and so sore last night that she couldn't help but be nice. But she in no way flattered herself to think that they had a friendship. A lot of relationships came and went here, along with the patients; however, she knew of at least a half-dozen relationships that had stuck solid.

But that didn't mean that anything was here between her and Gregory at this point. In fact, as she got up and had her shower, she couldn't think of anything that was between them at all. Still, she quickly dressed and headed out for breakfast and then to work.

As she walked into her office, she found stacks of folders waiting for her. She looked at an update note and realized several patients had had bad nights, and the night nurse had been backed up. As Meredith read through the names, she winced to see Gregory's name there as well.

She checked through to see who she would have to spend a little bit more time watching over, and only three of those who'd had night disturbances made that list. She wasn't alone on day shift either, which was a good thing. As she glanced at the stack of papers beside her, she groaned. They kept both paper files and digital files, and everything had to correlate and be updated. It was the only way to be assured that things were accurate. And some things, like scans, just didn't have the same visual on an iPad as they did when up on the backlit screens. She grabbed her list and started her rounds. She left Gregory for last, and, as she walked in, she found him still sleeping.

She frowned, realizing how much of a bad night he'd had to still be sleeping at nine-thirty a.m. She stepped out into the hallway and sent a note to his team, letting them know his bad night had resulted in a late morning, and he still wasn't moving.

Back in her office, she worked on the stack of files because now she also had her own to update. By the time she looked up again, it was already eleven a.m. She quickly grabbed her tablet and headed to check on Gregory again. As she knocked on the door and heard his muffled voice, she stepped in, looked at him and smiled. "Hey, sleepyhead."

He lifted blurry eyes and stared at her. "What time is it?"

"It's eleven am."

Gregory stared at her in shock; then, groaning loudly, he rolled over but didn't get out of bed.

"I hear you had a bad night," she said, using her most professional voice. She walked over and quickly took his temperature and blood pressure. His blood pressure was definitely up, but his temperature was fine. She looked at him and asked, "Have you been up yet?"

He shook his head. "No, not yet. Not looking forward to it either."

"Do you want me to stay here in case you have trouble?" He shot her a look. She smiled but stood firm. "You have to tell me to leave, if that's what that look was supposed to be."

"Yes," he said, "you can leave."

She frowned. "When you're a little more awake, take a look at what you missed this morning. Also potentially head for an early lunch so that you're a little more prepared for the PT this afternoon."

"I don't think I'm going to physio this afternoon," he said. He got up, grabbed one crutch and walked past her slowly, like an old man, bent over slightly. His gait was getting better as he made it to the bathroom. He was still hobbling but looked a lot less like he was crippled by the time he made it there.

She stood and waited.

When he stepped out, he looked at her and frowned.

"Yes, I'm still here," she said. "This is still my job."

At that, he didn't say anything but glanced at the floor. He made his way back to the bed and sagged. "I'm not going anywhere today," he said.

"Not even for food?"

"Not at this moment," he said. "Maybe later. I think I'll go back to sleep." He stretched out, rolled over and dropped his head on the pillow, groaning with each move.

Yet she knew he was holding back. She walked back outside his room, closed the door behind her, made several more notations and then sent a note to Shane, Gregory's physiotherapist. By the time she was back to her office and working again, she looked up to see Shane standing there, his arms crossed over his chest. "Is he sleeping again?"

"I don't know. Probably," she said. "I know he was pretty worn out late yesterday into this morning."

"I know," he said, taking a seat in her office. "I was still testing him yesterday, but I did put him through quite a few paces. I also watched to see when it was too much."

"I have a note here from Anna, who was on overnight, and apparently it was a lot too much. She says he woke up with pretty rough cramps and lots of abdominal pain." Meredith handed him the notes.

Shane looked them over, mentally ticked them off, nodded and said, "I'll take a look at him now." He got up.

As he walked from her office, she called out, "Don't forget. We might need to bring in one of his doctors on this too."

"I'm on it," Shane replied from the distance.

She could hear his footsteps disappearing. She worried about Gregory for a few moments and then realized that it wasn't her job. Not this part at least. He had a medical team, and they were a damn good team. They would take care of him in each of their specialized and distinctive practices, as she would take care of all her patients as their nurse. Another one from last night, who had had a bad time of it, she'd already visited twice, but he hadn't been doing so well either.

She grabbed her tablet and headed back to see him, sitting up in bed, looking a whole lot older than she'd ever seen him before. "Wow, Solson, you don't look too good," she said.

"Don't feel too good either," he replied. "I think I must have picked up the flu or something."

"Do you want me to bring you some food?" she asked.

He frowned, thought about it and then said, "No, I was thinking that maybe fresh air would help."

"And it might," she said encouragingly. "Do you want me to help you out on the cafeteria deck? Maybe snag a coffee on the way past?"

He looked at her, pathetically grateful. "If you wouldn't mind, that would help a lot."

She helped him into the wheelchair.

Solson nodded. "I was hoping there might be a shady spot where I can get some fresh air, maybe sitting closer to the doors on the deck? Have a juice or something for my stomach?"

"Well, let's go take a look," she said. "Did you have anything different last night? Any change in medication I don't know about?"

"No," he said, "it's such a weird thing. I had cramps, and my head just boomed, and my back started to hurt."

"Interesting," she said, "and it came on suddenly?"

"Yes, very," he said. "It didn't make a whole lot of sense. But I am feeling a bit better now that I am moving."

"Did you end up with vomiting or diarrhea?"

"Both," he said. "I wondered if it was maybe food poisoning." He stopped, frowned and said, "I did have some cookies last night."

"What kind of cookies?"

"They were butter cookies, but I've had them for a long time," he said. "I just woke up and got the munchies."

"Normally cookies dry out, but they don't cause that kind of an upset."

He gave her a sheepish look. "Well, I did eat the pack."

She stopped for a moment, walked around so she could look him in the face and asked, "You ate the whole pack of cookies? Was it full?"

He grinned and nodded. "I do have a sweet tooth."

"Well, that might make you have an upset stomach, with both vomiting and diarrhea," she said. "I'm scared to ask how many cookies there were."

He shrugged and mumbled something.

She wasn't sure what she heard, so she bent lower and repeated her question.

"Two dozen," he said, "maybe, give or take a few."

She tried to hold back her laughter, but there was no way. With her hand clapped over her mouth, she leaned against the wall and laughed and laughed. By the time she was done, he was grinning like a crazy man too.

"You don't do that enough," he said. "You should."

She smiled, shook her head and said, "I haven't heard anything that funny in a while. I mean, I hate to say that karma is right there, ready to bite you in the butt, however ..."

He nodded. "That's what I figured. I'm not sure it's all out yet either."

"Well, if it came out both ends, obviously your stomach revolted. So chances are something very light for lunch is about all you'll put down there today."

"That's what I was thinking. I thought I'd start with a glass of milk."

She grinned at that thought. "You do that." She led him gently through the cafeteria that wasn't busy yet and found him a spot outside where he was mostly in the shade, but he could shift if he needed to. "How does this look?"

"It looks good," he said. "I'll just sit here for a bit."

"Good, and I'll go get your milk," she said. Not giving him a chance to argue, she walked over to the large cooler and pulled out a carton of milk and brought it back for him. "Here you go," she said. "Now remember. Just take it easy at lunchtime. I know you always have a big appetite, but your stomach's really had a number done on it this time."

"Yeah," he said. "I guess I'm not a kid anymore."

"When you cross the thirty mark," she said, "your stomach isn't a kid anymore."

He chuckled, grinned and said, "Thanks, Meredith."

She patted his shoulder gently. "I'll check on you later." She walked back toward her office as a few more people came into the cafeteria. She took a side route and quickly walked down the line to see what there was for lunch. Apparently it was Mexican today. She smiled as she looked at the tacos, burritos, tortillas and guacamole, then said, "Dennis, this looks divine."

"Well, if it's so divine," he called out from the other side of the counter, where he was still loading up the sour cream and chives, "why are you going in the wrong direction?"

She grinned. "Because it's not time for my lunch yet," she said. "I'll be back in a little bit."

When she returned to her office, she quickly updated Solson's file. Most of the time he did well. But obviously a couple dozen butter cookies weren't what his stomach wanted last night. With those notes updated, she looked up to see one of the other nurses coming in. Rene plunked herself down and looked at Meredith, blew a wisp of hair off her forehead and said, "Wow, it's busy today."

"Apparently it's been busy for a while," she said, motioning at the stack of folders. "These here on the right side are still left over from the night shift." She pointed them out. "The rest are ours from today."

"I hear you," Rene said. "Most of the notes we can update as we go, but, when it comes to some of the other staff, we have to do the paperwork."

"There's always paperwork," Meredith said calmly. "Checks and balances. It's always about checks and balances."

"Right." Rene dropped her tablet on the table beside her and said, "I'll grab some food first, then get started on my own paperwork." She stopped, looking at Meredith, and asked, "Do you want to come?"

Meredith thought about it for a moment and then nodded. "Why not?" she said. "It's Mexican today too," she said to Rene.

"Wow," she said. "Let's go."

Laughing, the two women headed off.

GREGORY LAY ON his bed, exhausted. His muscles throbbed, and his body felt like he'd been tossed out into heavy uncharted seas and fought a twenty-mile swim against the tide before being smashed on the rocks and rescued just before he drowned. He'd already had a conversation with Shane, but Gregory wasn't at all sure that they were on the same wavelength. Gregory had overdone it and blamed himself, but he also blamed Shane for letting him.

"Well, it's an interesting reaction," Shane had said. "I was watching to make sure we didn't overdo things, but obviously something affected you."

"Yeah," Gregory said in a slightly bitter tone. "I can hardly even move today."

"And that also likely means a buildup of lactic acid in your system too," his therapist said thoughtfully. He walked over, sat down on the chair and appeared to be bringing up a file on his tablet. He clicked through several times and then shrugged. "Okay, well, I'll come back here after lunch. Then we'll do some exercises to loosen you up a little bit, making sure that you don't feel quite so bad, and see if we can get you back up on your feet again."

"Today?" Gregory asked in a rough, gravelly voice. He hated to be a whiner here, but none of this made any sense. If Shane had listened, why would they force him to do more? At the other place, as soon as Gregory was in pain, everything stopped until he healed.

"Well, a lot of the pain is from the muscles tightening up. As soon as you start moving again, the pain eases."

"Sure," he said. "What I can't handle is more pain. So whatever we do today, I'll need painkillers to even let you touch me."

"We can arrange for some of that," Shane said cheerfully. "What we can't do is let you just sit like this, where your muscles go cold and tight, creating a worse scenario tomorrow."

"Worse?" He damn-near glared at him. "One thing I can't do is get any worse."

"Exactly. So, do you want to work now so you can walk down to lunch—or at least wheel yourself down there on your own—or do you want us to bring you some food first? Only then you have to work with a full belly, and that won't be as easy."

"Not as easy?"

"It could be a little harder," Shane acknowledged. "There's just no right or wrong answer."

"Right," Gregory said, "so that sucks."

"Yes, it does. But those are the facts of life, … so make a

decision now." He stood here, hands on his hips, quietly waiting.

Gregory dropped back against his bed and said, "Now then. I don't think I could eat anyway."

"Exactly," he said. "Let's get those pajama bottoms off you, and we'll start on the ankles and the foot, working our way up."

"Sure, but that sounds completely backward," Gregory said. "It would make more sense to start at the thighs and work down."

His therapist smiled, while replying, "Well, we're working our way up first, and then we'll work our way down."

Gregory groaned. "Or you could just *not*."

"Well, it'll happen whether you like it or not," he said, his tone businesslike but determined, which pointed out to Gregory what a little whiny brat he was being.

He groaned. "Okay, let's do this."

And, for the next hour, Shane stretched, pulled, massaged and loosened up Gregory's muscles to the point that one leg and then his other shook out to not feeling too bad. By the time Shane had done Gregory's arms and chest and then was rolled over so Shane could work on his back, Gregory started to feel like a whole new man again.

"If I knew you could do this," Gregory said, "I would have called for you when I woke up."

"And that's exactly what you should have done," Shane replied. "Instead I heard it from Meredith."

"Yeah, she was here just after I woke up. I had to get up and go to the bathroom, and I guess I didn't look too good."

"Obviously," Shane chided. "That's just the way life is when you don't listen to your therapist."

"Right," Gregory replied. As he laid here, he realized his

body hummed with a sense of peace. "You have magical hands," he announced.

Shane laughed. "Years and years of experience. There's no need for pain here. Most of the time it's muscles that have been either not used for too long or we did too much. One of the other biggest issues is the fact that often you sleep too hard, too long and too deep, so the muscles don't even move around during the night. You sleep in one position. You wake up the next morning, and everything has seized up."

"Gotcha," he said. "Still sucks."

He laughed. "It does, indeed, but we're almost there." He stepped back a few moments later, looked down at Gregory and said, "Try to sit upright and see how you feel."

At that, Gregory rolled over, slowly sat up, rolled his shoulders and his neck, and said, "The shoulders are good. The arms are good. The neck is a bit tense."

Immediately Shane stepped behind him and quickly massaged the shoulder and neck joints. "How're your teeth? Do you grind your teeth at night?"

"I don't think so, but my jaw feels locked."

"That would explain the sore neck too." With those very experienced fingers, Shane gently but firmly massaged along the jawline and up along the TM joint under the ear and then moved up the outside of the ear, up across the temple and over the forehead before doing a quick down-the-head scalp rub.

By the time he was done, Gregory was almost ready to beg for more. "That last part of what you were doing," he said, "that's wickedly good."

Shane chuckled. "It is, isn't it?" he said. "Now get moving, and see how it is this time."

And, with that, Gregory slowly stood, hopped on one leg

along the length of the bed and then grabbed a crutch. He took a couple steps and turned around, calmly looking for his other crutch. He hobbled over, grabbed it and then did several steps around the room. "You know what? That feels pretty decent."

"Excellent. How about some lunch?"

Gregory nodded and said, "Yeah, that's probably good timing. I need to get changed though."

"Good. I'll see you down there. We'll do a session this afternoon," he said firmly. "It won't be hard, and we'll definitely do some lighter weights and multiple repetitions. Don't worry. We won't overwork it. I would suggest maybe an hour of that and then hit the pool."

At the sound of *pool*, Gregory lit up. "Now that would be ideal." He said, "Actually the hot tub too. That would really help to set this off."

"Maybe," Shane said. "But its food first, then some light workout, and afterward the pool before any hot tub time."

"Fine," he said in disgust. "Don't you ever give anybody a break?"

"No," Shane replied. "If we did that, everybody would want one." He laughed as he walked out.

Gregory pondered that, noting the laugh had left him feeling a hell of a lot better. He quickly got changed, and something about being dressed and ready to start the day seemed so different too. It felt good, like he had left the invalid part of him behind. He chose the wheelchair just because he didn't want to overdo it, and, as he rolled his way down the hallway and back to the cafeteria, he found most of the lunch crowd had come and gone. He rolled his way down the line, chose a selection of aromatic Mexican food and then headed to the sunshine, but, as soon as he got there, it was hot. Too hot. Struggling, he turned around, rolled back inside and found a table with a little more space for his wheelchair.

He hated the fact that he was still dealing with space issues while in wheelchairs, but it had been his choice, so it was what it was. He ate slowly, enjoying the food, but realizing, of course, he'd forgotten his water. It just seemed like everything was so much effort today. Even though Shane had done a heck of a job, everything appeared to be a lot more difficult. And maybe Gregory was just being forgetful from being so tired, but he looked over at the water several times and realized he couldn't avoid it. He rolled back and headed toward the drink section.

While he was there, he grabbed a bottle of water and then a cup of coffee. That made rolling his wheelchair a little harder, but he was determined to make it, and one wheel rotation at a time, he made his way to his table. Triumphant, he placed a full cup of coffee beside his plate and then opened the bottle of water. The trouble was, he drank it almost immediately.

Suddenly Dennis was there with a second bottle. "That was good work," he said in admiration. "I don't think I have ever seen anybody bring a cup of coffee over quite the same way."

Gregory shot him a look. "Right. I probably looked absolutely ridiculous."

"Nope, not at all," he said with a big grin. "It was good." He looked at Gregory's food and said, "How are you enjoying it?"

"I love it," he said, "but that's why I needed the water. It's a little spicy."

"We do like spicy food here."

"That's great," he said, "but some of it should come with a warning label."

Dennis smirked. "If this is too hot for you, I can get you something else."

"No, this will do just fine," he said, forking up another mouthful.

Dennis took off, leaving Gregory to finish his lunch in peace.

By the time he was done, he checked his watch and realized he was already late. Shane was likely waiting in the physio room for him already. But at least Gregory had dressed with that in mind. Moving slowly, he headed out to the hallway. There, he stopped and saw Meredith coming toward him. He frowned at her. "Are you looking for me?"

"Only to make sure that you're doing okay," she said gently.

And he hated that gentleness, that *Hey, I know you're injured, and I know you're hurt, and I just want to make sure you're fine* kind of thing because, like she'd said, it still was her job. And something about that struck him so wrong. It was just enough to piss him off.

He nodded stiffly and said, "I'm doing just fine, thanks. Shane was a good idea. Thank you for messaging him." And then, without another word, he turned the wheelchair in the direction he needed to go and rolled down the hallway, leaving her staring behind him.

He could feel her eyes burning into his back. When he reached this PT room, he tossed a quick glance back, and, sure enough, there she was, still staring at him.

Chapter 8

MEREDITH TRIED TO keep herself busy for the next few days and to not hover over Gregory. She didn't know whether it was the female part of her or the professional nurse part of her, but she figured it was likely a gentle mix of both. She also knew that that's the last thing Gregory wanted. He needed to move on with his life without feeling like somebody was affecting his progress. And that was fine with her. She had enough work to do. One of the other nurses had fallen sick, and Meredith was doing double duty right now. At the end of her day, she was tired and exhausted.

As Wednesday rolled around, she really needed to take some R&R just to feel better herself. As she quickly made her way through the day, she was busy without even minutes to spare until her shift was over. When she finally handed off her case files and clocked out for the day, she headed home to her on-site apartment, quickly changed into a bathing suit and headed back to the pool.

She was so tired that she didn't think she could do any laps but knew she needed to, just to destress. Nothing like physical exercise to wear some of that off, and she quickly dove in. She swam laps—one, two and three—and by the time she stopped at twenty, she realized she hadn't done as many as she needed to, but she already felt better. She did several more laps at a much slower pace. Instead of trying to plow through the water cleanly, she gently floated along the top and moved lightly.

A few more laps later, she took several deep breaths and floated to finish destressing. Finally, her body chilly, she headed over to the stairs. When she got out and wrapped herself with a towel, she noticed a few patients sat here, watching.

She smiled at them. "You could go in, you know?" she teased.

"We don't belong in the mermaid category," Bernie said. He was a big, burly man with a huge gut that they were working to reduce, and he was missing both legs. But they were missing very high up, so prosthetics would not be easy, if even possible.

She just smiled and said honestly, "With that tummy of yours, I'm sure you'd float anyway."

He grinned at her. "Like a beached whale or a turtle," he said.

She laughed. "Have you already had dinner?"

He patted his belly. "What do you think?" he asked. "You know me. When there's food, I'm never late."

She smiled, looked over at Stan beside him and said, "How are you doing? Surprised you are aren't still downstairs with the animals."

Stan, the vet, just smiled and gave her a tired nod. "I'm fine," he said. "Long day."

"Surgery?"

"Yes, plus I got two female cats and about eight kittens in today. The kittens aren't old enough to be fixed yet," he said, "but we did the moms, and then we had to round up fosters for the kittens. But everyone had to be chipped and inspected and examined and fixed," he said. "Fixed as in shots and ears checked, and a couple had ear infections."

She nodded. "Kind of sounds like my day," she said. "Hannah is sick for the second day now, and I'm just worn out doing double shifts."

"That's the thing, isn't it?" Stan said. "We can do everything just fine from Monday to Friday, bumping along quite happily with a regular workload, but then something happens, and our workload doubles."

She chuckled. "That's about it," she said. "In my case, staffing issues. I know Dani was trying to get somebody in temporarily to help but wasn't having luck. Then Hannah thought she'd be back today, but she didn't make it. But if she's not here tomorrow ..."

"A pretty nasty flu is going around the place," Stan said. "If she caught that, she could be down for a week."

"A week?" Meredith cried out in mock horror. "If that's the case," she said, "I'll need Dani to get someone in to help. It's okay for a day or two, but, after that, it gets to be an issue."

"Of course it does," Stan said. "I was wondering about getting a second vet in here."

"You mean, until Aaron comes?"

"Exactly," he said with a grin, "and that, of course, will still be a few years out."

"True. Neither of our issues have an easy answer."

"Yours shouldn't be that hard to solve. Maybe you can talk to Dani after dinner," Stan said. "You're looking pretty tired."

There was such concern in his voice that she smiled at him and collapsed on the chair beside him. "I am," she said.

"Just work?"

She shot him a veiled look and shrugged.

He nodded. "I heard something about you and Gregory."

"Gossip travels fast around here," she said with a half smile, wishing he didn't know anything about it, but, of course, he did.

"Exactly," he said, "the gossip is notorious. But remember that we're all friends. Nobody wants to see you hurt."

"Might be a little late for that," she said. "Well, maybe five years late."

At that, Bernie wheeled away in this chair, calling back, "Private stuff. I'll leave you two alone."

"Thanks," she called out. She looked over at Stan and said, "It's hard to see Gregory and not wonder about the 'what ifs' in life. We've never mentioned our history. It's like a great big black hole that neither of us wants to get sucked into."

"Understandable. You don't know where a conversation like that will leave you. Still, you need to know where you stand inside first. If you can't determine that, then any further conversations would just confuse the issue. Learn what's in your heart, then find out what's in his. A lot of time has passed, and he's been through a rough time."

Stan stared out at the open deck. "He's lost a lot in his life. Not only his career but his health. He has years to recover and faces an uncertain future. He also lost you. And, although we're sorry for what he's been through, we can't do anything but help support this next part of his journey. He's stronger than he knows. You have to be too." Stan's piercing gray eyes locked onto hers as he said in a low tone, "Particularly if you want to keep him in your life."

"I know that mentally, but I still want to rail at him that, if he'd chosen me over the military way back when, then he wouldn't be in this situation. Yet I also know that would be the worst thing I could do, denying him what makes him *him*. Yet it hurts me so to see him suffering," she said, her shoulders sagging, "He's struggling, like really struggling sometimes."

"Everyone here does," Stan said, his voice still low so it wouldn't carry across to others around.

"I didn't want to see him go off to war again," she muttered. "I feel very selfish about it now, but I know I couldn't have lived with the constant fear and worry about him getting hurt. Even after he left, I still worried and felt fear. It took a long time to stop doing that." She waved a hand toward the rehab center sprawled around them. "And then to see him here like this?" She shook her head. "I know it's selfish, but I'm glad I wasn't there at the time. Yet I feel bad that I wasn't there for him."

"It would have been incredibly difficult," he said. "At least at this stage, you're seeing him already on the mend. You're seeing him on the road to recovery."

She nodded. "That's it exactly," she said. "I've seen him turn the corner, and I know that it's still hard for him, and, of course, there's added pain because of our own breakup. But, at the same time, it is showing me a side of him that I'd never seen before. I've seen men come here broken and, at the end of their stay, stand up and walk forward into their new lives, making me feel so proud to have been a part of their journey. To watch them step into their futures, when they didn't actually think they had one when they arrived.

"Most arrived broken, hating their lives. Their hearts had been devastated at what had happened to them. Very few are happy and upbeat. And I mean, very few. They're challenged here. They're given tasks and end goals, and yet, through it all, they learn abilities and gain strength and find an inner sense of who they really are. And, in a way, I feel like I missed something very important for Gregory from the time that he was injured until now. Because he was in much better shape than a lot of people when first checking in here," she finished.

"I don't know him all that well," Stan said, "but he appears to be fairly well-adjusted. And that's a surprise. Of course, we have lots of that here, but, as you said, he came in already in really good shape."

"And yet, our rehab has been a shock for him too. I think he became a little too complacent, thinking he already had this. I'm not sure his last VA center was the best place for him. He's one of those guys who can fool you into thinking that he's doing everything, and it's all working well, but he's actually taking shortcuts. So some of the very important steps that are necessary weren't taken, and now, well, you know what our PT guys are like. Shane won't let Gregory off the hook at all."

Stan chuckled. "No, Shane is quite a hard character, but he's fair."

"He's beyond fair," she said. "But he's also extremely good at what he does, and he already worked out Gregory's character on the first day. It is unfortunate though that, between the two of them, Gregory was overworked from his very first PT session, so that he was quite sore that night and into the next day. The thing is, he wasn't in anywhere as bad a shape as I've seen time and time again. But, for Gregory, I think he was more than shocked that he was in such poor condition as to not survive his first PT session with Shane. And that's not easy for Gregory to accept."

"Even harder," Stan said, nodding his head, "Gregory arrived with a false self-confidence. Shane abruptly woke him up from that to see where Gregory really was, and now he'll have to work."

"But, at the end of it," she said, "he will be where he wanted to be."

"And yet, something about that concerns you."

"I think I'm holding him back." Meredith sighed.

"What's your relationship like right now?"

"Professional," Meredith said. "I'm keeping it that way. We haven't discussed five years ago. We're ignoring it, but that means it's always there between us."

"And why is that?"

"I don't want to get in the way of the work he has to do here. When he first arrived, and we were a little friendlier, he didn't seem to think he had any work to do, so he was much more relaxed. But now it's different, as if he's got more locked up inside."

"Of course he has, because he has a true challenge to face. It's not something you can help him with, and you're right. Maybe in that instance, you'll actually feel his pain because he knows he has to do this, and he has to do it well. And, on top of that, you're there watching him. No matter whether it's as an ex-lover or as an old friend, no one wants to come up short."

At that, she stared at Stan. "In what way would he come up short?"

"Well, think about it," Stan said, as if it was blatantly obvious. "Five years ago he was whole and physically fit— and God only knows what else you saw in him—but he isn't those things anymore."

"No," she said slowly, thinking about it. "He used to

have a big smile and a huge sense of humor. But what hasn't changed is he's still strong, loyal, and committed."

"But those are what he would consider as *soft skills*. You know those job applications where you have to give your actual skills, but they want those *other* skills? Right now Gregory's looking for the measurable *real* skills—the ability to walk, the ability to be independent, to look after his own physical needs. He wants to know that he has a purpose in his life and that he can hold a job and can support a family." Stan smiled sadly at her. "No matter what the other person in the relationship is doing, it's always important that the men know that they can handle looking after their family. Women can become the major moneymaker. They can become the CEOs. They can become all kinds of things in this world," he said, "but it'll never change that a man wants to know he can be strong enough, capable enough to be the breadwinner."

"I guess the men are still hunter-gatherers at heart, aren't they?" she mused.

"We so are, and, considering we're both exhausted"—he grinned—"why don't you quickly go get changed, as much as I like the view, and we'll get dinner."

"How about I just throw on my sundress?" she said. She picked hers up from where she'd dropped it to the side with her towel and tossed it over her head, letting it float lightly over her body. She reached out a hand and said, "Come on. Let's go eat."

He reached up, grabbed it, squeezed her fingers and let her hand go. "Let's go." As they walked over to the edge, he said, "Don't look now, but somebody's been watching us for the last twenty minutes or so."

"I saw him," she said with a smile. "Do you think us

holding hands bothered him?"

"Absolutely," he said. "Which is why I dropped yours. Now let's eat."

IT WAS HARD to watch somebody who you cared about being friendly with another man. The handclasp was one thing, but at least it didn't last too long. The thing that bothered Gregory the most was the fact that it was obvious Meredith and Stan were close. But then, why wouldn't they be? They'd both worked at Hathaway House for years; they were bound to be friends. Gregory wondered painfully if that was all they were.

There was an obvious age difference between them, but it wasn't so much as to raise eyebrows. Meredith had always been mature for her age, and she was absolutely perfect, so, of course, every man in town wanted her. The thing was, she had chosen Gregory at one time, and he'd been so honored and so delighted, … until it came time for him to leave. He hadn't come up against that issue before because he hadn't really cared enough before.

But, with Meredith, everything had changed, and it had hurt big-time. And how could he even begin to contemplate a relationship with her now? She'd already seen him when he had been so much more, when he had walked away from her, so why would she want anything to do with him now?

Yet he was here, full of hope, winging it on a kiss and a prayer.

Honestly, it was heartbreaking. He knew he shouldn't be even thinking about it like that, but it wasn't easy. As much as he wanted it and was delighted and had actively taken a path that would have put Meredith right in front of him, it was hard to know what to do next, especially with the current rude awakening to the truth about his physical condition.

Hathaway House had a lot more to offer than he had ever expected.

She deserved so much more. If he was smart, he would have just walked away from the military years ago, and he'd have spent the last five years with her. Not only would he have had the last five years but he'd be whole now because he wouldn't have been blown up by the damn IED.

He stared out at the pool, knowing that Stan and Meredith would come upstairs and would walk past him at any moment. As they approached, she smiled at him, but Stan asked, "Have you eaten yet, Gregory?"

He looked up in surprise. "Actually I have," he said. "I was just thinking about going for a swim to help digest some of the food I shoved down there."

"Just make sure you wait a little bit, please," she cautioned.

Of course, always the nurse, he thought. The two of them walked past and headed to the cafeteria. Gregory wondered if an invitation would have been in the offering from her.

He moved toward the water. He had on his shorts and knew he could make his way in the pool, yet he couldn't force himself now that he was here. He had wanted to get out. He could have gone up and had dessert or something with them. They'd offered a branch of friendship, and instead, he'd been churlish and refused. He deserved to be alone right now. As he sat here, frowning, he turned to look up to see Meredith standing on the top step, looking at him.

She frowned, and he frowned right back.

"Do you want company?" she asked him.

Immediately his back stiffened, and he shook his head. "I'm fine," he said, and she quickly disappeared.

He groaned and quickly pulled off his T-shirt. He put his wheelchair alongside the ladder to get into the pool, hit the brakes on it, stood and helped himself into the water. As soon as the first wave splashed over his head, he could feel some of his tension easing. Now he was just miserable, and, every time he saw her, he felt like he said the wrong thing. And that wasn't fair to her, and it surely wasn't the reason he came here.

Putting some of his muscles to use, he swam laps, trying not to roll with his uneven leg movements and to stay straight. It didn't take too long to get caught up in the natural rhythm, and, as soon as he did, his stiffness left. Once he did a few more laps and calmed his breathing, he lowered himself in the water.

Shane had had a hard talk with him today. Gregory hadn't in any way realized he was doing it, but Shane had taken him to task for not showing up for the job. Gregory had been hurt and insulted at the time, but then, when Shane explained about how Gregory was putting up a front and telling them everything was fine but was only giving about seventy percent because he was sore, Gregory could see what Shane was talking about.

It wasn't his usual way to act, but Gregory realized that the other rehab center had let him get away with a lot, whereas Shane wouldn't let him get away with anything. Gregory knew that he would thank Shane for it later, but right now it felt brutal.

Gregory didn't know how long he swam. It was hard to

keep track. But, when he finally stopped, instead of feeling exhausted, he felt energized. His body hummed with joy; his muscles swelled with pleasure. He pulled himself up beside the wheelchair and just sat here. It was such a beautiful way to end a day, and he knew he'd sleep so much better.

But, of course, he hadn't thought about a towel. He looked around for one to grab and saw Meredith walking toward him, a towel in her hand. She held it out to him. Taking it, he muttered, "Thanks," and quickly dried his face. "Are you done eating already?" he asked, still drying his hair and not looking at her.

"Yes," she said. "Stan got called back to an emergency."

"Ah," he said.

"What does that mean?"

He shrugged. "Sorry that your dinner date was cut short."

An awkward silence followed for a moment, and then she crouched beside him. "Stan is a good friend," she said, looking Gregory in the eyes. "Shane is a good friend. Many other males here are also my good friends. You'll see me sharing a meal with them, many times probably," she said. "We're part of a very large family here, and it's very peaceful, comfortable. When I have something I need to talk out, I can pick any one of them, and I know that they'll just let me vent. They won't tell me how to fix the problem. They won't tell me what to do. They'll just listen, so that I can get some of it off my chest."

He nodded slowly. "I'm sorry. I didn't mean to be child-ish."

"No," she said, straightening. "But it's obvious that something about my dinner with Stan bothered you, and it's something we have to talk about."

Immediately he shook his head. "No," he said, "we don't have to at all."

"Yes," she said firmly. "We do."

"Well, not today," he said. "I don't think I can handle more today."

"Well, I agree with you there," she said. "I've been doing double-duty for several days, and I'm exhausted. I had a hard swim earlier, and now I've just eaten, so I'm heading back to my place. I'll see you in the morning." She turned, walked alongside the pool, picked up a towel that he hadn't even realized was there on the back of a chair, threw it over her shoulder and disappeared.

She was right; they did need to talk. But he was also right in that it didn't need to be today. He was the one who would need some time to work up what he wanted to say. Because really, what could he say? *Sorry* seemed awfully useless now.

Chapter 9

I T WAS NOON the next day when she finally sat back and looked up to see Dani walking in, a smile on her face.

"You've done really, really well," Dani said. "I'm so sorry about the staffing shortage, but I just heard from Hannah, and she'll be back in tomorrow."

Meredith gave a huge sigh of relief. "Good," she said. "I've been trying to handle it, but it's getting away from me."

"Understood. Hanna will see if she can get in to do an hour or two today and maybe catch up on some of the paperwork for you, but she wants to avoid the patients until she's a hundred percent clear of flu symptoms."

"Absolutely," Meredith said. "It's always the rule, isn't it? The last thing we want to do is spread any germs around this place."

"Exactly. Now I told her, that if she wasn't feeling up to it, not worry. The paperwork would still be there tomorrow."

"It always is," Meredith said with a heavy sigh. "It always is."

"I am interviewing for more staff. I'm sorry I'm not further along on that process."

Meredith nodded and waved off her comments.

Dani looked at her and asked, "Are you doing okay with Gregory?"

Meredith gave an irritable shrug. "I am. It's not that easy, and I'm not exactly sure what I'm supposed to do, as we do need to talk and clear the air, but I can't seem to find the right time."

"You know you have to pick your time carefully, right?" Dani asked softly, checking to make sure nobody else was listening to their private conversation.

"I know," she said. "I was hoping to avoid him, and then I pushed the issue last night." She sighed. "But he said we couldn't talk yesterday, and I was too tired anyway."

"Maybe have a talk with Shane first, and see if Gregory's adapting well. The last thing we want to do is cause a relapse."

At that, she winced. "Right, that would push the conversation back a couple more weeks."

"Maybe just try to be friends for now?" Dani asked curiously. "I'm not sure what it is you're trying to do, whether you want to go back to him or not."

"I know. It's kind of hard. I want to be friendly. We can't go back to what we had because, well, ... I just don't think we can," she said honestly. "Maybe something better though. But I don't even know if I like him right now." She had a sad smile on her lips as she spoke. "I don't really recognize him."

"So you know what this is," Dani said. "This is the time to get to know each other, like really get to know him, to see who he is inside, not just the outside."

"That's all we ever see here, isn't it? So many are broken. So many are working on becoming better," Meredith said. "We see so much of the inner person all the time here."

"And I think it's very different here for him," Dani said. "And he needs time. He needs space."

"And that's exactly what I was trying to give him," Meredith said. "But it's not easy being his primary care nurse, which throws us together. Often."

"I know," Dani said with the sweetest smile. "I do understand." With a lopsided grin, the two women exchanged hugs. "Now let's hope Hannah comes this afternoon," Dani said as she headed out. "That will help relieve some of your workload. I really appreciate you stepping up while she's been down."

"You know me," Meredith said. "The super-responsible type." And, with a flippant look, she grabbed her tablet. "Speaking of which, I have to go."

"Don't avoid him," Dani called out to her retreating back. "Just treat him like one of the regular guys."

"Oh, he is," Meredith threw back, with a saucy grin, turning to see Dani. "Just with one big difference."

Dani chuckled. "And that difference, of course, is everything."

Meredith thought about that as she kept going because a lot of truth was in that statement. She already knew who he was in one way; this situation would just add another layer to her knowledge. Maybe this time she would make a better decision, and so could he.

GREGORY WORKED AS he'd never worked in his life. His water-based military training had been absolutely brutal, and, at the time, he'd cursed his way through it, finding strength in the brotherhood around him to make it through. But right now, he didn't think anything could possibly be worse than what he was doing. And when he finally collapsed, his body shaking, Shane squatted beside him and said, "Remember. On a scale of one to ten, you are to tell me when you're at a six."

Gregory glared at him. "And why would I do that?" he asked. "If I keep giving my body a chance to quit before it's done, it'll never push the level of achievement higher."

"Because, when you go past a six out of ten," Shane said patiently, "you're pushing your body well past the point where it can recover easily. And, instead of helping your body, you're hurting it. You're putting it into a stressful position it can't recover from easily. That's not what we want."

"I want to get better," Gregory snapped. "I want to be healthy again. I want to be strong again."

Shane straightened, looked at him and said, "What you really want is to turn back time to be who you were before. That's not happening." He closed his folder and picked up his tablet. "We're done here for the day. I suggest you either get back to your room and have a shower or maybe do some time at the pool." And he turned and walked out.

Gregory, still writhing with anger, wanted to follow him and yell at him and scream and rail at the injustices of life. Instead, he picked up the weights and did ten more reps, feeling the sweat pour off his body until he couldn't lift the weights again.

He groaned and collapsed on the mat and just laid here. He thought he was done being angry about his current life; he thought he was done being frustrated and hating his world. And yet, coming here, seeing Meredith, seeing her happy and joyful and laughing with all the other men made him realize just how much he wanted to be that man again.

But he wouldn't *ever* be that man again.

She was a nurse. She saw more broken men than he'd ever seen in his life. And he didn't give a damn because it was his life, his broken body he wanted her to see, but he didn't want her to see it as it was today; he wanted her to see it as it had been. Only his body wouldn't be that fit again.

And, to his humiliation, he could feel tears burning up in the corner of his eyes. He immediately squeezed his eyes closed to stop the tears from leaking out. The last thing he wanted was to be caught crying like a baby. When he'd laid on the battlefield in pieces, he had bawled in agony. But then every man around him—except for those dead friends whose eyes he could see staring skyward—were crying too. There was nothing like that horrible sense of waking up and realizing how vastly his world had changed.

For a long time, he'd wished he'd died on that field. But, in his last rehab center—for whatever reason—he'd been fine there. He'd been doing okay, until he'd come here, and they'd taken all that false reality away from him. They'd taken that mirage that he was comfortable living in, and they'd showed him where he *really* was and what he really could do—or not do.

And what he really looked like beside the rest of the men in the world.

Deep down, Gregory knew it wasn't Hathaway House's fault, but he wanted to rail at them and make it their fault. He knew as much as anything it was the fact that Shane wasn't a pushover, like his other therapist had been.

It was also Meredith's presence here. He'd come here specifically to see her, but he'd expected to still be that king of the walk. That same confident, capable person who had arrived on the first day at Hathaway House. Instead, he was more broken than he'd ever been, and he couldn't show her that confident person anymore because he didn't exist, had never existed. He was just someone Gregory had made up to make it through life when the reality inside him was that he hadn't even begun to heal.

At the sound of footsteps, he quickly sat up and struggled over to his wheelchair.

He was just hopping in and collapsing down when a woman's voice called from the doorway, "Are you okay?"

He mustered up a smile, nodded and said, "Just fine, heading back for a shower now."

The woman in scrubs nodded and walked away. He thought her name was Shannon. He again wondered if having Meredith around was helping or hurting him. He wanted her to be the goal at the end of the day, but he also knew he couldn't make that his goal, as it was something out of his own control. But just because he knew that didn't mean that he wanted that to be the truth. He wanted something so much better for himself. And Hathaway House was giving it to him, just not the way he expected.

Exhausted and depressed like he hadn't been in months, he made his way back to his room slowly. He had a shower, taking his time because he was so tired. As he let the heat roll down his sore muscles, he knew that he had pushed it too far. He had refused to listen to Shane once again, and he would pay for it tonight. Maybe even sooner than that.

Back at his bed, he took several muscle relaxants, and, rather than struggling to stay awake, he laid down, pulled a sheet over himself and closed his eyes.

Chapter 10

WHEN MEREDITH GOT to work the next morning, she found Dani waiting for her. In a serious voice, Dani said, "I need to talk to you."

Surprised, she nodded. "Here or in your office?"

"In my office." Worried, Meredith followed Dani to her private office, and she closed the door and motioned at the chair, just saying, "Be seated."

She got doubly worried. "Have I done something wrong?"

Dani immediately shook her head. "No, you haven't. However, it goes back to you and Gregory."

"Oh, in what way?"

"Some of the others on his team feel that your relationship is impacting his ability to heal."

Meredith sagged in the chair. "And I was trying to avoid him, other than doing my job, hoping that, if I wasn't around all the time, it would make it easier for him."

"I think we need to make it a little more than that," Dani said. "He hasn't requested this, but I'll be interested to see if he says anything about it. I'd like you to switch your care to exclude him. And I will ask one of the other nurses to pick up his room as part of their roster."

Meredith could feel a little bit of her shrinking inside yet again. "Okay," she said slowly. "Is that really necessary?"

"No, maybe not," Dani said honestly. "Shane says that Gregory's angry at himself, and he's pushing himself well past the point of normal. Shane thinks that's because a certain amount of Gregory's rage has come back because he's not where he was before he was injured, and Shane's wondering if it's because Gregory can see you around here."

"I didn't tell Shane about our history," Meredith said honestly, "but I probably should have."

"I told him," Dani said. "You know we can't keep something like that a secret from our patient's team. But Shane thinks that Gregory wants to impress you, that he wants you to see him as he was, and so he's pushing himself, and what we're heading toward is a complete breakdown."

Meredith chewed on her bottom lip, worried. "We've certainly seen that in a few of our cases," she said, "at least ones with that much rage still in them."

"Exactly," Dani said. "We understand the rage. What Gregory has to do is get past it and get to the acceptance part. And I don't know at what point in time we'll see the blowout. I don't want you to set it off, and I don't want him to use you as a catalyst. This needs to be his fight for his own healing and not because of what he lost and thinks he can never regain."

Meredith reached up, not surprised to feel tears dripping down her cheeks. Dani reached for a box of tissues and held it out to her. She pulled out one and dabbed at the corner of her eyes. "I had convinced myself that it would be easy to see him, and then I would be totally over him," she said. "But I'm not. And to see how hard he's working, to see what he's trying to do, ... I know he came here overconfident and had that knocked out of him in his very first session with Shane. But it was hard to see him drop down to no confidence."

"And again, we've seen it time and time again," Dani said gently. "He has to get through this yawning pit of despair so he can come out the other side and crawl back up to the light again. You know perfectly well he can get back to being the person he was when he arrived. But the person he was upon arrival wasn't real. That was fake. That was Gregory's fantasy, his imagination. No way is he as strong as he thought he was. And all Shane has done is show him that he was hiding his defects. Defects that would have caught up with Gregory sooner or later. Those weaknesses are what will put him back into a wheelchair in a few years."

Meredith gave Dani a watery smile. "The thing is, we both know that. But when it becomes personal ..."

"Which is why I want to remove the personal element," Dani said. "Let's try it for a week, and see if he notices."

"And it will be heartbreaking if he doesn't notice," Meredith said brokenly. There wasn't much else she could say, so she nodded and said, "Am I to avoid him in the rest of the place too? I hate to make it obvious like that because he will wonder if it's my decision."

"I don't think that's necessary," Dani said, speaking slowly as she thought about it. "We don't want him to think you're doing that. If he asks you what happened, just tell him that I changed your roster."

Meredith stood. "Okay, I can do that."

Dani looked up at her and smiled. "You're being very brave."

"I don't feel very brave," she said. "Since he arrived, I feel like I've been on nothing but a roller coaster ride. It's been very rough."

"I know," Dani said. "Believe me. I do know." And, of course, that just referenced Dani's crazy up and down relationship at the beginning with Aaron, another patient and a longtime friend of Dani's.

Meredith smiled, gave her a hug and said, "At least in your case you are at a point where you no longer have all those doubts."

"No," Dani said with a smile, "thankfully I'm well past that."

"When's the wedding?" Meredith teased.

Dani's face flushed. "Not sure," she said, "but we are talking about setting a date."

"Well, you know that everybody here will want to be part of it," she said with a laugh. "So you better plan for that too."

"Absolutely," Dani said chuckling. "But that just adds to the logistics issue."

"No, not at all," Meredith said. "Get a minister and have the ceremony here. And for the reception? You know the kitchen will want to handle that. Whoever is here at the time gets to attend, and, other than that, it's really not about anybody else. It's all about you and Aaron."

"True enough," Dani said. "We'll think about it."

"I'm sure you do nothing but." Meredith smiled.

"Well, it is kind of nice," Dani replied. "As you said, I already know that we're together, and that makes a world of difference. I don't get to see him anywhere near enough, and, for a couple years, that's the way it'll be, but after that? Well, it's a whole different story."

"Do you think Stan is seriously interested in working with Aaron?"

Dani beamed. "He can't wait for him to get here. He's needed a partner for a long time. Whenever Aaron is off, he comes down and helps anyway. He'll do part of his practicum with Stan as it is."

"Now that sounds perfect," Meredith said warmly. "I'm really happy for you."

And, on that note, she turned and walked out. She might be happy for Dani, but Meredith still had a long way to go to get her own life together. She could only hope it happened a little sooner rather than later because this was just too hard. She went to bed thinking about Gregory, and she woke up thinking about him. How fair was it to know that now she wasn't even supposed to work with him? That had been the one light in her day. So many times in a day she got to check up on him. And now, ... well, even that was gone. She understood the reasoning, and a week wasn't a long time to see if it would make a difference or not. But it would seem like forever, ... at least to her.

SEVERAL DAYS LATER Gregory finally asked the question on his mind. At first, he hadn't been sure, but now too much time had passed. "Why did Meredith ask to be removed from my team?" Gregory asked Shane bluntly.

Shane stopped what he was doing, crouched so he could look at his face and then said, "What are you talking about?"

"She's not part of my team anymore."

"I don't know," Shane said. "Doesn't mean it was her choice though."

"Of course it was," Gregory scoffed. "Obviously she doesn't like to see who I am now."

"I think you're doing Meredith a great injustice," Shane said. "Of all the things I know about her, she sees people very, very clearly."

At that, Gregory closed his mouth and went back to work. He didn't like these exercises at all. They were working on one of the strips down his back that had been badly mangled. Part of it was still there; part of it was damaged, and the scar tissue kept pulling. Shane kept working on it. Softening it, loosening it, telling Gregory that they could ease some of these knots and get it to stretch out properly. But, so far, Gregory didn't believe him. It just seemed like pain upon pain with absolutely no joy at the end of the day.

It'd been four days since he'd seen Meredith.

"Do you think she's avoiding me?" he muttered, not letting the subject go.

"No," Shane said firmly. "She's incredibly busy. We've had a lot of new people come on board, and I think she's just a swamped as everybody else is in here. Now, focus."

At that, Gregory shut up because he didn't have a job himself right now. And that's what Meredith's position here was—it was a job for her—unlike him, who was here twenty-four hours a day, whereas she didn't have to be. She could have a life outside of this place.

When he was finally done, his hands were shaking, but unfortunately, he was afraid it was a buildup of rage inside, a rage that had been building slowly for the last few days. He didn't know what to do about it, but he was terrified he would lash out and hurt somebody. He closed his hands into fists and clenched them tightly, trying to let out some of that energy. When he opened them again, Shane stared at him calmly but knowingly.

"You've got to let it blow, you know?"

Immediately Gregory shook his head. "I can't." His tone was harsh. "I might hurt someone."

"Maybe," Shane replied. "But you can't keep it inside."

"Why not?" he snapped. "It's what I have done so far."

"Sure," he said, "but a rage like that is not healthy, and it's holding you back. I get that you're not who you were. I get that life dished you something you didn't want to see. … I even get that you had choices that you could have made before that would have changed where you are right now, … but none of it matters. Because you can't go back. You can't change it. You can't fix it. All you can do right now is play the hand you've been dealt."

Gregory knew everything Shane said was true, but it didn't matter. Gregory glared at his hands, and he could feel the vibration starting deep inside. "I need to go to the pool or something," he said, his voice thick.

"Ever used a punching bag?"

He lifted his head, stared at Shane and frowned.

"If you haven't, now might be a good time to try it. If you have, I've got one down in one of the other rooms."

"What kind?"

"Get in your wheelchair, and I'll take you," Shane said. "You need an outlet, and you need it fast."

Once he was in the wheelchair, Shane grabbed the handles and pushed, not even giving Gregory a chance to go on his own power. Shane took him past more rooms, then brought him to a room he'd never been in before. Shane opened it up to reveal a beautiful hardwood floor with several hanging balls and punching bags. Gregory got up, grabbed his crutches mounted on the back of his wheelchair, hobbled over and said, "It's not exactly something I can do with crutches."

"No," Shane replied. "But I do have this over here."

Gregory walked over to see a generic prosthetic, probably useless for most cases, but it would give him the ability to stand. They quickly strapped it on, and he took several experimental steps. "Even this is so much better than crutches."

"Your prosthetic is on the way," Shane said. "We took the molds. We don't know if the stump has healed enough yet to support it, but we thought with extra socks and maybe a bit of a cushioning, you'd be okay with it. This, however, isn't it. This is just something for you to get around with for right now."

Gregory nodded. He stared at his good fist. That same damn rage sat in his gut, burning a hole. "I didn't even realize how angry I was," he said. "It's a red haze that's building."

"Because you're not acknowledging it," Shane said. "You're keeping it stuffed inside, and it'll just hurt you. It'll eat you from the inside out, and it will demand an outlet. Whether you like it or not, it will insist on coming out. It has to. Have you ever used a punching bag before?"

Although Shane had asked the question before, Gregory hadn't answered him. He nodded. "I'm not the best at it though. My hands won't handle much."

At that, Shane walked over to the side and picked up two gloves. He helped strap them on Gregory's hands, and, when they were secure, Shane said, "I'll hold the bag, and I want you to pound into it as much as you want and as hard as you want. Release as much of that anger as you need to in order to get your mind back on getting you in shape. Are you ready to release? You've got a ways to go yet in your therapy, and you're making it a very slow, arduous journey. We already need a couple months. But, if you don't deal with this, it'll take six months instead. I don't know that I can get you as high or as far or as fast if you can't let this out."

Shane may have said all that only to shut him up, but Gregory's instinct to reach up and pound into that bag was instinctive, and he struck out, pounding the bag once, twice, and then he couldn't stop. With Shane holding it somewhat steady and taking the force of the blunted blows, Gregory beat on that bag as if it were every damn commander who had made a wrong decision. For every wrong decision Gregory had made. For his body not recovering as fast as it had been blown up. For everything and everyone he blamed for his life and his fate and his so-called karma. For every damn thing in his world that had gone so very wrong.

Gregory just kept pounding ... and pounding ... and pounding ... and pounding, until finally, he could hear somebody's voice in the background. He slowly collapsed to his knees. He wrapped his arms around his chest and started to sob. His humiliation was complete when he heard another voice. Then both disappeared. All of it disappeared into the silence around him, and he realized that Shane had moved whoever it was out of the room and stood outside in the hallway with them.

Gregory sat here, feeling his body completely collapse in on itself. So much pain. So much anger. So much torment in his soul. It was as if there was no freedom, no way out.

As he had always done before, he slammed a lid down on his emotions and collapsed, so he lay on the floor and stared up. The tears were tears of exhaustion at this point in time, and he knew he couldn't even unlace his gloves. They were darn hard to get in and out of normally, but alone it was almost impossible. Especially today, ... right now ...

He took several deep, calming breaths, trying to find a center that would allow him to move forward in life. But he couldn't even sit up. How the hell would he go anywhere? Finally he heard the door open, and Shane walked back in.

"How do you feel now?"

"Empty," he croaked as he reached up one gloved fist. "Could you help me with these, please?" His voice was low and quiet. *Empty.*

Shane quickly unlaced them and tugged them off. He set them aside, then brought the wheelchair over. "I would suggest that pool now to finish off your workout, then a bit of time in the hot tub."

Gregory shook his head. "No," he said, "the only thing I want to do is go to my room and stay there."

"That's the worst thing you can do."

"It doesn't matter if it's the worst thing or not. I don't have the energy to go to the pool. I don't have the energy to do anything. I'd like to go back to my room and be alone now."

Shane hesitated. "You know something? I think the answer to that is no." He helped him into the wheelchair, then, without giving him a chance, grabbed the handles on the back.

"I don't want to go anywhere public," Gregory snapped in outrage. He tried to grab the wheels, but Shane was too strong, too fast, refusing to listen. "And I definitely don't want to go to the cafeteria."

"Doesn't matter what you want at this point," Shane said, his voice and tone brooking no argument. "Your therapy session isn't done."

"It is done," he snapped. "And I want to go back to my room. You can't force me to do anything." Hating it, his voice rose like a truculent child.

"Yes," Shane said, "I can. You'll have to get up off that

chair to stop me."

Gregory was so angry. Again. Where had that anger come from? How could there possibly be any more anger? He was exhausted; his body was pummeled from the therapy. Then he'd beaten his hands to death in the gloves, and his shoulders were killing him. There shouldn't have been any more anger, but it was rising yet again in another red wave.

"I'll have you fired for this," he roared. He knew he was attracting attention, but, shit, he couldn't stop himself.

Shane chuckled. "If it was that easy to fire me," he said, "I would have been fired a long time ago. I've been dealing with guys like you for over a decade," he said, "and I do understand a lot about it, and I understand that layers and layers and layers of rage are inside. The sooner we can deal with them, the better we all are."

"Didn't I get enough out already?" Gregory snapped. "You not happy with your job? Is that what this is? Are you just angry because you don't see another little successful check in a box beside your name?" he asked snidely. He hated the way he was acting, but he didn't know how to stop it. It was just too unbelievable. Suddenly they were at the pool level.

He glared at the beautiful gleaming water, even though part of him desperately wished to be swimming in it. But he didn't want Shane to know that.

Except Shane had absolutely no intention of giving him the upper hand. He hit the edge of the wheelchair with the ladder and locked down the wheels to the chair. He walked in front of Gregory and said, "You go in voluntarily, or I'll pick you up and put you in."

Gregory glared at him and said, "No way in hell you'll

get away with doing that."

Shane nodded, scooped him up underneath his arms, and then, with a quick flip, tossed him into the deep end of the pool. Gregory hit the water, and his outrage came in a scream of fury as he kicked and pounded and screamed underwater. Suddenly he came up, gasping for air, to find Shane already in the water beside him.

Gregory glared at him and said, "What kind of a sadistic move was that?"

"It was a good one," Shane said. "I haven't thrown a patient around in a few years, which is too damn bad as it's really cathartic."

"It's also not legal."

"Stop being such a crybaby, and listen to your therapist."

"Like hell," Gregory roared as he stroked away from him. There was something so damn calming, so peaceful and so good when doing that. But he was also exhausted. Four laps later, he found himself doing the breaststroke, trying to maintain his floating, and realizing that he'd burned out so much energy that it was all he could really do.

He rolled over onto his back and just floated, letting his body and mind relax. Without any warning, a huge sigh worked up from his belly and his chest. He could feel something inside him letting loose, a great big boulder that he'd been hanging onto. He didn't recognize it. He didn't know how, but, with whatever had happened this afternoon, he could just feel it pouring from his mouth and chest as he released heavy sigh after heavy sigh after heavy sigh.

And yet, again feeling tears in his eyes, he turned over to float facedown so that nobody could see. He didn't know what had just happened, but, for the first time in a long time, he felt a hell of a lot better.

But he'd be damned if he'd let Shane know that.

Chapter 11

A S THE WEEK went by, Meredith thought these were some of the worst days she'd ever experienced. Dani's request had been official, so Meredith avoided Gregory as much as she could. Of course, it was impossible to avoid him all the time, and she did not deliberately go out of her way to avoid him in public settings, like the cafeteria or the pool. However, she rarely caught a glimpse of him, and, when she did, it was always from a distance.

However, every time she did see him, her heart ached at the pain on his face. She understood that Shane was working him hard, but there was also a murmur of some kind of a breakthrough. And, for that, she was absolutely overjoyed. If it came because of her absence, that made her seriously sad, but, if that's what it took to get Gregory back on his feet, then that's what it took.

To keep her mind off of him, Meredith became super efficient and super busy. She kept herself occupied every moment of the day, until finally, Dani called her into her office to talk. Meredith plunked down on a nearby chair, her arms full of files and tablets. Looking at Dani, she raised an eyebrow. "What's up?"

"You," Dani replied bluntly. "Several of the staff members have noticed that you're very edgy, that you're working too hard and that it's obvious how you're stressed about something. The idea was to relieve the stress, not to increase it."

Her back stiff, she stared at Dani, trying to figure out what she was supposed to do now. "The idea was to reduce Gregory's stress, I believe, not mine." Then she winced at her cattiness. Finally, she sagged in place and said, "I can't stop thinking about him, and the only way I can avoid spending too much time doing that is if I stay busy. And, if I'm not busy, then I just wallow."

"Understood," Dani said gently. "And I do have an official word here from Shane saying that Gregory's not completely over it all yet, but he hit one of those walls and broke through it. A lot of Gregory's anger has been released from his soul. They're working on getting some more of it out, but Gregory has reached a turning point."

Meredith beamed. "I'm really glad to hear that," she said. "I'm really sorry it came because of my absence, but I understand."

"I'm not sure it came from your absence at all," Dani said. "In a way, actually it might very well have been *because* of your absence but for another reason. I think he was angry that you weren't there for him. Whether it was because he understands you didn't have a choice or not, I don't know. But that anger at what he perceived as a slight from you was enough anger to push him up and over the edge."

"Ouch," Meredith said. "So by me following your orders, it made him angry enough to blow, thus letting go of some of these issues?"

Dani nodded. "And that might be hard for you to accept," she said, "but you might want to consider the fact that this is probably exactly what he needed."

"So, now what?" Meredith asked quietly. "It's been a

week."

Dani nodded. "Shane's requested that you stay away for another, say, two or three days, maybe as long as another week. Then we'll bring you two together and see where Gregory's anger spikes again and how."

"Along with psychologists?"

"Maybe, if needed," Dani said with a serious tone to her voice. "The whole point of this is his healing."

"I know." It was on the tip of her tongue to ask what about *her* healing, except she wasn't the important one here. She was one of the staff, not one of the patients. And there was only so much that anybody could do in a situation like this.

"And I understand how hard it is for you," Dani said. "But remember that, when he's a whole person, it makes life a whole lot easier on everyone."

"Exactly," Meredith said, standing up. "Anything else?"

Dani shook her head. "No, you're free to go, but please, slow your pace down. Your absence did what we needed it to do, and you will get over this, and so will Gregory. You can both make up over this," Dani reiterated.

Meredith let her lips quirk upward into a semismile. "I hope so," she said, "because he's a good man, and I value his friendship."

"Are you friends?" Dani asked curiously, stretching back in her chair, her arms in her lap. "Did you ever get to that stage where you're actually friends too?"

"I thought we were getting there," she said, "but we haven't really had enough time. And, no, you're right, before it was much less of a friendship and more of a relationship."

"Exactly. So maybe take the time, once we pull the brakes off, to get to know him, know who he really is, and see if he's still the same person you fell in love with."

Meredith walked to the door, and she then turned. "The trouble is, I already know. As soon as I saw him again, I already knew I'd made the wrong decision last time. I just hadn't acknowledged it. Until I couldn't see him again." And she turned and walked away.

She headed back to the nurse's office and just stared at her monitor. There was absolutely nothing going well for her today. *Another two to three days.* She shook her head. "That'll be very painful."

"I know," a man said from the doorway.

She looked up to see Shane. She frowned at him. "I don't want Gregory to think that it was my choice to stay away."

"And we'll tell him eventually," he said. "But we had to spike that anger so we could find an outlet for it."

"And I understand that," she said. "At least in theory I do. But it hurts. I hate to think of him hurting because of something he perceives me to have done when I didn't."

Shane folded his arms across his chest. "I promise we'll fix it afterward," he said, trying to put her worries to rest.

She nodded and stared down at her paperwork. "Another two to three days?"

"If you could, yes, please."

"Of course. Anything for him."

As Shane retreated, he tossed back, "It'll go very fast."

She muttered to herself, "Not fast enough." She knew the damage had already been done no matter what they said, but it's what she had to deal with, and Gregory's health came first. That was her job. For the first time in a long time, she realized how much her job sucked at times. But there was no point in moaning about it, so she reburied herself in her work.

THERE WAS STILL no sign of Meredith. Gregory wondered if it was her choice or if she had been ordered to stay away. Maybe both. He'd been a pretty ugly sight these last few days, he admitted. He didn't know any other way to have it work, so he wasn't someone she should be around regardless. It's not like he was at this best. He didn't really know what he was doing yet because the slightest thing could set him off. When he mentioned it to Shane, he had nodded and said, "We need to get more of it out."

"I don't want to," Gregory said quietly. "I don't like seeing that part of my personality."

"Which is why it's even more important to release it all," Shane said, his tone equally low. "Particularly if there's anybody around here you want to spend time with. That anger is old. It's bitter, and it'll poison everything around you."

Instantly Gregory's face shut down. He looked around the room and said, "What are we doing next?" He watched Shane hesitate and then nod.

"Let's move on to the water exercises. I've wanted to give you some specific things to work on while you're there."

"Good enough," Gregory replied. "It's almost four o'clock anyway."

"So we'll spend a half hour going over some things in the water. Now I want you to practice this a minimum of three to five times a week, if you can."

"I don't even get to the pool that often," Gregory said.

"Well, from now on, we'll make it a part of your

workout. It's one of the best whole-body exercises that we can do for ourselves."

"Well, I guess these shorts I've got on are my swim shorts anyway," he said, "so let's go down." He led the way to the elevator, out to the patio, only to see Meredith leaning over the deck above. He feasted his eyes on her until someone called her away.

Without giving Shane any chance to *help* Gregory— particularly after the last time, when Shane had locked the wheelchair and threw Gregory in—he took a couple hops to the railing, being careful to not slip, and fell in. The water closing over his head wasn't the same kind of relief that he'd experienced last time, but then the last time had been so emotional that he'd been drained afterward. He'd even spent most of the last several evenings eating dinner in his room. Now this pool work would force him back in the public eye again, and he wasn't sure he was ready for it.

Gregory came back up slowly and floated. This time, Shane walked along the edge. He instructed Gregory to go through the paces of standard swimming techniques to see just where he was at.

Gregory shook his head and said, "I did this for a living." He swam like the dolphin he was, back and forth from one stroke to the other, rolling forward and backward and sideways. When he finally came to a stop, Shane grinned at him.

"Feels good, doesn't it?"

Gregory nodded. "It does. So, what is it you want me to do in here?"

They went over a series of exercises that seemed simple enough at first, but Gregory very quickly learned that *simple* with Shane was not simple because Gregory had to do it exactly as Shane said, and he wanted certain muscles isolated. No other muscle was allowed to come into play. And that was really hard as Gregory had found the gluteus maximus— or his butt—had a tendency to take over everything it possibly could.

Shane explained. "That's because it's the big stalwart muscle that knows it can handle this. It's always protecting and guarding the rest of the body. But, as such, the rest of the body gets to be weak and isn't gaining any strength, like it needs to be. So these exercises that seem like they're nothing will make a big difference."

Gregory trusted him so far. Shane had led him into the storm and then guided him safely back out again, so Gregory would certainly trust Shane as he went into the water and back out again. But it wasn't easy to sort through. As a matter of fact, it seemed like a lot of trouble, and for what? By the time Shane had explained exactly what to do and when to do it, Gregory felt his own body rebelling. Finally he stopped and said, "Six."

Shane assessed the truth of his words and the pain of the workout, then nodded. "Now it's dinnertime, if you care."

"Well, I care," Gregory replied. "It's just that I'll stay in the water for a bit. Feels like a little bit of energy needs to be broken down."

Shane studied his face for a long moment. "No more than another twenty minutes. We're not going back into the muscle-cramp scenario we slid into before."

Understanding, Gregory immediately headed back to swimming. As long as he focused on his laps, he could get his mind off Meredith. When he finally came to a stop, he wasn't tired, but all his senses had been on alert, making the swim not so relaxing. As he looked up and casually looked around, he still saw no sign of Meredith. She wasn't coming back.

He could feel his insides deflating. Had she left on purpose to avoid him? It seemed like that's what she had been doing these days. But then, looking sideways, he saw Shane and Meredith standing at the top of the stairs, talking—he hoped not about him. Because that would be humiliating. He knew that Meredith herself was very private and wouldn't want to be talked about, so he hoped that she would give him the same courtesy. He made his way to the side and, of course, realized too late that he had forgotten a towel.

He looked around and hopped up, standing on his one leg. He could walk if he had to, use his stump for balance for a moment or two, but it would just set him back from getting a prosthetic, so he sat down in his wheelchair, wet and all, and moved to where the towels were. There, he switched to the bench, took the towel, dried off his wheelchair and then proceeded to dry himself.

It was nice enough out that he wanted to just lie in the sun. He folded his towel, put it on the wheelchair and then wheeled over to one of the loungers, where he stretched out and closed his eyes. It had been a long time since he'd done something like this, and it felt good. He was starting to feel really good on the inside.

It wasn't anything like what he'd thought *good* actually felt like when he'd first arrived here because *this* felt like a holistic inside-out kind of good. He knew it didn't make any sense, and it was darn hard to explain, but it was helpful. And, with that, he closed his eyes and napped.

Chapter 12

MEREDITH LOOKED AT Gregory down below on the lounger. She didn't want him to sleep too long or to miss dinner or to get too burnt.

Shane leaned against the railing beside her. "You really care, don't you?"

"I do," she said. "I made a mistake five years ago with him. And I knew he was coming here, and I tried to prepare myself. But I honestly thought, after all this time, probably nothing was between us, but there certainly is on my side. But I didn't let myself believe it."

"I know it won't make you feel any better because of the enforced separation that we've requested, but he cares too."

"Oh, he cares," she said, "but I'm not sure it's the right kind of caring." She gave Shane a sad smile and continued, "I don't know if you're standing here to watch over him, but he could burn."

"I'll stay here and have a cup of coffee," he said. "I'm meeting up with a bunch of our new residents."

"Good. I'll get changed, have a shower and come back for dinner." She disappeared quickly. If it was the only way to stop Shane's conversation, then she'd take it. Back at her place, she realized she should have picked up a plate of dinner and brought it home with her; then she wouldn't have to worry about going back out there.

For a moment, she contemplated the idea of just staying in for the night and then decided she needed the social aspect too. She'd been working so hard these last few days that she'd isolated herself even more than usual. Forcing herself into shorts and a tank top with a light sweater, in case a breeze came up, she put on sandals and headed back outside.

She stopped along the pastures and smiled at the horses. Appie and Lovely were running across the field, absolutely delighted with the day.

Appie jumped and kicked, and the little baby llama tried to follow. Meredith laughed out loud, loving the mix of animals in nature. When something cold nudged her hand, she looked down to see Helga, the great big Newfoundland with the peg leg, beside her. She crouched and gave her a big hug. "Are you supposed to be out here on your own?" she chided. "Or is that the problem? You are out here on your own, and you're completely lost. Or lonely." She gave her a big cuddle and then straightened, brushing the dog hair off her, and walked toward the pool area, calling Helga to join her.

She looked up to see if Shane was still watching over Gregory, but he'd disappeared. That would mean Gregory was probably gone too, but then she saw him, still napping on a lounger. Helga was at her side the whole way. It was a problem trying to keep her out of the pool most of the time, and Dani, not wanting to have the poor dog suffer in the heat, especially with Helga's heavy coat of fur, had changed to a different filter system on the pool, so the animals could come in at times too. And just then, Helga got the idea, and she raced ahead and did a belly flop into the pool.

Meredith giggled and giggled, her cupped hands at her

mouth to not disturb Gregory's nap, while Helga swam back and forth. Then she hopped up the steps, stood at the top and gave an almighty shake, splattering water all over Gregory. He woke with a startled cry as he sat up to see Helga right beside him, shaking hard.

He looked at her, laughed and said, "There are easier ways to wake up."

"Maybe," Meredith said as she walked toward him. "But it's a fairly unique one, you must admit."

"Maybe not around this place," he said.

Helga walked closer to Gregory so she'd get a cuddle from him, and, as his hand came away completely coated in wet dog hair, he sighed. "This is definitely not the cleanest way to head in for dinner."

"And that's why there are outdoor showers, soap and a separate drainage system right over there." She pointed a few feet away from the pool.

He looked and smiled. "I don't think I even noticed that before." Getting up, he made his way to his wheelchair, rolled over where he could turn on a sprinkler head system and quickly washed up again. He looked at her and asked, "Are you going up for dinner?"

She laughed. "I'm starved, so, yes. You?"

"Maybe in a bit," he said, his tone turning more formal. "I've got to get changed first."

She nodded and immediately withdrew. "Enjoy," Meredith said. She scampered up the stairs as fast as she could. At the top, she walked over to the line starting to settle down, but some of her emotions must have shown on her face because Dennis took one look and asked her what was wrong.

She gave him a brittle smile. "Nothing. Maybe it's the

fact that I'm hungry," she said in an attempt at a teasing tone.

"I hope so," he said, "because I know you would enjoy this. I made southern fried chicken just for you." Immediately she held out her plate, and he gave her three big pieces.

She laughed and said, "The only thing I'll have room for besides this is some salad." He grabbed a second plate and put a big salad on it.

Seated outside, she felt a little melancholy, wanting to be alone, but not so alone that she was out in the field with the animals. She needed human contact too, and right now it seemed like her contact—limited as it had been—only highlighted how much she had spent every day wondering how quickly she could see Gregory. It wasn't like she didn't treat her other patients with great care, but, in her mind, she was always waiting for an opportunity to see him. She'd just seen him outside, but it hadn't the same effect as seeing him face to face.

There was no longer that same friendliness between them. Something was definitely broken. And, for that, she could blame Dani and Shane. And Meredith also knew that, if she brought it up to them, they would say what really mattered was the fact that Gregory was healing.

So she wouldn't cause any waves because the last thing she wanted was to lose her job and to never see Gregory again.

WAKING UP TO see her standing there, watching him, Gregory took all the strength and determination that he had to not break out in a big smile and reach for her hand. But it wasn't to be, and he'd soon remembered that she'd avoided him for the last couple weeks.

Gregory wanted to go back to his room and get changed, but he could have gone and had dinner with her. He could have spent a few moments in her company, remembering the good things they had enjoyed about each other before. Instead, he let her walk away, wanting it to look like he didn't care. Then again she probably didn't care. So who was he to create something out of nothing?

Angry and fed up and just sad with the whole scenario, he made his way back to his room, where he collapsed on the bed and stared out the window. He wasn't sure what he was supposed to do now.

He was adjusting a little bit more to their workouts. The only good thing about that was how tonight he had lots of energy and didn't need to just crash. The bad thing about that was how he had lots of energy and wouldn't just crash.

It also meant that, once Shane found out, he would change Gregory's program the very next day. According to Shane, they had to continually shift the program and make Gregory's body work to adapt all the time. But he was hungry, and he needed food. Shane had been very clear about that too.

As Gregory changed for dinner, he had to decide on crutches or the wheelchair.

He was still waiting on that prosthetic. He was hoping for it the very next day. He had thought it would be here already, but it wasn't. He grabbed his crutches, put them under his arms and immediately felt his muscles scream.

"So much for that idea," he muttered. *Wheelchair it is.* Gregory laid the crutches against his bed, sat down on the wheelchair and took himself back to the cafeteria for food.

He could smell it from outside the doors. He rolled his way forward to see Dennis's big grin greeting him. "Are you always this happy?" Gregory asked.

"I so am," Dennis said. "What's eating you today?"

"Nothing any different than any other day," he said. "What have you got that'll heal me and get me back up on my feet faster?"

"Well, a plate of veggies and a plate of meat. How's that?"

"Maybe some carbs because I'm tired," he said with a yawn. With three plates, he shook his head as Dennis piled them up with food on the tray on his lap. He made his way down to the cutlery and tried to get some water, but Dennis leaned around the canteen and said, "You go pick out a table, and I'll get you some drinks."

Maneuvering carefully, Gregory made his way to the far end of the deck in the sun. As he unloaded his tray, Dennis arrived with a bottle of water, a cup of coffee and a carton of milk.

"Why the milk?" he asked in surprise.

"Calcium," Dennis replied. "With all that work, you need calcium." And he smiled, moved his empty tray and said, "Enjoy."

Gregory stared at the food and just shook his head. There was enough here for two people, and that just brought him back to remembering Meredith. They'd had every meal together in those first few weeks. Hating the memories, and yet, loving them at the same time, he attacked his steak with more gusto than needed, but, as soon as he popped the first bite in his mouth, he immediately slowed down and moaned in delight. It was tender, tasty and cooked perfectly. After that, finishing his meal was no problem at all. Dennis came around with another bottle of water, motioned at his plate and said, "You only ate half your vegetables."

"I'm working on it," Gregory said with a smile. "But you gave me a lot."

"Should have eaten your vegetables first," he said. "And then the meat. Your body needs the easily digested nutrition."

"It does, so I thought I'd sit here for a bit, then finish eating."

"Good idea," Dennis said. "Don't make me come back and have to pick up leftovers." And he took off again.

Gregory smiled as Dennis walked away. How had everybody here gotten to be so friendly? He knew people at the other center too, but they weren't like this. They weren't invested in his care. Or maybe the truth was they weren't invested in him.

He had thought for sure Meredith was part of the group invested in his healing process, which made her absence these weeks all the more puzzling.

On top of that, she'd been always friendly when he did see her, so it was as if nothing was wrong, as if nothing had ever happened.

But something had, and it was definitely troubling.

Finally, he finished his vegetables, pushed the plate back out of his way and slouched in his wheelchair. His back was killing him. It was definitely time to go back to bed and to stretch out again, but it was sad because the weather was beautiful. A light breeze took away the hot stifling air that he'd noticed earlier, and, if he sat here long enough, the sun would go down, and a beautiful sunset would happen.

Except he'd be watching it alone.

And, at that, he realized how pathetic it was that he'd be

sitting here all alone, staring at the evening. He had to stop mooning over her. She was friendly, professional, and that was it. Their time together was gone, not to mention that who he was before was gone, never to return. It was better he accepted that now and moved on.

On that note, he pulled his wheelchair away from the table, turned and slowly headed to his room for the night. It would be another night hiding away. This time not from physical pain but from emotional pain.

Maybe soon, if he was lucky, he'd finally get over losing her.

Chapter 13

M EREDITH WORKED HARD for the next few days. She hated this arrangement that the others had forced on her, but she would do her part. It felt unnatural, and she felt certain that Gregory would know this wasn't her idea. It was easier to avoid him than to be so professional with him, not to mention it hurt her to see him suffer.

He looked lonely, and at times he looked worse than that. He looked despondent, and she could feel her own anger rising up within. But there was no outlet for her except more work—since she was avoiding the pool now that Gregory had his workouts there—so that's what she did. She dove into work yet again, cleaning up the shelves, getting the backlog of paperwork taken care of. Washing and scrubbing anything and everything to try to keep her mind off him.

On the third day, she sat down at her computer, feeling an edginess sliding through her system. She looked up to see both Dani and Shane frowning at her. Meredith immediately frowned right back. She didn't say anything but waited for them to speak.

"Houston, we have a problem," Shane said in a funny voice.

"What kind of problem is that?" she asked, returning her gaze to the screen.

"He's hit a wall," Shane said bluntly.

Immediately her gaze flew back to him. "Gregory? What kind of wall?" She tried hard to keep the worry out of her voice, but both of them heard it. Meredith could tell from their voices when they next spoke. She sagged back against her chair and said, "What's happening with him?"

"He's gone from anger—which is great, we've gotten rid of most of that—and now he's incredibly depressed," Shane said softly. "And I think that's back to you again."

She raised both hands in frustration. "What do you want from me?" she cried out. "It's hard on me too, you know?"

He nodded. "I know it is. That's why we're here."

She glared at him. "And what exactly are you here for?"

He glanced over at Dani.

Dani picked up the conversation. "We think it's time to stop the enforced separation."

"I see," she said mutinously, perversely not wanting to have anything to do with Gregory just because they said so again. She pinched the bridge of her nose, trying to tell herself to back off and to calm down and that they were looking at it from a perspective she wasn't detached enough to see. "And how am I supposed to do that?"

"Well, you could be friendlier to him," Shane said.

"He needs an explanation," Meredith said quietly. "Otherwise, I'm just blowing hot and cold and hot and cold again. Nobody needs that. Neither him nor me."

"And it's okay to tell him exactly what's happening," Shane said. "Maybe that's what needs to be done so that he understands that you didn't have a choice."

She frowned, picked up a pencil and flipped it end over end between her fingers. She studied the pencil but could only see Gregory's face. "I saw him this morning," she said abruptly. "He looked almost despondent. Depressed."

"Which is why it's time to shift things again. There was this massive well of anger inside him," Dani said. "With that drained out, he's now left with this empty hole. And, with nothing good to fill it, he's filling it with the negative."

Slowly Meredith nodded. "And I guess we have seen that before too, haven't we?" She stared at Dani and then looked at Shane. Both of them nodded. "It's easier from where you guys stand," she complained, though she felt more balanced. "It's hard from here. I'm not detached enough to accept the games you're playing, even though I've participated in them before."

"Which is why it was so important to have you back off initially," Dani said gently.

"And why it's equally important now that you stop backing off and step forward," Shane said.

The two of them stepped out and walked toward the hallway.

Shane called back, "I know it's not something you can turn off and on like that, but sometime today would be good." And the two of them disappeared.

Long after they were gone, she sat here, trying to work, but her mind was consumed with what she was supposed to do now.

She had seen that look on Gregory's face; she had seen that horrible sense of his loss. But she didn't know what was causing that. She highly doubted it was her, but, if it was, then she and Gregory needed to clear the air. Because Shane's words had struck a chord. She had a well of emptiness inside her too. And it had been there for five long years.

At lunchtime, she walked into the cafeteria, her mind still consumed with Gregory. She quickly made herself a salad and went to sit out on the deck. No sign of Gregory.

She dawdled over her salad, watching who came in, her antennae always up and looking for him, of course, but still, she saw no sign of him.

Finally, she finished eating, put away her dishes and headed down the stairs to the pool area, wondering if he was there. But it was empty. Stumped, more than a little upset at the situation and upset at herself for not being able to let it go, she walked out to the animals and wandered around. Off to the far side, a good two hundred yards away, down one of the lonelier stretches of the pathway, was a wheelchair with somebody sitting in it. In her heart of hearts, she knew it would be Gregory.

Frowning, not sure if it was the right time but unable to leave him alone like that, Meredith walked over to make sure it was him. Sure enough, he sat here, staring at the animals.

"I'm surprised to find you here," she said when she got closer.

Startled, he looked up at her, shrugged and said, "It's not like I can leave."

"Ouch," she said with a bright smile. "Maybe not, but I hear you have a prosthetic leg coming pretty quick."

"They've been telling me that for days," he said. "I think it's just a catch-all answer."

"Meaning, you haven't got it yet?"

"No," he said, "and it would be nice to get it. I'd love to walk independently."

"Understood. I'll take a look for it when I get back to the office." She frowned. "If I recall correctly, it should have arrived a week ago."

"That's what Shane said, but sometimes I wonder if Shane is telling the truth." On that note, he gave her a cryptic look, turned his wheelchair around and said, "See you later." And he rolled away from her.

She stood here for a long moment, wondering what else she could have said. But he'd left it kind of cut-and-dried and left her without much to say. She followed behind him at a slower pace and waited until he disappeared before she headed back to her office. As soon as she was there, she checked in with Dani about Gregory's prosthetic.

"It's been delayed twice," Dani said, sighing. "It should have been here already."

"I know that's part of his depression," she said. "He also seems to be either upset or maybe suspicious of Shane right now." She quickly explained the conversation she had with Gregory.

"Probably because of Shane's part in all this," Dani said. "Shane worked him hard in order to get some of that bottled-up emotion out, and no one ever really likes the messenger of bad news."

"I know," Meredith said quietly. "Well, maybe I'll talk to Gregory a little bit later, see how he is."

"I've shifted the roster, so he's back on your list again," Dani said.

"Okay, I'll do a checkup in another hour or so." She started her rounds again, checking on everybody, making sure those who needed medication got it and the rest were either at their appointed sessions or were resting and didn't need anything else.

By the time she got to Gregory—she'd left him for last—it was almost four p.m. She was hoping he was done with his therapy, but she also understood that Shane had tacked on the pool workout some days. She knocked on his door, heard a shout to come in and pushed open the door. He sat on the side of his bed, looking a whole lot worse for the wear. She winced. "Ouch, you look like you're sore today."

He shot her a hard look. "This is nothing. Today is actually a huge improvement over the last few weeks."

"Good," she said with forced cheerfulness. "You're back on my roster, so I'm checking to see if you need anything." She studied his muscles and continued, "I know you may not have been terribly happy with Shane's methods, but your body has really, really developed since you've been here." Meredith sounded enthusiastic, even to her own ears. She walked closer, studying the damage along his back. "Wow," she exclaimed. "That's a huge difference."

"Is there?" he asked, almost with indifference.

"I'll show you." Impulsively she put her pencils and papers down, picked up her tablet, took a picture and showed it to him.

He looked at it and just shrugged.

"Sure, you may not see the difference," she chided, "but here's the before picture." It took her a moment to pull up the before picture that she had in her files from when he'd first arrived and had come with medical photos showing the damage. She put the two of them side by side and held it out to him.

He studied one and then the other, and his eyebrows shot up. "Oh, wow. I feel like I need to frame that."

She nodded. "You do. I think one of the worst things people can do is not take that before picture because then they never have anything to realize how far they've come. You have come so far," she said. "You should be feeling damn proud of yourself."

But his gaze, when he looked at the photos, was hooded. "Maybe. I need to be proud of something I've done. Seems like all I've done the rest of my life is the wrong thing."

That was the opening she needed. "In what way?" He hesitated, but she didn't want to let him off the hook. "Joining the navy was exactly what you wanted to do," she said. "It was your passion. That means it was the right thing to do."

He looked up at her. "Even when I lost out on a wife and a family?"

Her breath caught in the back of her throat, but she nodded slowly. "For that," she said, "even if you're not talking about you and me, I do owe you an apology."

He reared back slightly and looked up at her in surprise.

She nodded. "I was thinking of me at the time. I wasn't thinking of you. I'm not normally selfish, but then I hadn't come up against something that I really, really wanted for myself until I met you. I wanted you, and I didn't want to lose you to the navy again." She continued, "So I'm sorry. I made the wrong decision back then, and I didn't think things through, and I didn't think of your perspective."

He stared at her, shocked.

She winced. "And I understand if that's not what you were trying to talk about, and I'm sorry because I probably shouldn't have brought it up." She snagged up her paperwork, gave him a quick glance and said, "I'll make sure I send you this picture."

And she disappeared. As soon as she bolted out of his room and down the hallway, she felt like a fool. But, at the same time, she felt a cleansing inside. She'd said what she needed to say. Maybe, just maybe, she could finally move on too.

GREGORY STARED IN shock at the doorway where she disappeared. His session today had been harder than normal, forcing him to adapt again. Even when he went to the gym for a workout, sometimes everything went smooth and easy, and the next time it was like moving through molasses, and he could not muster up any energy. Today was one of those days. Seeing her earlier had just made him even more upset, and then finding out he was back on her roster, and she would now be seeing him on a regular basis but only professionally, ... well, that hurt.

But to hear what she had just said? ... He didn't even know what to say. He hadn't been talking about their relationship. He'd been talking about other decisions he'd made in life. But maybe he should have been talking about their relationship. Instead, she had been the one to bring it up, but not in the way he'd expected.

She'd apologized for making the wrong decision, for not understanding his point of view. Well, he'd been exactly the same; he hadn't understood her point of view. He loved to think that she had thought he was something that she really, really wanted for herself. It's the way he'd felt about her too, but he couldn't walk away from his loyalty to country and his career. It was part of who he was, the most honorable part. As he'd stared at his busted-up body and thought what it had done for him, his *this is where I'm at now* body, it hurt that she hadn't even mentioned *now*.

She'd been all about yesterday, the past. And he was hung up on that, hating the fact that everything she'd said had been in the past tense. What he figured they needed to do was let the past go and see if there was anything they had to move forward with. He knew that he wanted a relationship with her, but he wasn't exactly offering her much at this point in time. He didn't even have a career anymore, whereas she was a nurse. And look at this place where she worked; it was fantastic. She lived here, all her meals, everything was taken care of. How could he pull her away from that for a life he couldn't even think about? He stared out the window, feeling his heart wrenching, as he realized that they were better off going their own ways.

Gregory straightened slowly, feeling his body had aged considerably since the injury. He quickly changed into swimming trunks, got back into the wheelchair, wondering where his damn prosthetic leg was, and made it down to the pool.

He locked the wheels, and, without giving himself any chance to think, he dove in again. Tired and moving a whole lot slower than normal, he just kept going, length after length after length. When he finally stopped, he was afraid he'd overdone it. When he tried to pull himself out and fell back into the water, he looked up to find Shane sitting there.

"Feel better?" Shane asked. "Or did you overdo it again?" His face was creased with worry, and his tone said that he knew exactly what Gregory was going through.

"No, I'm fine," Gregory said. "Just sad and grieving. A hope that I had held on to needs to go into the past and stay there."

Shane studied his face for a moment while Gregory wiped the water off and struggled up the ladder to sit on the edge of the pool.

"The thing about the past," Shane said finally, "is that you can't ever bring it into the present. But whatever was in the past, if it was good, there's no need for it to be bad now either. Remember the good and recreate it in the present and make something better out of it."

"Easy for you to say," he said in a harsh voice. "You're whole. You have a career and a future. That was me in the past. It's not who I am now."

"Well, I'm not listening to that bullshit," Shane said. "Because I know the truth. I know that who you are right now is better than I am," he said. "Do you think I don't know how much everybody who comes through this place has been through, whereas me, I haven't been tested like that. I haven't had my body torn apart like you guys. I haven't had to deal with the emotional and psychological damage of what you've been through. I didn't serve my country. I was in school, and I didn't choose to go into the military in any form."

Shane was on a roll. "I've often wondered how I would have fared if I had served. I don't think I would have done well. You are who you are," he said calmly, but his voice was low, so nobody else would hear. "Stop knocking that. You're a damn fine man. And any woman—particularly the one who we both know we're talking about—would be very happy to take you as you are. But you have to reach out and let her know that you care."

"How can I?" Gregory asked. "She basically apologized for our past, but it was a goodbye. It wasn't a *Hey, this is where we're at, and let's see where we can go.* It was an *I'm sorry*, almost like she needed to move on."

Shane shook his head. "No, that's not it at all. She doesn't want to cause you any pain, and we had to pull her away to help you get over the anger eating at you," he said, "and we're the ones who forced her to stay away from you. Now whatever happened today—I don't know what that was—but I can tell you that she spent the last week and a half dealing with her own sense of grief and her own loss and her own anger over what we did. Don't blame her for coming to the wrong conclusion. What you need to do is clear the air, and see where you stand now." And, on that note, he got up and left.

For the second time that day, Gregory stared in shock as someone walked away from him. Meredith didn't have a choice? She had been removed from his care so that he could deal with his own issues? How did that work? Meredith *was* his issue. And obviously, Shane and Dani knew that. It felt weird to think that everybody else was discussing his personal life. But he'd come here specifically to see Meredith, and, of course, he'd gotten so much more in a different way. Still, he really wanted her, but her words had seemed so final today. They were an ending rather than a beginning.

Was Shane right? Was she under the wrong assumption, or was Gregory? Or maybe they both were. Was it all about communication or the lack thereof?

Gregory stared down at his stump, realizing just how much better it did look. She was supposed to check into his prosthetic, and it wouldn't make that much difference—not about getting her back, that is—but it was almost like a symbol of moving on again. With it, he could stand on his own two feet.

It was such a simple sign of progress. Hell, he should have just made himself a peg leg and stuck with it. It was also very indicative of how he felt about himself in this world, that he couldn't stand on his own two feet physically or mentally, spiritually or emotionally.

Thinking to himself, he got back into his wheelchair and made his way to his room, where he changed into dry clothes. He grabbed the crutches and headed to the cafeteria. He stopped at the entranceway, hearing lots of conversations and loud laughter. He'd made a few friends here himself but mostly kept off to the side, isolated. He wanted to blame Meredith, which was hardly fair, yet it seemed like, when he was given a choice, he always went to a table where nobody else was.

Dennis called out to him. "Hey, Gregory, how are you doing?"

He hopped over and gave the ever-friendly man a smile. "Hungry and fed-up with life at the moment."

"Well, we got the cure for what ails you," he said. "How about lasagna and maybe some ribs on the side?"

He looked over at Dennis. "What, no vegetables?"

"Sometimes we need comfort food," Dennis said. "And, if vegetables aren't it for you, they are not going to cut it."

"Thank you," Gregory said. "And you're right. I need comfort food right now. So load me up." They went through the food, getting him a decent plate. Dennis grabbed a tray, filled it up and carried it for him. "You do look tired today," Dennis said.

"Tired, worn-out, fed-up." He nodded and said, "Just one more of those days."

"You'll have a lot of them for a while," Dennis said seriously. "But they will ease as you improve."

"I know," Gregory said. "I just wish I was there already."

Dennis led the way to a table out all on its own.

When Gregory hobbled behind, he said, "Let's change that up."

Dennis turned to him and raised an eyebrow.

A group of men sat off to one side at a table that would easily seat ten. Motioning, Gregory said, "Maybe I shouldn't be quite so antisocial all the time."

Dennis grinned. "Come on. I'll introduce you." He

walked over to the table with the others and said, "Hey, guys. This is Gregory. He could use a little company."

The men all smiled, shook hands and introduced themselves. One man pointed at the table and said, "Lots of room here. Grab a spot."

Gregory sat down and started to eat his dinner. He partially listened in the conversation, but very quickly the men turned their attention to him and started asking him questions. He was surprised at how nice it was to have a conversation with somebody who wasn't concerned about his health or his emotional status, and he thoroughly enjoyed himself. By the time he finally finished his meal, most of the men had gone, and he sat and talked with one guy named Steve.

Steve was almost done at Hathaway House. He had another week to go. Steve asked, "How long do you have?"

"Another couple months, I think," Gregory said. "When I got here, I was pretty cocky, thought I knew how to do this, knew what this was all about." He shook his head, a wry grin on his face. "And then I started working with Shane."

Steve laughed. "Isn't that the truth. We can be as cocky as we want when we get here because we've been through it all before we got here. In truth, we're way behind the curve because Shane is way ahead of the curve, and, for that, we should be damn grateful. But, when you're working with him, when you're in the middle of it all, it's pretty hard to find the energy to be grateful."

Gregory leaned back, looked at Steve and smiled. "And that's the truth I needed to be reminded of," he admitted. "I haven't exactly had the nicest thoughts about him lately."

Steve smirked. "Whatever they do here, they do for your sake. You may not like it. You may not like their methods.

You may not like the hard work right now," he said, "but you will like the end result by the time you take a look at yourself down the road. Has anybody showed you a before and after photo?"

"Meredith did one today," he said. "I was shocked, honestly. I didn't get much of a chance to look at it, but she said she'll send it to me."

"Those photos, they're gold," Steve said. "They've kept me going through so much here. I know a lot of the guys don't put any stock in them, but I do because, if I don't know where I've been, I don't recognize how far I've come." And, on that note, he slapped the table, stood and said, "And now it's time for me to head back to my room. I've got a video conference with my family tonight." With a big grin, he picked up a huge cup of coffee and walked on two prosthetics out of the room.

Gregory chuckled; Steve wore shorts and was completely casual about the fact that he had two mechanical legs. And, if he was so relaxed about it, why the hell was Gregory having such a hard time? Of course, it would be nice if he even got his first prosthetic, and maybe one that would fit. Possibly that was the difference. It was amazing just how far he'd come; Steve was right. Gregory hadn't given enough credit where credit was due. He didn't like Shane's methods, didn't like anything about what they'd done to keep Meredith away, but obviously, it had been good for her too. That distance had given her perspective.

And something about that brought up a wave of anger that he had trouble keeping down. As he sat here, the anger grew and grew. With perfect timing, he saw her arrive for dinner. She walked over to go out on the deck, and he waited until she was seated. Then he hobbled away from his table, headed out onto the deck, stood beside her and, in a low, hard voice, he said, "You had your say, but it's time for me to have mine."

She looked up at him in surprise and said, "I'm sorry. Did I do something to upset you?"

"Yes. I get that you're ready to let go of the past, and I certainly accept whatever apology you think you need for your part in our breakup," he said, "but you have to let me apologize too because I wasn't thinking about you. I wasn't thinking about anything but me, and that wasn't fair either."

She started to smile. "Okay, we both screwed up."

"Back then, yes," he said, taking a deep breath, "we both did. And I think, since I've arrived, we've both screwed up more."

She looked at him, and he could see the hurt in her eyes.

"Shane told me what he asked you to do. He said that Dani took me off your roster and that it wasn't personal on your part. For a long time, I thought it was, and I was really angry," he said. "And I think that's what Shane was trying to do, to make me angry enough to make me blow, to get that emotion out. And now the inside of me feels scraped raw, and I don't really know how to handle it. But, when I'm sitting here thinking about what you said, I'm angry all over again."

"I didn't say that to upset you," she protested.

"No, of course not," he said, his tone almost caustic. "You said it for yourself. I get that you're ready to move on. The problem is, I'm not."

She stared at him in shock.

Gregory nodded and continued, "Now you figure out how to deal with that." And he spun around and crutched out of the cafeteria. When he got to his room, he was grinning because, this time, he felt in control. This time, he felt like he'd done something positive to move his own life forward.

And, damn, that felt good.

Chapter 14

MEREDITH SPENT THE next two days in hiding. She alternated between red with anger and white with fear. She avoided Gregory until she could be calm enough to talk to him. She thought she'd had it all worked out until his words the other day. Even now she didn't really have a reason to back away, except that she felt it was something that she needed to do to regain control.

Finally, Shane stepped into her office and frowned at her.

She frowned right back.

"You need to talk to him," he said, shoving his hands into his jean pockets. "Whatever is going on is holding him back."

"I don't think so," she said calmly. "He pretty much tossed a gambit at me, and I haven't decided if I'm going to pick it up or not."

"Or you've decided already," Shane said with a nod of his head, "but, for whatever reason, whatever he said or did is confusing you."

She took a deep breath. "I haven't talked to him because I don't dare," she said. "I might be glad to go in there and blast him myself."

He grinned. "Maybe that would be better," he said. "Blast away, get it all out in the open. Then you can kiss and make up."

"And yet, I'm not sure kissing and making up is on the agenda," she said, turning her gaze to the computer monitor in front of her. "It's not always that easy."

"No, but I do find we make most things in life more complicated because we don't actually communicate. We leave everything as this big nightmare, instead of clarifying what it was that people were trying to say. But I can't have you hindering his progress, so you best decide what you'll do before I have to step in and make sure that the entire team knows what's going on."

She glared at him. "That's blackmail."

"That's called having a relationship at Hathaway House, where everybody knows everything," he corrected. "I get that you are not quite ready, but I am telling you that you need to get ready faster." And, on that note, he turned and walked off.

She sat here, trying to control her breathing for a long moment, because she didn't know what the hell she was doing. Shane was right about that; she was confused. She was torn, and she cared so damn much that she didn't know how to get over her current situation.

Gregory had said he didn't want to find closure, that he wanted to have a relationship. So why was she arguing? Why was she sitting here, fighting it? All she wanted to do was have him wrap his arms around her and hold her close, like he used to when it felt like it was just the two of them alone in the world, when nobody else could quite understand how special what they had was. And now she didn't understand herself.

"He's right, you know," Dani said quietly as she walked inside. "No, I wasn't trying to listen, but I couldn't help overhearing. Most people don't understand what's going on, but, of course, I do."

"I'm confused," Meredith said, her tone hurt. "I don't even know what to do anymore."

"Well, usually the best way to handle that," Dani said, "is to talk."

"I pretty much said goodbye. Said that I was fine, how he could carry on his life, that I had been able to find some closure."

"Well, I'm sure that pissed him right off." Dani laughed. "Nobody likes to be told that somebody's ready to move on from them."

"He more or less told me that I could be as ready as I want, but he wasn't ready, so I had to deal with it."

"Well, you're not ready either," Dani said smoothly. "Hurt feelings utilize words all the time to gloss over the rough edges and to have nobody else understand exactly what it was that you were trying to say. But the truth of the matter is, you care. You've always cared. He cares. He's always cared. The two of you are at cross-purposes, yet shouldn't be."

Meredith nodded slowly. "It's just so silly."

At that, Dani laughed and laughed. "All relationship stuff usually is. The bottom line is whether you care enough that you want a relationship with this man in the shape he's in, as he is right now. And the issue for him is whether he's prepared to step up and be the man who he can be, and does he love you enough to pursue you in a relationship that will last through the end of time for both of you."

"When you put it that way ..." Meredith said, rolling her eyes.

Dani grinned. "A little bit of that wisdom was hard-earned through experience, but that really is the bottom line."

"It's not that easy to get there. I've pretty well ignored him for the last few days."

"Oh, you haven't ignored him at all," Dani said. "You are hyperaware of everything that he does and says. And that makes it even more obvious to the rest of us that you guys need to sort this out."

"Sure," she muttered, "it sounds easy, but …"

"Most things in life aren't," Dani said. "So why don't you take some time this afternoon? I happen to know he has an extended lunch break because our psychologist had to run into town to help somebody at the hospital, so Gregory is free for that session. You have your lunch hour and the first hour afterward where he is not booked up."

"That's like making an appointment," Meredith said, wrinkling up her face.

"So then, make it a meaningful one," Dani said. "Talk to Dennis. Maybe get a picnic and take Gregory to visit with the animals where there won't be any chance of you guys being overheard and then hash this out. It's really that simple."

But the fear was gripping and choking Meredith.

Dani nodded. "I can see the fear inside you. Every day we watch these men face their fears. Some days they do it well. Some days they don't," Dani said softly. "But we've also seen incredible acts of courage from people who we didn't think had it in them. They stand, step up and face the new challenges. Can you do any less?" And with that prophetic question, Dani turned and walked out.

Meredith sat here at her desk, her face in her hands for a long moment, and then she got up and walked into the kitchen. It was still a little early, but she saw Dennis standing out on the deck, enjoying the late-morning sunshine. She walked over to him. He turned around and gave her a beaming smile, but his smile fell away when he saw her face. "Uh-oh, problems in paradise?"

She gave him a half a smile. "Yes, but I'm hoping to maybe hash out some of the problems."

"What can I do to help?" he asked.

"A picnic lunch for two," she said, "if that's possible."

"For you and Gregory?"

She nodded. "We've been at crosscurrents since he arrived," she said. "It's time to clear the air and see where we stand."

He frowned at her and said, "You don't have to make it sound like a death sentence."

"It's kind of the opposite," she said. "He said he's not ready to walk away."

"But?"

She shrugged. "I guess there's no *but*. I just feel very confused about the whole thing."

"Then go back to the beginning," he said quietly. "Go back to the origin, to the start of it all, and remember what it was that you felt. And, if what you felt back then is the same thing you feel now, only more mature and a longer-lasting kind of emotion, then go with it. What you don't want to do is be a year from now, looking back at this moment, and wishing you'd done more, feeling like you've lost something very, very valuable because you weren't willing to reach out and offer something different."

"That's another way to look at it that I hadn't considered," she admitted.

"Well, think about it. How did you feel this last week

when you couldn't see him?"

She stared out over the pastures. That's what came from working with a tight-knit group. "You heard about that, huh?"

"I did," he said. "Probably most of us did. But we also know you were miserable. Is that how you want to be all the time?"

"But I won't be like that all the time," she argued. "It would be a settled issue."

"And that would make it worse," he said. "Right now, you have an easier time of walking away because you're not really walking away. He's still here, so that's still something that you have an option to proceed with. But, once you make that decision, then it becomes that permanent kind of a thing, and it's very hard to open that door again."

"I know, and I don't even have any real reason for feeling this way."

"Sure, you do," he said. "Your feelings don't need to be validated by anything other than the fact that they exist. What you must do is figure out why they exist and make a decision to move forward or not."

"I really love him, you know?" she said softly. She wrapped her arms around her chest, feeling the chill even though they were out in the sunshine. He reached an arm around her shoulder, hugged her close and said, "And that's the only answer there really is." He stepped away and called out as he left, "I'll have it ready for you at noon. Don't come in through the main part of the cafeteria. Just knock on the door, and I'll give it to you."

"Okay," she said. "Thank you."

He gave her a big grin. "We're going to have a lot of weddings around this place," he said, "and I can't wait." With that, he disappeared.

She walked back to her office and thought about what she was trying to set up, wondering how she would get Gregory's agreement. The easiest way would be to just ask him. And maybe he'd be okay with that too. She had to do her rounds anyway.

Meredith quickly took care of patients and stepped into his room. He had just returned from a session with some-one—she hadn't checked her tablet to see who it was. He looked up at her in surprise. She held up her tablet and said, "Checkup time."

Obediently he sat down and let her go through the motions of doing what she had to do every day.

"Are you ready for lunch?" she asked.

"I was planning on it," he said. "I'm feeling a bit stifled inside."

"Well, I have a plan," she said.

"What's that?"

She hesitated.

He looked at her and raised an eyebrow and said, "What's up?"

"We need to talk," she said.

Immediately his smile fell away. He stiffened, nodded and said, "Yes, we do."

"So, meet me at the elevator, maybe in twenty minutes?"

He frowned, considered her face for a long moment, then nodded. "That sounds ominous. Is there some bad news I need to know?"

She gave him half a smile. "I wouldn't do that to you." And she turned and walked away, but her stomach was hurting, and her palms were sweaty. It bothered her that she was making such a big deal out of it all, but she really needed to know where she stood, and she needed to know where he stood because she couldn't do the hot and cold anymore. It was just too devastating and too traumatizing to her sense of well-being.

Meredith finished her work and waited for the last five minutes to go by. It seemed super slow, but she was also terrified that something would happen or somebody would come in and take her away, and she wouldn't be able to meet Gregory.

Finally, she headed to the cafeteria and knocked on the door. Dennis met her there, handed her a large basket and said, "Enjoy."

And he closed the door in her face.

TIME ALONE WAS one thing. Time alone with lonely thoughts was something else altogether. What was she up to? Did he even want to know? Hell yeah, he did. It was killing him. Twenty minutes was nothing, but it was also a lifetime. He went over every possible option and still came up blank.

That had been their relationship so far: clarity followed by confusion. And this was no different. Moodily he sat in his chair and stared out the window, waiting for the time to pass. This trip had brought him so close, and yet, in many ways, he was still so far away from getting what he desperately wanted.

They were friends. Dare he hope they were good friends? But he hadn't told her about his reason for being here at Hathaway House. Would she appreciate hearing it or consider his actions in a negative light?

He knew they couldn't go on like this. Someone, somehow, needed to clear the air between them.

And it might as well be today.

Chapter 15

S HE MET HIM at the elevator on time. He took one look at her and saw the basket in her hands, and his gaze lit with pleasure. But almost immediately the light disappeared from his eyes. "So is this good news or bad news?" he asked again.

"I don't know," she said, "but I figured that, of all things that we needed to do, it was to come to an understanding."

"Agreed." He gave a clipped nod and rolled the wheelchair into the elevator. They went down to the bottom level, and there was Racer, sitting in somebody's arms, just staring outside. He looked at Racer, smiled and said, "I don't get to spend enough time with the animals."

"Once you start the heavy PT regime, it's hard to do everything. It takes about six weeks to get adjusted."

"Well, I should be there then," he said. "Actually it's been longer."

"Well, we've had some setbacks, haven't we?" She headed out and down. He followed her, rolling at her side down to the pasture, and then she remembered something. "Oh, your prosthetic came in," she said.

His face lit up with joy. "So, maybe this afternoon with Shane ..."

"I think so," she said. "That should make your life easier." She took him to a lovely spot, where they could sit and watch the animals and talk in private.

"What will make my life easier," he said, "is solving the problem between you and me. And the problem between you and me goes way back. The thing is, we've both apologized for who we were in the past. But we haven't addressed anything about who we are right now."

She pulled out a small blanket then sat down in a grassy spot. "Do you want to sit there in your wheelchair, or do you want to sit down here?" she asked.

"I want to come down there with you," he said. He locked the wheelchair, stood up on his good leg and made several hops before he finally collapsed on the grass beside her. He sat up, looked around, and said, "This is really nice and private."

"And I figured we needed that."

"Yes," he said, "I agree."

She opened the basket, laid out the small tablecloth and unpacked lunch.

"Wow, Dennis went over and above," Gregory said as he eyed the wine, a couple glasses and what looked like big platters of food.

"Yes," she said. "I think he enjoys things like this."

"I don't imagine he gets too many opportunities."

"No, I'd say mostly when there are problems," she said with a half laugh. Gregory opened the wine, poured her a glass, and handed it to her. She set it gently off to the side as she unwrapped what looked to be croissants stuffed with smoked salmon, also some biscuits and jam, a fresh fruit platter and even some gourmet cheeses. In the warm sunshine, a gentle breeze easing the heat, both of them sat apart, yet both were so aware of each other.

At this point in time, they sat here gently and ate.

"So what do you want to talk about?" he asked, not looking at her.

"Us," she said bluntly.

"Is there an us?" he asked.

"There could be," she said, "but I don't want to be going back and forth. I don't want to be apologizing for what was before. I don't want to even be thinking about what was before."

"Is it that easy?"

"Maybe if we're both determined to move forward, yes," she said quietly. "You're a very different person since you've arrived here." Immediately after she said that, she sensed him withdrawing. She shook her head. "No, I don't mean physically. I mean emotionally."

He looked at her in surprise. She nodded. "Yes, your body's changed. I'm a nurse. That doesn't bother me in the least," she said with a wave of her hand. "I get that, for you, it's huge, and I'm sorry. I'd have done anything I could have to save you from this. But there isn't anything I could have done. There isn't anything I can do other than to help you become the best and strongest that you can be."

She waited for him to say something, but he didn't. She took a bite of her sandwich, washed it down with a drink from one of the bottles of water and said, "Emotionally you're deeper, richer, stronger than I ever thought you would be." At that, she saw his shoulders straighten. She nodded. "Not what you expected me to say, I presume."

He shook his head slowly. "No," he said. "I think we tend to see only the deficiencies in our own selves. We rarely look for the good things."

"When you arrived, you were cocky, arrogant, confident, and I knew that you would take a beating ... because I've seen it happen before. Many arrive here thinking that they can ace their time here. We have those who are closed off from accepting help, and we have those who arrive open and willing to try, and then we have those who are full of themselves. They think that they've already been through rehab, so how hard can it be?"

At that, he snorted. "They haven't met Shane," he muttered.

At that, she laughed out loud. "And you're right there. Shane is a force to be reckoned with. But he runs a hell of a team, and he's the boss. What he says goes, and everybody else toes the line because he's good at what he does."

"As I've come to find out," he said. "If he had said that weeks ago, I may still have been on the disbelieving side of life, but I do believe it now."

"Exactly," she said, "and, in the process, I've learned a lot about who you are inside."

"Is that good or bad?" he asked hesitantly when she didn't speak again.

"Good." She looked over at him and smiled. "I'm also learning a lot about myself."

At that, he frowned at her. It was swift, deep and a bit hard.

She shook her head. "I still like myself," she said, "but I don't like who I was back then."

"I thought we weren't going there."

"Which is why we have to have this talk," she said. "Back then I was shallow, insecure, full of myself and thought too much of myself. I wanted you to leave your love and come be with me and make me your passion instead. And that was wrong. I've already told you that I'm sorry for all that. And then you came to me and said that I wasn't allowed to walk away and that you didn't want to have closure."

"I didn't want there to be closure from us, so you could walk away from what we had," he said. Then he stopped, confused. "That's bringing up the past again, isn't it?"

She nodded. "Which is why we're here," she said in a dry tone. "I would like to state for the record that I admire who you are, and I respect the journey you have traveled, and I'm incredibly heartened by the man I see before me now." She reached across, slid her fingers into his and added, "He's a very different man than the one I knew five years ago. But this one is vastly superior."

His fingers clenched tightly on hers. "This one's damaged," he said, his voice harsh but low. "Have you forgotten that?"

"No, I mentioned it earlier," she said cheerfully. "You're the one who sees the damage. I just see a challenge that you have already aced. I think it's incredible how far you've come and so fast. Shane thinks you've done an unbelievable job. He said that, when you got rid of that anger, there was a hollowed-out space inside though."

"That was where the anger used to be, but that anger filled the void from where *you* used to be," he said. "So, in truth, that void is still there."

She looked at him.

He reached up gently, brushed his thumb across her lips and said, "Unless you'd like to come home again."

Her eyebrows shot up. "Is that where I will be? Is that my home?"

"I don't know," he said, "that's definitely where you belong though."

She smiled and whispered, "Yes, please."

HE REACHED ACROSS and gently kissed her. It was a baby's breath of a kiss, just a gentle stroke of lips on lips, skin against skin, but it was heart against heart and love against love.

"I don't think I've ever had a more lonely five years in my life," he said, "but, when I woke up in the hospital and realized how damaged I was, how broken, it finally came to me how much I'd lost because I knew that you would never accept what I was now."

She opened her mouth, but he pressed a finger against it to stop her from speaking. "No, it's my turn," he said firmly but gently stroked her arm. "I needed to come and see you, see what this place could do for me, so that I might get back on track and be as whole as I possibly could. And, yes, I needed to do it for myself," he said impatiently. "But I also needed to do it to see if anything was left between us."

"Well, that was darn lucky for you that I was here," she said, laughing. But then her smile fell away. "It was a coincidence, wasn't it?" He gave her a secret smile as she shook her head. "There's no way you could have known."

"Couldn't I?" he asked. "Did you keep track of me all these years?"

"Well, I would search for your name every once in a while, but it's not like anything ever came up."

He laughed at that. "True," he said, "often nothing does come up. But, in your case, I had heard about Hathaway House. While on the website, when I was studying the staff, ... guess who's on the team photo page?"

She stared at him in shock and sagged back slightly. "You're right," she said. "I am up there."

He nodded. "And then I had to figure out if you were still single and whether you had anybody permanently in your life. And, of course, I can't tell you how many phone calls I made anonymously, asking if you were the woman I was looking for, saying the one I was seeking was married and had been living in California five years ago."

At that, she laughed. "And, of course, they would have said that, no, I was single."

"Exactly," he said, giving her a fat smile. "And that's what I needed to know."

"Are you saying you came here for me?" she asked in a daze.

"I came here on a hunch and a prayer that maybe, just maybe, you would let me back into your life," he said gently. "Even if I don't deserve it, I want it. I fought for it. I came here, and I've done the damnedest I could to put myself forward. … Never expecting the progress I've made. Or Shane. Or his plans that kept us apart. But the real goal in all of this was to have you back in my life." He looked at her and smiled almost nervously. "So, what's your answer?"

She teased and asked, "What's the question?"

He held out his hand. "Shall we take that path forward? See who we are to each other now? Take it to the end of the line, hopefully, seventy years down the road when we're both old and gray and shorter, curled up in matching rocking chairs together? And, if we're lucky, making a much better job of it than we have done so far?"

She leaned forward, brushed her lips against his and whispered, "I'd like nothing better. So my answer is yes."

And when he finally wrapped his arms around her and held her close—the Gregory she knew from five years ago now merged with the present-day Gregory—made the moment absolutely perfect.

Heath

Hathaway House, Book 8

Dale Mayer

Chapter 1

HEATH HANKERSON HAD fought his surgeon hard to sign off on his transfer to Hathaway House. As he was healing at a tremendous rate, the surgeon had finally been persuaded to let Heath sign on with somebody else, and that had let him take the open bed at Hathaway House.

"I've heard a lot of good things about Hathaway House," Dr. Macklin said. "I'm surprised you got in. But then, the fact that you did means maybe this is where you need to go."

"I think it means exactly that," Heath said in a quiet voice. "I want this opportunity. I've heard some pretty decent things myself."

"A lot of other good rehab centers are around the country though," Dr. Macklin said, as he studied Heath's face with care. "You could probably pick and choose."

"That's exactly it. And I have done exactly that. And I'm choosing Hathaway House."

"In that case, there's nothing more to talk about," the doctor said. "You're progressing well, and I would like to get regular updates. We've done a lot of surgeries, so it'll take quite a bit of time to recover. At this point I have no idea how well you'll do, but I'm hoping for a full recovery."

"I know it's up to me now."

"I'll write up detailed notes for the physio team there to continue the work you've been doing."

"I'd appreciate that," Heath said.

"Wouldn't hurt you to send me an email every once in a while too," Dr. Macklin said. And then he laughed. "I still get emails from patients I treated twenty years ago."

"That's because you care," Heath said with a grin.

"I do. It's not easy. We see people in pretty rough shape when they initially come in. We do the best we can, and sometimes it works, but sometimes it doesn't. At a certain point, the medical technology can only do so much for you. In this case, you've done pretty well though. Now it's up to the physio and to your own will to be better."

Heath nodded, and, just as he slowly moved out of the office, Dr. Macklin called out behind him.

"Do you have a specific reason for going to Hathaway House?"

Heath turned, looked at the doctor, and smiled. "Well, Houston was always home. I don't have any family left, but something is drawing me back there. As for why Hathaway outside of the location ..." He pondered for a moment and then said, "I guess the only answer I really have is just this gut feeling about it."

The doctor looked at him thoughtfully for a long moment, then nodded, and said, "Sometimes, as you know, the gut feeling is all we have to go on. In this case, I think it's an excellent call."

As Heath made his way to the elevator, he hoped the doctor was right. Heath had gone over the Hathaway House website with a fine-tooth comb and had talked to several people that he'd known to get help there. Some had tried to get in and had been refused because no bed had been available in time. On the other hand, a couple guys had come out of their treatment there and had glowing praises.

At the end of the day, all Heath personally had to go on was that gut feeling of his. He could only hope it would work out in his favor this time. He didn't have a whole lot of options left.

HAILEE CISCO WORKED her way down the hallway, moving the mop slowly across the white-tiled floor. As she did, she pulled the bucket behind her. It was two in the morning, and she was just about done with her cleaning shift, a job she had just started about a month ago. Hathaway House was one of those places that needed to be maintained and kept absolutely crisp and clean. A lot of sick men and women were here, and nobody could afford infections.

The fact that a large animal center was also downstairs just added to the need to be extra careful about cleanliness. She was all for the animals, but she knew that they added another level of possible contamination for the humans here. These patients couldn't afford that. Their bodies were weak and already struggling.

So she worked hard. She took care and pride in her job, even though it was a job that she hadn't ever considered doing. Right now, it was a balm to her soul and a soothing hug to her very stressed-out body. She felt like she'd walked through a war herself to get where she was. Of course it certainly didn't have the same kind of impact that a lot of these men—and women—had gone through. But every night that she came through here, she took a moment or so to reflect and used the cleaning as a way for her own soul to get back on track.

She focused hard and kept her head down while she

worked and cleaned the hallway. As she did, she eviscerated the stain from her body, her soul, and her emotions. She was a long way from being whole, but she owed Dani a lot for giving her this chance. Dani had tried hard to provide Hailee with a different job, one that dealt with more people to take her out of her shell, but Hailee couldn't handle it yet. She couldn't interact with people. She couldn't bear to feel the hurt that came with making friends or the pain that came with trusting the wrong person or the betrayal that sometimes happened between family members and friends.

Automatically she pushed the mop into the big bucket of water and pulled it out slightly, then used the ringer to take most of the moisture off the heavy twisted cotton ropes. She had never used a mop like this before. But it worked well, and that's all she cared about. She dropped it to the floor and sent it slowly across the floor.

Swish. Swish. Swish.

Back into the water, rinse, wash, and repeat. She worked slowly but steadily. She knew she was avoiding the far corner, as she did every night. She was hoping that maybe this time she wouldn't hear what she'd listened to every other night. Something that tore her apart, something that made her own heart bleed. The patients' stories that came out of this place were enough to make anybody cry.

When she had first heard a man behind the doors sobbing quietly to himself, thinking that he was alone, it tore her insides apart. Not only for his pain that she could do nothing about, but also for invading his privacy. She had no name for him, and maybe it was better that way because it hurt enough even without a personal connection. Then again all of it hurt. Which defeated her ultimate purpose.

She didn't come here to be torn apart further. She came

here to heal. It had been Dani's suggestion, and they had been friends for a long time. So she'd trusted her friend, who seemed to understand healing at a whole other level, and here Hailee was.

Hailee had worked at one of the large warehouse stores in the city. She'd often arranged for supplies to be delivered to Hathaway House. Yet again that also wasn't what she wanted to do. She was an accountant by profession, and somehow she had ended up working on the warehouse floor and then finally walked away from that too. Sometimes one had to start fresh. You could only hang on to the pain for so long before it was absolutely mandatory to make a change. Dani had offered Hailee this lifeline, and she'd taken it.

It was as if cleaning here would help her clean her soul. Dani had reassured Hailee that she had nothing to be ashamed of since her soul held nothing but goodness, and life was just sometimes contrary like that. But Hailee hadn't managed to let her past go. She hadn't managed to find peace the same way Dani had. Her friend was so happy. It was such a joy to watch Dani every time Aaron came home. She just bounced full of life.

Hailee wanted to feel that same joy again.

Hailee knew Dani's wedding was in the planning stages, but it would be a long way away. And, for Hailee, she could only hope that maybe she'd be lucky and be invited. Hopefully she'd still be working here. She took several more steps, rinsed her mop, and whooshed again. Then she slowly worked down the long main hallway.

She loved working at the rehab center. It was an incredible place. It hadn't taken even a few weeks of being here to see that. She was astonished at how warm and caring everyone in the center was. She had previously known about it and had realized that anything Dani was involved in had a lot of heart. But it was one thing when you're on the outside hearing about what happened here at the center. It was an entirely different thing to actually see the emotions, the people, and the heart beating in this place.

Or the pain …

As soon as that thought popped into her mind, she shook her head and started scrubbing the floor that didn't need to be cleaned yet again. She wouldn't dwell on the pain. There was always pain. And, if she couldn't help herself, she sure couldn't help anybody else. And she was a long way away from helping herself.

She carried on mopping the floor, moving her Beware of Wet Floor sign as she went. Even though it was calm and quiet in these early morning hours, it didn't mean that people weren't walking through the hallways. Nurses were moving from room to room, taking care of patients as needed. Hailee gripped her mop tighter. As long as she wasn't personally involved with anyone here, she could handle being here. Staying detached was the only way she could deal with doctors after what she'd been through.

It was a miracle she could do even that.

Chapter 2

HAILEE HADN'T THOUGHT it possible that she would end up at a place like this, but Dani had been adamant that her center was different. That not just the patients healed here.

Hailee sighed, knowing that the last door was coming up. This was a short hallway off the main one, and, as she came to the end, she knew she would reach the door where every night she cringed—or softly cried with him—at the pain eking from that room.

It wasn't because she wanted to avoid it but because she knew she couldn't. It was almost a penance, as if somebody needed to witness his pain so he could release it and let it go. *Or maybe it was her own penance.* Regardless she knew it sounded foolish, and she didn't understand it herself because he would probably be horrified if he thought someone could hear him. And it was definitely a man's voice; she avoided reading his name on the medical file in the box affixed to his door to confirm that. She'd yet to have anything to do with any of the patients. But then, part of that was due to working a night shift. A position she'd asked for.

She kept her head down and worked away at scrubbing the floor. This was her last pass, and, after this little bit, she was done. She went to the far end and worked her way backward.

When she got to *the* door, she smiled in joy. The room was silent. No signs of someone struggling on the other side. She walked, moved, cleaned, scrubbed, and did her penance for her own soul's sake tonight. As she was just about done, she heard it start again. Her breath caught in the back of her throat. He was crying about his pain. But in many ways it was about her pain too. He was crying the sobs that she couldn't let out, the sobs that were deep within herself. She stayed where she was, her head bowed, as she wished him well, wishing him a more peaceful night. Even though he cried, surely tonight it seemed his pain was less.

Satisfied with that little bit of hope, she gathered her bucket and headed back to the utility closet in the laundry room, where she could clean the mops and put away her cleaning supplies. Another night done. And hopefully another little brick of goodness to build a wall to survive the new world she lived in. It wasn't fair, and it wasn't easy, but it's the one that she had. Once people got their minds wrapped around their current reality and could see their way forward, they could do so much more than when avoiding that reality.

But, of course, the problem often was people got hung up on where they were and couldn't get to where they were going. In those moments, it seemed like the distance was so damn far that they couldn't find a way to get there. Yet, in fact, it didn't need to be that way at all. People could cross any amount of distance without any issues. They just had to believe in it and put in the effort. That's the most laborious and time-consuming part. But it was all about taking that first step.

Hailee had attended yoga and meditation sessions be-cause they were both so darn crucial for stress relief. And one of the things she loved was when they were told to visualize themselves in a cloud, where the only thing they could see was a little bit of a space where they stood. And then they were told to take a little step forward into the unknown, into the unseen. It was amazing to listen to people calling out that they were falling and were too scared to take action because they couldn't see what was in front of them.

And, of course, that was the lesson. To trust that a step would be there, that you would be okay, and that, as soon as you put your foot out there, another step would form under it, so that you wouldn't fall. But so many people struggled with that concept. Hailee had used it many times for herself, trying to get through what she needed to get through in life. The last few years hadn't been easy. Yet she had not only survived but she'd also become a much better person for it. She smiled at that as she returned her cleaning supplies at the end of her shift.

Hathaway House might be perfect for the patients here, but it was the right place for Hailee too.

HEATH LAY ONCE again on his bed and stared up at the dark sky just outside his window. It seemed like darkness was his friend these days. Or maybe an enemy. It gave him the privacy of being alone, but with it came the most incredible nightmares and the most horrific images that he never wanted to see again. There should be a way to stop it. He knew that all kinds of meditations and drugs and things could deal with it, but, in his heart of hearts, he knew that part of the problem was he didn't want them to stop. Because, as long as he relived these memories, he never forgot his friends who blew up beside him.

He lived. They died. But, as long as he remembered them, they weren't forgotten.

Two of his friends were scheduled to head back to the US with him two days later for their leave. Both of them were excited. They had girlfriends they were heading home to. Heath, on the other hand, didn't. He was the only unattached one. They'd been joking and laughing when he drove too close to the shoulder, and the truck hit an IED. He'd taken part of the blast, but his friends had lost their lives.

And, every night, he drove that same damn road, wrenching the wheel to prevent the accident because now he knew what would happen when he hit that shoulder. But there was no forgiveness. There was no change. There was no going back. There was no fixing this, and every time he thought about his best friends and their girlfriends and their bright futures, it always came back to the same questions: *Why me? Why was I the one to survive? Why was I the one to stay here and to suffer through all this pain and the guilt? Why couldn't they have lived, even if they'd lost their legs? Their women would have loved them regardless. Their families wouldn't have cared as long as their sons, brothers were still there to love and had something to look forward to.*

But it was just him, staring up at the ceiling and the lovely apparatus that came with these beds. He hoped he was past his need to use the hoists, but he certainly had initially.

Heath had heard the doctors talking about mental blocks and resistance and all kinds of other psychobabble. Heath wanted to ignore the docs. He wanted to say they were full of crap, but he knew, deep in his soul, what they were talking about. His own guilt was eating at him and was keeping him from functioning as he should. He wasn't even sure he cared. What he wanted to do was find a way to be a better person, so he didn't ever have to live with this horrible guilt again. Yet the sin was there, the terrible mistake, and he knew it would never go away. And that's the way of it. It was his penance.

His life goal now was to live the best life he could to make up for his friends' deaths. Heath should have been the one who died. That he didn't was something he would have to live with for the rest of his life.

He closed his eyes, hoping that maybe this time he could sleep. Sleep was necessary for healing. He also knew that the docs thought Heath needed to continue seeing the psychologist. The psychologist felt that Heath needed to talk more. And he needed them to just go away and to leave him the hell alone.

The black abyss was one that he rightly belonged in. He shouldn't even be here, shouldn't be taking up a bed. He didn't even know how he'd really come to be here. In one of his more positive moments he'd applied to a bunch of places, and, sure, this had been one of them, but he hadn't really thought he'd get in. When the acceptance letter came, he'd been given a bunch more paperwork, and he hadn't cared either way but figured he'd started something so needed to carry it through. He'd signed them and passed them on. Next thing he knew, he was transferred here. But it hadn't really settled in as to where and to what he'd been transferred to.

As he lay here hating himself and the world he lived in, he could hear the cleaning lady go by—every night as regular as clockwork. He heard the *swish* of the mop as she dropped it back into the bucket, trying to be quiet but failing. The requirements of her job necessitated some noise. There was something about the mundaneness of her actions, knowing that she was out there and that he, therefore, wasn't alone.

Yet, after his nightmares every night, seeing his two buddies blown up once more, his tears welled up. He always tried to hold them off, but it was hard. Deep down, he silently wished that somebody could know he was in such pain. Yet that was foolish because, in his rational mind, he didn't want anybody to know. However, she was a silent witness to his own pain. He hated it, but it was a connection he needed, only hadn't known it until she started her nightly ritual. It was just one more thing in Heath's life that was so wrong.

And still, to hear her out there, swishing back and forth, he'd often imagined what she must look like. He figured she had to be at least in her fifties and gray-haired. He wondered if she'd left a half-dozen kids at home. Maybe even grand-children? Perhaps she had a husband who was retired. Heath didn't know why it was easier to imagine her as older. Maybe it was the thoroughness with which she cleaned everything.

He could tell time by her movements too. Every night it took her exactly twenty minutes to get to his door. The tears would have already started and now stopped when he finally heard her mop. That sound always made him hold back the tears a little bit better. He hated it, and yet he waited for it. Sometimes teary-eyed. Sometimes sleepy-eyed. He wondered now if he woke up just in time to hear her. He often considered opening the door to see her. Not to embarrass her by any means and not to worry her or scare her, but just for that connection to somebody who had obviously heard his pain and was still here, day in and day out.

Maybe to know he hadn't scared her away.

Heath never cried in the morning. He never cried during the day, even after Shane put him through the paces. That new guy, Jeff, was supposed to be just as wickedly good too. Or wickedly bad, depending on your viewpoint. Heath seriously hurt after his physical therapy sessions, but Shane kept saying that Heath was getting better, getting stronger. He would just smile and nod, knowing Shane was full of crap.

Because Heath wasn't getting any better; no way he could get better. Who could possibly want him to get better? He held too much pain, too much horror, too much of everything. He wasn't suicidal; he just wished that life had been a whole lot fairer and had taken him and had left his friends to live their lives and their dreams with their partners who cared for them. Heath was alone and had always been alone. He knew nothing else. The light in his life had been his two buddies. He'd been an orphan, and nobody else had been in his life like they were. They'd known each other since they first enlisted. He shook his head, trying to figure it out.

"You've been there with me for the longest period of time that I've ever known anyone," he whispered. "But still you were taken from me." And more like a parent who'd lost their child or a brother who'd lost his siblings, Heath had been left, bereft and alone. And he hated it. He'd do damn-near anything to not be this way anymore. *Bereft. Alone.* Anything *but* go out to meet and to enjoy the entire community of other broken people in this rehab facility.

Because to acknowledge them was to accept himself.

Chapter 3

HAILEE SAT IN the hallway, holding her coffee, taking a breather before she started work at her second job of the day. She'd come in from her low-level bookkeeping job in town—where she holed up in her office with her head down and with no one to distract her—straight to Hathaway House. This was her life, and it sucked, but each was honest work, and each brought in its own paycheck.

Her phone buzzed with a text. She smiled at her lawyer's message. It was simple and didn't say anything really. But the message **Making progress** made her smile. He was trying to reduce her medical bills from Jacob's intensive treatments. That Jacob hadn't made it through didn't matter to the debt-collection laws or to the hospital. It didn't matter that she'd struggled to keep food on the table while her infant son had struggled to take each breath.

He'd been gone a year now. A year of deep soul searching, working multiple jobs, and fighting for a greatly reduced hospital bill that would set her free and clear within her own lifetime. Her lawyer also considered going after the company that had laid her off when her son's health issues had hit hard at the company's health coverage. Of course they didn't fire her. They found a way to make her position redundant.

But the hospital bill was the more important issue. She sighed. And could only hope that this nightmare would be over soon.

Voices reached her around the corner from the direction of the offices.

"Did we get a new cleaning lady?"

Hailee stiffened with worry. She couldn't see who was speaking and didn't recognize the voice, but dozens of staff members were here, so it could be anyone. "Hi, Anna. Yes, a friend of mine is cleaning for us. Yes," Dani said, her voice easily sliding down the hallway. "Problems?"

"No," Anna said. "I was just commenting on the fact that everything seemed so clean, and a lemon scent is in the air when I come in first thing in the morning now."

"That'll be Hailee," Dani said. "She loves lemon. As long as nobody complains about it, then I'm happy to let her use it."

"No, it's quite nice," Anna said, her footsteps clipping across the floor as she walked. She seemed to pause and then asked, "Do you know her well?"

"I do. She has gone through some rough times lately. This job isn't one that she would normally do. I have a great need for an accountant, and she is one, but I haven't quite convinced her to come here full-time."

"She's an accountant, but instead she's doing the cleaning?" Anna asked in surprise.

Hailee winced. She hadn't asked Dani to keep that to herself, but Hailee was a reserved and private person and wouldn't want others talking behind her back. Although it was human nature, she'd like to avoid their curiosity if possible.

Dani added slowly, "And I'd appreciate it if you don't pass that on. We all have to do what we need to do for whatever reason we feel is right."

Prophetic words. Hailee smiled as she sipped her coffee. Dani was a wise woman.

"I don't have a problem not talking about her," Anna said. "I'd love to meet her, but I don't ever see her. She's not here when I arrive, and she must show up after I've left."

"That's the way she likes it too. Sometimes it takes time to adjust to being around people."

"Not sure cleaning on the night shift will do that," Anna said doubtfully.

"No, but we have to do what we need to do in our own time frame."

"That seems to be one of the Hathaway House mottos here," Anna said. "Everybody makes progress in their own way."

Hailee peeked around the corner.

Anna stepped out of Dani's office into the hallway, then stopped, and, with a big smile, turned back to face Dani again. "Speaking of which, I was down with Stan. Did you see that new cat he's got down there?"

"A new cat?"

"If that's what it is," she said. "It's huge. I have no clue. But it's missing a full back leg, like it was taken right off at the hip, but it's got the temperament of a teddy bear."

"Wow," Hailee muttered. She wished she could take a look. She had yet to be in the veterinarian clinic. They had their own cleaning staff.

"I hadn't heard," Dani said. "I may take a look at this guy myself."

"You should," Anna said, now standing in Dani's doorway. "She's huge. As in seriously huge."

"Is she really?"

Anna stopped, tossed her head to the side a little bit as

she considered the question, then nodded. "She definitely has an extra pouch on her. I think she must have had a litter, and she's holding some of that belly weight," she said with a laugh. "A common complaint all mothers have."

"Generally the animal world doesn't care about it though," Dani said. "It's just us crazy human females."

"Isn't that the truth," Anna said with a chuckle. "Anyway, I'll talk to you tomorrow."

Anna tossed Dani a bright smile as she headed down the hallway, away from Hailee.

On that note, before Dani stepped out and realized that Hailee had heard them, Hailee got up and headed off to start her shift.

WHEN HEATH WOKE up again, gasping, his breath seizing in his chest and his body completely covered in sweat, he didn't need to check his clock to know that it would be right around two a.m. He waited for the sounds outside in the hallway to slowly penetrate through the massive din of screams in back of his mind. He could hear his friends screaming over and over and over again. Some cruel twist of fate had this exact same moment frozen in time being relived in his nightmares.

It could have been ten minutes earlier, or it could have been ten minutes later, but it was always when the truck blew up, and he could hear the screams and roars and then the deafening silence. Except the silence was broken by his own sobs. From his friends, there was nothing. Not a sound. And that was worse than anything.

He'd once again be laying there on the desert ground,

staring up at the sky, and hoping that he was wrong, hoping that they were just knocked unconscious. But he already knew that they were gone. Such an emptiness resided inside his soul. The only brothers he'd ever known, the only real friends he'd ever had, the only people who had ever given a damn about him were gone. Worse, he'd been responsible.

He didn't quite understand what had happened, but he knew that Shawn had reached over and grabbed the wheel. They were joking and laughing, and he'd done it as a joke, but his movement had driven the truck to the shoulder of the road. Heath had been too surprised to react fast enough. He *should* have jerked the steering wheel back faster to keep them on the roadway. But he hadn't, and then he had no time to respond.

It was just over.

It was becoming quite a habit now, but, as he lay here, his body tense in the cool air and slowly drying as the sweat evaporated around him, he could hear the sounds he expected. The *swish-swish* of the mop going back and forth across the tiled floors. He smiled and settled back into his bed—almost as if hearing her helped him to stay grounded in this world and a long way away from all the nightmares and the cries around him.

Comforted by the sounds proving she was out there, he closed his eyes and let the repetitive sounds, moving back and forth, ease his soul, bringing him back to the reality of where he lived now. This was his life. And, even as the screams faded, the sound of the mop became louder and louder. It was a comfort; it was a reassurance. It was a connection to another living soul.

And, more than that, it fired up his curiosity about her. Whoever the poor woman was, the last thing she needed was some scary-ass dude like himself opening the door and frightening her. He could get up and open the door at any time; he knew that, but just something about the mystery of her kept him glued into the bed. He closed his eyes and let sleep take him once again.

Chapter 4

WHEN HAILEE SHOWED up for work the next evening at eight, she was surprised to see Dani still working in her office. Dani looked up and called her over. "I hope you didn't stay late for my sake," Hailee said worriedly. "Am I not doing a decent job?"

Dani looked at her in surprise. "Oh my," she said, "you're doing a wonderful job. And several people have commented about the fresh lemon scent."

"Is that okay?" Hailee asked, still worried if her friend and boss had waited for her intentionally.

"It's more than okay," Dani said warmly. "Stop being so worried."

"It's hard not to be," she said. "At least now."

"It'll be fine. Just chill."

"Got it," Hailee said, laughing. "And, if there's no problem, I need to get to work." And, with that, she took off. Sometimes she headed to the laundry area to see how that was going. She came in and helped out in that department a few hours a week. She was totally okay to do whatever was needed, and some weeks it was a little more than others.

As she walked into the laundry area, Dennis from the kitchen brought in another big load of kitchen towels. She grinned at him. "You know what? You guys almost dominate the laundry these days. Sometimes way more kitchen laundry here than bedding."

"Lots of people eating," he said. "Lots of cooking happening. Lots of kitchen towels. But we're nowhere near what the bedding or the linens are or the towels for the showers."

"Just seems like it," she said. She took the large hamper and wielded it toward one of the big machines and quickly filled one washer. She added in the soap as required, closed the door, and started it. When she turned, Dennis stood there, his hands on his hips, studying her.

"What's up?" she asked casually, as she walked over to the utility closet, where her mops and brooms and dustpans were. She would clean the kitchen and dining room area tonight. She turned toward him. "When does the dining room close?"

"Never, really," he said. "Drinks are always available for any of the patients. Are you gonna vacuum?"

She nodded. "I just thought I would start there a little earlier tonight."

"Go ahead," he said. "Are you doing the bathrooms too?"

She nodded. "I'll vacuum first and then hit up the bathrooms."

"Good enough," he said.

As he stepped back, she nudged the hamper at him. "Here you go. You can refill it. I will send another up with folded towels when that load's done."

He grabbed the hamper, grinned, and said, "It's nice to see a friendly face down here."

She stared at him in surprise. "Everybody is friendly here."

He shook his head. "Don't often see anybody in here. Most of the time, I put the laundry on myself."

"That's hardly needed," she said. "There's like four people doing laundry at this place every day."

"Yeah, but why add more work for other people if it's something you can do yourself?"

She nodded. "Well, I agree, but most people don't."

He shrugged. "But we," he said, pointing his finger at her and then him, "are not normal people."

"No, we aren't," she said with a smile. She watched as he disappeared, whistling, happy and cheerful as always. He was one of the most upbeat people she'd ever met. She used to be optimistic. She used to be bright and cheerful, but life had dealt her one too many blows, and she didn't even feel like she had the time or the effort anymore. And that was such a defeatist attitude.

On that note, she grabbed her commercial vacuum and headed up the service elevator to the dining room. With Dennis quickly moving chairs and tables for her, she got started. When she turned around, he was wiping down the tables and the tops of the condiment bottles with a cloth, then wiping down all the chair seats too. She smiled. "You make my job easy."

"You've got enough to do," he said. "At least a dozen public bathrooms are in this place."

She chuckled. "Hey, but I'm not doing the private bathrooms, so it's much better."

He rolled his eyes at that. "If you need a hand in the bathrooms, let me know."

She shook her head. "I'll lose my job. If we're too efficient, you'll cut my hours in half."

He frowned. "I don't want to do that."

She chuckled. "I'm kidding. You have lots of work to do for tomorrow yourself."

"Yep, but I'm waiting for somebody. We're seeing a movie in town. So, for fifteen to twenty minutes, I can do a little bit of extra work too." At that, he started refilling the salt and pepper shakers.

She left him to do his kitchen duties. She wasn't exactly sure what position he held, but he was everywhere, from the kitchen to the dining room to the laundry area. He was one of those guys just happy to lend a hand, and she wished more people were like him.

She headed to the bathrooms, gloves on and armed with lots of cleansers and her mop. She didn't mind doing the bathrooms. She had such a great sense of satisfaction when everything turned out sparkling clean. She moved steadily from one bathroom to the other. By the time midnight hit, she was damn-near done. But now it was time to start the floors. That always took her a couple hours.

She checked her watch and realized she was running a little bit behind. She headed back to the utility closet and switched out some of her cleansers. And then, with the mop and her bucket filled with hot water and the floor-cleaning solution, she started mopping on the main floor and then moved upward. It would take her over two hours tonight. It looked like the floors were dirtier than usual, which meant changing her bucket of water more often. But she was up for it. Every time she did this, she imagined each stroke cleaning the pain and sorrow of her own soul.

She moved steadily through the hallways, washing and scrubbing, moving the mop back and forth to a natural rhythm that seemed to ease something inside her. The routine movement and the sense of hard work, knowing that she was doing something necessary and in some way contributing to somebody else's healing, it all helped. Maybe that was good for her own soul too. She moved in a steady rhythmic motion, absolutely loving to see the clean floors as she moved backward down each hall. By the time she came around to the final hallway, she knew she was running almost half an hour behind. She headed down with a bucket of fresh water and started working on the floor.

She heard a sound. She stopped, frowned, and then softly called out, "Are you okay?"

A ghost of a voice answered, "No."

She immediately went to the door, knocked, and opened it slightly, poking her head around the corner into the dark room. "Do you want me to call a nurse?"

"Yes, please."

She immediately closed the door and raced to the closest nursing station. Tina was there. Hailee told her about the patient in the far room. Tina followed her and headed inside the room that Hailee had only ever stuck her head into once. She could hear their voices on the other side in the darkness. She hadn't actually seen the patient, but he needed somebody. Happy that she could help, Hailee picked up her mop and resumed working again.

By the time she finished, her soul was a little lighter, and she realized that, on a scale of one to ten today, she was running around an eight.

Considering she'd been working closer to the six or seven range every day for the last three weeks, this wasn't bad. But today, well, was a little bit better. She cleaned up her mop and put away her bucket, then headed back to check that she'd collected everything. She'd left her Wet Floor sign, and she snatched that up.

The door to *his* room opened. Tina walked out, smiled at Hailee, and said, "Thanks for calling me."

Hailee nodded slowly. "I didn't know what I heard. I felt terrible even knocking."

"In this specific case," Tina said, "it was the right thing to do."

"I'm glad to hear that," she said. "I really don't have much to do with any of the patients here, so I never really know."

"Not to worry," Tina said with a smile. She headed back to the nurse's station.

Hailee followed ever-so-slowly. She returned to the utility room to put away the floor sign but returned to the main floor to once more look around and make sure she was done for the night.

Tina saw her. "Time for the end of your shift?"

"I hope so," she said. "It's been a bit of a long day."

"Is this your only job?" Tina asked with a frown.

Hailee hesitated and then shrugged. "No, I have another job too."

Tina nodded. "I figured as much. It's probably not enough hours here, if you've got bills to pay."

Hailee's smile slipped. "Bills to pay, yes, that's one way to look at it." She turned away, and then she looked back at Tina and asked, "Will he be okay?"

"Who?" Tina asked, looking at her in surprise.

"The patient I called you for."

"I hope so," Tina said with a smile. "He's such a handsome man with his dark Moorish looks," she said. "You probably couldn't see for the lighting, but he's got dark hair, thick eyebrows, and an immaculately chiseled jaw."

Hailee nodded and hesitantly said, "He seemed like he was in a lot of pain."

"Well, he's doing better now," Tina said. "He has not

been too forthcoming about asking for help, and sometimes, well, sometimes you just don't know when people will need more care."

"I can understand that," Hailee said. She wasn't even sure why she was talking to Tina. It was so opposite to what Hailee usually did. But finally feeling a little awkward, she smiled and said, "Have a good evening."

"You too," Tina called out.

As Hailee grabbed her purse and readied to leave, she found herself taking the long way around and going past that same door. As she walked by, she whispered, "Good night. Sleep well."

In her mind, she wondered if he heard her but knew no way he could have, unless he had acute hearing. But, if he was lying in bed, waiting for morning to come, and could hear her footsteps, maybe he had heard her speak. Embarrassment burned through her, and she quickly rushed past. When she thought she heard his voice call out, she stopped and swore and then retraced her steps. At the door, she asked, "Are you okay?"

"Open the door, please," the voice commanded.

She hesitated and then turned the knob and pushed it open slightly. She stuck her head around the corner into the darkened room. "Hey," she said. "Can I do something for you?"

"I just wanted to say *thank you*," he said.

She straightened and stepped in slightly. "Why?"

"Because you called a nurse for me, and, if you hadn't done that, I'd be in a whole lot more pain right now."

She nodded and said, "You're welcome."

As she went to leave, he whispered, "Stop."

She hesitated again and looked toward him. But she

couldn't see him for shadows. "Do you need anything else?"

His voice was hesitant, almost like hers, when he said, "It's just nice to talk to somebody."

Her eyebrows shot up. "You're in a center full of people," she said. "Don't you visit with others?"

"Not really," he said. "I haven't been good about putting myself out there."

She could sympathize in an instant. "I'm not very good at it myself."

"I hear you every night," he said.

"Oh," she said. "I didn't realize I made so much noise. I'm sorry."

"No," he said. "You don't understand. It's a good noise."

She frowned. "How can it be a good noise?"

"It reminds me that I'm alive and that this is the real world. It tells me that I'm not still caught up in my nightmares. Yet sometimes I wonder if being in my nightmares is the only place that I'm comfortable anymore. But then I wake, and I hear your mop moving back and forth on the floor."

She could sense the surprise in his own voice, as if he was shocked he was talking to her. She understood the sentiment. "As long as it's not stopping you from sleeping," she said slowly.

"No, not at all. It's restful. It's …" He seemed to reach for a word and then stopped because he didn't know what he meant. "It's security," he whispered.

That just floored her. Because that was the last thing she'd expected. "The sound?" she asked. "The normalcy of it? The rhythm of it?"

"All of the above," he said. "It means I'm safe. It means I'm not still on the roadside, staring up at the sky, wondering what happened to my world."

Her heart softened. "I'm sorry. It seems like you've lived through some traumatic events. I just … I can't imagine trying to put it behind you and moving on."

"And yet, that's what they tell us to do, as if it's so easy. It's not," he said, his voice deepening. "It seems impossible to let go and to move on."

"I understand," she whispered.

"Do you?" This time there was almost a detached sarcasm to his words, as if he'd heard that many times and thought that people were just plain pathetic.

"Not just the patients have been through rough times in their lives," she said with a little more strength to her tone than she expected. As if she didn't want him criticizing her, but, at the same time, she didn't want to explain either.

"You're right," he said in surprise. "And sometimes I need to be reminded of that."

"I'm sorry. I'm not trying to be insensitive," she whispered.

"No."

She could see his hand wave in the darkness.

"It's fine. I would much prefer people talk to me and treat me as a normal human being instead of somebody to be coddled and spoken softly to, in case I erupt."

"Is erupting something that you do?" she asked in surprise.

"I didn't think so, but it still seems as if everybody walks around me as if I'll explode at any moment."

"Interesting," she said. "Maybe they aren't anticipating an explosion as much as a cracking."

"WHAT'S INTERESTING ABOUT it?" he asked, wondering about her last words. "I would have said I was a fairly balanced personality. But since I've arrived here …"

"I imagine nobody wants to cause you a setback or to do anything that would in any way slow your healing."

"And how would they know what would do that?" He was genuinely curious.

"I don't know," she said. "But, for me, it seemed like, as soon as disaster struck, everybody either sank out of sight and completely jumped ship or spoke as if I'd suddenly lost my hearing instead of my child."

A gasp came from the bed.

She frowned and winced. "I'm sorry. I didn't mean to say that."

"No," he said. "I appreciate the honesty. I'm surrounded by people in similar situations, trying to recover from their own hell. I know I can't be sympathetic to anyone else because I can't even be sympathetic to myself. I feel incredibly vulnerable here, and yet, at the same time, I have this sense that I don't deserve to be here."

"Wow," she said. "How is it you could possibly think you don't deserve to be here?"

"Two other people died," he said. "I should have been with them."

"I wanted to die too," she said, tears in her eyes and pain clogging her throat. "All I ever wanted was to be with my son."

"But our wants don't matter," he said. "Because, for whatever reason, we're forced to live with the losses of those who were with us."

"I know." Then, unable to handle anymore, she said, "I have to leave." And, with that, she closed the door and left.

Heath stared at the closed door for a long moment, hating that she'd left but realized that it had been a turning point for him regardless. He just didn't know in what way or how. He tucked himself under the blankets and pulled the pillow under his head to support his neck and then closed his eyes.

This time, he fell asleep with a smile on his face.

Chapter 5

THIS WAS A pattern they set every night. Hailee worked her same routine, cleaning everything else before the floors, all the while waiting for the moment when she came to his room. Then slowly mopping the hallway floor outside his door. Something was almost spiritual about it. Yet she knew that anybody else would think she was a fool. It was such an odd feeling, yet almost one with a sense of honor to know he was listening to her—dare she say, *for her*? Her mopping sounds helped him feel grounded in this reality and kept him away from his nightmares. Who'd have thought it?

On the second evening in a row, he'd called out to her.

She'd stopped and spoken with him again. And then again on the third night. And a pattern had developed, and she didn't know if it was healthy or not, but it was an encounter she looked forward to now. This continued for seven nights in a row, and she was due to be off for the next two. She'd taken several more shifts to stay for these last two nights, and she'd slowly learned a little bit from the nurses about his condition.

She understood that he'd been driving a vehicle which blew up and that he blamed himself for the loss of his friends. Her grief and his held such similarities that she felt a kinship to him. Yet, at the same time, she knew that he wouldn't appreciate the sympathy.

He was so wrapped up in his guilt that he didn't know he could turn and walk through a doorway and leave some of that guilt behind. And how did she know that? Because she hadn't been ready to see it either. She'd done everything she thought she could do, but it hadn't been enough. So her guilt had continued to destroy her. Her child hadn't been meant to live in this world for very long, and the six months that Jacob had been in her arms were the most blessed that she'd ever experienced. But he'd been born with a severe heart condition, and multiple surgeries had just made his life one of pain and agony—and her own just as bad.

For any loving mother would have gladly borne all those surgeries and all that pain and agony for the sake of her child. A mother's greatest anguish is to watch her child suffering from anything, whether physically or emotionally.

When five-months pregnant, she'd found out in her doctor's checkup that there were problems with her pregnancy, and her ob-gyn had suggested she let go of her unborn child. But she couldn't do it, couldn't even begin to contemplate such a thing. He was her son. He lived and breathed within her already, regardless if she had yet to give birth to him. He deserved to have every breath he took and deserved to fight for the next one.

But her husband hadn't agreed. They'd fought bitterly. He'd turned and walked.

And the person she needed most at that moment had abandoned her and their unborn child. That had been one of many very long and very hard lessons for her from there on out.

Her son had been gone from her life for one year now. Twelve lonely months of trying to pay off medical bills so large that everything she threw at them just bounced off the total due, not even making a dent. She had no reprieve.

She wasn't even sure she could ever get clear of this massive debt. Her husband had divorced her, and she was free and clear of him, but he refused to pay any medical bills, citing that he had agreed with the doctor for her to have the recommended abortion. So it was her fault that she was suffocating under the mountain of bills—not his fault. The lawyers had been grim-faced over it all, and there'd been no happy resolution.

She'd gotten up and walked away from him and the attorneys and the paperwork that she had signed, knowing that it would be a long time before she could ever trust or believe in anybody like that again. But, at the same time, she had been bravely taking one step in front of the other. When she thought about Jacob now, she still fought tears but also wore a smile every second.

Hot tears burned the back of her eyes even now, but they weren't pouring down her cheeks. And what she did every day honored Jacob's presence in her life by honoring those debts she had to pay and honoring her commitments to relinquish her guilt, possibly to forgive her ex-husband at some future date. After that, maybe she'd finally take a step forward. She planned to never have another child. The pain and loss were too incredibly debilitating to go through again.

And, like these military men feeling survivor's guilt, all she could think about for the longest time was that it shouldn't have been Jacob who died. It should have been her ...

Even though she hadn't done anything to contribute to Jacob's death, she'd brought him into this world, knowing he could have a hard and painful life.

It also felt like she hadn't done anything to add to his

life, and yet she'd been there as much as she could every day. Jacob never really made it out of the ICU. The hospital had done what they could to reduce the bills initially too. But still, some of them had to be paid. And she didn't have a support system or a network of family and friends to help pitch in, not monetarily, not emotionally, not physically.

It'd been all she could do to make a minimum payment. But she was doing what she needed to do, and that was working two jobs to keep some of the bills at bay. She paid a bunch of them down, but it would be a couple more years before she could even begin to see her way clear, and that's only if the hospital agreed to the latest proposal made by her attorney.

She had a friend who was a lawyer, and he'd submitted proposals that seemed like pennies on the dollar, so she could climb out of this hole. They were still waiting to see if the hospital would agree to this amount or would come back with a counteroffer, but even that reduced figure would be way more than she could get clear of anytime soon.

As she worked the mop back and forth along the hallway, she knew that he would be without her for the next two nights, and she worried that he would not get back to sleep if he woke up in the night. Could she tell the other cleaning lady to come and do this piece last? Or would that just seem so bizarre and cause an investigation into her relationship with a patient? A relationship based entirely on healing.

And yet, how could she begin to explain it? It was obscure. But the connection was there, a little bit at least. In fact, that connection and that sense of doing something for another human being was helping her too. How odd. So she didn't want to lose whatever it was, and she didn't want to slow down his healing. If her mopping the floor helped him return to sleep, then she was all for it, no matter how bizarre it may seem.

As for her looming hospital bills, she couldn't just spend her life comparing the numbers to see how far apart the hospital bills were from what she earned. The fact of the matter was, she was doing the best she could, and she would keep doing that. She would keep putting one foot in front of the other for as long as she could. Until she dropped from exhaustion. And, when she came to such a stopping point, if it wasn't enough, then it wasn't enough, and she'd find another way.

As she got to his door, she smiled as he called out. She stopped, placed her mop against the wall, walked to the door, then stuck her head around the corner, and said, "You should be sleeping."

"Can't sleep," he said. "Not until I hear your mop."

"On that note," she said, "I won't be here for the next two nights."

SILENCE.

"Why not?" he asked, dread in his heart. He really did not sleep well until she came past his room with her mop.

"It's my days off," she said apologetically. "I took an extra couple shifts, so I was here for the last two nights. But I do need a break."

"Of course you do," he said immediately, hating that he would lie here awake at night and wonder what she was doing. He didn't understand their connection but acknowledged that it existed. They shared … something. Some odd, twisted relationship between her mop, him, and his sleep.

He smiled bravely and said, "I hope you'll enjoy the next couple days."

"I'll be at another job," she said slowly. "So I don't think *enjoy* is quite the right word."

"You have two jobs?"

She hesitated, then nodded. "Medical bills."

"Right," he said softly. "Thankfully that is not a burden I have to bear."

She smiled and closed the door slowly behind her.

He laid there though, thinking about that pain of losing somebody and then still paying for the medical bills on top of it. What a horrible reminder. And given what she had said about her son, she had a mountain of debt to pay off. More years of remembering you were paying a bill that somebody had incurred while trying to save your child who couldn't be saved. Just the repetitive acknowledgment of that pain would be brutal.

He wished he could do something, but she was one of a million people he suspected with those kinds of medical bills, and how wrong was that? How do you ease that burden of so many? Or in what way could her burden be lifted? The last thing he had was money. Or not much. He was fine, his needs taken care of, but no pot of gold in the bank awaited him.

The government paid all his medical bills. He didn't know what he was supposed to do when he was back on his feet again. He would need retraining to make a living because he couldn't live off his benefits for long. He might find himself like her, cleaning floors to survive. Wouldn't that be a twist of fate? He should have enough to not have to do that, but she was doing honest work, and he could see how that honest work meant a lot, especially to her. Anything she could do to get back out from under her massive medical debts would be a huge boon.

He closed his eyes and thought about it, wondering if maybe he could help in some way.

Chapter 6

HAILEE MADE HER way up the long ramp to the main floor of Hathaway House. She'd sent Dani an email early, asking if she could have a meeting with her. She was hopeful that her request would be granted, but she had yet to get up the nerve to even ask for it. But now she had been forced into making this change. As she walked into the front reception area, she recognized a new girl who had started a few days ago. "Hey, Caitlin. How are you doing?" she asked.

Caitlin looked up with a bright smile. "Hey, Hailee. How were your days off?"

Hailee shrugged and said, "It was fine." But of course it wasn't. She'd worked. That's all she ever did. But that wasn't for anybody else to worry about.

As she walked past, Dani called out, "Hailee, come on in."

She walked in and closed the door. "Hey, Dani. Sorry. I didn't mean to make this cloak-and-dagger-ish. I just wondered ..." She stopped.

Dani pointed at the two visitor chairs. "Hey, sit down. Relax. You're not due on for quite a few hours, aren't you?" She looked at her watch, frowned, and faced Hailee. "Or do you need to change your shift?"

"No, my shift is fine," she said, then hesitated.

"I can't help if you don't tell me what the problem is,"

Dani said gently, a sly smile on her face.

Hailee laughed. "You've already helped so much that it feels wrong to ask anything more of you."

"That's not the issue at all," Dani said. "All I've done is give you a job, and I'd give you a better one, if you'd let me."

"But I can't afford to let go of the one job," she said. "Yet it seems I might be forced to."

Dani frowned at that. "Well, if you tell me what you're making at both of them, maybe I can help."

At that, Hailee hesitated. This isn't what she had expected, and she didn't know what to say about that patient's need for Hailee's nighttime floor mopping, but then she hadn't been here for two nights anyway. Maybe he had managed without her. She sagged into the chair. "I was wondering if you had a staff room available," she said in a rush. As Dani's eyebrows shot up, Hailee took a deep breath and said, "I really need to cut back my expenses."

"Those damn bills, huh?"

"Yes," she said. "The lawyer still hasn't heard back on the latest proposal for the medical bills."

"*Hmm*," Dani said, frowning. "They should be lucky you're working as hard as you are, trying to pay them back."

"But it's so much money."

"Let me take a look at what I have available," Dani said.

"I know it's for your medical staff," Hailee rushed in to add.

"It doesn't matter who it's for," Dani said. "If I've got something that will help, then I'm all for it. Do you really think it'll help though?"

"It'll save me some back and forth traveling time for sure," Hailee said slowly. She'd been thinking about this a lot over these last several hours. "I don't know how much you charge your residents for the housing."

"I don't," Dani said. And then, with a clipped nod, she added, "That alone would help you, wouldn't it? Do you have much furniture to move?"

"I sold everything. I've been living in a tiny studio apartment in town."

"So how hard would it be to move you here?"

"Just loading up my car might take two runs." She tried to keep the anxious tone out of her voice, but it was hard because Dani could save Hailee quite a bit of money. Yet how was she supposed to ask for something like that? She wasn't very good at asking for help.

"You don't have much at home, so that'll make your move easier," Dani said, as she checked through the screens on her monitor. "You're right. We do have a lot of staff in residence here."

Hailee sat back and watched as Dani continued to click through her records. Hailee wondered if Dani even had any free spaces or if everything was full.

"And your employee numbers must move up and down all the time," Hailee said. "So, if you need to keep an empty apartment for incoming staff, then I understand totally."

Dani smiled at her. "If I had an accountant on staff, she could find this instantly." Dani tilted her head and raised her eyebrows at Hailee. "But I don't. And I can't even answer you about availability until I check through these records," she said. "So either grab a coffee and come sit back down and let me do this *or* disappear and let me do this."

At that, Hailee burst out laughing. "Got it," she said. "I'll go grab a coffee." She stopped at the doorway and looked back at Dani. "Do you want one?"

Dani looked up, smiled, and said, "I'd love one, thanks."

With that, Hailee headed toward the cafeteria. She was rarely here during the day and never midafternoon, but, since she'd finished at her bookkeeping job early, she was here now. She desperately wanted to stay here. Just a place where she could live and work and save a little bit more money so that she could get out of debt faster. A year here would help a lot. The lawyer had made it very clear that, if she made an attempt to pay the hospital bills, then there was a good chance that he could negotiate that bill down a good 50 percent—or even 75 percent. That would get her back on her feet in the foreseeable future, while she was still capable of working. Indeed, it would make a huge difference, and she could probably get most of it paid off within several years. But, without this write off, she might as well declare bankruptcy right now, and that was a very depressing concept. Did that even clear medical bills?

In the cafeteria, she was surprised to see a number of people, from patients to staff. Some were sitting together, and some were sitting alone. Lots of meetings seem to be happening. From what she saw, some of the therapists were off in a huddle to one side. As she walked down the aisle, she accidentally went in along the foodservice line.

Dennis popped up and said, "Can I get you something?"

She shook her head. "I'm not starting my shift yet. I just came to get coffee for Dani and me."

He stopped, frowning at her, and asked, "Are you paying for food elsewhere?"

She looked at him in surprise. "Of course I am!"

His frown deepened.

She smiled and said, "Remember? I don't live here."

"*Hmm.*"

She could see it bothered him. "Don't worry about it,"

she said carelessly. She walked over to the coffee area and poured two cups. She didn't even remember how Dani liked hers. She turned to see Dennis still staring at her. "Do you know how Dani takes her coffee?"

He chuckled and said, "A little bit of cream."

She smiled, added a splash of cream, picked up the two mugs, and said, "Thanks." As she headed out, she continued to feel Dennis's eyes boring into her back. She hadn't even considered that extra cost. And now she worried if she'd asked Dani for way too much. She had already given Hailee a job. But to expect Dani to cover Hailee's housing costs was too much because Hailee hadn't taken into account her food costs here too.

Although she didn't eat much, it was still an extra expense. And she hadn't even looked at her own budget to see how much it would have saved her because she wasn't eating well now because she didn't dare. She shook her head. As she walked in, she announced, "Forget about it."

Dani looked up at her in surprise, saw the coffee, and smiled. "Thanks. What do you mean, *forget about it?*"

"I wasn't thinking," she said. "But, for me to live here, I'd also be eating here, and that would be an added cost on you."

Dani chuckled. "Are you serious?"

Hailee sat down, frowning. "Of course I'm serious," she said. "I don't want anything to impact your ability to run this place."

"The food is good and all," Dani said, "but one more mouth really doesn't make a whole lot of difference in the overall scheme. In case you hadn't noticed, we offer a ton of food all the time." Then she stopped and looked at her. "But, of course, you don't know that, do you? And you probably don't even eat here, do you?"

Hailee shook her head. "No. I was just talking to Dennis, and he basically hopped up to ask me what I wanted to eat."

"That's Dennis," Dani said. "One of the most willing staff members we have here."

"He didn't sound pleased that I didn't eat here," Hailee said with a frown, still feeling bad at her oversight. "Does everybody eat here?"

"If you work here, you're welcome to eat here," Dani said. "It's one of the perks. We do have a lot of extra people, and yet there are leftovers all the time."

If Hailee could even get some of the leftovers, that would save her even more with her food bill. She shook her head. "You've already done so much for me."

Dani sighed. "I want you to tell me point-blank how much money you make at the other job."

Hailee hesitated.

"Okay, let's go by ranges," she said. "Do you make over forty?"

"Hell no," Hailee said. "I don't. Why?"

"Adding in your earnings from this job, do the two of them pay you fifty?"

Hailee had to stop and think about it, and then she slowly shook her head. "Close maybe, but no."

"So then, how about you come in as my accountant? Which is what I've been trying to get you to do for months. I'll pay you what I paid my last one, which was fifty-eight a year to start, and we can move up from there later. Plus I have a room for you. It's actually scheduled for my accountant," she said with a smile. "And, yes, that's my added bonus to entice you to take this job. And, of course, all your meals would be free here. So basically you would have fifty-eight grand minus taxes at the end of the day."

Hailee stared at her, her jaw dropping. "Seriously?"

"Absolutely," Dani said with a nod. "I should be paying more than that for the accountant. That's something you can help me figure out when you're in the position. We'll do some shifts in the bookkeeping work, so that I can see where all the costs are coming from. I have it here in front of me, but, at the same time, I'm sure I could do some better record-keeping."

"Are you positive you need an accountant?" she asked. "You handle all the books."

"I do," Dani said, "and it takes me forever."

"So do you need an accountant part-time?" Hailee countered.

"No, I need a full-time accountant." Dani laughed, and the sound was joyous and bright, putting a smile on Hailee's face.

"I get that you care, but I don't want you being overly concerned about me," Hailee said.

Dani shook her head. "If you come on board as my accountant, we both get the benefit of that."

Hailee looked at her, smiled gently, and, with a deep *whoosh*, said, "Thank you. I accept."

"Good," Dani said, her smile widening, lighting up her face. "Now, how long before you can start?"

"Well, I got notice from my landlord that my rent is going up next month, plus layoffs will happen soon at my day job, which is why I was asking about a place to live," Hailee said with an unhappy frown. "My boss in town is already asking for people to step up and quit, to avoid forcing others into a layoff. If I do quit, I'm not supposed to go back anymore. And this month's rent is due as it is, so I already talked to my landlord about maybe being late this month."

"In that case, we'll send somebody back with you, and you'll get moved in today," Dani said. "Okay?"

Hailee shook her head, amazed and stunned at how fast everything had just shifted. "Are you sure?"

"Hell, yes, I'm sure," Dani said. "On the downside, I might have to hire somebody to replace you for cleaning. People have noticed what a great job you've been doing."

"Well, if you don't need a full-time accountant, is it possible that I could still do some of the cleanings?"

"No, that won't work."

"It'll work if we say it works," Hailee said stubbornly and hoped she hid the tiny note of desperation in her voice. She had an ulterior motive for continuing the cleaning, but that was a completely different topic.

HEATH TOSSED AND turned on his bed. He'd come back in from physio exhausted, but nothing was helping him sleep. Since his cleaning lady wasn't here, he couldn't wake up and hear the same rhythmic motion that immediately put him back to sleep again. He knew it was stupid. It was one of those little things that he didn't dare tell anybody about because it made no sense.

Not only that it made no sense but it also made him sound like he was off his rocker, and he *really* couldn't afford more of that. He already knew that everything he said and did was analyzed and then ripped apart to look for hidden meanings and nuances as to why he was struggling so much.

He'd told his medical team that he was having nightmares, and they'd offered all kinds of suggestions to help
relieve some of the stress, but nothing would ease his guilt.
He understood survivor's guilt was a real thing, and so did
they, but, so far, nothing they had suggested was helping.
And he wanted it to, but, at the same time, he hadn't told
them the entire story. He kept it locked in the back of his
mind. He was too ashamed to tell anyone. He didn't think it
was essential to share; it was something he had to work
through himself. But now, after two days without decent
sleep, nothing was going right. He was short-tempered and
angry, and all his interactions caused him more and more
stress.

On that note, a hard knock came at his door. He
groaned. "I'm sleeping," he growled.

The door opened instead. Heath glared at his intruder.
Shane stood there with his hands on his hips and glared right
back.

"What do you want?" Heath muttered. He shifted, hating the wince that crossed his face at the pain rippling up
and down his body. But Shane immediately moved to
Heath's side and, using competent hands, shifted Heath's
body until he lay flat on his stomach. Shane pulled the
pillow out from under Heath's head and said, "Just lie there
for a moment."

It was all Heath could do to not immediately retort back
with something much harsher. Then Shane got to work on
Heath's neck. When he felt a moment later the tension
release, Heath whispered, "Thank you."

"Is this why you're having such a crappy day?" Shane
asked, as he worked up and down Heath's spine.

Heath knew that Shane could feel the knots and the agony from the torn muscles as they had healed but left scar tissue that tightened so badly they wouldn't stretch. It was all Heath could do to stop the tears from coming into his eyes. He turned his head so his face was pressed against the sheet, holding back as much as he could.

Shane suddenly stopped and said, "No point in me releasing the knots in your back if you continue to hold it all within your head and your heart. I've seen bigger and harder and tougher men cry. You have to let this go."

Heath couldn't stop the shake of his head and the instinctive tightening of his back.

Immediately Shane grabbed Heath's trapezius gently and squeezed ever-so-lightly. "These? These shoulder muscles are sending the rest of your chest muscles off-balance," he said. "And this tension is from you resisting. You need to calm it down." He shifted Heath a little bit lower in the bed and then resumed work. His hands were coated in something. He massaged lightly and then not-so-lightly, as he continued to work layer after layer at the insertion points on each and every muscle on his back.

When Heath realized he no longer shook with the pain but was actually shaking with relief, he didn't know what to say. The tears had stopped flowing, and finally he could lay his head to the side and take a deep, normal breath.

"And after that deep breath," Shane ordered, "take another one. I want you to think of your chest now." As he said this, Shane placed his hands on either side of Heath's rib cage. "Think of your chest as a box. I want you to imagine your shoulders and arms as the sides of the box. ... And I want your head ..." He placed his hand on the top of Heath's head. "To act as the knob on the lid of this box. When you breathe, try to push out all four walls of the box, then lift the lid, meaning stretching your head up. I want you to maximize that image with each breath and then slowly release it."

With that visual, Heath had no problem following Shane's instructions. After three deep breaths, he could already feel some of his tension easing.

"If you were standing right now," Shane said, "and in front of a mirror, where you could actually see your body working, you would note your body starting to straighten up and to align properly, using that box method. And when you do get up, I want you to practice that box exercise three times and widen that box as much as you can by filling your lungs, then lifting the lid off that box as high as it will go. Can you do that?"

"I can do that," Heath said. "My chest is feeling a lot better."

"Yes, it is," he said. "You're missing half a rib, and your muscles have to compensate for it," he said. "But, when you end up so strained all the time, they can't even begin to work because they're trying to pull against that tension you hold there. Then what happens is all your back muscles seize up, trying to do the job that the front muscles are supposed to be doing."

"What you're saying is, I need to relax more." A note of bitterness was in his tone. "I can't even sleep right now," Heath whispered.

"If you can't find ways to sleep on your own, the drugs do help."

"They give me terrible nightmares," he muttered.

Shane's hand stopped for a brief moment on his back. "Interesting," he said.

"What's interesting about it?"

"Sometimes drugs get in under your subconscious and work things to the surface. I'm not much for chemical inducements, but sometimes it's needed to get your body to rest. Muscle relaxants would also help, but I understand that you're struggling with a reaction to those."

"Yes," he said. "I'm getting terrible water retention from them." He lifted his ankle, since there was only one left to show Shane.

Shane immediately said, "Okay, I'll get down there in a minute." By the time he had worked all the way down, massaging Heath's massive quads and thighs down to his calves, Shane gently stroked a couple places and then pressed down, Heath almost screamed at the unexpected pain.

"I gather that's painful," Shane said in a half-joking manner. "We'll work on that area next."

And he kept working, easing and smoothing out some of the tension and the swelling in the ankle. "This is a lot of the reason why you're getting some of this water retention." And finally, after at least fifteen minutes of massaging that leg, Shane shifted and said, "I'll leave it alone now. It's had enough." And he reached over and placed his hand on Heath's knee and what was left of his other leg. "Now, how is this one?"

"It's fine," Heath muttered. But he was already tense and afraid that Shane would start working on it.

"And yet it's apparently not," Shane said with a note of humor in his voice.

"Every time you touch me, it hurts."

"But does it still hurt?"

"Not the other parts, no, but I know the process of getting there is painful."

"It can be, yes," he said. "Let's get you into the wheelchair."

"And if I don't want to?"

"Well, you can resist all you want, but it'll just hold you back. So why would you not go into the wheelchair?"

"It depends on where you are taking me," he said.

At that, Shane laughed. "I would suggest the hot tub."

Immediately Heath shifted so he was sitting, and he stared at Shane with a doubtful look. "Are you joshing me?"

"No," he said. "I'm not. But it occurred to me that that's one of the things we should be working on. You can also do exercises in the hot tub."

"Is that all you think about? Exercises?"

Shane chuckled. "No, maybe not. But you, dear sir, need to get your body back into alignment. And it's not doing that on its own." He pulled up the wheelchair and set it beside the bed. "Get in."

"Are these shorts okay?"

Shane nodded. "Yep, those are fine. Let's grab a towel and get you down there." He tossed the towel over the back of the wheelchair and pushed Heath out the door.

"Am I supposed to be powering my own wheelchair?"

"Nope, not right now," Shane said. "I don't want you messing up the work I just did."

"And pushing my own wheelchair would mess it up?"

"Depends on your technique," he said. "The mood and the tension that you're under right now could very well do that."

At that, Heath subsided. He couldn't believe he was going to the hot tub. His body was craving something, and he hoped the hot water would work for his muscles. He needed sleep, and he needed it in a big way.

Chapter 7

A S SOON AS she walked out of Dani's office, Hailee felt a whole lot better. But then Dani called out, "Hey!"

Hailee stepped back in again. "Hey what?"

"I've got Robert on-site with one of the trucks that we use for deliveries in town," she said. "He's free. I want you to get in your car, take him to your place, pack up, and try to move in here tonight, if you can."

Hailee looked at her in surprise.

"You can't stay where you are. Go ahead and quit your town job. No point in you going back and forth," Dani said. "And you can start work tomorrow morning, if you're up to it. Otherwise we can hold off another day."

"I really have nothing much to pack up, and, although it probably won't all fit in my car, I don't need a big truck."

"Well, we have a pickup. Would that be better?"

At that, Hailee smiled. "That would be perfect." While she stood here, talking to Dani, a grizzled old man walked toward them. There was a spring to his step, and he dangled keys in his fingers. He poked his head in Dani's office and asked, "What's up?"

"We're moving Hailee here to one of the residences," she said. "She doesn't have much and figures it's too much for the big truck but maybe one of the pickups. Can you go with her and give her a hand?"

"Sure," he said. He looked over at Hailee. "You'll finally join the funny farm, will you?"

"Well, I've already been here for a while," Hailee said with a big smile. "Now I guess I'm moving in full-time."

"It's the best place to be. Now come on. Let's go. I got to meet the missus coming in to pick me up later. She wants me to do some drapery shopping or some such thing," he said with a big eye roll.

Hailee laughed. "Do you have the time? Otherwise I don't want to take you away from your wife's appointment."

"It's twenty minutes to town. I don't think you got much stuff, if Dani says you don't," he said. "If nothing else, I can meet you, drop you off, go meet the wife, then come back to pick you up."

"That might not be a bad idea," Hailee said. She hadn't been looking forward to packing up what little she had in front of him.

"Good enough," Dani said, waving her fingers. "Now get lost so I can get some work done." But there was a laugh in her voice and a smile on her face.

On their way to the parking lot, Hailee called her boss in town to quit her day job, so somebody else didn't lose theirs. She'd talk to her landlord in person soon. When she hung up, she was at her car and gave Robert her address. "I'm probably a slower driver than you."

"Yeah, you probably are. Follow me into town. I'll get you there in no time." He winked at her, making her chuckle. He walked over to one of the pickups parked off to the side, hopped in, turned it on, and pulled out. He waited for her to get in her car, turn over the engine, and come in behind him.

And that's how they drove back into town. He did drive

faster than she usually did, but it didn't seem like a dangerous pace. They made it to her apartment in no time, leaving her feeling incredibly upbeat. Then he parked outside and said, "Show me your place, so I have an idea of what kind of work we got before us."

She nodded and led him to her second-story studio.

He looked around at the small space, shook his head, and said, "Wow, not much here."

"And it's not my bed or my couch," she said. He looked at her in surprise, and she shrugged. "It's been a rough couple years. I had to sell everything to pay medical bills," she said quietly.

Instantly understanding flashed on his face. "Those outrageous medical bills could kill anybody," he muttered. "How long do you think you need to pack?"

She shook her head. "An hour or two maybe?"

"Do you have any boxes?"

"No," she said, looking around. "I've got a few pieces of luggage that I'll take my clothing in, but I don't have anything for my kitchen stuff. I can use garbage bags for the bathroom stuff and linens."

"I'll get some boxes," he said. "You start pulling out stuff to pack. We should be done with this in a couple hours, if not half of that." Without another word, he disappeared.

She couldn't even begin to process how quickly her life had flipped around, but she pulled out her suitcases, opened them up, and dumped in her clothing and personal stuff. She didn't even worry about how well she packed. It was more important to just have it done, so she could move out. As soon as she had the suitcases full, she grabbed a couple big black garbage bags that she had and stuck in her comforter, blankets, and bedding. She could do laundry at Dani's. With that done, she headed to the bathroom, and, in smaller garbage bags, she quickly loaded everything of hers here, wrapping up breakables in towels.

By the time Robert came back with a few boxes, she was mostly done.

Robert looked at her in approval. "Not too shabby. You're not worried about getting it all neat and tidy, are you?"

"It seemed more important," she said with a laugh, "to just get it done."

"Exactly," he said. "And you don't have very much here anyway." He went to the kitchen and pulled out a few dishes, then looked at her and asked, "Is this all yours?"

"The dishes and the cutlery are the landlady's. The coffeemaker is mine. The teakettle is mine. The food in the fridge is mine, and the food in the cupboards is mine," she said. With four boxes folded into shape and a fifth one now ready, they quickly unloaded the cupboards. Robert folded together two more boxes for her to pack up the fridge. Then they hauled everything out, and, before long, she stared at one last box that was half empty.

While she walked through the small space, cleaning cloth in hand, confirming she had everything of hers out, the landlady walked in, took a look, and said, "Oh, good. I have somebody interested in this room now. In which case I can let you off this month's rent."

"It's perfect timing for me too," Hailee said, "as I'm almost done cleaning up." She'd already done the bathroom and the kitchen area. "I'm just figuring out if I missed anything."

Together they went through every corner and looked under the bed. Then the landlady handed over her inspection report to Hailee, as she returned her key to the landlord, all while Robert was here to collect the last box. When Hailee stepped out and shut the door behind her, she stood for a moment, feeling a massive shift in her world. Then she ran down the stairs, feeling better today than she'd felt in a long time.

Robert waited for her at the truck. "Do we have everything now?"

She nodded. "I wonder if I could have gotten this all in the car."

"Not without two trips," he said. "Much easier to do it this way," he said. "And we'll get back in time," he said. "I'll still make the wife's appointment."

She laughed and said, "I'm following you. Let's go." And she got in her car and returned to Hathaway House. As she crossed the gates into the massive property, she could feel something inside ease further. If nothing else, she could give back to the world here. Surely somebody could use what she had to offer. As long as the lawyer kept fighting for a reduction in her medical bills, maybe she would see a light at the end of that tunnel someday too.

Robert pulled out in front of one of the buildings on the far side as Hailee parked beside him. They stood together on the sidewalk, and he motioned to one of the doors. She was surprised that she had already been assigned a room. She followed him and asked, "Do you know where I'm staying?"

"Yep. This is the hallway." And he opened it up, and she could see doors on either side leading down. "Each of these opens to their own private patio on one side, and we've got housing for thirty here. You're number four." As he said that, he opened up number four and let her in. It was twice the size of where she'd just come from, and a small loft held a bed. She looked up there and smiled. "Beds are here too?"

"Dani gave you one of the first ones," he said, as he headed back to the truck to grab the first of the boxes.

She raced behind him, laughing with joy. "I'll love being here," she cried out.

"It's a good place to be," he said. "Dani is a good woman."

"She has been a lifesaver for me," Hailee said.

Robert nodded. "She has a habit of picking up people who need help and giving them what they need so they can fly solo again."

"Well, that's an apt description. I hadn't really considered myself in that light, but that's the way it is."

"I didn't mean no insult," he said. "She's just known for helping out people."

As Hailee looked out at the paddock nearby, she could see several horses, a filly, and what looked like a little llama too. She stopped for a moment. "I don't even remember seeing these animals here."

"Well, that big black one is Dani's own personal horse, and the little llama is named Lovely. That partner right beside Lovely, that pretty multicolored horse there, spent all its time with the llama. And the other horses are strays or spares or whoever knows. Dani fosters and adopts anybody who needs a home."

For a long moment, Hailee stood here, realizing that she had just become one of Dani's fosters. It was an uncomfortable feeling. Especially for someone like Hailee, who hated to ask for help. Yet, when forced to ask, she really needed any help she could get. But, at the same time, she also knew that Dani had given Hailee a gift. A chance to get back on her feet and to find her way again.

Robert walked past her with another armload. "Come on, come on, come on," he said. "Otherwise you're explaining to the wife why I'm late."

She shouted out a bark of laughter and raced to his truck, grabbing the garbage bags. With one over her shoulder and the other one in her arms, she returned to her little apartment. Then did it again and again. And finally they were done.

Robert walked back outside and said, "Welcome to Hathaway House. You'll love it here." Then he hopped in his truck and drove away.

Hailee stood at the open hallway door and realized that it was never locked, so everyone could come in the same way. She went to her new apartment, typed in the code Robert gave her, and it unlocked in front of her. Then she stepped inside, walked outside through the double glass doors to her patio, and, from where she stood, she could see the paddocks and some of the horses from her apartment. She turned around in a big circle with her arms wide and laughed. "Thank you! Thank you! Thank you, Dani!"

Then she went inside to unpack and to get her house to rights before she returned to the main building. She knew she was supposed to go to work in the morning. But part of her desperately wanted to see how Heath was doing. She just didn't understand if that was something she was even allowed to do. Maybe she'd sneak by his room at two in the morning. But first things first. She needed to get settled in. Then everything else could come later.

HEATH SAT IN his wheelchair near the hot tub the next day,

once again persuaded by Shane to make his way down here. Heath wasn't quite as stiff and sore as he had been the previous day. Yesterday he'd had a hard time enjoying the heated water because it had soaked into his aching muscles and then zapped the strength away from him, the weather itself having taken what little bit he had left.

As Shane helped him out of the wheelchair and into the water, he said, "It shouldn't be too bad today."

"Well, it's better," Heath acknowledged, as he shifted in the water, almost groaning as the heat soaked into his body again. "I don't understand how it can feel so good, yet, at the same time, it exhausts me."

"It's the heat soaking into your muscles," Shane said, as he stepped down ever-so-slightly into the hot tub. He started working on Heath's shoulder. His rotator cuff had been badly damaged in the blast, while muscles holding the atlas bone underneath his skull had been weakened. Heath often got headaches when he sat up too much. "I want you to sit on this lower level over here."

Heath discovered the different levels to the hot tub. Shuffling slowly, he sat down on the lowest seat, feeling the warm water rise under his chin, soaking into the back of his neck. He rested his head along the wall to the hot tub and just groaned in relief.

"Now I don't want you to stay here too long," Shane warned. "Five minutes and then shift out."

"You mean, *fifty* minutes and then shift out," Heath said with a smile.

"Well, that's the first smile I've seen out of you in days," Shane said, "so we'll make it ten."

"If you get a laugh, can we make it twenty-five?"

"Nope, no more deals," Shane said. "I'll be right here.

I'll grab you another towel too. We didn't bring one from your room today."

"That's because we came straight from PT," he said. "You didn't let me get to my room."

"Nope," Shane said. "And I'll also bring over Jeff. He's one of our newer specialists on staff, and he'll work with you while you're in the water."

"Crap," Heath said, opening his eyes to glare up at Shane. "When am I off duty?"

"When were you off duty when you were in the navy?"

"Basically never," he said.

"And now you're recovering from your injuries until you're 100 percent, so the answer is basically *never* here too."

Heath hated to hear it, but he also understood the reasoning behind it. He just wished there was some get up and go that could be pumped into his system, so he didn't feel like everything was a waste of time, energy, and effort, because well, ... at the core, of course, he didn't feel like he deserved any of it.

When he opened his eyes the next time, he felt an inner sense of being watched. He saw a young man, olive-skinned and heavily muscled, standing and staring at him, his hands on his hips.

"You *better* be Jeff," he said.

"Oh, I'm Jeff, but you sagged into that spot on the hot tub as if your bones and your muscles won't hold you up anymore."

"They won't," Heath acknowledged. And, true to form, he just let his body float up until the water churned around him, and he floated on top of the bubbles.

"Interesting," Jeff said, as he walked around the large hot tub, studying Heath's body.

"Interesting in what way?"

"Even floating, you're favoring your full-leg side."

"Well, doesn't that make sense? There's less of me to float on the right side," he said. "So I'm floating higher there because less weight's pulling me down."

At that, Jeff laughed. "Nope, that's not it at all. But you're still pulling away from your injured side."

"I would think that's normal."

"Some people pull away, and some people roll toward it," Jeff said. "Some people are more protective of that side, whereas other people still refuse to acknowledge that the injured part exists."

At that, Heath's eyes flew open, and he stared up at the bright sky above him. "Well, that sucks."

"Why is that?"

"Because that's me," he said. "I'm still pretending it doesn't exist. And, if I don't acknowledge it, maybe I don't have to actually live with it."

"Maybe," Jeff said, as he squatted down, still studying Heath but from his foot position. "It won't work long-term though."

"Well, apparently it didn't work short-term either," Heath said in disgust. "Don't you guys let us have any illusions?"

"No," Jeff said. "I used to run PT in the military." He shrugged. "Not a whole lot I haven't seen before."

"You don't look old enough to even have made the grade to get in," Heath said in disgust.

"That's because I'm healthy," Jeff said with a surprising answer. "I haven't been through a major trauma like you have. So the lines, the worry, and the stress aren't etched into my skin yet. I've lived, but it's been relatively easy so far."

"For that, I hate you," Heath said, his tone quiet and barely audible above the bubbles.

"No, you don't," Jeff said. "You'd like to be me, but you also know that your time is past."

"Yeah," Heath said. "A long time ago."

"But that doesn't mean," Jeff continued, "that you can't still be a whole lot better than you are."

"It doesn't feel like it," Heath said. "It feels more like I'm heading into the backside of sixty."

"If you don't get fixed up soon," he said, "you'll hit a body age of sixty very quickly. In the meantime, we can do a lot to keep your body improving to the point of being in its thirties again."

"Meaning, I'm already forty or fifty, per my body?"

"Yes, unfortunately," Jeff said bluntly, not pulling any punches. "Just like with any physical trauma, it ages your body. But it's the mental decline and that emotional stress which ages the rest of you so much faster."

Heath groaned. "So what do I have to do?"

"Get started, Heath. We have a lot to work on."

Chapter 8

T HE NEXT FEW days followed a simple pattern. Hailee would get up, shower, and then head to the cafeteria to grab a coffee, presenting herself at Dani's office by eight. The first morning, Dani was there on time to show Hailee where her new office would be, as well as her new computer and their filing system. As Dani walked out, she said, "Get yourself familiar. We'll have a ton of work soon enough, and I won't always be here at the same time. I'll start horseback riding in the mornings again, as much as I can."

"That sounds wonderful," Hailee said. "You should take more time off."

Dani tossed her a bright smile. "That's why I hired you."

Hailee just rolled her eyes at that. "Glad to hear it," she said.

"I do have a bunch of employee benefits materials and reimbursement stuff for you," Dani said. "We'll get to that in a bit. I've got a meeting here at nine. A phone conference." A secretive smile split her face as she headed back to her office. But then Dani was involved in a lot of different things. Not to mention trying to jump up funding for the several beds that she kept open for people who didn't have money.

It was one of the reasons Hailee really appreciated her friend's life philosophy about making sure that everyone helped others in need. No one person could help everyone because bills still had to be paid, but it was essential to help *someone* when you could. Like Dani was doing for Hailee.

But Hailee fully intended to give Dani excellent value. If Hailee hadn't lost her first accounting job, right after Jacob was born, she'd still be working at that same place, where she'd already worked for seven years. When they realized she was draining their medical benefits, she'd been laid off in a very suspicious manner. She couldn't seem to fight that because, according to them, all of a sudden, they'd lost several big clients and needed one less accountant.

She understood why they'd done it from a strictly numbers perspective, but it had been heartbreaking for her, along with too many more heartbreaks at the same time. And so disloyal to a long-term employee like her. It was highly illegal too, but, when Hailee's lawyer said that he could only do so much pro bono work for her and asked her if she wanted to go after her employer or try to get the medical debt reduced, she'd immediately gone for the reduction in her medical debt.

She sent him a quick email, telling him that she now had one full-time job at Hathaway House and gave him a new work email address where he could contact her. He sent a quick response, telling her that he was really happy for her and that he expected to have some news here within a week or so. She smiled and typed, *I hope so. I've lost weight because I can't afford to eat.*

She added a happy face because, now that she was here at Hathaway House, she *could* eat. Speaking of which, she hadn't had food yet. She frowned at that and wondered just what the deal was. She didn't want to take any food from Dani if it wasn't allowed and neither did she want to abuse the eight-to-four work system by eating on the job.

When the new girl at the front, Caitlin, hopped up and came around the corner, she stopped when she saw who was behind the desk in Hailee's new office. Caitlin smiled and said, "Wow, that's perfect," she said. "From cleaning lady to an accountant."

"Well, technically I was a cleaning lady *and* a bookkeeper, working two jobs to replace my original accountant's job, now back to being just an accountant," Hailee said with a chuckle. "I'm not proud. Workers work."

"But a very different paycheck," Caitlin said with an eyebrow raised.

"Absolutely," she said. But she didn't offer any information to clarify how she'd gone from the highs to the lows and back to the highs again.

Caitlin motioned down the hallway. "I'm getting coffee. Do you want one?"

Hailee smiled and hopped up. "Maybe. I'll come with you. I'm not exactly sure how the system here works."

"Oh, that's easy enough," Caitlin said, as she filled her in. "For lunch, we try to give way to all the patients. We have more time available to us to get there because we can come and go as we need to. The breakfast bar opens at six in the morning, but I've never really made it that early, so don't hold me to that. Maybe ask Dennis. And then dinner is between five and seven, I believe. I don't eat breakfast, but I'll often pick up a muffin and take it back to my desk."

"I wondered if we're allowed to eat on the job," Hailee confessed. "At my old job, I was allowed a cup of coffee but no food because of the possibility to drop crumbs into the keyboards."

"I think everybody here would starve then," Caitlin said

with a laugh. "But you're right, that was like my last job too. Dani doesn't mind, and her only restrictions on the food are, *if you take it, please eat it.* Because they don't want to waste any food. Here, the kitchen is very good at using up leftovers, and that has gone a long way to keeping her food costs down. Plus I see a lot of the staff willingly eating the leftovers for their meals."

"Makes sense to me," Hailee said. "I'm happy with leftovers too." She walked into the cafeteria to see Dennis with a big smile on his face.

"There you are. I've seen you in the evening, in the afternoon, and now in the morning."

"And you'll see me a little more often now," she said. "I'm working as the new accountant."

"Perfect," he said with a beaming smile. "I didn't see you here for breakfast though."

"I wasn't exactly sure what the protocol was."

"*If you work here, you eat here,*" Dennis said with a fat smile. "That doesn't mean necessarily I won't give you leftovers ..."

She chuckled. "I'm pretty sure your leftovers are way better than no leftovers."

He chuckled, and she headed straight for the coffee, but he frowned at her. "Too much caffeine on an empty stomach is not good."

"Maybe not," she said, "but I just started. I don't really want to ruin my job already."

At that, Dani came up behind Hailee and said, "I should have gone over that with you anyway. I'm glad Dennis just said something. I often come in and do some work, and then I'll take a break and have breakfast. Put in the hours, get the job done, and I won't bother you about when you work and where you eat."

At that, Dennis handed over a beautiful omelet to Dani.

Hailee smiled and said, "Now this looks great."

Dani snagged an orange juice and some cutlery, and, with a wave to everyone, headed back to her office.

Caitlin said, "See? That's what I mean."

Hailee looked back at Dennis. He lifted up a second omelet and said, "One of the guys ordered it and then decided he didn't want it," he said coaxingly.

"But what's in it?" Hailee asked, eyeing the omelet.

"Steak and mushrooms," he said. She stared at him in surprise. He nodded, walked over, added a few hash browns and a couple fresh orange slices, then gave it to her. "Now eat up. You can't do the job if you have brain fog."

She chuckled. "Does that argument work for you?"

"Well, you're holding the omelet right now," he said, "so I guess so." He chuckled and headed into the kitchen, then turned and said, "Lunchtime starts at eleven and finishes at two. If you come a little later sometimes, it's better because it can get really crowded in here. Otherwise aim maybe for early."

"In other words, if it's busy, just come back?"

"Patients come first," he said, "but the staff is a very close second. Dani would tell you that she can't help the patients if she doesn't have a pleasant staff."

"I understand that philosophy," Hailee said with a big smile. "Besides, Dani is a sweetheart."

"She is," Dennis said. "And, because of her, this place does very well."

"Good to know." Carrying her omelet and coffee, she followed Caitlin back to the office area. As Hailee walked behind the receptionist, she asked, "Does anybody worry about getting fat here?"

"Well, I haven't worried about it," Caitlin said. "But, if I stay here much longer, I might have to." She held up the cinnamon bun she was taking back to her desk. "At least your meal is nutritionally sound. Mine's food for the soul. Yours is food for the body."

"Well, if my body wasn't so starved," Hailee said, "I'd have gone for soul food too."

And they both chuckled and headed to their respective desks.

SEVERAL DAYS LATER Heath sat in the outdoor dining section on the deck, letting the sunshine bathe his face. He was still gathering the energy to go back inside and get food. He'd gotten his coffee, and he was working on a second cup when Dennis had come around with the pot. Otherwise, Heath wouldn't have that still. The heavy massage sessions with Shane and the heavy workouts in the hot tub with Jeff had slowly built up some of Heath's muscles, but the pain and exhaustion had really whacked him out. He still wasn't sleeping at night. In fact, it was getting worse.

As he sat here, he thought he heard a familiar voice—*the cleaning lady.* He turned his head and listened intently to make sure. He twisted ever-so-slightly, mindful of his back and his neck, turning to see if he could put a body with the voice. He noticed one of the women from the front offices and another superslim, almost too slim, woman with dark hair and curls down over her shoulders, wearing a simple pair of white capris and a flowery blouse. She held a plate of food, and she had a big smile on her face.

He studied her for a long moment, but he couldn't hear her voice anymore. Disappointed and frustrated, he shifted back, staring outside past the deck. His cleaning lady was supposed to take two days off but hadn't come back in like a week now. And since then, he hadn't had a decent night's sleep. Something was magical about whatever they'd had before, and he needed that back.

Yet he could hardly ask some stranger to come and mop the floors at nighttime for him to sleep. Talk about a dependency issue that made no sense. As he sat here, wondering if he would make it to the cafeteria line or not, Dennis walked over and placed in front of Heath a platter of fried potatoes and eggs with ham and sausages. Heath looked at it, then up at Dennis in surprise.

"Saved you a trip," Dennis said. And he disappeared.

That was one of the things about Dennis. He saw things that other people didn't recognize, and he acted without other people needing to say anything. Heath didn't know if that was a good thing or not, but, as far as he was concerned, Dennis was solid gold. Somebody who saw a need and handled it without being told was an exceptional individual.

Heath dug into his breakfast with gusto. He may not have chosen quite the exact same things, but it didn't matter because it was fresh and hot, and it was in front of him. By the time he pushed away his empty plate, he was more than happy that he'd chosen to just sit and relax. Sometimes you had to stop and smell the roses instead of rush, rush, rush.

And it would have been a rush to get in before the long lines started, and then he would have felt self-conscious for stumbling forward on his crutches in front of a big crowd. He was getting a prosthetic foot for his right leg, and he knew he'd have to learn to walk all over again with it, but he was up for that. The crutches made life difficult, but it also made a hell of an improvement to being an invalid in bed or in a wheelchair. He had to make note of these tiny stages of success. If you didn't mark every one, they were easy to miss. Then it wouldn't feel like you were making any progress at all.

He'd been grateful, so grateful to get into a wheelchair, so he could buzz around independently. But, when he got out of the wheelchair and onto the crutches, standing upright—like homo sapiens were meant to be—was something completely different. He'd loved it for a long time. Yet, all of a sudden, his crutches just weren't enough. And he found himself struggling with that too.

It seemed, once you got something you wanted, you turned around and wanted something else. He was pretty sure it was human nature that made him so contrary, but, at the same time, it was also human nature to reach for something, to achieve it, and then to create a new goal and to reach for that. He just had to make sure he kept reaching. Because pretty darn soon, if he didn't make an effort, he would stop reaching, and he didn't dare do that. He was trying hard to progress.

However, his continued lack of sleep each night was killing him.

And somehow he had to get rid of those damn nightmares. And the guilt.

That ever-residing guilt.

Slowly moving, he stood, wavering ever-so-slightly, using the table for support. Then he grabbed his crutches and wobbled back down the hallway to his room.

He stopped, thinking he heard that voice again. He moved forward ten feet to where two hallways joined up and heard it again. Then he walked forward a step, yet leaned back. He looked down both hallways and saw Dani and Caitlin at the front reception area, standing with another woman. The same tall dark-haired one he'd seen earlier. They were talking together, but he didn't recognize the one woman's voice.

Then again the women were laughing, not whispering in the dead of night. The nearby office door read Accountant. Obviously this unknown woman wasn't his cleaning lady. Not here in the middle of the day. Not here chatting with other office workers. Something was wrong here. His feelings and hopes dashed, he slowly turned and walked back down the hallway.

He didn't know who his cleaning lady was, but he sure wished she'd come back, if only for him to get another good night's sleep.

Chapter 9

HAILEE LOOKED UP to see Caitlin standing at Hailee's doorway but looking down the hall at something. Caitlin stepped out of sight, and Hailee could hear Caitlin speaking with somebody else. Frowning, Hailee hopped up to see Caitlin talking with one of the patients. Hailee smiled and headed back into her office. When Caitlin reappeared a few minutes later, Hailee looked up and asked, "Problem?"

"No, I don't think so," Caitlin said with a shrug. "But he seemed hesitant to come forward, and I didn't want him to feel like he couldn't talk to us if he needed something."

"Of course not," Hailee said in surprise. "What was he looking for?"

"He didn't really say," she said. "I saw him earlier. He was walking down our hallway, as if listening to something. And then he seemed to shrug and turned around and moved on."

"Maybe he was looking to see if Dani was here?"

"Maybe," Caitlin said, looking relieved at the suggestion.

"As long as he knows he can talk to us anytime, it's all good," Hailee said, comfortably digging back into the pile of work on her desk, smiling to realize she had, indeed, settled in here. It had taken a few days, but Dani had quickly dumped a stack of paperwork on top of Hailee's desk. Hailee was doing a combination of pure bookkeeping work as well as accounting, but she was good with that.

As Dani cleaned off her desk, more and more was getting dumped on Hailee. Her day was quickly filling up. Plus the bookkeeping was behind in terms of producing proper documentation needed for Dani's next investors' meeting with the bank. Hailee would take a few days getting all that taken care of too.

But, all in all, she settled in much better than she had expected. She reached for another stack of invoices, studied them, and shook her head. These were from weeks ago and should have been entered around the same time. It just went to show how quickly the work ran away on Dani. She should have hired an accountant a while back. Had Hailee known she was ready to tackle this job on the level Dani needed, Hailee would have jumped at the chance earlier.

As far as her meals were concerned, she took to that like a fish took to water. Three meals a day was something she hadn't had in a long time. Most of her clothing hung on her shoulders and thin frame now. She used to have a good twenty extra pounds on her long before Jacob was born. After that, it just melted off. So she could stand to gain a little bit, but she wanted more muscle. So she couldn't just eat cinnamon buns. She'd have a thicker layer of excess padding around her instead. Much better that she ate a little bit more in the calorie department as to the healthier foods, indulging in cinnamon rolls occasionally, and went for long walks.

So far, Dennis had treated her almost like a best friend—or maybe his role was more of a mother hen because he came along and watched over her all the time. He would even come to her office, once he found out where she was, if she didn't show up for lunch. Speaking of which, her stomach started to grumble. She looked out her office at Caitlin to find her working, head down, dealing with the phones and schedules, trying to sort out some of the day trips that were happening. Plus they had a bunch of deliveries that would come here and others that Robert would drive into town and pick up. Hailee decided she'd finish one of her stacks, and then she'd take a break and get some breakfast.

As soon as she had that work completed, she got up, walked toward Caitlin, and said, "I'm getting some food. Do you want me to bring you anything?"

Caitlin looked up, distracted, then shook her head until she realized what Hailee had asked. "No," Caitlin said. "I ate early this morning. I'll have a snack and then call it quits a little bit early today too. Heading into town for a dentist appointment."

"Ouch," Hailee said. It had been so long since she'd even made it to the dentist that she probably needed to go in for a checkup herself. But not until the bills slowed down.

"Well, we get that covered here," Caitlin said, "so I figured I should at least take care of my teeth while I can."

At that, Hailee stopped, looked at her, and asked in a low whisper, "We get dental here?"

Caitlin looked up in surprise, then nodded quickly. "Yes. You might even get a better plan too," she said. "I know I was amazed when I found out I could go in and get checkups and even cleaning covered. I think it's two cleanings a year and one checkup or something like that. Believe me. It's more than I've ever had, so I'll take advantage of it."

Hailee thought about it as she walked all the way to the cafeteria. She didn't know the last time she had had any dental coverage. As such, she took good care of her teeth because she couldn't afford to have anything go wrong.

When she entered the large cafeteria, she realized it was almost ten o'clock, and the patients would probably be coming for coffee. She looked to see if any breakfast food was left. A lot of the trays were gone, leaving mostly sweets. She walked through, looking for anything not too sugary.

Dennis caught sight of her and walked up. "You missed breakfast, didn't you?"

She smiled and nodded. "For some reason, I thought maybe there would be some leftovers."

"There is," he said. "What would you like?"

She thought about it and shrugged. "A little bit of fruit, yogurt, and granola would be nice."

"Coming right up," he said and disappeared without asking any details.

She frowned at that, but he came right back with two large parfait glasses layered with something delicious-looking. She stared at both and said, "I didn't want anything too sweet though."

"These are plain Greek yogurt with fresh berries and granola," he said. "I make them up a couple times a week, and these two happen to be what was left." She looked at him and hesitated. He held them up and said, "Raspberry or blueberry?"

"Raspberry," she said instantly. Then she accepted it, looking at it with a smile. "You're sure it's healthy?"

"Of course it's healthy. No extra sugar added. It doesn't need it."

She smiled and nodded. "This should hold me until lunch."

"It will," he said. "You can always have an early lunch too."

"Right," she said with a smile. Then she stepped back

and made herself a small pot of tea at the drinks station. With a fresh cup on the side, she carried her tray back. As she headed across the cafeteria though, she stopped and viewed the massive deck outside in the sun. She'd seen it before but had yet to make it out there. She wandered outside, knowing that she should go back to her office, yet she caught sight of the pool and the hot tub below. Again, things that she had seen but hadn't really taken in. Down below, she could see men put through the paces by their therapists, while other men wandered around with crutches, talking to people in wheelchairs.

A great social atmosphere came with this place, almost as if everyone was part of a large extended family. Hathaway House didn't have any hospital feel or look to it, and she appreciated that. She couldn't imagine anything worse for these guys. She didn't think they could either. A certain sense of freedom was here, and she loved that.

As she looked down, one man with dark hair leaned against the edge of the hot tub. He looked exhausted. She frowned as she studied him and then realized that maybe it wasn't exhaustion on his face but pain. She hesitated, put her tray on the table, and leaned over the railing to see if anybody was with him. He opened his eyes and looked up at her. She stared down and gave him a half smile and then pulled back. She didn't want to seem like she was interfering or being nosy. Yet there was something about him.

Dennis came outside with a big dishcloth and started wiping down the tables. "I thought you would take that back to your office."

She hesitated, then nodded, and said, "I haven't been out on the deck in the sun, so I'm taking five to just sort it out." She pointed over the railing. "I also hadn't taken time to really see the pool or the hot tub."

"Wow," he said, "you are missing something."

He joined her at the corner, and she stopped and stared at what was in his arms. "What is that?"

"Not *what* is that," he said. "It's who. This is Chickie."

He walked closer, and he held a tiny pet bed and inside was one of the smallest animals she'd ever seen. "Oh my." A short tail wagged at her tone, and she reached out a gentle hand and scratched his tiny head.

"His back legs are paralyzed," Dennis said. "He often sits up front with Caitlin, but he has had a couple rough days, so I often keep him in the back with me when that happens."

"Is he better back there?"

"Chances are somebody gave him food he shouldn't have," Dennis said. "Chickie's stomach is very delicate. One of the rules we have is that nobody's allowed to feed any of the animals. They're all on strict diets."

He motioned to the pasture, where she could see the big Newfoundlander. She'd seen it from a distance before but hadn't met him yet.

"I've been here three days on the day shift," she announced, "and I haven't seen any of the dogs."

"They're all around, but you're so tied to your desk," he said. Then he stopped and nodded. "You were doing the cleaning before, weren't you? They would have all gone to their beds. We don't leave them to run around at night."

"In that case," she said, "I'll have to go make everybody's acquaintance."

He smiled and said, "Well, you've just met Chickie. We also have a big Maine Coon around here with three legs, and I know that Stan has been working hard at getting another cat trained to be a therapy cat."

"That'd be a heck of a job," she said. "I can't imagine any cat allowing itself to be trained for anything."

He chuckled. "Absolutely. And I'm not sure this cat will be prepared to do anything, but he's incredibly intuitive, according to Stan."

She hesitated.

"You've never met Stan either, have you?"

She shook her head.

"Well, why don't you leave that tray here, and we'll come back for it in a minute?"

"Or I eat it right now," she said, "and then we go."

"Well," he nodded and said, "sit down. I'll finish my cleaning, and then I'll take you down and introduce you to Stan."

She frowned and glanced back at the offices.

"Stan is part of the office workers here. You should meet him."

"If you say so," she said. "I just don't want to get into trouble."

He laughed. "Dani should have introduced you right away, but I know she's really busy with these meetings."

"She is," she said. "And honestly I'm the one prepping her documents for those meetings, so I'll take a rain check. But maybe this afternoon?"

"Absolutely. Whenever you have time."

She picked up her tray and headed back, but her mind was full of animals and Stan. If she'd only known, she would have been there on day one.

HEATH WASN'T SURE who it was that he'd seen up on the

deck, but it looked like the woman from one of the offices. He shifted in the water and slowly pulled himself out, so he now sat on the edge of the hot tub. He looked around, and Shane came toward him with a couple towels.

"Enough for the day?"

"Yeah, I think so," Heath said. Beside Shane was the big Newfoundlander dog. Heath reached out a hand and called out, "Hey, Helga, come on, girl."

Helga raced over and jumped up so her paws were on the back of the hot tub which gave Heath so much more access for belly scratches.

He cuddled her gently. "You're so fortunate to be here," he said. "Do you know how many welcoming hands there are here for you?"

Helga barked in his face. Heath smiled and looked at Shane. "You're lucky too that you get to have these guys around your workplace."

"Hathaway House is very unusual that way," Shane said with a nod. "But it also works out very well. These animals need a lot of care and attention too. So we rehab both here. Plus I think the animals benefit from all the humans being around, just like the humans benefit from all the animals being around." As he looked past the hot tub, he saw Stan leading the small llama outside again. Shane called out, "Is she okay?"

Stan looked over and raised a hand and said, "She's fine. I was just checking her hooves, but she's doing great." Then he opened up the paddock to lead her inside and took the harness off her face and let her go. Up close was a multicolored horse waiting for the llama. Immediately the two raced off together and then stopped and cuddled up.

Heath stared and smiled. "You don't see that too often."

"No, but now they're both fixtures here," Shane said.

With one towel wrapped around his shoulders now, Heath used the other one to dry off and then slowly turned so his legs were out of the water. "The animals really add another element."

"I think more animals are coming," Shane said. "Oddly enough, I think one comfort animal is a pygmy pig."

Heath stopped, turned, looked at Shane, and asked, "Seriously?"

"Not only does Dani collect strays," Shane said with a head shake and a broad grin, "but so does Stan. Sometimes we're all asked to help out, depending on what the problem is. We had an injured female lab give birth here, but she needed surgery herself, so we had to bottle-feed her pups until she was capable again."

"That would have been fun," he said. "I could get behind something like that." He looked over at Helga, who seemed to immediately realize he was a soft touch, so she dropped her head on his lap. "The only problem," he said, "is how do you keep the facilities clean when these guys are shedding hair everywhere?"

"Which is why we have such a high level of cleaning in the place," Shane said. "And all the filters in the pool and the hot tub specially filter out the hair because we can't keep the animals out of the water."

He looked at the pool, then at Helga, and asked, "Does she swim?"

"Don't even say that word," Shane said hurriedly. "Given half a chance, she jumps in on her own. We've got her mostly trained, so she doesn't go in without an invitation, but an invitation is something that she tends to take on herself."

"Right," he said. "I wouldn't mind being in the pool myself."

"How much swimming have you done since your accident?"

"None," Heath said, staring at the water. He was just hot and sweaty enough from the hot tub that a cool dip in the pool was enticing. "You got any problem with me going in it?"

"Go for it," Shane said. He walked over to Heath's crutches and brought them to him. "But I don't want you to exhaust yourself."

"No, I already did that with you this morning."

Shane chuckled. "Let's get you into the water, if that's where you want to be."

Carefully, moving slowly on the wet cement, they made it to the side of the tiled pool. Heath handed off his crutches and just let his body fall forward. As soon as the water closed over his head, he happily sunk to the bottom. When he slowly surfaced, Shane stood there, watching him with a frown on his face.

"I'm fine," Heath said.

"Well, you looked like you were just a solid slab of meat when you fell in."

"This is so nice," he said. "I used to be a hell of a swimmer. It's been a long time though."

"Swim away," Shane said. "You've got about ten minutes. After that, you're done."

And Heath took Shane for his word.

Heath immediately broke into a front crawl, feeling his body roll with the unused muscle motions. He was surprised to find just how sore he was. His arm didn't quite fully go up and over, so his form sucked. Both legs kicked, but he only had one foot, so one leg was active, and the other one just felt like it was sticking out there doing nothing. It was such an odd feeling, but he was mobile, and he was doing it on his own. He raced forward to one side and then back to the other. By the time he had completed three full laps, he could feel his energy waning. He pulled into the shallow end and sat on the step, just catching his breath.

Shane walked up beside him. "And?"

"Well, it felt good to swim and to support myself in the water without needing crutches," he said, "but it really reminded me that I'm not in the shape I used to be in and that the muscles don't want to go in the direction they're supposed to go."

Shane grinned. "Isn't that the truth? But now that you've been in here, and I see that you can swim, I'll incorporate it into your weekly workouts."

"I'm okay with that." Heath looked over at the hot tub, then at Shane, and asked, "Are we done for the morning, or is there more?"

"No, you're done, but I want you in your room now, so I can take a look at your back."

"Great. I thought I could hop in the hot tub a bit longer."

Shane shook his head. "No, your energy level is already way too low. We may have to use a wheelchair to get you to your room as it is. The crutches would be hard with your current energy levels."

As he looked at the crutches, the rest of his energy started to drain, making him realize how tired he really was. Heath nodded. "I'm afraid you're right. I didn't even realize it until now."

At that, Shane walked over to the side and grabbed one

of the many waiting wheelchairs, then pulled it over, and said, "This time I'll take you up. Next time you're on your own."

Chapter 10

S EVERAL DAYS LATER Hailee started to get to know and to identify the different staff members and patients. During her night shift work of cleaning, she didn't get to meet very many people. But now any number of individuals came through the offices at any given time. It was one of the oddest feelings. When she had started her cleaning job, she'd been so grateful to Dani but hadn't really recognized how different it was to work here on the day shift as compared to working the night shift.

She saw very few people at night. If she ever saw even three in her entire shift, she'd have been surprised. But now that she had this daytime job, dozens of people were coming and going all the time. The other job had had a sense of privacy, something she'd been happy to have at the time. Yet now, she felt like she was part of something. She was involved in the hustle and bustle of daily life here at Hathaway House.

She'd been included. Maybe that was what was different. This kind of felt like she belonged.

Cleaning in the nights almost felt like she was whispering silently through the halls, not letting anybody know she was here. And now it was a completely different thing. She was slowly getting to know more of the staff, and, of course, some of the patients came up with headaches of their own.

Usually about paperwork or phone calls or connections and appointments that they needed to make and couldn't get made on their own without some help or maybe needed to go into town. So patients were continually talking to the women at the front desk if not with Dani and Hailee.

It was interesting. Hailee had her own office and a door that she could close, if and when she needed the privacy to get the work done. And yet, with it open, she was still part of the inner circle of how everything operated. A very different feeling than she'd had at night. However, one thing was missing.

And she didn't even know his name.

She'd gone past his door several times and hesitated, wanting to go in and to say hi but had struggled with that. She felt like she'd be interfering, an interloper in some ways, or maybe he didn't want to see who she was. If their positions were reversed, she'd be feeling bereft and deserted if the cleaning lady had abandoned her. *Abandoned.* And that just made her wince because was there any worse feeling in the world? She didn't think so. She'd been there and had experienced the same thing herself, and it was crippling in a way.

A couple conversations happened outside her office that were low-key, and she hadn't been invited to join in, so she hadn't a clue what was going on. But it was odd. She kept her ear perked out of curiosity but never really heard too much. She heard the name *Heath*, which made her think of moors and long walks with dogs and walking sticks. The broody type of male. But she didn't have any real basis for that kind of an intuitive image.

As she kept working away through the accounts and cleaning up matters, checking things out and making sure everything was up to date, Dani stopped in and looked at her with half a smile, then asked, "Have you got a moment?"

Hailee smiled and said, "For you, always." Dani came in and closed the door and sat down. The fact that she'd closed the door immediately put Hailee on edge. "Is there a problem?" she asked lightly. But inside, her stomach screamed. Dear God, she so didn't want to lose this job.

"No, no, no," Dani said, immediately shaking her head. "Sorry. I didn't mean to make it seem like this was a big deal." She turned to glance at the door, then frowned. "But I guess, by shutting the door, that would be an immediate assumption, wouldn't it?"

"I don't know enough about how this place works yet to know if it's a problem or not," Hailee said, "but almost every instance where the boss comes in and shuts the door tends to make employees cringe."

"Well," Dani said with a half smile, "this is something different."

Hailee sat back. "What's up?"

"First," Dani said, "how do you fit in?"

"Well," Hailee said. "Surprisingly well."

"Good," Dani said with a self-satisfied smile. "I knew you'd be perfect for here."

"And how would you know that?" Hailee smiled. "We've been friends for a long time, but I don't know that we've ever really worked together."

"No, but I understand who you are inside," she said. "And I'm so sorry for all the trauma you've been through."

Hailee's smile fell away. She stared at the papers in front of her, but she nodded. "Thank you. It's one of those things that life throws at you that you have to walk through alone, and nobody can really help you emotionally. Even if hands reach out to give you some assistance, they can't walk in your shoes with you," she said, raising her gaze. "It took me a long time to realize that and to just buckle in and ride through it."

"You might not have anybody who can walk in your shoes," Dani said gently, "but it doesn't mean having people walking beside you can't make the journey easier."

"Very true," Hailee said with a half smile. "Unfortunately the person who should have been there for me wasn't."

Dani nodded again. "Sometimes I think we're destined to go through really crappy relationships so that, when we do find something special, we recognize it."

Hailee looked at her in surprise. "Well, that's a different take on it. Here I thought we were supposed to find something special right off the bat and set ourselves up for life. Isn't that what we're taught? To get an education, get married, have kids, and be the perfect wife?"

"There's no such thing as perfection," Dani said. "And I don't think our mothers knew a whole lot more than we did at our age either." She sighed. "The generations aren't getting more stupid. I think they're getting smarter," she admitted. "But people are changing, expectations on relationships are changing, and the role models and what each brings to the table are changing. So it's a case of finding what works for you and only you."

"And have you found it?" Hailee asked quietly. She'd heard an awful lot of good things about Aaron but hadn't actually met the man.

Dani beamed. "Yes," she said. "Finally. But, like you, I went through a rough time first. But I'm pretty confident that what Aaron and I have will go the distance. Anyway, that's not why I came here."

"Okay," Hailee said, slowly crossing her hands as she

placed them on top of her desk, so she could sit tall and focus on Dani. "What's up?"

"One of our patients," Dani said, "and I'm just hearing about this now, was wondering who the cleaning lady was who's disappeared."

Hailee's eyebrows rose. "Interesting," she said. She turned slightly to look out the window on her left. "Is his room down that short hallway that leads to one of the fire exits? On the left-hand side?" she said, closing her eyes. "I think it's the first of three doors?"

Dani, her voice rich with laughter, said, "Exactly. That's him."

Hailee smiled. "I wondered if he'd miss me."

At that, Dani's eyebrows shot up. "So tell me more," she said. "What's going on between the two of you?"

Hailee shook her head. "Nothing, honestly. But I used to mop that hallway last every night that I cleaned," she said with a small deprecating smile. "And he used to wake up about that time." She laughed, then sobered. "One time I thought I heard him cry out. I knocked on the door and poked my head around the corner to see if he needed some assistance. After that, we spoke several times. Not too often."

"Well, his name is Heath," she said. "Heath Hankerson. He was asking about you, and now I understand why. He's struggling to sleep."

"He said that he had a hard time sleeping. The drugs weren't agreeing with him, and they left him groggy and brain foggy, so he hated taking them because of the way they made him feel."

Dani nodded. "It's amazing just how many of the drugs these men react to," she said sadly. "They come out of the hospitals—often heavily drugged on pain pills, sleeping aids, antibiotics, and any number of medications required to survive their surgeries—and then they go one way or the other. They develop a supersensitivity to some of them, or they find they can't survive without them. And they need stronger and stronger drugs."

"Well, I definitely got the impression that Heath went the other way," Hailee said.

"Yes," Dani said with a nod. "That's exactly right. So he struggles with taking any sleeping medication."

"I've never seen who he is," Hailee said with a chuckle. "His room was always dark, and I only had more or less ambient lighting in the hallway, just from the night-lights while I was mopping. I tried to keep the lights turned down. A little harder to see that way, but, as long as you're methodical, you know you've reached every corner anyway."

Dani nodded. "Now that I know who he's talking about and why he wants to know what happened to you," Dani said rising, "I'll go talk to him myself."

"Are you short a cleaner?"

"Yes," Dani said, "but you're not going back to that."

"What difference does it make?" Hailee said with a smile. "I mean, I worked a full-time job and then came here and worked too."

"Yes," she said. "But a lot of laws regulate something like that within the same company, and you don't need to do both jobs now. Remember? That was the reason for pulling those two wages together to give you this job."

Hailee bit her lip and nodded. "I understand," she said. "I just feel bad for him."

"I'll talk to his therapist and see if we can come up with something else to help him sleep through the night." And with that, she opened the door and left it wide open and disappeared down the hallway.

All Hailee could think about was the name Heath and the man himself, wondering if she should dare visit him and say hi. Yet, after Dani's visit, Hailee felt it would be much better to keep her distance.

HEATH SAT ON the edge of his bed, rubbing his eyes. He'd just woken up from a short power nap. He hated the damn sleeping pills he was forced to take, but, without sleep, he couldn't function at all. So it had been a painful compromise. But not one he liked. It didn't seem fair that he should have to use drugs to get the rest his body needed. He was exhausted inside and out, so why the heck couldn't this work out better for him?

When he heard a knock on his door, he called out, "Come in." He looked up to see Dani standing in the doorway. He glared at her. "Is there a problem?"

She laughed. "Nope, not at all," she said. "But I hear you've been asking about one of my staff."

His frown deepened. "And?"

She took several more steps into the room. "Are you always this grumpy or just when you don't get sleep?"

He glanced at the bed behind him. "I just woke up from a nap," he said, "so I should be getting sleep."

"But apparently you're not," she said quietly.

He didn't look at her this time. Instead he twisted and gently collapsed on the bed, wincing at the unnatural movement. "I keep trying to," he said, staring up at the ceiling. "But I don't seem able to."

"You're having trouble sleeping, or, when you wake up,

you're having trouble going back to sleep?"

"Going back to sleep," he said. "I figured it's exhaustion that gets me under in the first place. It wears off, and my body sleeps enough that it's looking to wake up and do something else."

"Is there a connection to this cleaning lady?"

He stiffened and then glared at Dani. "I didn't say that," he growled.

"Okay," she said, "then tell me why you want to know anything about her."

He just shrugged.

"Well, I'll hardly give you any information," she said, as she walked a little closer, "unless you tell me something too."

He gave her a small wave of his hand. "It doesn't matter," he said. "She's probably gone anyway."

"Yes, and no," Dani said.

He rolled his head to the side and stared at her. "That sounds very evasive."

"Actually it's not," she said. "She's still here but in a different capacity."

"Why? Did she not like cleaning?"

"She had other skills that we needed a little more," Dani admitted.

"Of course," he said. "Everybody else is important." What he left unsaid was everybody *except for him*. And then realized he was being a petulant child. "Well, hopefully she's happy." If she had another job, then she wasn't coming back, and that meant he would have to find a solution to his sleepless problem one way or the other. He didn't know what he was supposed to do, and exhaustion was dragging him down and affecting his performance in all aspects. He couldn't even eat properly. His stomach was continually churning up in knots.

"Would it help if she came and talked to you?"

He shook his head. "No," he said harshly. "She's already moved on, so whatever."

Dani hesitated.

He glared at her. "If there's nothing else …"

She nodded quietly. "I'll talk to you about it later then." And she turned and walked out, closing the door quietly behind her.

He wanted to say, *Don't bother. Absolutely nothing to talk about.* Because obviously the woman wouldn't be cleaning at two in the morning anymore, so what difference did it make? He groaned and scrubbed his face. "You'll have to deal with this one way or the other," he said to himself. Sleep and nightmares went hand in hand. He had tried a lot of different things, but nothing seemed to work. And now that he'd had enough sleep to make it through the rest of the day, he knew there was no point in trying right now.

When someone knocked again, he groaned and called out, "Come in."

A petite woman entered. She smiled at him and said, "I'm setting up yoga classes. Does that hold any interest for you?"

He shook his head. "I doubt Shane would even allow me to go to the class, at least not yet. I don't bend like a pretzel very well."

"Well, the idea of a yoga class," she said, "would be to start at whatever level you're capable of moving at and then stretching and moving toward improving that range of motion."

"If it requires anything more than lying in bed or sitting in a wheelchair," he said quietly, "you've already maxed out my range of motion."

She gave him a bright smile. "Not quite," she said. "I've seen you in the pool, so I know you can do some stuff."

He glared at her, but her smile stayed in place. Finally he groaned and said, "At nighttime, I have a hard time sleeping, so that'll probably just rev me up."

"No," she said. "One of the reasons that we do yoga is to help people sleep, so they don't need sleep aids."

At that, he snapped, "Did Dani set you up for this?"

"Well, Dani is my boss," she said with a laugh. "We thought maybe there would be enough interest in yoga classes to run a couple."

"Well, let me know how it goes," he said. And then he slowly shifted and rolled over toward the window. "Close the door on your way out, please." He waited to listen for her footsteps as she exited his room and heard the door slowly closing. With that *snick* of the door, he allowed himself to relax.

"And now what the hell am I supposed to do?" he muttered. "You're miserable inside and out." And that just made him feel worse.

Chapter 11

A FTER SEVERAL MORE days Hailee finally decided that she couldn't stand not knowing for sure if they were talking about the same patient. She knew they were, ... but that niggling doubt remained. She got up and walked down the hallway and got the room number. She should have done this a long time ago. Then she came back, and, as she did so, she asked Caitlin, "Heath's in Room 221, correct?"

Caitlin quickly glanced through her files and nodded. "Yes, that's correct." She looked over at her and said, "Problem?"

Hailee smiled and shook her head. "No, I just needed to check it for our records." She walked back into her office and sat down, wondering if she should set up a meeting with him. She was bound to see him sometime but didn't want to come face-to-face with him unexpectedly. But every time she'd been in that area when mopping, she couldn't see his face. So, whether that was a good thing or a bad thing, she didn't know.

It *had* put him in the mystery-man category. And the mystery man was almost perfect for her. Yet she didn't want to deal with any more men who wouldn't be real—that had been her husband. Unfortunately now she was sitting here, thinking that mystery men were probably perfect precisely because they *weren't* real. She had had enough of reality. At the same time, her mystery man was also a fantasy, and she didn't need that. But it was nice to have, and it stopped her from feeling lonely.

She still needed to recognize who he was, so she didn't come upon him unexpectedly and not realize it was him. But she wasn't sure how to do it. She could ask Dani, but that felt wrong now, after Heath had been asking about her. Hailee wouldn't sit there and haunt his hallway either because that felt worse. So how else was she supposed to know? There would be photos in their patient files, but that felt intrusive, like she shouldn't be looking there without good reason. All in all, that thought made it a little creepy. She had to do something about it, but she just didn't know what. She put it off yet again.

As she headed into dinner that night, she was once again amazed at how much her life had simplified by being here. With Dani giving her residency here, that meant Hailee's food and board was free, freeing up more of her paychecks. Although she hadn't had one yet, it would be automatically deposited into her bank account. And, maybe for the first time, since she could eat enough now, she could reduce her own stress levels.

As she walked up to the cafeteria line, she was happy to see that she'd timed it just about right. She'd been working later these last few days to get caught up and to get Dani's books all ready for the big meeting she had coming up. In the meantime, Hailee had allowed most of the dinnertime crowd to go through first, and she left afterward to have hers. It was after six now, and about eight people were in front of her with various forms of mobility. She loved that here too. Nobody was in a rush, and everybody was entitled to take as much time as they needed to get from point A to point B.

Sometimes people helped. Yet sometimes they didn't, and it was a case of just watch and hope that the patients made it without crashing. Other times though, multiple people all moved as a large group. And she loved that too. Loved the camaraderie and the friendships she'd witnessed here. She never heard any grumbling in the line. Everybody was joking or teasing others. Dani worked hard to keep the positive atmosphere here.

Dani had done a phenomenal job, but the more it grew, the harder it would be to keep this way. Hailee didn't know how much of a warning everybody got when they first arrived after being hired on or accepted in, but she couldn't imagine Dani being anything but blunt and open about what her expectations were for people here and what their expectations needed to be for their own progress. Hailee herself hadn't received any such speech, but then she and Dani went way back. They knew who they each were on the inside. Although Dani had had a tough time initially, she'd pulled through and had done an incredible job trying to help everybody else.

For herself, Hailee had seemingly gone the wrong direction and had ended up in more pain than she could have imagined by getting married and getting pregnant. There'd been so much agony that she often forgot about the rest and focused solely on the pain. And maybe she needed to focus more on the good things in her life. She stared aimlessly around her, stopping the line from moving forward. Snapping out of it, she stepped up smartly to see Dennis's big grin.

"What're you doing? Sleeping?" he chided her gently.

"Maybe," she said. "Heavy thoughts, at least."

"Well, you park them right now," he said. "No heavy

thoughts when you're eating my food. Food should bring happiness, not sadness."

She smiled at him. "Well, I hadn't heard that before."

"Well, you're hearing it now," he said. "Food should be a comfort. It should feed the soul and feed the heart, and it should definitely feed the body. Otherwise you're eating the wrong kind of food."

"For so long," she said, "I put food in my mouth because it was available to keep me going."

"Well, your luck has changed," Dennis announced. He motioned to the array of food in front of him. "What can I get you?"

"Vegetables," she said immediately.

He nodded and lifted a lid. There was a beautiful stir-fry with mouth-watering broccoli in some kind of a light sauce.

"That looks lovely," she said. He served her one scoop. As she considered it, and she said, "Three scoops total please." He added two more; now her plate was mostly full.

"What will you have for protein to go with that?" he asked.

She smiled at him. "What have you got?"

"I've got a beautiful piece of sea bass here for you," he said.

"And I'll take it too," she said. "I can't remember the last time I had fish."

He just stared at her, shook his head, and reached for a lovely piece of fish that he placed on the side of her plate. "Now, potatoes, rice, anything else?"

She shook her head. "Nope, nothing. I'll add a green salad as I go through." She was wondering if she would even have room to eat some salad, but it looked good. She knew that they made it fresh every day, everything from Greek to

Caesar. Grabbing a small bowl, she added a Caesar salad to her tray and then moved over, bypassing the coffee and reaching for a large glass of water.

Slowly she made her way outside to the deck, where she sat down all alone. She still hadn't collected any friends who she could have a meal with. She was hoping that that would happen, but so far it hadn't yet. Even as she sat here, she could hear friendly groups forming all around her.

She knew she was new, although not as fresh as anybody suspected, but had hoped that maybe she would have made a little more strides in the friendship area. Perhaps it was her air to stay away. And that's something she had garnered after her husband and she started having a lot of trouble. She hadn't wanted to get into that well of self-pity, where all she could talk about were the problems in her life, so she avoided people until she got her balance back.

But now, as she sat staring out across the hills, she realized she was more than ready to have some friendly conversation.

Almost as if her wish was fulfilled, somebody with a tray, standing on two crutches, stopped at her side.

He looked down at her and asked, "Do you mind if I share your table?"

She looked up at him in surprise and glanced around, then realized that all the tables were full. She immediately shook her head and said, "Not at all. I didn't realize this was the last free table."

"Doesn't matter if you're willing to share," he said with a smile. He placed his tray several seats over from her, as if he wanted space too. But still, at least she wasn't entirely alone. And then she realized that she recognized him from the hot tub the other day. Although maybe not necessarily everybody would have recognized him, for what made it more memorable for her was because he'd been in such pain. His muscles weren't at peace. And she'd seen way too much of that with her own son. She ate quietly, and finally, when she looked up, she caught him staring at her and glancing at her plate.

"You eat only vegetables?"

"Sometimes," she admitted. "I missed out on all the fresh vegetables for a long enough time. And I know for a fact I need the nutrition to get my body back to what it needs to be."

At that, curiosity piqued his gaze. "You don't look sick."

"No?" she said. "That's the thing in a place like this. The people who are physically injured are reasonably visible. The rest of us have our own problems, only they aren't as visible."

"Yeah? What kind of problem are you dealing with?" And there was almost a derisive tone to it.

She immediately felt her walls coming up. "Nothing much. Just long-term stress. And I'm smart enough to know I need my nutrients to help get back over the hump of what that does to you."

He nodded. "Sorry. I didn't mean to pry. In a place like this, you tend to forget—just because you're not missing an arm or a leg or your back isn't all gimped up or you're not carrying around half-a-dozen steel plates in your body that add ten pounds to your frame—that the people who work here can also have problems. And, of course, we all do. We just don't like to acknowledge them."

His apology surprised her. She looked at him and gave him a quick nod, then said, "It's not an issue. I just feel bad even complaining when I work here, and everybody is triumphing, overcoming such incredible challenges."

"Sometimes some people are overcoming more than others," he said, his lips turning down in the corners.

"Anybody who is here," she said, "anybody who's trying to survive, they deserve all the kudos coming their way. It's not easy to work with people who are struggling, and it's not easy to be somebody who's got a problem which seems insurmountable in my own head, but it really isn't because I see how much you guys are growing and changing. In fact, you're my role models. Don't ever think less of yourself for the journey that you're taking right now."

His eyes widened slightly, and he looked at her with a tilt to his head, as if she were unique or maybe odd.

She shrugged. "I know," she said. "I'm not normal."

"Nothing is normal," he said. "Not in this life. We are all who we are, but we don't usually learn these substantial lessons until we get through some of life's worst difficulties."

"Yes," she said, "I can agree with that. And I'm finding a lot of hidden benefits to being here that I hadn't realized originally. As if seeing what you are all working on is showing me where I need to work on things too." And it was surprising that she understood the truth of her own words. If she hadn't come here, she would have been wallowing in her personal losses and in her own grief, finding it very difficult to pick up her feet and to move forward. Instead she'd started to see the changes in her perspective. She still had a lot to work on, but it was a start. "It's the best thing I ever did, coming here," she said.

And, with that, she picked up a large piece of broccoli and put it into her mouth.

"INTERESTING WAY TO look at life," he said. Heath looked

down at his plate. It was heavy in starches but also heavy in protein. But hers was full of bright colorful vegetables, and he realized she was right. A lot more nutrients were available to him that he wasn't taking advantage of, mostly because he was a meat-and-potatoes kind of guy. But that didn't mean he shouldn't be helping himself to the vitamins and minerals that were on offer. He glanced back at the cafeteria line and realized how much farther he would have to go just to get some veggies. Next time would be soon enough.

"Is there something I can get you?" she asked.

He looked at her in surprise and then shook his head. "No, not at all," he said. "I can't eat much more than this anyway."

"So what were you thinking of then?"

"I thought you were right," he said. "I haven't really eaten much in the way of vegetables, and I'm sure my body needs it. And even supplements, which I do take, aren't the same as getting the vitamins and minerals that I really need from food."

"If you want me to get you a bowl of vegetables, just say the word," she said. "I'd be happy to."

"Nah," he said, hating to put anybody out.

She looked at him and frowned. "Are you one of those tough guys who can't ask for help?"

His gaze narrowed at her.

She just beamed a bright smile. "Not that I know anything about men like that ..."

That surprised a laugh out of him. "In a place like this," he said, "I imagine we all are guilty of that problem." He watched as her lips pinched together. And then he gave a clipped nod. "You too, I suppose." And his shoulders relaxed, as she nodded.

"Exactly. Me too. I keep trying to accept help when it's offered, but it's hard. You shut people out, you keep them on the outside, not wanting them to see the depths of your pain and your confusion and what you've been through because you know that they can't even begin to walk in your shoes."

"I think the fact that we walk in our own shoes," he said, "is what gives us our own unique perspective in life. You certainly don't want anybody else to walk in your shoes. Sure, we provide them with some empathy into our situation, but you don't want them to suffer like you have. You just want them to walk in their own shoes and to handle their own challenges with their heads up, knowing they're not alone."

She sagged back and looked at him. "That's very prophetic."

He shrugged. "I have my moments. And, on that note," he said, "I'll ask you if you would mind getting me a bowl of whatever that mixed veggie dish is. Because I should be eating vegetables."

She laughed, hopped to her feet, and headed back to the cafeteria line.

He smiled as he watched her. Tall, superslim—as in too thin—with long dark hair and a smile on her face. A smile of somebody who had earned it. Somebody who'd walked through the trials of life and had come out on the other side with more inner calm. She might think that she hadn't gotten very far in life, but he could see the challenges she had surpassed. The milestones marked her actual growth.

Almost like people should have rings like trees, so you could see the maturity on the inside and not just on the outside. It would help to match people's ages up with their own growth. Not that he wanted people to look old, but he wanted people to recognize that wisdom didn't always come on an easy pathway or just from the passage of time. Mostly it happened after hard years of journeys on steep paths that were convoluted and from decisions that maybe were better taken a different way.

But nevertheless, after you've traveled that path, and you've come to the other side, there you are, standing proud and firm. Yes, looking a little more aged and a little worse for wear in some cases, but these signs weren't something that you should hide with makeup or whatever. They were wrinkles in maybe a thicker skin that you should wear with pride. Not to show everybody and boast, *Look at what I've done*, but to know that you have surmounted that challenge, and that it was something worth going through as you now stand on the other side from a position of strength. These were the trials and tribulations of this thing called the human condition.

Wouldn't it be nice if any of that came with warnings, like in roadside alerts, that said, *Hey, if you didn't want to do any of this, then you shouldn't have come to this pathway?* When we started this journey, we needed the reminder that it could change in a heartbeat. Just like it had for him. And he suspected that that was a very similar issue for her too.

Just then, she came back toward him with not a small bowl but a large bowl of bright green veggies in her hand. She smiled at him. "You do need colorful veggies," she said, "but what you desperately need is dark greens. So here's a mix."

He looked at it. "Your bowl is brighter," he said, as he studied some of the steamed veggies before him. "I don't even know what some of this is."

"Try it," she said. "And then I'll tell you what they are."

He hesitated but then realized that she was watching him, her own gaze narrowed but with laughter in her eyes. He sighed. "I did ask you to get them for me, didn't I?"

"You absolutely did," she said. "And remember. What we take, we eat."

"You could eat most of this," he muttered.

She shook her head. "Nope. You try it first."

He picked up something that looked a whole lot like spinach but tougher and took a bite. He frowned, but the flavor was rich and deep, and, as he chewed, he thought it wasn't all that bad. When he caught her looking at him, he smiled and said, "I don't know what I just ate, but it was pretty decent."

"That was Swiss chard," she said. "Go ahead and try the lighter greenish leaf on the side."

"Spinach, right?" He picked it up and tasted it and frowned. "It's great."

"That was steamed spinach," she said. "And that's not all. You have broccoli and some kohlrabi in there too. That's an unusual thing to add to a dish like this, but it adds hidden depth and density to the plate."

He looked at his bowl and asked, "Which is the kohlra-bi?"

"May I?" she asked as she took his fork, leaned over, and poked part of a slice of a light green stalk with a white end. "Something between a cucumber and a turnip." She returned his fork to him.

He bit it, surprised to find a bit of a crunch to it, and then nodded. "That's really good." He dug in his bowl, found another piece, and popped it into his mouth.

"The rest of that," she said, "you should eat with no trouble."

Chapter 12

EVEN THOUGH DINNER was over, she carried his words throughout the rest of the day. She still didn't know what his name was, and he didn't wear a name tag. She'd seen name tags on a lot of the patients, but it probably depended on the individual men as to whether they wanted to be identified. As she, herself, didn't particularly care to wear a name tag.

For the next few days, she looked around for him but didn't see him. Then, at dinnertime, she was walking through to the deck, all alone, looking for a place and realized that she'd come out a little too early as the tables were mostly full. Off to the side at a table, all alone, was the same guy. She walked over and said, "Hey. Mind if I join you?"

He looked up at her and smiled. "Absolutely. It's time for me to return the favor," he said and motioned at his table. This time it was only a table for four though, so she sat down across from him slightly to the side. He looked at her and laughed. "So do you have any meat in there?"

She pointed at the two skewers of souvlaki Dennis had given her. "And lots and lots of veggies," she said. In fact, she had this massive Greek salad too. "I gather it's Greek night or something," she added.

"Absolutely," he said. "They do all kinds of food themes

here. And it's pretty impressive."

"I'm quite surprised," she said. "The food is unbelievable."

"It certainly is," he nodded. "But I believe that's part of their actual philosophy here. The food needs to help feed you and restore you to your balance, so it needs to be something that you want to come and eat and not just eat to survive."

"Eat to thrive," she said with a nod of her head. She picked up her spoon and stirred the cup of coffee she had.

"Don't you drink coffee all day long?"

She looked at him in surprise. "Some days I do," she admitted. "But Dennis made me a special coffee tonight," she said, "something Greek."

"Oh," he said, frowning. "I must have missed that."

She smiled up at him. "Really? I don't think you miss much."

He grinned. "Maybe not," he said. "Although I haven't seen you around for very long."

"I've worked here off and on," she said, "for about six weeks total now."

"Good for you," he said. "I'm Heath, by the way."

He caught her just while she was inhaling and taking a bite. She immediately started coughing, and, by the time she was done, he held her a glass of water and looked at her worriedly. She took several deep breaths, then took a sip of water to clear her throat, and then said, "Sorry. Man, that went down the wrong way." She hoped she had covered up her shock at finally seeing who she'd been visiting with at night when on mop duty.

"Are you okay?" The concern was evident on his face and voice.

She smiled, nodded, and said, "That'll teach me. I guess I was a little too hungry."

"Two hatches," he said. "One for air and one for food. Don't mix them up."

At that, she burst out laughing.

He grinned at her. "Haven't you ever heard that before?"

"No," she said, "I haven't."

"Then you don't have any kids either," he said, "because that's something you get to tell them all the time too."

At that, her laughter fell away, and she stared at her bowl. "No," she said. "I don't."

As if sensing that the mood had shifted, he nodded and started working on his plate again.

She continued to eat for several minutes. "How long have you been here?" she asked when she could, trying to restore the camaraderie that had been there before the topic of children was mentioned.

"Too long and yet, not long enough," he said. "Maybe about six weeks. But I'll have another couple months anyway. I've hit a snag and slowed my progress."

"Sometimes you need longer," she said, "but, even from the time I've been here, I've seen some fantastic progress."

"And I have too, in some ways," he said. "And then the hardest things cause you to slip backward, and you just don't know what to do about that."

"I'm sorry," she said. "If there's anything I can do to help, let me know."

"You could give me your name," Heath said.

"Hailee." She smiled. "Is there anything else I can help you with?"

He chuckled. "No it's my burden to bear."

"But remember," she said. "Just because it's your burden

doesn't mean others can't be there to give you a helping hand."

He looked at her appreciatively. "So you did remember our conversation."

"Not only remembered it but I've also thought about it a lot," she said, "because you're right. And some of the pathways that I've taken haven't been the easiest, but they have had their own rewards. I keep forgetting to focus on the rewards and not on what seemed like punishments."

"I think *punishment* says I need to place blame," he said slowly. "And I'm a bad one for that too. Part of my problem is guilt. I feel so guilty for an accident that happened when I was driving that cost the life of my friends. I keep forgetting that I need to rejoice in the fact that I am still alive. And that they didn't suffer."

"I'm sorry," she said sincerely. "Losing someone is not easy."

He looked up at her sharply, his gaze assessing.

She immediately dropped her gaze to her plate. And then her shoulders sagged, and she nodded. "Yes, I've lost somebody too."

"And that's a bond that we don't really want to have," he said quietly. "But we both understand how much of a loss that can be."

Her lips kicked up in the corners, and she nodded, but she didn't answer him. She felt his gaze on her again. She continued to work through her giant bowl of Greek salad. When she was halfway through it, she realized she might have taken too much. "You know what? When you're so hungry," she said, "you just don't how much to serve yourself."

"You don't realize," he said, in a parody of her words,

"that when you're so hungry, you take big bites out of life because you think you can handle it all, but you can't."

She sat back and stared at him. "Where did that come from?"

"I was just sitting here, thinking about how anxious I was to do so much and then thinking that, just because I wanted to do it, I could do it. But I realized just how really big a bite of that plateful I was signing up for."

"Isn't that the point in time where you step back and take smaller bites?" she asked curiously.

He grinned at her. "Is that what you did?"

"No. I fell into this dark bottomless pit. I forgot all about taking bites and handling what was happening in my world and came close to giving up," she admitted.

"So did I, but I think climbing back out of that pit is the lesson here. If you can't jump up and grab the whole thing all at once, you're supposed to do it little by little."

"But little by little, it doesn't feel the same," she murmured.

"No, but the progress is there nonetheless. It's just you can't keep counting on it day to day because the day-to-day progress doesn't show. But, if you were to check in once a week or once a month, you would see a more significant increment, and, therefore, it would be more visible."

"But when it's not measurable?"

"Like dealing with loss? Or guilt?"

She nodded. "Yes, precisely that."

He smiled and said, "You know what? According to what everybody's trying to tell me, that's exactly what we're supposed to do. It's to not look at our achievements and to not grade them on a day-to-day basis but more to acknowledge that we've gotten through another day and hopefully without feeling as guilty as we did the day before."

"I wonder if I'll ever get there."

"I can tell you will. I'm not there yet myself, but I have seen some progress in my own life," he admitted. "But I don't want you to tell anybody about it." He laughed. "Because they might make me sit in more of those therapy sessions." And he scrunched up his face into a comical frown.

She burst out laughing. "Oh my, aren't they the worst?"

He stared at her. "Have you been to any of the ones here though?"

She immediately shook her head. "No. I attended some, and you know something? They were trying to get my head straightened around, but I'm not sure that they even understood that it takes time before you can even see that your head is screwed up. You're so caught up in the loss and the whirlwind of pain that you don't *want* to hear much, and your doors are shut, so you *can't* hear whatever it is they're trying to say."

He leaned back in his chair and studied her for a long moment. "You really do understand, don't you?"

Her lips quirked. "And you have no idea what I'd do to not understand."

"Yes, I do," he said, "because I'm the same."

She dropped her gaze once again to her plate and realized that, although he was the same, his pain was different.

"And I can see that you're trying to separate your pain from mine," he said, leaning across the table, his hand reaching out to cover hers. "That your pain is more personal, that your pain is more intense. And it probably is because it wasn't a husband, a brother, a father, or a child in my case. But they were my two best friends, and they were my bros. I was raised in a foster family, and these were the only two men in my entire life that I ever bonded with. So it felt like having my arms, my legs, and my heart ripped out over and over again every time I woke up to realize that I was alive and that they would never be at my side again."

She could feel the tears forming in the back of her eyes. She stopped and pushed her plate back ever-so-slightly, then pinched the bridge of her nose. Her other hand was still held in his. She squeezed his for a long moment, and he pressed back. When she finally had control of herself, she looked at him and said, "It's probably not a good idea to bond over pain."

"I've got a suggestion then," he said, those large dark eyes of his warming up. "How about we bond over recovering?"

She gave him the smallest of a smile. "I think I can get behind that."

"Good," he said. "Not every day, but maybe every couple days and perhaps once a week, let's check in with each other and see how we're doing."

She took a deep breath. "Maybe," she said, cautious of offering too much of herself.

He smiled. "And, just like me, you're scared and hesitant to get involved because *what happens when we get involved?*" he murmured.

"It hurts when we lose that connection," she said.

"But we know that going in. We understand that both of us have this burden on our backs. And it's not like we can stop or put down that burden immediately. We can't put it down because we'd feel even guiltier, but what we must understand is that our burden doesn't have to have the weight we're giving it. We're assigning that weight to it. But, if we straighten up, we can still acknowledge that we lost part of our life but not let it be the hefty forty pounds on our back that we're continually carrying."

"Wow," she said. "Wouldn't it be nice if we could lighten that load?"

"Is there any reason we can't?" he challenged. "Think about it. We bear the load because we want to. That's what the psychologists around us don't understand. They think that we don't have any option, and we're guilt-stricken. We carry that load because we love those we lost and because we don't ever want to be parted from them."

"Right," she said slowly. "So, in other words, we need to incorporate them more into our life but in a lighter way so that we don't feel the burden."

"Because it isn't a burden," he corrected. "I don't want to let go of my two friends. I imagine one on one shoulder and the other on the other shoulder. The guilt is something I'll have to work through, but I don't want to work through it if it means letting them go."

"And that's what everybody wants us to do. Let them go."

He nodded. "Which is why I haven't made the progress that everybody else wants me to make here," he murmured. "And maybe it's because I also can't reconcile and verbalize what I mean. Of course a lack of sleep isn't helping. I'm cranky and cantankerous."

"Sorry about the lack of sleep. I think you're doing an outstanding job verbally on all this," she said. "And, if you can't tell the psychologist, why don't you write it down? Write how you feel and what it is that you want out of this. And keep your friends so that you can look from your left shoulder to your right shoulder with a smile on your face and can remember how much they meant to you and can still mean to you because you have those memories."

It was his turn to sit back. And then slowly he nodded. "And what do you think? Can we make some kind of a commitment here to help each other?"

She smiled ever-so-slightly. "As long as it's not formal and as long as you understand that if my world blows up ..."

He waved away her protestations. "Everybody's world is blowing up. I'm not talking about forever here. I'm talking about for the here and now."

"Deal," she said immediately.

NOBODY WAS MORE pleasantly surprised than him when this agreement between the two of them not only ended up with them actually following through and checking in with each other regularly every week and sometimes every couple days but also to find their relationship deepening and broadening in some ways. Only as he understood how much she needed his participation in this did he realized how much he also needed hers.

They weren't lifelines reaching for each other, not realizing what they needed until they found it. They were both on floatation devices, doing their darnedest to stay up there, surviving—and just knowing that they weren't alone in that massive agony kept them floating and moving toward their goals.

It was a surprise when, at the end of one of his sessions, Dr. Garrick, the psychologist, looked at Heath in shock and said, "I see a great deal of progress," she said. "Do you care to share how and why?"

Heath gave a laugh. "Amid all these patients here, and the staff so eager to help, I finally stepped out and connected with somebody who's also going through a tough time." At that, the psychologist frowned. Heath shook his head. "No frowns, Doctor. It's not too much. It's not dark. It's not light. It's just … reality."

"Care to share with whom?"

"No," Heath said. "Just know that I'm in a happier place right now, and I think it's because of this person." He was careful to withhold Hailee's gender in case that raised all kinds of flags with the doctor too.

He could see that the doctor remained a little worried, almost felt like the doctor believed this should be questioned. Yet, at the same time, progress was progress.

"It's fine," Heath said quietly. "I, at least, am seeing a pathway forward."

The doctor made a decisive nod at that. "And we're definitely happy to see that. I just want to make sure that you're not getting into something that'll cause you more trouble later."

"I don't think so."

"Good. In that case, we'll check in with you in a couple days. How's that?"

"Make it next week maybe," he said.

"I can do that," she said. They set up the next time.

When he got up and grabbed his crutches, she said, "You're also moving easier."

"I am," he said. "Lots of things in my world are feeling easier right now."

"Good," she said. "Now if only you were sleeping better. I look forward to seeing your progress on that next week then too."

He used his crutches to get to the door, where he stopped, turned to the doc, and said, "It really does feel better from this new position."

She looked up at him in surprise, nodded, and said, "And that's excellent news. The fact that you can even see yourself in a different place from where you were is enormous progress."

"And I know exactly who to thank for that," he said with a chuckle.

"Make sure you thank them," the doctor said. "Sometimes people don't realize how much of a benefit they are because nobody takes the time to tell them."

He cocked his head to the side, looked at her, and nodded. "That's a good point," he said. "Maybe I'll do just that." And he headed out, wondering if he could find where Hailee was right now while he remembered. He made his way down the hallway and up to the front to the offices. He stopped at the front desk where Caitlin was and asked, "Any idea where Hailee is?"

"I think she's in her office," she said, "but she has a meeting with somebody right now."

He nodded, looked over at the door he thought was hers, then uncertain, asked, "Is that hers?"

Caitlin smiled and nodded. "Yes, she's the accountant."

At that, he was surprised that they'd never discussed what she actually did at this place, and he was glad that she had a professional job that would at least help her to make her way in the world. He leaned back against the wall and realized that, just because he couldn't hear the words through the door, the voices were coming out, though muffled, distorted. He didn't want to listen in, but, at the same time, something important here tugged at him, something that he needed to figure out. He wasn't sure what it was, but it was bugging him.

Finally he gripped his crutches and headed down the hallway. As much as he wanted to see Hailee, he needed to figure this out first. There was something familiar, yet something odd that he was getting. But what was it? As he hobbled back to his room and entered his doorway, it continued to puzzle him, but he couldn't place it. And it would bug him until he figured it out.

Hailee's voice sounded similar to the cleaning lady's, just … not quite the same.

Chapter 13

I T WAS AMAZING how quickly Hailee had adjusted to her new schedule as an accountant, but she was worried about Heath. She hadn't told him that she was the cleaning lady and neither had she told him that she knew he was still struggling to sleep. When she saw him next, it was a few days after their weekly check-in. She had a cup of coffee in her hand and saw him sitting out in the deck, soaking up the sun. She detoured to head toward him, finding that she was craving a few minutes of their connection. It was a dangerous path for her, given that she didn't want to enter into any kind of relationship at this point in time, but he was a friend and solace, a place to rest her weary soul every once in a while. And she was starting to feel more for him than she was ready to admit.

As she came upon him, she asked, "You're not sleeping still?"

He opened his eyes slowly and looked up at her, then smiled. "Some days are better than others."

She frowned and nodded. Inside, she vowed to find a solution. It was the least she could do.

He looked at her coffee and said, "Is this a break for you?"

She nodded. "As much as I take a break, yes. I would have made it back to my office, but then I saw you sitting here."

He smiled. "Got a moment?"

"Of course," she said. She pulled out a chair and sat down. "The sun is hot," she exclaimed in surprise.

"I didn't notice," he said.

"Not too many people can handle the Texas heat all the time," she murmured.

"I was raised in Houston," he said, then opened his eyes and looked back at her. "Not that I have any family left, of course."

"Interesting you came back here," she said. "And that you didn't want a complete change."

"A change I wasn't really ready for," he said. "I think I was still trying to make connections to forge parts of my life into some semblance of a new reality that still contains some of the old as I continue forward."

She understood what he meant. When your foundation was ripped apart, like his had been, you grasp at straws to try to weave them together into a lifeline of something you know, something you can live with, something that you can move forward with. Because she'd done the same thing. That's why she was still here. Part of her wanted to run away and go to the opposite side of the country, and the other part of her couldn't leave everything she'd known.

And yet, she also knew it wasn't terribly healthy to sit here and spend all her time thinking about her child, thinking about her lost marriage, and thinking about all they could have been together. Instead she plunked down her butt and straightened her shoulders and dealt with the debt that she'd been left with. Speaking of which, she still hadn't heard from her lawyer. She frowned, making a mental note to contact him when she went back to her office.

"That looks like you just remembered something unpleasant."

"I did," she said. "I have to contact my lawyer."

"Sometimes I wonder if a lawyer is of any value when you spend as much money securing their services as you might have lost without them."

"I've thought about that a couple times," she said. "In this case, he's doing this pro bono."

"Wow," he said. "I'm happy for you."

"This lawyer spends his time dealing with the medical bills that some people are enslaved with for life," she said. "I just happened to luck into him and have him helping me to figure out how to reduce mine. It's pretty overwhelming."

"Well, let's hope he can help you," Heath said quietly. "I get that we're supposed to pay for services and for the treatments given, but sometimes it looks like the costs are incredibly overpriced."

"Like ten dollars for one aspirin. And there's no justification for it," she said. "You get this long list and this horrific dollar figure at the bottom of the page, and it just makes no sense at all."

"Well, if it's good news, hopefully you'll share it with me."

"I will," she promised. "I just don't know how long it'll be until I get any good news."

He nodded. "I think I heard about a couple charities that helped people retire medical debt too."

"That would be an interesting option," she said, looking at him in surprise. "It's certainly something that, unless you're caught up in this nightmare, you don't understand the magnitude of these bills. And then, when it is something that happens to you, it just becomes crushing."

"And your husband?"

She gave him a flat stare. "He skated. Then I was let go of my job. Lost my health benefits."

He nodded grimly. "You haven't had an easy time of it, have you?"

She nodded and said, "Nope, I haven't. But, like you, I'm dealing." She pushed her chair back. "And now I had to return to work."

"Just don't forget to contact the lawyer," he said. "One of these days, you've got to catch a break."

"One of these days I will," she said. She gave him a small wave and headed off. But, in the back of her mind, it was hard to imagine any kind of break that would help her. With her luck, her "break" would more likely be a broken leg from falling down the stairs or something equally stupid. Although she worked and lived in a medical facility, she wasn't so sure she'd get that kind of treatment here. And how sad that she now had full medical and dental at a point in time when she didn't need it, not with her new salary. And yet, when she did need it, she'd lost it all. She shook her head, desperately trying to keep the depression from overwhelming her yet again.

When she returned to her office, she sat down and brought up her email, then typed out a note to her lawyer, asking if there'd been any progress. She also asked as to whether anything could be done about the former employer and whether there were charities that helped to chip away medical debt that she could access. She put a note at the bottom, saying, *I know I'm obviously way too hopeful, but, if anything else could take this monkey off my back or at least help me bear that cost to be paid, it would be helpful.*

She quickly sent it before she gave herself a chance to

rethink it. And, with that done, she returned her attention to the day's work.

HEATH WATCHED HER go, shifting in his chair to see her walk away. He'd wanted to ask her if she was the cleaning lady, but it had seemed so very wrong, and, after having heard her voice in person just now, he'd immediately begun doubting himself. And, even if she was the former cleaning lady, so what? Was he supposed to ask her to go back to mopping the damn floors at two in the morning? That obviously wasn't an answer.

Even if she did need a second job, she could do much better than a cleaning lady for wages. But then maybe he was wrong. Perhaps cleaning ladies made a lot more money than Heath thought. It was just all so damn sad. And the last thing he wanted was to lose their relationship. If he were honest, he'd been interested in seeing their relationship develop further. It was nice to have Hailee here as a connection, somebody he looked forward to seeing.

When he shifted back around, Stan stood there, his hands on his hips, staring at him with a big grin on his face. Heath had finally met Stan a few weeks earlier but hadn't had a whole lot to do with the vet, but he was looking forward to more time with the animals. "What's that look for?" he asked with a half smile of his own.

"Do you think you can make it downstairs?" Stan asked.

Heath's eyebrows shot up. "Well, I can, even without an elevator, but why?" he asked cautiously.

"Because I have some unusual guests downstairs," he said. "I'm bringing some of the guys down one or two at a time to come meet them."

"I'm game," he said. "I was down there once, but it seemed like so much chaos that I didn't want to add to it. I left." He slowly straightened, using his crutches.

Stan looked at Heath's crutches, then looked at him, and said, "Let's take the elevator." And together, the two of them headed downstairs. Once inside Stan punched the button down to his place.

"Why me?"

"Why not you?" Stan asked. "I wanted to bring Hailee too. I saw the two of you talking, but she got up and left before I had a chance to invite her."

"I think she feels like she can't come down because she's working."

"Probably," Stan said. "I'll send her a message in a little bit."

"Okay," he said, mystified and wondering how he'd been the one invited. He rested on his crutches until the door opened, and he slowly made his way out. The elevator hallway was off to the side. They had to go through big double doors to get into the vet clinic. Once in there, he was surprised to find it mostly empty. "Not very busy these days?"

"Everybody is in the back," he said, and he opened up another set of double doors and led Heath into what looked like a large treatment room. Dani stood in the middle, her arms full of something big and wholly furry and fuzzy.

Heath stared at it and asked, "What is it?"

Dani smiled, walked closer, and a huge paw came out and batted him in the face.

"They're bobcats," Stan said. "This is Mama, and she has two kittens here too."

Dani added, "She has been at a local zoo. It's more of a rescue, but the cats hadn't been checked over, and her claws were causing some trouble. So all three have come in for Stan to take a look at them." The bobcat in Dani's arms wiggled, twisting almost like a smooth silken bundle and reaching for Heath.

With his crutches, it was hard for him to hold the big cat. He immediately sat down, and Dani shifted the huge feline onto his lap. Instantly a massive engine kicked in, and she rubbed her head against his. But it was more of a head-butt than a rub.

Dani quickly caught his crutches threatening to fall, which would cause chaos with the cats by the sudden noise. She put them to the side against the wall.

Heath's arms wrapped around the massive cat as its tongue came out and snaked once across his neck, like sandpaper swiping against his skin. He laughed and reached up to scratch the mama cat's ears. "Wow," he said. He turned to look at Dani, but she now had a much smaller version of his.

She sat down beside him and said, "You don't get to see these guys very often."

"You're not kidding," he said. He was amazed at the power and intelligence in its gaze. "She is beautiful."

Dani nodded. "These guys are fixed, and so is Mom. But like, wow. I love it when Stan gets to deal with animals other than the normal dogs and cats."

"Are you down here often?" Heath asked hesitantly.

"Every chance I get," Dani said. "It's either here or out in the pastures with the horses."

Stan stood behind them, checking the paw of the other bobcat kitten, and, when he was satisfied, he handed off the kitten to another man standing here. He had one leg in an odd-looking prosthetic at the end. He immediately sat down to cuddle the kitten.

"This is a huge advantage to being here," Heath said. The big feline tried to settle into his lap and, using Heath's chest and shoulders, hooked her claws in. Even as he gasped in pain, he smiled because the feline immediately draped across his arm. "What does she weigh? Thirty, forty, fifty pounds?" He gasped.

"If she's too much for you ..." Dani said, immediately standing up.

He shook his head. "No, not at all," he said. "I was just amazed at the size of her." Only then Stan came over and had some kind of a treat in his hand. He held it out for the big cat in Heath's arms, and she immediately snagged it up with one of her paws. She sniffed it carefully and then ate it with complete aplomb.

"She's so tame," he said.

"Yes, and no," Stan said. "Tame in the sense that she's well used to being handled, but that doesn't mean, if a rabbit or something went across the front yard, she wouldn't go after it in two seconds."

"Right," he said. "That makes a whole lot of sense." He stared at her, mesmerized. "She's still beautiful." He held her for another few minutes, until she got bored and started looking around for something else. She slid off his legs and stalked something that only she appeared to see as she headed toward the doorway.

Stan called out, "Let's make sure she doesn't go out that door."

"I hear you," Dani said. She turned to the man holding the kitten. "George, are you taking these guys back now?"

He nodded. "Yeah, now that they're all checked over. I'll get them loaded back up again."

Heath realized that the big female had a harness on. He didn't even notice that earlier. "Does she walk on a leash?"

"No, not well," George said with a half grin. "I have a cage for these two babies to move them, and I have converted the back of my truck into a complete cage. I'll just move Mama up into that and take her back."

"She appears to like field trips just fine," Heath said. He stood and watched while a leash was clipped onto the back of the big female's chest harness. Then he smiled and asked, "Her name is?"

"Rascal," George said with a smile. "I thought she was male at first, and then, all of a sudden, we've got two kittens."

At that, Heath chuckled out loud. "Well, that's a pretty rascally move on her part."

"It sure is," he said. With the kittens moved into their big carrying crate, a typical crate that any dog or cat would have been put into, Stan picked up the container, and they moved all three of the animals outside. Heath sat back down again at a spot where he could watch them load up the family of bobcats into the truck.

Dani stood at his shoulder.

"That's pretty special," he admitted.

"Absolutely," she said.

Just then another cat, a huge black cat—missing one ear and his tail looked to have been hacked off somewhere along the halfway mark—hopped up on its back legs, putting its front paws on Heath's knees and just glared. Heath looked at him for a long moment and said, "Okay. So the look in this guy's eyes is not terribly friendly."

Dani smiled, reached down, and scratched the battered cat between the eyes. "He's amiable, but he's probably pissed off at you because you gave the bobcats time and attention, but you have yet to greet him."

Hesitantly Heath reached out a hand and gently chucked the black cat under the chin.

Almost immediately the cat's eyes closed, and he leaned in. "So, does he always look like he's ready to tear a strip off you?"

"That's about right. He's a rescue, and, as you can see, he has suffered a little bit."

"I can see that," he said. "Still, he's beautiful too." At that, the cat immediately took advantage and jumped into Heath's lap, then settled in with his eyes closed. "Is he falling asleep now?"

Stan walked over and took one look. "Well, at least he found you."

"What's his name?"

"Mystique," he said.

"I think Mystique and Rascal should have their names switched," he said.

"I do too," Stan said. But he shrugged. "The thing is, this cat responds to the nickname *Misty*." When he said his name sharply, the cat immediately spun his head back and around and looked at him.

Heath just chuckled. "Is he a permanent resident too?"

"We're trying to adopt him out," Stan said, picking up the great big black cat from Heath's arms, while Stan urged them all back inside. Stan carried Misty to the counter, put him down, and gave him two treats. Mystique sprawled out flat to eat them. "But he was returned because he didn't settle in well."

"Why not?" Heath asked, as he dropped into a waiting room chair, hanging onto his crutches.

"Honestly I think he missed us," Stan said. "He does get a fair bit of attention here."

"I've seen Helga, Chickie and a couple other animals, but I've never seen this guy."

"Well, now that you've met him," Dani said, "he'll find your room."

"Seriously?"

"Oh, yeah, absolutely. It's almost like, if you don't make his acquaintance, he won't make yours. But, once he knows you, he'll be all over you."

"Well, he's welcome in my room anytime," Heath said. He grabbed the chair for support and slowly stood, then positioned his crutches under his armpits, smiled at the other two, and said, "Thank you. You don't realize just how much you miss animals until you come down here and get a moment to be with them."

"You can come back anytime you want," Stan said. "And, of course, we've always got the animals outside looking for some love too."

"Animals beyond the horses and the llama?"

"And the dogs that wander around."

As soon as he made it to the elevator, Heath headed upstairs. Stan was supposed to contact Hailee about the bobcats, but they were gone already. Still, Heath wouldn't let an opportunity like that pass by without talking to her. She was his go-to person, his go-to friend. She was quickly becoming something else in his mind. He just had to reconcile who he was now with who he'd been, and he knew that she had her own hurdles to relationships as well. In both cases, it was likely all about trust.

He didn't trust himself, and she didn't trust anyone else.

He shook his head and changed his mind from going to her office, choosing instead to head back to his own room. He didn't want to think too much, but sometimes he just needed space and time alone. As he headed there, he met up with Shane.

Shane looked at him for a long moment. "We didn't have a workout today. Have you been in the pool?"

"No," he said a little belligerently. "All I really wanted was some time alone."

Shane nodded, as if picking up on his tone. "You can't go more than two days without something. You understand that, right?"

"We had PT yesterday," he said in relief as he walked past. "I just needed some downtime today."

"So you just come up from being outside?"

At that, he stopped and smiled at Shane. "Yes, and no, I was holding a bobcat in my arms. Stan had a female and two kittens in."

Shane's face fell. "That's not fair. I'd have been down there if I had known."

"Well, maybe I was just lucky today. I was sitting on the deck when Stan came up to tell me that I needed to come down and take a look at the animals he had."

"You're lucky," Shane said. "Stan is a special guy. He understands animals, and he *says* that he doesn't understand humans, but I think he's wrong. It seems like he understands people more than we expect. You know that you can go down there any time, right? And put your name on a list if they need help?"

"I didn't know," Heath said. "Maybe I'll do that. It was great to have some exposure to the animals."

"It looks like you brought a friend with you," Shane said with a chuckle and pointed behind him.

Awkwardly Heath turned, using the crutches to keep his balance, to see Mystique, the big black male, racing behind him. And, sure enough, he stopped right at Heath's feet, then looked up at him, and meowed.

"Wow," Heath said as he struggled to bend down and give him a scratch. "Last I saw him, he was downstairs in the vet's waiting room."

"He's a bit of a survivor, this guy," Shane said, as he too reached down and scratched Mystique. "Are you heading back to your place now?"

"Yeah," he said. "I was just looking for some time-out." He shrugged. "I know that seems odd, but I'm still adjusting to being with people all the time."

"It can take a bit to adjust." Shane nodded. "But what you don't want to do is step out so long and so hard because, by then, it'll be challenging to get back into being with people."

"Sounds like my last year," Heath admitted.

"Well then, why don't you join up with one of the guys playing pool or one of the board games going on? Dinner is not for another hour so."

"Maybe," Heath said, but he hesitated.

"Or go for that swim," Shane said. "As soon as you start to slide deeper into that black hole, it's important to remember that even a walk around will kick in some endorphins and make things not quite so bad."

"If I could get some sleep," Heath said, "it wouldn't be so bad at all." And, with that, he headed back to his room, Mystique tagging along.

Chapter 14

A COUPLE DAYS later Hailee once again came across Heath. This time he had collapsed on one of the large couches in a common area, looking morose and upset. She stepped in front of him. "You look like you could use a friend," she said quietly.

He looked up at her. "I need sleep. I just can't seem to sleep past two o'clock in the morning."

She frowned. She felt guilty that she had in effect abandoned him when she gave up her cleaning lady job to be Dani's accountant. Obviously he needed her back as the cleaning lady again. "How about white noise, instrumental music, or meditation?"

"It seems like I've tried it all," he growled. He gave an irritated shrug and then struggled to his feet. "I've got to go to PT." And crutched away from her.

She stood in the middle of the room with a frown, watching him as he left.

When he got to the where the room morphed into the hallway, he turned, looked back, sighed, and said, "I didn't mean to snap at you."

Her eyes were gentle. "Of course not. I understand."

"I know," he said. "And it's almost as bad."

"How do you figure?"

"Because I don't want you to have to understand. I just

would like to be healthy so that nobody has to go out of their way to actually understand what's going on in my world." Then he waved a hand. "I don't even know what I'm saying."

"No, but maybe I do," she said quietly. She walked toward him. "You want to be normal, so nobody has to go out of the way or make any extra effort."

He nodded. "Something like that. But this lack of sleep …"

"Nightmares still?"

"Yeah," he said. "It's always the nightmare of the crash. They just never seemed to go away. I had a method before of getting back to sleep, but it looks like nothing works anymore."

She frowned as he stormed off on his crutches. When she walked back toward her office, she stopped in at Dani's office and said, "He's still not sleeping."

Dani, preoccupied, looked up, but obviously confusion was in her gaze. "Who's not sleeping?"

"Heath."

Dani nodded, comprehension filling her gaze. "No, he isn't. It's a definite problem."

Hailee stood in the doorway for a long moment. "Meditation? White noise? Music? Have any of those things helped?

"No, not at all." Dani looked at her in surprise. "Good thought though."

Hailee looked out over the window not sure what to say. Except…

"I'll talk to his team and see if there is anything else we might try." Dani frowned down at her desk as if already wondering who to contact.

"I know," Hailee said. She took a deep breath and added, "On a side note, I was wondering if you needed another cleaning lady. I could do a few hours in the evening.".".

"No," Dani said firmly. "One job for you. You are making enough now you don't need to do that."

"Hey, maybe he was falling asleep to my mopping," she joked. "We could try it," Hailee said slowly, "if it worked, maybe we'd find another way to make that work out for him permanently?"

"You mean, like having my current cleaning lady come by at that hour? Because you certainly aren't going back to that." Dani looked at her pencil, tapping her desktop.

"Well, that's possible," Hailee said. "But it doesn't mean her mop strokes will have the same rhythm, and we can hardly teach or expect another cleaning lady to maintain my particular rhythm so somebody else can sleep."

"I'm glad you said that," Dani said gently, "because that is an imposition."

"It might be worth a try." Hailee didn't know what else to do or say so quietly withdrew. But she couldn't let go of it as she went through the rest of her day and evening. She did go to bed at ten, but she set her alarm for two. As soon as she woke up, she quickly dressed and headed to the central part of the building.

There, she went into the utility closet and pulled out her mop. She filled her bucket with hot water because, if she was out here and she would be mopping, then she might as well do an excellent job of it. When she passed one of the other cleaning ladies, the woman just ignored her. And that was the way Hailee wanted it. She went two doors down Heath's hallway and proceeded to slowly and methodically mop the floor.

Coming back up against Heath's door, she spent a few extra minutes there, slowly mopping. She didn't know if he was awake or asleep or if she was making any difference tonight, but she kept up the rhythm as she had done before for him. By the time the hallway was done, it was well past three.

She emptied out her mop bucket and put all her equipment away, then went back to bed. The next morning, she got up, tired, yawning in the middle of her coffee, as she headed to her office. By then, she needed food so went for a coffee break and grabbed an apple. She walked out on the deck, lifting her face to the sun. A few minutes later, she heard a voice behind her. She turned, saw Heath, and smiled. "Wow," she said. "Don't you look better."

He nodded. "Maybe I finally turned the corner. For some reason last night I slept really well."

"Did you wake up?" She didn't know how to take the news. Great that he slept, but she was so tired that it's obvious she couldn't do this every night.

He frowned, searched her face, then shrugged. "I might have, but I fell back asleep again. I know I'll need lots more sleep like this, but, man, that really made a huge difference."

She smiled. "I hear you. Nothing like getting a good night's sleep."

As she headed back to her office, she felt good. She didn't know if it was from her own mopping, but the fact was, he'd had a good night's sleep, and she herself identified with just how valuable that was for healing. She didn't know if she should even try to keep it up, but she thought, if she did it for a couple nights and then didn't do it, maybe she could tell if Heath was sleeping better because of her mopping. She felt foolish getting up every night doing this, but she was determined to try and see him through it. Nothing in the world helped a soul heal as much as the proper rest.

She went through that new routine for the next three nights. Getting up and mopping his floor, putting away everything, not saying a word to anyone, and then falling back into bed. On the fourth night, she didn't do it. And, when she got up Friday morning, she'd slept better because she hadn't gotten up in the night, but now she was racked with guilt.

Instead of going to the cafeteria first, she headed to her office and started in on her work. She didn't hear from anybody and, of course, why would anybody know about her experiment, much less be worried about it? But finally she had to find out, and it was lunchtime. It was early, so she got up and headed to the cafeteria, looking for him. She saw no sign of him. She looked around, and then, after she'd eaten, she grabbed a coffee and a muffin to take back to her office and headed by his room. He was coming out as she went past. She stopped, smiled at him, and said, "Hey."

He nodded and said, "Hey."

But it was apparent he wasn't too happy. She frowned. "Not a good night?"

He shrugged. "I guess I can't have good nights every night. I did for the last several nights, and I thought maybe I had turned the corner, but last night was one of those rude awakenings that I really didn't need."

"Aah," she said, "I'm sorry." Inside, her heart sank. She felt guilty but gave him a warm smile and said, "Maybe you'll have another good night tonight."

"Maybe," he said, but he didn't look at all convinced.

She walked away, feeling terrible, because there had to

be a start and stop to this, and she just didn't know what to do about it. She quickly turned and headed back to her office. As a test, it was minor and inconclusive, but it was definitely leaning toward the fact that maybe she had been the reason that he had been sleeping. And that made her feel even worse for not following up with it.

Surely she could do something for him. But, for the rest of the day and that evening, she determined she would return and do the mopping. And it was two o'clock when she headed back up again. This time, when she walked into the hallway, Dani stood there, her arms crossed over her chest, frowning at her.

Feeling guilty, but not knowing what else to do but to continue with her plan, she held up a finger to Dani and slowly and methodically mopped the floor. When she was done, Dani standing there and watching her in amazement, Hailee gathered up her bucket and grabbed her mop and pointed to the far end of the hallway.

Once they walked there, Dani asked in a low voice, "Why?"

Together, the two of them walked through the silent building and back out to the big deck, where usually Hailee would go downstairs to her own apartment. There, with the two of them under the moonlight, Hailee explained about Heath not sleeping without the mopping sound. Dani looked at her in surprise. "Well, I knew that he was looking for the cleaning lady from weeks ago," she said. "I hadn't realized it was connected to his sleep pattern."

Hailee nodded. "And I only started again a few days ago. He just looked so ragged all the time, and I thought that, if I could at least help him get a good night's sleep, he would heal."

Dani's small smile started at the corner of her lips, and, before long, her whole face held a big beautiful smile. "You really care about him, don't you?"

"I shouldn't," Hailee said hurriedly. "It's terrible to care."

"No," Dani said, immediately reaching out a hand to squeeze Hailee's fingers. "It means being human."

"But it hurts," Hailee said in a low voice. "It hurts so damn much."

The two women stared off in the distance. "The thing is, words can say a lot," Dani said, "but they don't show the person on the inside. So then, when you listened to the words, but you didn't actually see who was under them—when their actions and their words didn't match—you felt abandoned and bereft. Yet now, in your case, you didn't tell anybody what you were doing, but your efforts were there because all you were trying to do was give Heath a good night's sleep. Do you know how few people would get up in the middle of the night to come mop the floor outside his room so that he could sleep?"

"You know how many people would think I was nuts for doing it?" Hailee said, a small smile playing at the corner of her mouth. "Or how crazy he is for needing that?"

"It doesn't matter as to the wisdom of it or whether anyone understands it," Dani said. "After we've seen as many patients as we have, we realize that we're all unique, and, for whatever reason, that sound cemented something for him, and it allowed him to fall back asleep. And, when he lost it, and I didn't realize it was that severe, he couldn't rest anymore. Shane said that he'd taken a couple steps back, but I hadn't really understood why."

"Well, the real trick," Hailee said, "is if Shane says this

last week that Heath has improved because I've been doing this for the week. Then I stopped last night, and Heath had a terrible night, so I returned tonight so he could sleep again."

"Wow," Dani said. "That's devotion."

Hailee stopped and frowned because, in some ways, she didn't even think about it and, indeed, hadn't labeled it. "I don't really want to think of it that way," she muttered.

"Too bad," Dani said, "because you do not see your actions for what they are."

"Why?" she said defiantly. "I'm just trying to be nice."

But Dani's eyes saw a whole lot more. "Are you telling me that your heart doesn't flutter when you get close to him? That you don't spend a good part of your day wondering if you can detour so you can pass his room or meet up with him in the cafeteria? And that you don't look forward to the meetings that you have planned with him?"

"All of that just means we're good friends," Hailee said. "Or that we're heading toward being good friends."

Dani's smile was luminous in the darkness. "Oh, it does, indeed," she whispered. "But it also says so much more. There's a connection between the two of you. And, if you're lucky, it'll become something so much more."

"But then I have to trust," Hailee whispered back. "And I lost so much last time."

"You lost everything important," Dani said with a nod. "But that doesn't mean it will happen a second time, and it doesn't mean that it wasn't worth going down that path in the first place. Do you regret having Jacob in your life?"

Hailee looked at her in horror. "Of course not. He was everything to me."

"So, when you lost him," she said quietly, "you lost everything important. But, if you hadn't gone down that path, if you hadn't tried, you wouldn't have had him in your life in the first place. So I'd like to believe that everything happens for a reason. And, even though your husband turned out to be a waste of human space and absconded before he had to deal with the pain of losing his own child, that just makes him a weak person with a whole lot more lessons to learn.

"And I'd rather see you fall back in love again, even if it hurts a second time because through that hurt we grow. And through that hurt, great things come, like Jacob. Yes, Jacob wasn't on this earth for long, and it hurt you tremendously to lose him. But just imagine how empty you would be inside if he hadn't even shown up in the first place?" With that, she patted Hailee gently on the shoulder and gave her a quick hug. "Now that I know what you're up to in the middle of the night, I'm going to bed."

As she walked away, Hailee turned and called out, "How did you know I would be there?"

"The other cleaning lady," she said. "She asked why I was hiring somebody to do just that hallway and what was she not doing good enough."

Hailee laughed. "She's doing a good job," she said. "She just wasn't doing it at the right time or with the right rhythm."

Dani smiled and nodded. "So I came to see for myself, ... and this isn't over by the way." She shook a finger at her. "We do need a better solution than this."

"Well, it'd be nice to get my own sleep," Hailee said.

"Absolutely," Dani said. "And that's something you have to consider."

"Maybe," Hailee said, "but I still don't want him to end up with no sleep."

"I hear you, but that's not always the same thing."

"No, it isn't, and that's why we have to sort through this."

"Maybe we can," Dani said. "I'll see what I can do."

And, with that, Hailee headed to bed herself.

THE NEXT MORNING Heath woke up, feeling rested and relaxed. He rolled over slowly, feeling a sense of inner peace in his life. "Finally," he muttered. "I was so afraid those few nights would just be the oddity, and I'd never sleep again." When a hard knock came on his door, he called out, "Come in." He watched in surprise as Shane headed in.

Shane saw him in bed, stopped, and said, "Wow, does that mean you had a good night or a bad night?"

"A good night again," Heath said, slowly shifting in the bed, so he was leaning against the headboard. "I literally just woke up a few minutes ago. I gather I'm late?"

"Not necessarily," Shane said. "I can push you back a bit if you want."

"Well, coffee and some food would probably be a good idea." At that, his tummy rumbled.

Shane smiled. "Well, absolutely nothing is better for you than a good night's sleep, so the chances are that we'll just push this back to this afternoon, if you've got time. Maybe we'll do a pool session instead."

"Perfect. The pool sounds great. What time is it?"

Shane, heading back to the hallway already, turned and laughed at him. "It's past ten-thirty." And he was gone.

Heath stretched out in the bed. "Is that what good sleep's all about?" He slowly sat up and stretched again. Even though he was stiff, and some parts of him were sore, the rest of him felt so damn good that it was almost impossible to sort it out. He tried to remember whether he'd woken up in the night and thought he'd surfaced once or twice and then had fallen under again.

Maybe he wasn't thinking about his cleaning lady anymore. Perhaps he was finally past that hurdle. He got up, showered, dressed, and, by the time he made it into the cafeteria, he was already heading for the lunchtime crowd. Dennis took one look at him and said, "Wow, you look bright-eyed and cheerful."

"I slept solid and slept late too," he said. "Now I'm starving."

Dennis immediately loaded him up with fried chicken and a big plate of greens. "Here you go."

He crutched to an empty table on the deck and sat down out in the sunshine. He sat here for a long moment, sipping his coffee and looking around him. When Dani happened upon him a few moments later, he looked up, smiled, and said, "Quite the place you got here, Dani."

She stopped, looking at him in surprise, and said, "Don't you look good today."

He raised an eyebrow. "You're like the third person to tell me that. I didn't realize just what a good night's sleep was doing for me."

"Last night?"

He nodded. "All of a sudden, I started to sleep again."

A small smile played at the corner of her lips. "Perfect," she said. "There's nothing better for you." And, with that, she disappeared. He saw her talking to Shane down at the far end, but he ignored them. He was totally okay to go to the pool this afternoon and to work out there, but he wanted food first. He attacked his lunch with gusto, and, by the time he made his way to the pool at two o'clock for his afternoon physical therapy session, Shane was there, waiting for him.

"Let's see what a good night's sleep has done for you," he said, and he proceeded to put him through the paces. By the time he was done, it was almost four-thirty, and Heath was in the hot tub.

"I think I did much better today," he said, staring up at the sky.

"There's no *think* about it," Shane said. "Now just repeat whatever that magical moment was that gave you all that sleep again."

He smiled and said, "I wish I knew."

As he went to bed that night though, he thought about it and wondered if he was still waking up at two o'clock or maybe just the silence now was setting him back to sleep again. He drifted off to sleep quickly. And, when he woke up later, he checked his watch to find it was yet again two a.m. He sighed and settled in and realized he would probably not get in a good night's sleep this time. As he drifted into a half dose, he heard in the background the same mopping sounds. He smiled, feeling that same sense of comfort, and he closed his eyes and drifted yet again back under.

He didn't know who was out there, but he was grateful that somebody was back, mopping the floor, almost as if just for him.

Chapter 15

W HEN HAILEE CAME into work the next morning, both Dani and Shane waited for her in the hallway. She frowned at them both. "What's up?" They just shook their heads and waited until she unlocked her door and stepped inside. "Okay, now you've got me worried," she half joked. "What have I done?"

Shane smiled said, "You haven't done anything except be a perfect human being."

"Why is that?"

"Because Heath is progressing beautifully," he said. "I understand you're the little bird that may have been out there mopping the hallway in the middle of the night." She winced at that and glared at Dani.

Dani shrugged and said, "You can't expect the world not to find out."

"Does Heath know?"

"No," Shane said. "But you should probably tell him."

"Why? It'll just make him feel guilty."

"How so?" Dani asked.

"He won't want his sleep at the cost of my sleep," she said bluntly.

"Maybe not," Shane said. "So we need a solution."

"Not sure what that is though," she said.

"Well, I have a suggestion," Dani said. "It might take a

little bit to make it work though. I don't want to say too much about it, in case I can't get it to come together. Let me think it through and get back to you."

Hailee nodded and settled in for the day. When she looked up, it was already eleven, and, sure enough, Heath was at her doorway with a bright smile on his face. "Hey," she said.

"Well, it looks like I'm doing well for sleeping, but you? I'm not so sure."

"Hey, I'm not sleeping too bad," she said with as bright a smile as she could muster.

"No," he said, "maybe not, but I can see you're not sleeping precisely the same as I am."

"Well, I don't think you were sleeping for a long time, so it's hardly a surprise that you're doing better now that you're finally getting some sleep."

He nodded. "Got time for lunch?"

"Sure, why not?" she said. And she looked at her desk, smiled, and said, "I just need a couple minutes to put stuff away."

"I'll head down because I'm slower than you," he said. "I'll see you there."

She smiled and locked up her office and headed in behind him. She caught up with him just as he went into the cafeteria. "Good timing," she said.

He smiled and stepped up to talk to Dennis. "I want all of it," he declared. Dennis burst out laughing but gave him a huge plateful. Hailee snagged it and carried both of their plates down the aisle.

Soon Heath and Hailee were both sitting outside. Not in the sun because it was too hot but off to the side in the shade. They'd both been working on their individual problems. At least she thought so.

"How are you doing these days?" she asked.

"The world is a better place when you have sleep," he said almost complacently. She immediately felt guilty for even considering not doing the mopping. He just nodded and looked at her and said, "But obviously you're not feeling the same way."

Dani's words were in her mind as Hailee thought about that. "I'm learning to let go a little bit more," she said quietly. "It's not easy though."

"Nothing worth doing ever is," he reminded her.

She smiled. "Isn't that the truth?"

"Will you avoid relationships for the rest of your life?"

"Of course not," she said, and then she stopped and thought about that. "That was a trick question too."

"Not at all, but I figured it was probably more comfortable to ask you that one outright instead of beating around the bush."

"Do you even know my history?" She appreciated his honesty, even as she worried what he'd say if he knew it all.

"Some of it, yes," he said. "The rest? … Well, it isn't too hard to connect the dots."

She quickly filled him in about Jacob's painful fight for life, right from day one, followed by the pain and the sense of betrayal she'd gone through with her husband, and the final straw—Jacob's death.

Heath listened quietly and sadly. "And, of course, it's no wonder why you don't want to trust anybody again."

"Maybe," she said with a half smile. "I might have been a little too quick to make that decision. Somebody reminded me that, if I hadn't met my husband, and if I hadn't married him, and if I hadn't had Jacob in the first place, there would have been this massive hole in my heart about a joy that I wouldn't even know that existed. So, even though it was painful, I would still have wanted Jacob in my life."

"Meaning that, even though you lost him, he was still such a joy that you're grateful he came to you in the first place."

"Exactly," she said. "And, therefore, I can't really begrudge my husband either."

"Are you divorced?"

"Yes," she said. "He divorced me. As soon as possible to get away from the situation."

"Well, maybe you'll be ready soon," he said.

"Maybe, but it would probably take somebody else in my life to make me care enough."

"Right." And, at that, he fell silent.

She looked up, realized that she, in a way, had cut him off from that and said, "And maybe it's time to do that." There was an odd silence, and she looked up to see him staring at her intently. She smiled at him and said, "I really enjoy the time we spend together."

"I'm glad," he said softly. "How have your nights been?"

"They've been great. I'm not sleeping as well as I could, but then I'm still dealing with stuff," she said with an airy wave of her hand.

"And how do you feel about being honest and open and not keeping secrets?"

"Sometimes secrets need to be kept," she said honestly. "If they'll hurt somebody to share them, I don't think they should be told." He just nodded and kept eating. She wondered where the question was going. "What about you?"

"It's like little white lies," he said. "I don't think there's any point in telling them if we don't have to, but sometimes telling a little white lie could save a world of hurt, yet it could cause a world of hurt in some instances. In the end, I don't really believe in hurting others unnecessarily."

She smiled at that. Because, of course, he didn't. "And are you dealing with your losses?"

"A little better than I expected," he said. "Now that I'm sleeping. Now that I've got an email." At that, he fell silent.

"What kind of an email?" she nudged.

"From the sister of one of my friends. It was an odd email, awkward, I guess. And I still haven't read it thoroughly."

"Maybe you should," she said.

"Maybe," he said, then shrugged. "But I read enough to realize that she doesn't blame me. Instead she thanked me for being in her brother's life. And that her brother, my best friend, had always spoken about me and how much he really loved spending time with me." At that, he seemed to choke up.

She reached across, gently laced her fingers with his, and said, "And I can see that. I'm thrilled she took the step to tell you that."

He nodded, smiled, squeezed her fingers, and then continued eating. "Me too."

HEATH HEADED BACK to his room after lunch, surprised that he'd even mentioned the email to Hailee. But, of course, she understood. So far, there hadn't been a whole lot that they hadn't had some level of understanding on. So, if she was the cleaning lady, why wouldn't she have said anything to him? Was it not important to her? And that just brought him back to being afraid that maybe he'd been wrong the whole time.

This time, he was determined to stay up and see who it was. He didn't want to put her on the spot, but, if it was her, well then, he didn't know what it meant. His heart raced when he thought about if it had been her, then what would it say? And, if it wasn't her, he had almost a deflated feeling to it. But also guilt and something he didn't want any more of. He couldn't turn off his mixed emotions for the rest of the day.

By the time he headed to bed that night, his whole mind-set was in turmoil. He hadn't seen her all afternoon, and then, at the end of the day, he'd seen her yawning. He frowned with that same need to sort it out, and he went back to his room and waited until the dinner hours were almost done before he headed in and got his.

He passed the evening answering emails and talking to his best friend's sister. She was married with two kids, and, as soon as he'd responded to her email, she phoned him. They'd spent a lovely hour talking and reminiscing about the men that had both been so special to them. When he hung up, he'd felt raw, heartsore, but also happy. And he realized that he'd reached yet another stage of grief and was actually capable of letting some of that guilt go. He headed to bed and, with a smile on his face, crashed right away.

When he woke up, it was once again two a.m. His body was into this weird rhythmical cycle that made no sense. He listened intently, but he couldn't hear the cleaning lady outside. He tossed and turned and then thought he heard something. He hesitated and listened intently. And there it was, that same rhythmical back-and-forth footsteps, with the rolling of the bucket and the swishing of the mop. He got out of bed, quietly grabbed his crutches, and crept forward until he stood right at the door. He could hear the cleaning lady's motions. He wondered, did he dare find out who it was. If it was some other lady, it might scare the crap out of her.

He leaned on his crutches and slowly and quietly opened the door to see who might be out there. He only opened it enough to stick his head out, and the hallway was dark. But there was a long, lean form, calmly and methodically mopping the floor. He couldn't tell for sure who it was. He wanted to see her face underneath the ambient light of the hallway. When she went around the corner, he would get just that second to find out. She yawned, then reached for the bucket and the mop, nudging them out of the way.

She turned, and his heart raced. It was her. Hailee. Ever-so-softly, he closed the door and thought about it. His heart raced with joy, but, at the same time, he knew it had to stop. He didn't know how or why she was doing this, but he could guess. It was one of the sweetest things he'd ever had done for him in his life.

He headed back to bed with a big smile on his face, and he fell asleep instantly.

Chapter 16

S HE WAS YAWNING the next morning when she made it to her office. She put down her purse, turned on her computers, and then realized she couldn't do anything without coffee. She hadn't even had time for breakfast because she'd overslept. As she walked into the cafeteria, it was still full of people. She smiled and walked straight to the coffee, and Dennis called out, "Tut, tut, tut. You need more than coffee."

"You're a mother hen," she said to him.

"I am," he said. "I like to take care of all my chicks, and you're one of them. What would you like for breakfast? Something with more protein, like sausages and eggs, or something like yogurt and fresh fruit?"

"Yogurt and fresh fruit," she admitted, "with maybe a bit of granola?"

He pointed to several freshly made parfaits.

She nodded and said, "Is there one with seeds?"

"How about I make you one right now?" He grabbed an empty parfait glass and filled it in the layers that she requested. By the time he was done, he looked at it and said, "You know what? That looks mighty fine."

She smiled. "You're right."

She grabbed a spoon with the parfait glass on one hand and her coffee in the other, then headed back to the office.

As soon as she got inside, she sat and started eating. Dani called her extension and asked, "Hey, you got a moment?"

"Sure," she said. "I'm eating, but whatever."

"My office in ten minutes or so?"

"Perfect," she said. She sat back, checked her emails, finished her parfait, and tossed back the last of her coffee. Then she got up and headed to Dani's office. She greeted her friend with a bright smile, but Hailee's smile immediately fell off when she saw Shane and Heath here. She looked at them in surprise. "Sorry. Am I intruding?"

"Not at all," Dani said with a warm smile. "We're waiting for you. Close the door behind you, please."

Slowly closing the door, she took the last chair available and sat down. She wasn't sure her legs would support her at this point anyway. "What's up?"

"What's up?" Heath said, his voice was a little harsher than she'd ever heard from him. "I don't want you losing sleep to help me sleep."

She stared at him, wordlessly. "Sorry?"

"I saw you last night," he said. He shook his head. "You know I'm not exactly sure why you're doing what you're doing. If it's for the reason I think it is, then I really, really appreciate it, but I don't want to sleep if it means you don't get any."

"Uh," she said but then fell silent. She really didn't know what to say.

"*Uh?*" he repeated with an eyebrow raised.

She shrugged. "It's just, whenever I do mop the floors, you sleep. And when you were struggling so much for so many weeks without it, I realized how much it meant to you. And that I was being very selfish when it was something so simple that I could do to help." She didn't know why this conversation was happening in Dani's office, but both Dani's and Shane's attentions were going from Hailee to Heath, depending on who was speaking.

"I get that," he said, "and that's precisely why I thought you were doing it." And then he sighed heavily. "But you're also tired, and you're getting run-down. You're rising before two in the morning to come mop that hallway," he said in exasperation. "I wake up. I hear the mop, and I fall back asleep. Immediately. And I get that. But you were up earlier, getting dressed, coming up here, then spending an hour mopping that hallway. That's got to be the darnedest cleanest hallway in the entire place. And then I'm supposed to go back to sleep in just minutes, knowing that you've come up here, spent like ninety minutes of your own time in the middle of the night to mop so that I can sleep?" He shook his head. "I'll admit that I fell asleep last night with a smile on my face," he said, "but I don't want you doing it again."

She didn't even know what to say. She was ultimately embarrassed and felt extremely awkward. Not to mention hurt. "I hear you," she said. "And, of course, I won't if you don't want me to do." She tried to stand, moving the chair back out of the way.

Shane lifted a hand and said, "Stop."

She looked at him, refusing to look at Heath.

"He's not asking you to stop for the reason you think he is."

She frowned at Shane. "What other reason is there?" She used all of her experience of many years gone by. If life wasn't turning out the way she wanted it to, she'd put some steel in her spine. If she was getting a talking-to or things were turning out differently than she wished them to, well, that's fine. She'd face it and move on. She'd been here before.

"He doesn't want you to lose sleep because it makes him feel guiltier. And we're trying to stop the guilt."

Her mouth formed a small *O*. "I hadn't considered that."

"No, of course not," Heath said. "You were trying to do something beautiful for me, and it just makes me feel worse."

She frowned at him. "You could just take it as a gift that somebody wanted to give you," she said in a tart voice.

He grinned. "Well, I would. It's actually something I was talking to Dani and Shane about earlier," he said. "So I would ask you if maybe you could mop the floor once or twice again, perhaps more if we need to. And I know it's stupid, and I know that nobody else would even understand why the sound is putting me to sleep—except that I now remember my mother always did this in the evenings. After I went to bed, that's when she would clean.

"And I now recognize that that was the sound and the feeling of the comfort of home for me. It was the meaning of family. It was what I had before I lost so much. So, when you did that, it was like bringing back my childhood security blanket and wrapping it around me. And, for that, I am forever grateful because I think you've probably come up with the answer to how I can get over my insomnia."

She stared at him, a question in her gaze. "Okay. I guess that's a good thing?" she asked hesitantly. "I'm honestly still in the dark."

"I know," he said.

At that point, Dani stepped in. "We'll have you mop in the night again, when everything's quiet and soundless, and we'll record it. I do have some sound experts in town, and, once we've got the recording that we need, we'll give it to Heath as his own personalized white noise that he could use to go to sleep. Whether we give it to him as a CD or an MP$_3$ format that he can play on his phone, I don't know yet. But we're hoping it will give him that same security-blanket feeling so he can sleep at night."

She sat down with a hard *thump*. "But that's wonderful," she said. "I didn't even think of that."

"Which is why we're all here in this room together right now," Shane said with a smile. "It's not that what you're doing was wrong. That's far from it. You actually solved a massive issue for us. We're just trying to find a way to make it happen without you losing your sleep too."

Hailee grinned. "Hey, as long as it works, I'm totally okay with doing this again."

HEATH HAD BEEN delighted with the solution. It had been something that they set up later without him even being aware of it because they wanted it to be as natural as they could. So several nights later he was presented with the MP$_3$ player and with a CD and an MP$_3$ file that he could play both on a small desk speaker system and also on his phone. So, at any time that he woke up in the middle of the night, he could just hit a button and hear the same sounds over and over again.

Now, four days later, with the first night under his belt with that recorded sound, he realized just what a blessing it was. Sometimes he wondered just how many memories he had left of his mother. He'd been young when she had died in a car accident, but he eventually remembered falling asleep to the sounds of her cleaning all the time.

And now here he was, once again falling asleep to sounds of somebody who cared enough about him to get up in the middle of the night to do that for him. He wanted to do something special for Hailee, but he wasn't exactly sure what. He'd sent out several emails, asking for more information, but, so far, there hadn't been too much response. He wanted a few moments of just some peace and quiet to talk to her about some options also and to let her know how he felt about her, more than just her mopping in the middle of the night to get him to sleep.

When he went to lunch, a look on his face must have relayed something because Dennis immediately asked in a low tone, "You okay?"

Heath looked up with a smile and said, "Yeah, I am. I was just thinking that maybe, instead of being in here, I'd find a way to get outside with the animals today."

"Well, why don't you have your main meal here," he said, "and I'll fix you a coffee and a couple cinnamon buns to-go, then you can take the elevator and go outside in the wheelchair or on your crutches and go to the horses?"

"That's not a bad idea," he said. "I need to touch base with the animals again."

"It sounds like you got woman troubles."

"Ha," he said. "Pretty hard to have woman troubles in here."

"Oh, I don't know," Dennis said. "I've watched a lot of couples form in this place. So, if it is, you just talk to old Dennis. I got a solution for you."

"Yeah, right," he said, and then he shook his head. "I'll eat lunch, and then I'll go down and spend some time thinking."

"Maybe you should do that," he said with a smile, and, sure enough, as soon as Heath finished eating, Dennis arrived with two big cinnamon buns and a cup of coffee in a thermos. "The buns are hot out of the oven," he said, as he then wrapped each of them in foil. "Take these with you, and maybe go visit with the animals," he said, putting the buns and a thermos in a reusable grocery bag. "Maybe over there where the llama is or someplace that you're comfortable."

Heath nodded. "That's a great idea." He slung the bag over his shoulder and slowly made his way downstairs and back outside on his crutches. He should have brought the wheelchair, but he preferred to do with the crutches as much as he could. He headed over to the long grass, and, rather than trying to get up onto the fence, he sat down against a post, his crutches beside him, wondering just what he was doing and where he was heading. When he heard a female voice call out to him a few minutes later, he looked over to see Hailee walking toward him, with a cup of coffee in her hand.

"Hey," she cried out, "may I join you?"

He smiled and said, "Absolutely."

She sat down beside him. "Ooh, cinnamon buns." She looked back up at the cafeteria and then shrugged and said, "It's too far to go."

"Well, I've got two," he said, "so how about you share with me?" And that's what they did, splitting up the cinnamon buns with an awkward, and yet peaceful silence between the two of them.

"So, how did it work?" she asked, studying his features.

He looked at her with a smile. "Perfect. You have no idea how grateful I am."

She shrugged. "Can't say gratitude is anything I particularly want," she said with a laugh. "But I'm glad it worked out."

"I understand," he said. Just then his phone beeped. He pulled it out and checked to see what the email was about and laughed. "On the other hand," he said, "I have something of a gift for you too."

"Really?" she said. "And what's that?"

He held out the email that was on this phone and said, "Read that."

She took his phone from him and slowly read it, her eyes widening as she stared at him in shock. He nodded and said, "I wasn't kidding when I said people are out there who work to help forgive medical debts."

"I actually heard from my lawyer, and the hospital has renegotiated my bill down by 75 percent," she whispered.

He looked at her in surprise and laughed. "Well, maybe between these two events, we can get you cleared of all your debts."

"And that," she said, "sounds too good to be true."

"Oh, I don't know," he said. "I think we often forget that good people are out there too."

She looked at the email again and said, "Is it for real?"

"They said so," he said. "They're offering $30,000 toward your medical debt."

"I don't have much more than that left to pay off," she said. "At least if what the lawyer says comes to pass."

"It probably will. We don't realize just how much of that medical debt is inflated. So, in this case, there's a good chance that you'll do just fine now."

"Wouldn't that be wonderful?" she said, laughing.

"And, if it is," he said, "what would you do with your

life now? Would you leave?"

She stared at him wide-eyed, then shook her head, and said, "No. I love it here. It's been the perfect place for me." Then she stopped and looked around. "How long are you here for?"

"Another month and a half, I think, maybe a little longer," he said. "And then I'll probably settle close by in Houston."

"Ah, good," she said.

Then more awkward silence came.

He finally took the bull by the horns and said, "And, even if I do move to Houston, I was hoping we'd be close enough to see each other. If your trust issues have come this far."

"Have your guilt issues?" she asked.

He nodded slowly. "I'm working on it, but having Wendy, Ben's sister, to talk to has really helped a lot."

She smiled and nodded. "You're right. And I've made some progress myself."

"Perfect," he said. His voice thickened. "So, do you think that's something you might be interested in?"

"What's that?"

He shook his head. "Let's not play games. I'm a straight shooter, and I think we've both had enough of the dishonesty in life to want to talk straight."

"If you're asking if I'm interested in seeing more of you? Absolutely," she said with a gentle smile. "But I was hoping we didn't have to wait until you went to Houston."

He looked at her and smiled. "Seriously?"

"I came out here to tell you about the email I got from the lawyer, and, as I was walking here, I realized that somehow you've become the friend I've never had," she said.

"Even when I was married, my husband wasn't somebody I could talk to like this. He wasn't somebody who I cared to share enough of my life with."

"So maybe you married the wrong person completely," he said with a smile.

She nodded and said, "It took me a long time to realize that I didn't do him a service either. And that I should have chosen somebody better for myself."

"So now what?" he asked.

"Well, I was kind of hoping," she said with a kink of her lips, "that maybe you'd be interested in the job."

"You mean, if I'd be interested in being a replacement?"

She shook her head immediately. "No, of course not."

"Good," he said, with a little more force than he intended. "Because I'm not a replacement for anybody. On the other hand," he said, "if you feel about me the way I do about you, I'd highly suggest that we entirely skip the whole talk of replacements and just start fresh and maybe create something unique between us."

She looked at him, then smiled, her eyes widening.

He leaned across and gently grasped her chin with two fingers, then tugged her closer. "At least if you feel the way I feel …" And he kissed her ever-so-gently.

Her lips curved under his, and she whispered, "I don't think you could possibly feel the way I feel about you because I think your heart would hurt too much."

"No," he said, "it's not about hurt. It's about being open enough to accept what's coming so that you're free and bright and happy."

"That sounds nice," she whispered. "I can definitely sign up for that."

And this time, when their lips met, it was a kiss of promise, and it was a kiss of hope. But, more than that, it was a kiss of growth for both of them, for a future neither had expected to find but was there waiting for them nonetheless.

Epilogue

CHANGE OFFERED THE chance for a new beginning.
Iain Macleod stared down at the acceptance letter and the rest of the papers that he had to fill out in order to make his transfer to Hathaway House happen. He took a slow and deep measured breath.

Everybody here knew him as a class clown, somebody who threw off the problems and stresses in his life without a care. Most looked at him sideways, wondering how he managed it. But he also knew he was at the end of his rope—knew that he couldn't keep up the facade. It was time for a change, and it could only happen if he left here and went where people didn't know him. A place he could go to find the depths of his soul, to find a way to live with the future as he had it right now. Because it looked pretty shitty from where he sat.

He didn't want to hear any more about "probably never walk again" or "probably never be fully functioning in society again." Just so many damn *probablys* that he didn't even want to contemplate it.

He had both hands, and he had a sturdy back, and that was more than a lot of guys had. Iain was missing a leg, but he still had one. It was kind of shriveled and didn't do so well, but that's because he'd had a lot of muscle torn off it. He'd also had the recommended surgery to put new muscle back on, and, so far, it was an unknown as to how well that would work. He roomed with three others, and he lived with hundreds, all in the same type of nightmarish scenario that he was in. Everybody was different, and everybody was unique, and yet all so much the same.

It hurt. All of it hurt. Humor and laughter had been his shields, which might have fooled everybody else, but they weren't fooling him.

He'd gone as far as he could, staring at himself, seeing the joker and the ultimate joke that life had thrown at him. Yet he knew, if he wanted to make anything out of his world, he had to cross that abyss and had to learn to live with the best that he had, which was what that surgery had given him. To maximize this point, he needed therapy that went well past what he had access to here, and that was stupid. This was a VA hospital. He should have had the best of the best right here, but he knew from what he'd seen that he didn't. From what he'd heard about Hathaway House, he knew there was more. He'd contacted several people who had been there and had left much improved. They'd all told him the same thing.

"Go. You won't be disappointed."

Taking that chance, he'd put his John Doe on an application form, and he'd sent it off. He hadn't told anybody here, and, if he had, nobody would have been more surprised than him when he'd been accepted. Now after more paperwork, more medical appointments, and a painful transfer, maybe he'd have a chance at a new life. Or at least a chance at living the life that he'd been given as best as he could.

And really, was there more to anything in life than that?

Iain

Hathaway House, Book 9

Dale Mayer

Chapter 1

A FTER MANY DELAYS, medical appointments, measurements, and tests—more than he could even think about—Iain found himself heading toward the long driveway to Hathaway House. It wasn't the suggested ambulance transfer, as he had a friend heading back to Dallas, so he'd hitched a ride. Big mistake. The trip had been excruciating. And he wasn't at his destination yet. The VA hospital had strongly urged him not to do this, but, if he'd learned one thing in life, his stubbornness always got him what he wanted and usually with a kick in the ass to go with it.

His buddy looked at him. "You sure you want to do this?"

"We're almost there," Iain said quietly. The pain started at his back and hips. Then it filtered downward. His left leg, dear God, throbbed and burned. So did his right leg for that matter.

"You really didn't want to take an ambulance, huh?"

Iain looked at Bruce. "Would you?"

"No," Bruce said with half a smile. "I just didn't want to see you suffer."

"I don't want to suffer either," Iain said quietly, "but I didn't have too many choices."

"It's a long road trip."

"And I've spent most of it drugged out," he said.

"The VA medics said that you would suffer for this and that it would put your healing back by weeks," Bruce warned.

"Warning noted," Iain said. "I still refuse to arrive in an ambulance."

"You're stubborn," Bruce stated. When shortly thereafter he accidentally hit a pothole, it was all Iain could do to hold back his automatic moan of pain. He felt every muscle in his body tighten down, even as Bruce cried out, "Lord, I'm sorry. Hang on a minute." He dropped his speed way down. "I wasn't watching," he said. Then he glanced at Iain. "Are you okay?"

Iain slowly let out his breath, feeling his back seize like he'd never felt it before. "I will be."

"I knew this was a bad idea," Bruce said. "No point in going to a new rehab center if you're more damaged and broken than when you left the last one."

"I'll be fine," he said.

Bruce snorted. "And I'm done listening to that shit."

Iain grinned. "You're a good friend."

"Well, I understood your request," he said. "I just couldn't see somebody who's been through what you had been transferred by an ambulance."

"Exactly," he said. "And I know ... pride goes before a fall, but no way ... could I do that. It was just ... too much. Just too much on top of ... the rest," he muttered, taking shallow inhales, breathing through his nose, trying to force his body to relax. But every few seconds he froze up, expecting another lunge, another bump, and another surge of agony through his body. With relief, his gaze caught on something ahead. He reached out and grabbed Bruce's arm. "Stop for a moment."

Slowing down and then finally braking on the shoulder of the road, Bruce frowned at him. "What's up?"

And Iain pointed to Hathaway House in the distance. "I just wanted a moment to look. How often do you see something like that?" A huge estate-looking house had been built onto the hill, surrounded by green pastures, and beyond perfection in Iain's opinion.

Bruce looked at it and said, "I wish we could get out and walk around for a little bit," he said. "But I don't think that's a good idea for you, is it?"

"No," Iain said. "Definitely not." He looked at the road ahead. "It's gravel, but it's been well-graded, nicely packed, and obviously they've done a fair bit of maintenance."

"It was my fault earlier. I hit that pothole," Bruce admitted. "Like I said, I wasn't paying attention. I figured we were home free, and I eased up my guard."

"It's not your fault," Iain said and continued to stare at the huge white building ahead of him. "It's such an odd look, one-third apartment building, one-third institution, and another one-third thrown in of an old Victorian estate." He sighed, grimacing at the pain, hoping his buddy didn't see that.

Bruce pointed to the pastures all around. "Look at the pastures. Looks a bit like Kentucky, doesn't it?"

"Yeah, it does," Iain said with a smile. He caught sight of the horses in the pasture. "I know I heard about animals being here too," he said, "but I didn't realize ..."

"Horses. Wow," Bruce said, "that'll make your heart happy."

"It will," Iain said, "if I get a chance to even see them close up."

"Well, we'll find out soon," Bruce said. "You ready to

take this last step?"

"Yeah," he said. "I so am. It might be painful, and it might not be the way I thought it would work out, but I really need this change."

"Are you making it a new beginning?"

Iain smiled. "You know me too well."

"I know you were the best at making the worst situations more livable," he said. "I've been out in the trenches with you, seen you at work, cheering up the others or just distracting us from the horrors we lived through. I've been out doing routine training with you in the Middle East, near our temporary base, when we got caught in the middle of attacks, and I've seen how you somehow turned a crap deal into something that smelled like roses."

"I don't know about the roses part," Iain said with a slow smile, "but I know that I was darn glad not to be alone at those times. Thanks for sticking by me."

Bruce looked over, reached across gently, and the two gripped hands, a static handshake of sorts. "You can do this," he said.

"I know," Iain said. Then he took a deep breath. "Let's go. Let's get to this next stage of my life and whatever it'll bring."

"Stop thinking that your life is shit. It doesn't have to be. I know that Gloria walked away from your engagement because of this, but all women are not like that."

"I'm trying not to think about it," he said, "but her words are a little hard to forget."

"She had no right to say that crap," Bruce said. "You know what? Thinking of her just now, what she did to you? What she truly is?"

"Don't bother," Iain said. "I've called her worse in my

mind already. But she's right about some things. I'm not whole. I'm not 100 percent, and she's in prime breeding condition, looking for a family and somebody to be there for her. I'm hardly a good prospect anymore."

"And that's just bull," Bruce said. "If I had five minutes with that woman …"

"You'd have sat there and stared at her in shock and not said a word," Iain said, chuckling. "Because she would have shocked the shit out of you, just like she did me. Plus, that's who you are. You'd never raise a hand to a woman any more than I would. And you know yourself that, once those nasty words leave your lips, they can never be unsaid."

"I know," Bruce said. "But, she's a piece of work." When Iain didn't respond, Bruce added, "And thankfully she's somebody else's problem. You deserve better. And Gloria had to leave your life to make room for that other woman, that better woman, that woman who was meant for you, to enter your life."

Iain sighed, gave a one-armed shrug. "Not my focus now. It's all about the rehab here."

Bruce sighed too but shot a smile his buddy's way.

They drove up the wide driveway, a massive parking lot off to one side. Bruce looked at it and said, "I'll pull up to that ramp at the front entrance, and we'll help you get up there. And then I'll come around and park."

"I'll be in the wheelchair anyway," Iain said, "so how about you just park your truck, and we'll go from there."

Bruce nodded and pulled into a parking lot not too far away. He turned off the engine and looked at his buddy and said, "I'll get the wheelchair."

"You do that," Iain said. "If I was feeling better, I'd hop out and try to make my way to the back of the truck, but today …" He shook his head. "No, I'm not quite ready to admit this was a nasty mistake, but I am ready to accept some help."

"We all need assistance sometimes," Bruce said cheerfully. He got out, shut his driver's door, and walked to the back. He lifted the latch to the back of the truck and then dropped the tailgate. He pulled out the wheelchair and set it up.

Iain, in the meantime, shifted slowly in the front passenger seat, opened up his side door, and, with great care, made his way so he stood on the pavement. He grabbed onto the door to steady himself. He didn't have the energy to shut it. Pretty sad state of affairs.

He took a moment to focus on gathering his breath. Taking in three slow breaths, trying to get deeper each time, he calmed his racing heart and slowly let his body untense. As much as it would right now anyway. He turned, concealing the shudders running up and down his spine, knowing the painkillers had worn off hours ago. He'd been so sure he'd be okay during this trip. After all, how different would the ambulance ride be from traveling by passenger truck?

Talk about how the mighty had fallen. He took a moment, leaning against the door and just closing his eyes, taking several more deep breaths. When he could, he opened the rear side door and pulled out his bags. He dropped them on the ground, knowing he couldn't carry them anyway. He gingerly shut that door, grabbed his sunglasses from his collar, put them over his eyes, concealing the agony that resided there, and stiffened his spine.

As Bruce pushed the wheelchair toward him, the two men looked at each other. "I know this might not be the best time," Iain said, "but I really do appreciate that you've been there for me over all these years."

Bruce glared at him. "Enough of that talk. We're friends. Best friends. That's what best friends do."

Iain didn't argue, but he knew better. He'd seen many, many other men lose contact with friends and family because nobody could handle the condition they were in. He'd been blessed with Bruce. "If you want to believe that," Iain said, "I'll accept it. But I know the truth. You've gone over and above many, many times, and it's made me that much better a person."

Bruce, choking back tears, walked past his buddy and closed the front passenger door. He snagged up the two bags, tossed the big duffel over his shoulder, then plunked the other one gently in Iain's lap and said, "Let's go, buddy."

"Yeah," Iain said. "I wish I just knew to what."

"Will you be the clown here?"

"No," Iain said. "I need to walk away from that."

"You always were the darndest chameleon," Bruce said quietly. "Why the change now?"

"Because I know that something more important needs to happen here, and superficial is one thing, but I can't do that anymore. The last surgeon says the right leg is as good as it'll get. So, no more time for a facade. It's time to get real. This is all about dealing with who I am right now. It's one of the reasons I had to leave that place, as no one back there would understand the change in me or the change in what I had to do next."

"You could have done this there," Bruce muttered. "You didn't give them a chance."

"Maybe I could have, but I felt drawn to this place, so I'm willing to take the chance."

"I think that's why a lot of your buddies don't make the

change," he said. "That's why the attendance back there is so heavy. They get sucked into the same mind-set. The *this is all there is* mentality. It's because people are afraid to change."

"I've never been *afraid* of change," Iain muttered, "but I can't say I'm terribly enthralled with dealing with this one. This one came as a shock. Nobody *chooses* these kinds of monumental changes. And it takes so long just to recover enough from the last surgery to endure the next horrific surgery, which knocks you back on your ass in that hospital bed. It's a long process, and you have to remain strong throughout it all.

"And I'm probably midway in with my rehab, and I've been struggling to get through each day for the past eight months as it is. I expect it'll be another eight months here. That's why it sucks so bad when others abandon guys like me because they can't deal with the aftermath. Yet me and the others? We have no choice but to deal with the matter." He looked down at his right leg, the stronger of the two. The whole one of the two.

"You may not be happy with your physical condition yet, but Hathaway House? That's a good change. I can feel it."

As Bruce pushed him up the ramp toward the front door, Iain could only hope his friend was right and that this wasn't Iain's biggest mistake of all.

ROBIN CARRUTHERS JUST happened to be outside, taking a breather. She worked at the veterinarian floor of the Hathaway House building. She was a vet tech who had only been here a couple weeks and had already found it almost like home, but she was one of the few staff members here who had a residence at the center as well. She couldn't quite believe what Dani had built up here over these few short years, both on the physical property as well as the personnel.

Stan, the one and only veterinarian in this place, at least for now, was a little in love with Dani but appeared more as her father figure, although he wasn't all that old. Those two had a great relationship, and, when it came to helping animals, Dani bent over backward to do anything that needed to be done.

Robin herself had considered going into veterinary school but just couldn't swing the money. She was doing so much more here than at a normal vet tech position. Primarily because they were short on hands. She shook her head. She figured she'd be doing more here anyway. It was the usual attitude at Hathaway House. Here, the people went above and beyond. Not just the staff but the patients were pleased to be here, so thankful to have such a wonderful workplace atmosphere.

She had been at other positions elsewhere, and this place topped them all. She couldn't ask for a better crew of folks to work with. Dani had employee benefits that entailed educational assistance and also allowed for educational leave for her employees too, where she would take those employees back upon completion of their studies. Not many bosses would do that for their employees. Robin sometimes wondered if she should go back to school. But, for her, she wanted more to have a husband and a family and to eventually work part-time. She wasn't as career-driven as so many other people she'd met in life. And Dani was just fine with that as well.

Robin stood here, stretching her neck and shoulders,

watching as a big black double-cab truck, heavy with chrome, but looking a little worse for wear after what could have been a long road trip, pulled into the parking lot. It was barely in her line of vision as she watched a man hop out of the driver's side and go around to the back, while the passenger, ever-so-carefully, slid his way out from the front seat. He stood shakily but on his own two feet. Then she realized that was a lie. He was standing on one foot. She was close enough to see that it hurt him to do so.

And when he closed his eyes and leaned forward to rest his head against the door, her heart went out to him. These poor guys. They were taught to man up, to not cry. Yet sometimes a good cry washed away the hurt. And, to make matters worse, these were military men. So she guessed they were too trained to hold all that pain inside, regardless. She had seen all that and more in her brother, Keith. And, with her ringside seat, she had witnessed all the pain he had to deal with from others' lack of empathy. She shook her head. *Sometimes family and friends, those closest to us, hurt us the most.*

As a vet tech, she wanted to bring some joy in the animals' lives she watched over as well as these hurting soldiers' lives. But, more than that, there was something almost spiritual about how just the presence of an animal could brighten a patient's day. She figured it was because these animals accepted us, without question. They didn't judge us, ever. They greeted people like it was the first time they had ever met, day after day. These animals, even the hurt ones down in the vet clinic, had boundless love for others.

Too bad humans weren't always like that to other humans.

Then what some humans did to animals? She shook her

head. Granted the abused animals were tough to see, and her heart went out to them each and every time, but even they rebounded and learned to love and to trust again. It was truly miraculous to watch that transformation. It gave Robin hope to deal with her own problems. Eventually.

She'd seen a lot of the patients upstairs and had some interactions with them. Not a ton, because she was so busy downstairs, but the staff brought a lot of the men and women from upstairs down to see some of the animals, and she had taken some of the animals upstairs to visit the patients.

This guy obviously was a new arrival, and not a moment too soon from the shape of him. He straightened as if he were living on guts alone.

She noted him taking what must be his last energy to put his sunglasses over his eyes. *He's hiding his pain.* Tears came to her eyes immediately.

When his buddy brought around a wheelchair and helped him into it, and when they slowly made their way to the main entrance ramp, she slid slightly out of view, so he wouldn't think that she'd been watching him at his most vulnerable moments. But this close and personal insight into the agony and the torture that these people who came here were living with? Well, that was something she generally didn't see.

She saw them at various stages of their day, sometimes with smiles on their faces and sometimes with tears drying on their cheeks. She herself was one of those people who couldn't leave anyone in pain, and it hurt her to know that so many people one floor above where she worked were suffering. But then she was working with suffering animals down below too, and it was hard. It was always hard.

Some were good stories of healing, and some were successes, but also many cases just wouldn't have a happy ending.

And she realized, not for the first time, as she watched this man slowly being wheeled up the long ramp to the front entrance reception area, that it was the same thing up above for the human patients too. She'd been so busy since her arrival here that she hadn't had time to even think about those hurting people above. She saw them almost as an auxiliary part of her job, but that human insight just now connected her in a way she hadn't expected.

She wondered who this guy was and what his story was. She could only hope that maybe Dani would make his life so much better. Of course, not just Dani but also Dani's team. And the man was in so much pain himself that Robin felt waves of it pummeling her, taking her breath away.

Yet everything that Dani had put together here was miraculous and would give this new guy hope, just like it did for the others before him. Dani and her team had replicated success after success for these military men and women. And that success had spawned the downstairs clinic.

"Robin?"

She heard Stan calling her. She peered around to see him through the window, his arms full of a gigantic rabbit. She smiled as she walked back inside to him and said, "You want me to take him?"

"Why don't you take him outside with you?" he said. "He really would like the sunshine and the green grass."

She took the massive furry bunny back out to where she'd been standing. They used a specially fenced-off yard for these rabbits because she was trying to keep the grass clean enough for the bunnies to eat it, and so she didn't want the dogs urinating here.

They had any number of different animals here that just wanted a safe place to get outside. The horses—and the llama—had the biggest fields of course, but some dogs could be allowed to roam free because they would come back with a whistle or a call. Some of the resident dogs here were housebound though, like Chickie and various other therapy animals, especially the three-legged versions. It surprised even Robin when new animals arrived who quickly became a permanent fixture here at Hathaway House.

This was a place where strays were welcomed. Robin smiled at that.

Moving into the small yard, Robin put down the big hopper. Immediately his great rounded nose twitched and trembled as he made several big hops, exploring his territory. She retraced her steps to close the four-foot gate behind her, so she could be inside with him and not have to worry about him hopping away if she turned around for a second or two. She grinned. "You look like you're doing just fine now after your surgery."

"Well, he should," Stan said. "He's healed now, so hopefully that back leg should work properly again."

She studied the bandage. "He's keeping it pretty clean. I thought he would have chewed off the bandage by now."

"I put some stuff on it to stop him from doing that."

"I've still seen them chew through that before," she said with a laugh.

Stan grinned at her. "Isn't that the truth. Where there's a will, there's a way," he said, chuckling.

She glanced back around where the ramp was to the front entrance.

"Looking for somebody?" Stan asked.

She turned and smiled up at him. "A young man just arrived," she said. "Something about the way he stood and the way he got out of the vehicle that hit close to home."

"That's right. Your brother is up here, isn't he?"

"Not yet," she said. "He's coming in about six months hopefully. He has to stabilize somewhat before he travels. Plus I don't think his bed is available until then. Even so, his arrival could be sooner or later, Dani tells me. Some of these patients leave sooner than expected, but some leave later."

"And that acceptance here, I think, is huge for his healing," he said. "Keith should do really well here."

"Well, that's one of the reasons I recommended it," she said. "In the meantime, it'll be nice to spend some time with him on a daily basis."

Stan hesitated and then said, "You know that sometimes these guys aren't the easiest to be around when they're recovering, right?"

Her smile softened. "I know," she said. "I'm not expecting miracles. But any progress would be wonderful."

Stan raised his pointer finger. "You haven't been here long enough or haven't been exposed to the human patients enough to see that miracles truly happen here." Stan nodded. "Dealing so much with the hurt animals, we don't always see what happens with their human counterparts above us. These animals are wondrous creatures. They don't realize they are missing a leg or have a cast or that half of their stomach was taken out due to cancer or a bullet wound. But our wounded warriors one floor up? Those guys and gals are dealing with some horrific hand that was dealt to them. And they have to show up every day for rehab, which is another word for *torture* in my book." Stan laughed.

"I admire each and every one of them," Robin said. "Not

sure I'd last a day. Then I catch a glimpse of someone as I get lunch two days in a row and am just amazed to see how much they have improved over the past twenty-four hours."

Stan agreed. "On the flip side, I see some backtracking, not making forward progress. Those are most likely dealing with some extra baggage on top of just their physical healing."

"Their mind-set."

"You got that right," Stan noted. "Attitude plays a big part in regaining health. Those heavy thoughts and hurtful words and just plain negative thinking can set a body back. Sometimes we humans are our own worst enemies, working against ourselves. So don't let your brother dwell on the negatives. You either," he said, wagging a finger at her, his face blooming into a full smile.

Chapter 2

"GRANTED, I MOVED here almost a month ago, so I am not able to see my brother as often as I would like to. Regardless Keith and I are close, but he has never been easy to be around," Robin said. "He's always had dark moods and a temper. But after his accident ..." She shook her head. "Nothing's been easy about it."

"And you visit him? Where he is currently?"

"At another rehab center. I saw him just before starting here," she said. "He looked like he was really struggling, suffocating in the four walls they had given him. And his progress had completely stalled."

"In that case, change is often the best answer," Stan said. He tapped her gently and pointed down at Hoppers. "What do you think?" Hoppers had made it to the far corner and was busy nibbling away on some clover in the grass.

"Seems like he'll be happy here for a while," she said. She stepped out of the fenced section with Stan, closed the gate behind them, and said, "As long as we don't leave him out too long."

"He'll be fine," Stan said. He gave the fence a shake and said, "He's not going under or over."

"He *could* go under, given enough time," she said, "but I presume this section was fenced with that in mind?"

"Yep, sure was," he said. "Chicken wire down two feet."

She groaned. "That's enough to make me cringe."

"And hopefully Hoppers too," Stan said with a chuckle. They walked back inside the vet clinic.

It was four o'clock, and they had no more scheduled patients, were down to a skeleton staff, and thus expected no more public traffic. "Are we done for the day?" she asked, reaching up a hand and rubbing her temple. "Seems like it was an extra-long day today."

"We had half the patients," he said, "but the people who came with their pets weren't necessarily the easiest."

She nodded and smiled. "The trouble is, people get just as emotionally worked up over their furry families as they do over their human families," she said. "And sometimes we just don't have answers for them."

"Sometimes I think we never have answers," Stan said soberly. "At least not the answers we want for them or that they want to hear. I've got to face a bunch of paperwork now. You want to check to make sure everybody's good for the night?"

"We're keeping three overnight, I believe?"

"Yes," he said. "I'll come in at midnight and check on them."

She nodded. "And I'll do the four o'clock check then. What about staying overnight at the clinic? Do you ever do that?"

"Way too often," he said. "But, as long as everybody handles their checks throughout the evening and night, then we can leave our patients for a few hours."

"Good." She walked into the back. A cat had had its tail run over, but the tail itself wasn't the problem. It had been pulled away from the body to a certain extent. They'd performed surgery to remove some of the remaining tailbone so the skin could close. But an injury like that often resulted in major damage internally and could affect his ability to defecate. So they were keeping a close eye on him at the moment, and he was out cold still. She checked his vitals, smiled, and moved on.

The next one was a dog who'd had a steel plate put in his back leg. He was a little bit more awake than the cat but not by much. He was also today's surgery. She bent down gently, stroked his face, and checked his vitals. She adjusted his medication and moved on to the third one, another dog who had been left intact to reproduce. He was now fixed, only he hadn't handled it well, and they were keeping him overnight because of the heavier-than-normal bleeding post-op. He appeared to be doing fine now.

That done, Robin cleaned up the back room, organizing some of the supplies that had come in.

Annette came in from the front desk and said, "I'm off, unless you need anything."

"No," Robin said with a smile. "Go have a good evening."

"Will do. See you in the morning." Annette waved, locking the main door behind her. That was the door to the public. The staff still had access to all the rest of Hathaway's yards and pool facilities—one of the huge perks of being here. Not to mention the food. She'd gained at least two pounds since she'd arrived. A pound a week didn't bode well for the end of the year. With that thought uppermost in her mind, she frowned, walked back toward Stan, and said, "Everything's cleaned up, and our three patients are doing fine for the moment. If you don't need me, I think I'll get changed and have a swim before dinner."

"Oh, that's a good idea." Stan looked up, arrested at the

thought. "I need to get back to swimming too."

"Come with me," she said. "The PT guys and gals should be done with their therapy sessions by now, shouldn't they?"

Stan checked his watch. "It's four-forty," he said. "I normally wait until five before I go in, just to make sure."

"Five would work," she said. "It'll take me a bit to walk home and get changed anyway." She stifled a yawn. "And I am tired for some reason."

"Some days are like that," he said. "I'll meet you at the pool at five then?"

She nodded, smiled, and said, "That's a deal." She headed out the back door, stopped for a moment, and realized that she'd left Hoppers outside too. She came back in and called out, "Stan, we forgot Hoppers."

He chuckled. "I was going to bring him in," he said, "but if you want to grab him …"

She went back out to the front. There was Hoppers, stretched out on one side and enjoying the sunshine, his legs fully out in front of him. She opened the door and called him. He looked over at her, completely calm and relaxed, not otherwise responding to her call. She walked over, bent down, and picked up the big lug, cuddled him close, and then walked him back in.

Hoppers was a semipermanent resident in the place. They were trying to find a special space for him, so he could be left to roam the grounds, but his area needed to be safe. They weren't exactly sure how the new dogs would handle such a big rabbit. Would the dogs feel threatened? Would the dogs treat it as prey or food? She shuddered. She was already attached to him and surely didn't want him hurt again. While he was big enough to hold his own, the rabbit obviously had no defenses against an attack, like maybe another pet would.

She put him back into his large glassed-in space, with plenty of air holes for ventilation and a strong wire gate atop, where they kept him overnight inside the vet clinic. He immediately headed off to his sawdust and curled up, as if to go to sleep. She closed the door to Hoppers' cage and said to Stan, "He's back in his space. I sure hope we can get him an outdoor yard, where we can leave him outdoors a little more often."

"And probably we could leave him overnight in the yard he just came out of," Stan said.

She nodded and said, "Maybe, but I feel better having him inside. I'll meet you in a few minutes at the pool." And she headed off to her on-site apartment. She smiled at the thought. She had been very lucky to land this job and even more so to have free room and board added in as huge perks on top of her generous salary.

Nothing like a swim at the end of the long day, especially in a place like this. She couldn't wait until her brother arrived. And maybe, just maybe, they could move past all the problems that they had themselves. They would definitely have more time together to work through those. And face-to-face. *That had to be better, right?*

After all, nobody here was problem-free, including her.

IAIN SAT ON the bed, almost in too much pain to even hear the words from the owner-manager of the place. Dani reached out and in a firm voice said, "Lie back down again." He looked at her, wanting to glare at the woman, but he didn't have the strength. She just gave him a clipped shake of her head. He eased back down and closed his eyes, feeling the trembling running throughout his body. That was never a good sign. Of course he knew what it meant. *You've overdone it. Again. You've got to learn to ask for help.*

"I understand that you came by truck," she said, "and I get that. You're not the first one. You won't be the last one either, no matter how we try to talk you military guys out of this. But I can tell you that it sets you back at least a day or two. Maybe more. That's for your doctors and your PT specialist to determine. Now, if you just relax and don't do a whole lot for the next couple days, we should be able to minimize the damage."

He opened his eyes and looked at her. "I just couldn't stomach the idea of arriving by ambulance."

"I get it," she said softly. "I do."

And, from her tone, he believed her. He smiled. "You've seen everything, haven't you?"

"Well, I think so," she said cheerfully. "And then somebody does something that surprises me." She handed him an Apple tablet and, pointing, said, "Besides your mandated bed rest, for the remainder of today, you'll need to go over paperwork, and your team and others will come in here to visit and to talk with you. Your schedule is in the tablet too. But I'll start first with one of your doctors and some pain meds."

"I still have a few," he said. "They're in my pocket. I can take those now and then later, when the doctor has a chance to assess my condition."

"That's fine," she said, "as long as they are standard-issue."

He grinned. "Yes." He pulled them out of his pocket,

shifting with a little bit of awkwardness. "This is all they are." And he handed her the medicine bottle.

She looked at him, studied the label, opened the bottle, checked that the inside matched the outside, and nodded. "Okay. I'll get you some water," she said, walking into his en suite bathroom. When she returned and watched him take two of his pills, she added, "I'll go get your doctor now." As she walked to the doorway, she turned. "In the meantime, take a look at what I've given you."

As she walked out, he flicked through the tablet, amazed at the technological level at which they were operating, but he realized, of course, it was necessary in today's day and age. His body was still on fire, but the fact that he was in a bed had taken the pressure off his spine, and the rest of him was holding. He kept telling himself that he had a strong back, but he kept putting it under so much physical strain and stress that he wondered if his back was still strong enough.

He looked at the data regarding the members of his medical team and who had been assigned to him, but none of the names meant anything to him. He had a doctor, two nurses, a therapist, and a psychologist. At that, he frowned.

Dani walked back in and asked, "What's the frown for?"

"Psychologist?"

"Everyone here sees a psychologist," she said. "Him or her, we have two on staff."

He looked up at Dani. "And how often?" He hated how that little bit of suspicion was evident in the back of his voice, but, of all the medical professionals Iain didn't trust, they had to be at the top of the list. Something was just so off-putting about knowing that people were trying to read something into or glean something from every word he said, and that made him not want to say anything.

She smiled. "We'll start with once every couple days, until the doc has a chance to assess your condition. Then it'll ease back to once a week, maybe once every couple weeks," she said cheerfully. "As long as you're making progress, as in you're doing well emotionally, as in you're stable and sound, then there's no reason to suspect you need more than that."

He winced. "You'll really put me through it, won't you?"

"I so am," she said. "Remember. You came here for the whole package, not a partial job."

"And if I want to change my mind?"

She laughed, and he knew that she hadn't taken him seriously.

"I get that," she said, "and I understand. But that time's past. It's a whole different story though, now that you're actually here."

"I guess," he said, giving in. "It's just weird to think of anybody poking around in my brain."

"No, that's the brain surgeon," she said. "These guys poke around in your mind."

He just glared at her, and she laughed. "Now I've already given you the rules, and I've told you all about how the system works. It's after five, but you are not coming down to the cafeteria for dinner tonight," she said.

His frown deepened. "And yet I'm hungry," he said, worried he'd miss dinner.

"Good," she said. "I will take it upon myself to see what's for dinner. I'll come back and give you an idea of the choices, so you can tell me what you want."

His eyebrows rose in surprise. "Don't you have better things to do than look after me?"

She stopped midway to the door. She turned and looked at him and said in a very calm, quiet voice, "I have nothing better to do than to look after you and every other patient in this building." And, on that note, she walked out the doorway.

He laid here in bed, listening to her as she walked down the hallway, her strides casual yet determined. He realized then what was unique about being here. He'd never felt like he'd mattered to anybody else in any of the other centers he'd been to. He had always been just a number, and every number meant more money to the institution.

Obviously it meant more money here too, but he never had that same heartfelt reaction, that sense of belonging, or that the sense of being someone who mattered. He took a long, slow breath and let it out. Then he picked up his phone and sent Bruce a message. **Thanks again for bringing me here**, he texted. **I can't go to dinner myself, but they'll bring me something, and I've been put on bed rest to recover from my travels.**

Bruce answered almost immediately but this time with a phone call. "Are you okay?" Bruce asked. "I didn't want to leave you there, but it seemed like I was in the way."

"You couldn't stay at that point, but you do get to come back, if you're around and available for a visit," he said.

"I'll do that," he said. "You know I'm gone for the next ten days anyway. But after that …"

"Hopefully after that, I'll have moved on and forgotten that lovely drive. Especially that pothole," he said with a short laugh.

"You would be the one to remind me of that," Bruce said with a chuckle.

"Well, I just wanted to say *thank you* again," Iain said. "I know you've got to get home and to get ready for your trip, but I wanted you to know that I'm fine."

"That's all right," he said. "We're living and breathing change right now for both of us."

"Exactly." Iain knew his friend had just separated from his wife and was still trying to patch things up. They were doing a trip to sort things out and to see if they could make it work. "Good luck on your trip. You know I wish you the best."

"Yeah," Bruce said. "You know I care about you too, buddy. You continue to do the best you can, and I'll be there for you." And he hung up.

Caught up with emotions, he wanted to send Bruce's wife a message and tell her what a great guy she had, if she'd only smarten up and find a way to figure that out. Then Iain realized it wasn't his job. No matter how much Bruce might have told him, his wife hadn't told her side of the story. And it just wasn't Iain's place. He really liked Laura too. But it was up to them to work it out, not Iain.

Just then he heard footsteps nearing his door. Dani walked in, a piece of paper in her hand. She held it out and said, "We'll try and get the cafeteria guys to post the menus online sometime soon. It would save trips like this."

"Trips like this?" He reached for the piece of paper and smiled. "Seriously, you're having a Mexican night?"

"For those who like Mexican food, but other options are offered as well."

"I love Mexican food. And, if you've got enchiladas, I would be happy to have some."

"You'll need your plate one-quarter full of vegetables too," she said. "We don't chintz in the food department, and we expect nutrition to be a high priority."

He raised his eyebrows. "I love vegetables," he said mildly. "So either a plate of hot vegetables or a big salad on the side would be fine."

"When you say big …?"

He smiled, held up his hands in a circle, like for a midsize bowl, and said, "I don't know how much I can eat after that trip, but I am hungry, and it seems like I could use a good-size bowl."

"Good. I'll send Dennis down in a little bit when he catches a break at the line," she said. "He'll introduce himself. He runs the cafeteria. So, anything you want, you can have."

"Perfect," he said in surprise. He settled back against the bed, just happy to have his muscles relaxing a little bit.

"And one of your medical doctors will be in fairly quickly," she said. "He wants to check you over and see how those muscle relaxants are working." As she stopped in the doorway, she smiled at someone down the hallway and said, "Dr. Burgess is here now."

Iain could feel himself tensing before the older gray-haired man in a white lab coat stepped in. But his smile and friendliness were sincere and caring. At that, Iain relaxed, knowing that, although he might be in trouble for pushing his body too far today, he didn't think Dr. Burgess would interrogate him.

Chapter 3

S EVERAL DAYS LATER, the man she'd seen arrive crossed Robin's path again. She was walking around the ground floor with one of the big new cats in her arms. This one was missing a leg, but his temperament was being tried out as a therapy cat. The staff had found that having the formerly injured animals around gave the human patients in the facility additional hope and that they would bond in some way, furthering their rehab efforts.

So, this was Max. He had a patch of fur missing off his hip that had refused to grow back, but apparently he was doing much better. He was mobile—a little too mobile to be let loose right now—and happy, and, as soon as you even looked at him, that diesel engine of his kicked in. She was going from room to room, asking the human patients on the floor above the vet clinic if they wanted to say hi. She hadn't met anyone saying no yet. Even those with that initial *stay away from me* vibe instantly broke into a big grin, their walls completely down. It was amazing to watch, each and every time.

As she approached the next room, the door was open, so she stuck her head in and said, "Hey."

A man looked up, and she was surprised to see who it was. The new arrival she had seen. She smiled and said, "I have Max here, if you'd like to say hello."

He looked at her in surprise, then at the cat in her arms. "Wow," he said, "can you actually carry that thing?"

"He is on the heavier side of twenty pounds," she said, "so part of his rehab includes losing weight." She walked in, held Max out, then placed him gently on the bed.

The patient looked at her—held his gaze there for quite a while—smiled, and said, "I don't think I've seen you around here before." He reached out a hand. "I'm Iain. I arrived a few days ago."

She nodded. "I'm Robin. I'm one of the vet techs downstairs."

He grinned. "Well, that explains why I haven't seen you." He reached down to pet Max. "Wow, look at this guy." Max immediately walked up his chest and butted him in the head. Iain chuckled. He wrapped his arms around the cat and said, "The advantage of a cat being this big is you can really hug them," and he held Max close for a moment, just letting his face rest against the big cat's head. Max took it for a long time. "His temperament is beautiful," he muttered.

She smiled and reached down to pat Max. "We're testing him out as a possible therapy cat," she murmured.

He looked at her with interest.

She shrugged. "We work with a society in town, and they work with animals that can go to children's wards in hospitals and also to visit with terminal patients—difficult cases where anything like this might put a smile on their faces."

"I love hearing that," he said warmly.

She studied him, her smile growing bigger. "Besides, Max put a smile on your face, didn't he?"

He winced. "Yeah. ... Did it look like I wasn't too happy with life when you first came in?"

"Not so much," she said. "But it's obvious you're not lying here relaxed and comfortable."

He looked at her in surprise.

She shrugged. "I deal with animals all the time. Humans are just bigger animals."

"That's the truth," he said. "Sometimes we're easy to deal with, and sometimes we're not."

"The same for all animals," she said.

Max, not liking to be ignored, immediately head-butted Iain again. He chuckled and scratched the big guy under his chin. "He looks like a tabby with those big rings, but he's so much larger."

"We're not exactly sure what other breed is in Max," she said, "but his previous owners had him declawed, and that's not a good idea when around other animals and, of course, never when outside. They have no way to defend themselves if they are attacked."

"Well, as a therapy cat," he said, "it would probably be okay."

"Well, for the moment, I'm mostly carrying him around, or he would get away from me really quick," she said. "I'll have to get him used to a harness though, for that kind of therapy work."

"That should be fun," he said, laughing. "Anytime anybody needs a chuckle, you should grab a group of us and put the harness on Max in front of us all, so we can watch this guy get out of it in two seconds flat."

She grinned, loving his humor. "Are you settling in okay?"

The smile fell off his face, and he nodded. "Yeah. I had a rough arrival," he said.

"You're not the only one to say that," she said. Max stood up and walked down to the end of the bed, sprawling down where Iain's left leg ended. She walked over to him, picked him up in her arms, and said, "I'll take him to visit somebody else now." She walked to the door and smiled at Iain. "Take it easy."

"You too," he said with a lingering smile.

IAIN WAS INCREDIBLY surprised by the visit but was also heartened by it. Robin, ... well, she radiated warmth. A special kind that he was not used to. And Max? He laughed at the thought. Robin and Max's visit highlighted how different Hathaway House was. Yet again. One of the things that he missed in his life was not having pets. He'd been raised in a family with lots of kids and lots of animals. Only his human family remained, but nobody knew how to deal with him right now. He'd given them the same joker personality treatment, but they'd already known that was the fake Iain, and so he'd avoided them at all costs, since they kept asking him questions he would rather not answer. He should have taken a picture of Max to send to them, as they would have understood Iain's joy in seeing and holding a pet again.

Only they would have also seen that he was in bed still, with a sheet over his legs. *Leg*, he kept reminding himself. He had one, the whole right leg now. He took a deep breath and reminded himself that he *had* one leg and that he should be grateful to have that. How it had been touch-and-go and how he could have lost that one too. Something he didn't really want to focus on. For that matter, he had to be grateful that he had like 75 percent of his left leg.

As he relaxed here, he looked up to see Shane, standing at the doorway, studying him for a long moment. Of course they had met on his first day here, but Iain's full medical team soon found out he was in no shape to start his recommended PT rehab plan. Not yet. And he wouldn't recover in two days' time either, despite what Dani had said initially. That may have worked with the others before Iain, but he had really done a number on himself this time.

Shane asked, "So, on a scale of one to ten, how's the body?"

"Three."

"Right. That trip of yours caused some inflammation and swelling on your spine," he said. "Plus the leg joint is not too happy. I was thinking about the pool or hot tub to ease the swelling a bit. What's your preference?"

"Either would be great," Iain said instantly. "I figured the pool and the hot tub were rewards for after I'd done some hard work, not after a mistake like this."

"I think just getting you down there and getting you mobile in the water, where we can get some of the joints moving without any weight on them, would be a good place to start," he said. "Do you have swimming trunks?"

With dismay, Iain shook his head. "No, I don't. I didn't really consider the pool as an option for me."

"I'll be back," Shane said, and he smacked the door and left.

Iain didn't know if that meant that shorts were available or what Shane would do, but Iain really didn't want to lose out on an opportunity to get into the water if he could. And Shane was right. The inflammation was worse—seems no movement was not good, although too much movement was definitely bad—but Iain had been trying to minimize it with heat and ice and anti-inflammatories.

Of course he almost reverted back to that old joker personality of his, where he would laugh it off. Instead, he should have been open in acknowledging it and asking for help. But some here had seen it immediately. He wondered if Robin had said something because she'd been the last one he'd seen. He frowned, wondering about that insightful part of her, wondering if she saw enough—or too much—and then realized it didn't matter if it had been her or not. He was grateful that somebody had noticed because he himself hadn't.

Shane returned about fifteen minutes later, holding up two pairs of trunks. "Different sizes," he said, "let's see which one we can get you in and out of the easiest. After swiveling his legs to the side and pushing the sheet back, he allowed Shane to help him get dressed and then into a wheelchair.

"Well, I'm glad the first pair fit," Iain said, gasping for breath. "I didn't realize how much the movement would hurt."

"And that's something you've got to keep an eye on," Shane said quietly. "No strong silent types needed, please. We've got enough of those around here. Take an interest in your own healing and be active in your own treatment."

"I hear you," Iain said, "but I might need a few reminders."

"Not a problem," Shane said cheerfully. "I've got no problem doing that for you, particularly if I see that you're showing some progress. What pisses me off is when I see guys with potential who won't apply themselves."

"Do you get many of those?"

"Too many," he said, "but not for long."

"Meaning, you ship them out?" And that was the last thing he wanted to hear.

"No," Shane said. "I definitely don't ship them out," he said with a laugh. "But we do shift that attitude real fast."

Chapter 4

ROBIN STEPPED OUTSIDE with a cup of coffee in her hand and brushed the hair off her face. She could hear several men laughing and joking nearby. *Happy humans nearby*, she thought with a smile. That was the thing down here. Happy animals made happy sounds, like barks, purring engines, but too often in a place like this they were silent or resorted to aggressive barking because the animals didn't want to be here. Like now. They'd just finished a tough surgery, and she could use the break. Stan came out beside her with a cup of coffee in his hand. The two looked at each other and smiled.

"It went well," Stan said. He motioned at the sun chairs out in the front. "Let's sit down and relax for a minute."

She walked with him over to the side and realized that they were approaching the patio where the pool was. "Is it okay to sit here when the patients are outside?"

"Absolutely," he said. "The more we intermingle, the better. It stops the alienation and that line between *them and us*."

It made sense, and she was happy to collapse for a moment. "That Jack Russell," she said and then stopped and shook her head, "I thought we would have to put him down."

"We might still," Stan said, leaning his head back, his

369

face up to the sun. He took a deep slow breath and let it out. "But, with any luck, he'll pull through."

"I can't stand to see anyone in pain," she murmured. Her gaze swept to the side, where at least six men had gathered in the pool, some doing laps and some doing what looked like PT exercises. Two men were in the hot tub. No females were around at the moment. And just then, two women came, both in shorts and T-shirts with clipboards in their hands, so they were probably therapists. Robin smiled as she watched the men get put through the paces. And then she recognized one in the hot tub was Iain.

Stan, his voice low, commented, "Anyone you fancy?"

She snorted. "It's been a long time."

"It doesn't matter how long it's been," he said. "When there's a spark, there's a spark."

She smiled, nodded, and said, "True enough. But I haven't been here long enough."

"Liar," he said with a chuckle.

She grinned. "What about you?" she asked. "Anybody here for you?"

"No, I haven't had a serious relationship in over a year," Stan said. "I'm wed to my work."

"I hear you," she said. "It doesn't change the fact that, when it happens, it happens, but you have to be in a position where you can meet people so it can happen."

He burst out laughing. "Good point," he said. "I thought maybe somebody would be here for me over time, but, so far, it hasn't happened." He shifted comfortably, then lifted his coffee and took a sip. "Man," he said. "My lower back is killing me. I have to get that height adjustment fixed on the surgical table."

"Yeah, that mechanism needs to be repaired," she mur-

mured. "That awkward bending we did today was due totally
to the wrong height."

"I'll make sure somebody calls about it this afternoon."

"If I get a chance, I will," she said. "I know we don't
have long to enjoy these five minutes because the appointments are starting this afternoon, but, boy, oh, boy, it got
busy this morning."

Stan grunted his agreement.

She smiled as she watched Iain in the hot tub, and then
Shane approached him, and Iain slid up and over and, rather
than standing, he shuffled on his butt over to the pool before
sliding in. She could see his left leg missing most of the calf,
and his right leg—from where she sat—was purple and angry
and about half the size it should be. She winced.

"Looks pretty raw, doesn't it?" Stan asked beside her.

She rolled her head toward him, her eyes welling.
"God," she said. "What he must have gone through."

Stan studied him, but she didn't dare turn and look
back.

"What he's *still* going through," Stan murmured. "He's
got to build that muscle back up. It looks like some of it has
been surgically reattached. It'll take a lot of time and effort."

She nodded. "It'll be worth it though," she said, "because that'll give him one good leg. Presumably at that point
he might have a prosthetic for the other."

"I think so, but it depends on the damage. I've put prosthetics on many animals, and sometimes it's for the good,
and sometimes the animal was better off without it."

She smiled. "I think it's all about adaptation. Speaking
of which," she said, standing. "We have to adapt to the fact
that our break time is over."

He groaned. "You are a slave driver."

"If you won't get help in," she said, "we pretty well have to be our own slave drivers."

"Aaron is coming," he said. "Just can't happen fast enough."

"He's also pretty green, right?" she warned.

"True, but he's gifted," Stan said. "I'd be more than happy to have him join in."

"Good to know," she said. She walked back with him and said, "Do you want to bet we have twenty people in the waiting room?"

"I hope not," he said. They opened the door, and she laughed.

"Maybe not twenty," she said, "but at least a dozen."

He groaned, and they both walked in with smiles on their faces and got back to work.

IAIN LOOKED AT the calendar in shock. It had been two weeks. Two weeks, when it seemed like he'd arrived yesterday. It had taken much longer than two days to get over the inflammation from his long truck drive, and he still hadn't seen Bruce. He was due back in another couple days, having delayed his return for whatever reason. Iain hadn't heard from his buddy yet.

As he got dressed this morning, Iain realized that, so far, everything had been pretty easy and smooth. They were proceeding based on what his body could handle, and he appreciated that. But he also had the sense of not making any progress. When he looked back to where he'd come from two weeks ago, he realized his progress so far was basically getting back to normal, getting back to where he'd been.

How depressing was that? The knock on the door brought him out of his musings and back to the present.

Fully dressed, he looked up and called out, "Come in." He was surprised to see the woman who had brought Max the cat last time. He raised his eyebrows.

She smiled and said, "I know you're heading out for the morning, but I was just wondering if you wanted to say hi to somebody."

"Sure. What somebody is this?"

She opened the door wider but didn't step closer. She held a leash in her hand.

"Did Max finally learn to wear a harness?"

She chuckled. "No, Max is still a project in the making," she said. "Come on, Hoppers." She pushed the door open more and in hopped one of the biggest, fluffiest rabbits he'd ever seen in his life.

He stared in shock. "Did you feed that thing steroids?"

She smiled. "He's a giant breed," she said, as she bent down, scooped him in her arms, and brought him over, closer to Iain.

Instantly the rabbit leaned forward, his nose twitching and his whiskers wiggling as he tried to sniff Iain.

He reached up a hand, gently stroking the bunny's face and his long soft ears. "He's adorable," he said warmly. He shook his head. "You know what? I kind of like your job."

"You do when it's nice," she said with a smile, reaching down to kiss Hoppers, still in her arms. "But parts of it aren't so nice."

He nodded soberly. "I can imagine." He scratched and played with Hoppers's big ears, admiring his legs. "Will he be another therapy animal?"

"Could be. He basically lives here now," she said. "It's

good for him and for you guys to see him and visit with him. We're hoping to build him a little pen, that he can come and go from, on a regular basis, which will allow him to spend a few hours outside without us."

"That's a good idea," he said. "Wish I was back on my feet. I used to be pretty handy at building that kind of stuff."

"Well, as soon as you're mobile, we could use your help," she said, holding out the rabbit again.

Iain reached out automatically, and, when Hoppers landed full weight in his arm, he *oof*ed. "Wow," he said. "This guy and Max are a mated pair."

She burst out laughing. "He's got some heft to him, doesn't he?"

"Amazing," he said. In awe, he reached down toward his face and his smooth silky neck. "He's beautiful. Do you think the clinic would mind if I putted around with a hammer and some nails?"

"No, I don't think they'd mind in the least," she said. "You'd have to clear whatever project you envisioned with Dani and your medical team, but, other than that, I'm sure they're happy to have some free labor."

"Maybe, depends if I can get clearance from Shane."

"That'll be a challenge." She grinned. "Now you can have your breakfast. I just wanted you to meet Hoppers." She scooped him back out of his arms and walked away.

He studied her as she left, wishing he had a reason to call her back. "Robin?"

She stopped at the doorway, then turned toward him with one eyebrow up. "What's up?"

He shrugged and said, "Nah, it's okay."

She frowned deeper. "Well, it's not okay," she said. "You did call me."

He shrugged. "I just wondered if there was a way for people to get up and out of here too into the pastures, like the rabbit? If I ever get *peopled out?*"

Her initial confusion cleared. "You mean, like wanting to head down to the pastures to spend some time over in our corner of the woods instead of here?"

He nodded. That was close. It wasn't quite what he wanted to say, but it headed in the right direction. "Something like that," he said with a shrug. "It'd be nice to sit down, have a coffee with somebody, and get to know them, instead of being surrounded by hundreds of somebodies."

She grinned, surprised and flattered to think that he wanted to have coffee with her. "My break is at noon," she said. "I plan on sitting out in the pasture, so feel free to join me if you want, and I'll introduce you to the horses."

"I miss horses," he said in a low voice.

"Are you used to horses?"

He nodded. "Yeah, I am," he said. "I've been riding ever since I was a kid." He looked down at his mangled right leg, and his left leg missing its foot and beyond and said, "Make that past tense."

"Doesn't have to be," she said. "We have horse therapy here on a weekly basis." She frowned. "Didn't you know about that?"

He looked at her, shook his head slowly, and said, "No, I hadn't heard about that. I knew horses were here …"

"Mention it to Shane," she said. "He may not think that you're quite ready yet, but it's an option down the road. And, if you're a good rider, we have lots of other people here who ride horses. I think you have to talk to Dani about that though, because she handles all the horses."

"Well, Dani is right here," Dani said, interrupting the

two. She stepped into Iain's room and looked at them. "I just happened to be walking down the hallway. What's up?"

"He was wondering what the horse therapy thing was," she said. "He's used to being around horses, been riding forever."

Dani looked at him with a smile. "And, if you're a horse person," she said, "it's got to be hard not to have them close by again."

"It is," Iain admitted. "Just seeing them outside again is pretty special."

"So true," Dani said. "I'll see when the next opening is in the horse therapy, but I guess we must get clearance from Shane first."

"Shane," Iain said with a shake of his head. "It sounds like he's the go-to man in this case."

"We use horseback riding as therapy, and it's a recurring thing here. So if you miss the next session—or four—you'll catch it later," Dani said seriously. "And, if it's the right thing for you, then that's perfect. But, if it will hinder your healing, it's not a good thing."

"Right," he said. "That makes sense."

"Absolutely, but I have seen you in the hot tub already, so Shane must be thinking of moving you to the pool. That's something you can look forward to as well," Dani said with a smile. "Is that okay with you?"

He thought about it, realized that Shane had been the one who had been here every day for him so far, and he nodded. "Shane is a good guy," he said with a smile. "And, speaking of which, I need to get moving so I'm not late for my appointment with him."

"Never do that," Dani warned. "He doesn't like slackers."

"So far I don't feel like I've been doing very much," he said drily. "Slacking just seems to be the way of it here. I expected much more."

Dani looked at him in surprise for a moment. Then she nodded. "I think your arrival slowed things down."

"Well, I'm ready to have that slowness taken off my chart and make some progress," he announced.

She smirked. "Watch what you say. You could come back to your room today feeling very sorry to have spoken those words."

"Maybe," he said with a shrug. "But it's better to feel like you're doing something and feeling the pain of it than to be doing nothing and feeling nothing rewarding either."

"Then tell Shane that," Dani said. "There's lots you can do once you reach this point, you and your body."

"Will do."

Chapter 5

ROBIN WONDERED OVER the next few days how Iain had done with Shane *unleashed*. She'd gone out to lunch that afternoon, as she had mentioned to Iain, thinking he would join her, but Iain hadn't shown up. She'd gone out a few days later, and again she saw no sign of him. Now she stopped expecting him to show up at lunch, thinking that either something must have happened or he hadn't been quite so ready to make that lunch date with her. He'd seemed to be the one making that initial gesture, but maybe his health hadn't been as strong as he'd hoped.

Still, she didn't want to go to his room and make it seem like she was pushing him. It was dinnertime on Friday, her last day before two days off, and she walked upstairs after a shower. It had been another tough day with so many people in the clinic. It wasn't a surgery day thankfully, but lots of individuals were picking up animals, so it seemed like a never-ending revolving door of activity today. As she walked toward the cafeteria, she saw Stan at the top of the stairs, waiting for her. "You ready for dinner?"

He nodded. "I was thinking about taking mine and going back to my apartment," he said. There was such exhaustion in his expression, and the lines on his face etched a little deeper.

"I hear you," she murmured. "I just figured I'd sit in the

sun and soak up some of that late afternoon heat."

"Don't burn," he warned.

"Nope, I won't," she said.

They separated at the line as Stan got his to go. He must have arranged it ahead of time because he ended up getting a tray with silver domes on top. He smiled at her as he disappeared back down the stairs.

She got into line, and Dennis looked at her and said, "You look as bad as he does."

She wrinkled her nose up at him. "Okay, now that sounds pretty bad."

Dennis went off on peals of laughter. "Vegetables," he said. "That'll help perk you up. You need nutrition."

"And I love my sautéed vegetables," she said, "but I was thinking something like a big salad first."

"How about a big chef's salad?"

"Or a cobb salad?"

"You pick," he said. "Happy to make it for you."

"How about a chef's salad with some fried chicken on the side," she said, when staring at some in front of her.

He chuckled. "What is it about fried chicken that gets everybody every time?" he asked with a big smile.

A voice beside her said, "And here I thought it was just me."

Startled, she looked over to see Iain, standing on crutches. He towered above her.

"Wow," she said. "I knew you were tall, but I didn't realize how tall."

He grinned down at her. "I'd probably still be taller than you, even if I stood on my stump."

She shook her head and grinned. "Can you get a prosthetic for that?" She motioned to his missing foot and calf.

"Working on it," he said easily. He hobbled forward as she moved her tray down.

Dennis looked at him, grinned, and said, "Man, I like to see you on your feet."

"Me too," he said. "Whatever you're making for her, make one for me too, will you?"

"Supersize it though?"

"I can get behind that," Iain said.

She laughed. "What if you don't like what I'm having?"

"He was talking veggies and nutrition," Iain said. "That's something I definitely need to focus on."

She nodded. "I guess what you put in your body is just as important as the rehab work you do, isn't it?"

"Absolutely it is," Dennis interrupted, not giving Iain a chance to respond. "You guys go pick your places. I'll come and deliver."

"Are you sure?" she asked, frowning at him.

"Of course I'm sure," he said.

"Okay," she said. "I just don't want to add to your work-load."

"And I thank you for that." Dennis beamed. "But this is a pleasure. Go find a table, and I'll bring it."

She walked forward, slipping out of the line and heading toward the juices and water section. Iain was right on her heels. She pointed to what was in front of them and said, "I want just water but maybe coffee afterward."

"That's a good idea," he said. "I think I'll have some milk to go with mine."

She nodded. And, not giving him a chance, she grabbed one of the bottles of milk for him and a bottled water for her, then asked, "Anything else?" With both on her tray, she snatched up the cutlery they needed and said, "I might as well carry it. It's not like we both need to."

"That's a good idea. I'm not great at walking with crutches and also carrying trays yet," he said with a smile. "I've seen lots of guys do it though."

"Come on. Let's go find a place to sit," she said. "Inside or outside?"

He hesitated. "You know what? I'd like to do outside, but I'm afraid it'll be deadly hot, so how about half and half?" He pointed at a table with the shade line down the center.

She chuckled. "That's perfect because I was thinking I'd like to sit in the sunshine." As they made their way to the table, she didn't offer to help him navigate. Something she'd been warned about when she first started working downstairs was to make sure the patients didn't think that she was pitying them or taking it easy on them, pride being a very subtle and sensitive yet critical issue. After they sat, and she opened her bottle of water, she took a drink, smiled at him, and said, "How are you adjusting?"

"Well, I'm adjusting," he said. "Not terribly fast though."

She waited for him to continue that thought.

"I told Shane a few days ago that I was ready for more, but, after a test run—which is why I missed lunch with you that day—he thought I needed another week, to get the inflammation down more. So, I'm still waiting."

She nodded. "Any other surprises?"

He hesitated.

She lifted her eyebrows and said," You can talk to me, you know?"

"Can I?" The corner of his mouth quirked.

"Yep," she said. "When I moved here, I found it difficult

to adjust myself."

"Adjust to what?"

"The multiple changes in my life. Change from a big city to this. Change from having a relationship to not. Change from my previous job to this new one. I had a lot of adjustments, and I decided to make it a new beginning for myself. But, as such, I didn't have any foundation or any history to go on here. Nothing to draw on in my experiences to make it easier."

He cocked his head to the side as he studied her.

She gave a self-conscious shrug. "I guess that doesn't make a whole lot of sense, does it?"

"It makes more sense than you realize," he said slowly. "At the VA hospital where I was, I was the class clown. I was joking and laughing, and I knew that it was just a facade and that underneath nobody could really see the pain I was in. I promised myself I wouldn't do that when I got here."

"I like the sound of that," she said. "Because, of course, the class clown is hiding something. It's usually pain or embarrassment or lack of confidence."

He smiled. "In my case it was the inability to deal with the body that I currently live in. I kept hoping and hoping that the surgeries would work. And, of course, the jury is still out as to whether they really will."

"You're walking," she said slowly. "In my book, that's a huge success."

He looked at her, startled, and then he nodded. "And that's what I just came to realize," he said. "When I left that place and came here, I was determined to find out who I really am. I want to be who I am on the inside, not just the person on the outside everybody saw."

"And that sounds very deep too. I think, when you get

an opportunity to be at a place like this," she said slowly, "you almost have to wipe out everything that came before. You can challenge the good things, the things that worked, taking them to a new level. Things that pissed you off from the old life almost have to be put in a box and stowed away, so you can give this experience a chance, without that prior stuff hindering your vision. A fresh start to take each new experience from a whole new perspective."

"Easier said than done," he said with a smile.

"I'm just as guilty. I came with what I thought was a broken heart, only to realize very quickly that I wasn't brokenhearted. It was more like a dent to my pride," she said with a self-deprecating smile. She lifted her water bottle and took another big sip. "My heart wasn't touched. My pride took a blow when I realized he preferred somebody else to me."

"I'm sorry," he said.

She shook her head. "I'm not," she said. "The best thing I did was come here. If I had stayed with him and had tried to make it work, we both would have been unhappy. Where's the joy in that?"

He gave a shout of laughter. "A perfect way to look at it," he said. "I'm trying to take this as a new experience and come to terms with who and what I am right now."

"What you are," she said firmly, "is a man with a disability. But you are not a disabled man. Those are two very different things."

He stared at her in surprise. "I think I like that," he said slowly.

She nodded. "It's all about perspective," she said. "What you've already done since you've been here is great."

"No, right there, you're wrong," he said. "I haven't done

anything yet. I don't even feel like I've had to apply myself."

"Maybe the harder thing for you was to do nothing," she said seriously. "You came here in bad shape. You were ready to do the old gung-ho, charge-forward thing. But instead, what you had to do first was ease back, relax, and let your body destress and deal with the extra damage because of that trip."

He glanced at the table. "Maybe," he said. "I'm not very good at doing nothing."

"And, after two—now three—weeks of doing nothing, as you say, you're feeling like you haven't made any progress. Yet it's the opposite. You should be slowly improving to the point that now maybe you can get to work. The real work you came here for."

Just then Dennis arrived, carrying large plates of food. He placed them on the table, stepped back, then looked at them both expectantly.

She smiled up at him. "Thank you. It looks lovely."

"And," Dennis said with a huge toothy grin, "it tastes even better. I'll be back in a little bit to make sure you're doing okay." And, with that, he strode off again.

Iain watched him go. "Does he ever walk, or is he always in a race?"

"I have seen him casually walk," she admitted. "Just not very often."

Iain smiled, nodded, and said, "It's like a lot of things in this place. There's a time for everything."

"And your time, so far," she said, "has been to rest and to recover. Your time to move forward will happen soon enough."

He nodded. "This afternoon, I think. Shane said yesterday it was time to switch things up."

"See?" she said. "You may not want to eat quite so much, at least not before your workout. Because, if Shane says he'll switch it up, chances are he'll *really* switch it up."

"It'll hurt tomorrow, won't it?" He wrinkled up his face. "I can handle pain, but I don't really like it."

"Nobody likes pain," she said. "We can all handle a certain amount of it. But nobody wants to get to the point where we tolerate it so much that we don't even feel it. Because to feel pain is to feel alive. And to recover from that hurt is to recover from what we went through. That means, realizing that every step we take moving forward are the steps that we're doing for ourselves, to improve our lives and to improve our future, now that we know that we actually have one."

He shook his head. "Heavy words."

"Enlivening words," she corrected. "Now let's eat."

IAIN SPENT THE next few days thinking about her words. Robin had a unique take on life, and maybe he needed that too. His reason for coming here was to experience a whole new beginning, but he had been very disappointed at his start so far. Shane explained he was just checking to see what Iain could do and what he couldn't do, trying to see where his weaknesses were and finding out what needed to be done.

But it sounded like the same old song Iain had heard time and time again. He felt that this was as good as his legs would get. This was what he had; this was all he had, and he had better make the best of it. When he woke up in the morning three days after that prophetic conversation with Robin in the cafeteria, Iain had gotten dressed and was sitting here when a knock came at the door. He called out, "Come in."

Shane poked his head around the door and said, "This morning's session might be a bit rough. I just wanted to warn you to eat light."

Iain looked at him in surprise, then slowly nodded. "Nothing has been hard yet," he said.

"I know," Shane said with a big smile, "but now it's time to get down to work." And he disappeared.

Iain wasn't sure if he believed Shane or not. It seemed like just more talk. The trouble was, if this was all Iain had to live with, was it even worth doing more? He figured it would be something he had to ask Shane about. But maybe it was too early to judge. Maybe Shane didn't know. Maybe Shane was being an eternal optimist.

For himself, Iain could feel that sense of wanting to just give up. That sense that nothing mattered. That this was it. He might as well leave the rehab center, save everybody the time and effort, and get a job somewhere. He didn't have a clue how or what skills he possessed, but he was sure that nobody would take an amputee. Why would anybody take on someone who obviously has physical issues when they could get an able-bodied individual instead?

Although some companies were definitely helping out veterans more than others. He'd even heard about that group in New Mexico, helping vets get back into the employment field. He was pretty sure he'd met Badger a couple times, and he was the one heading this new group. Iain wondered if he should contact Badger and see if similar work was being done here in the Dallas area that Badger might know of for someone like Iain. Hell, Badger's group had advanced prosthetics. Maybe Iain could get something that would work for him too. Make him more employable.

Refusing to allow himself to be daunted by the thought, he opened up his laptop and quickly sent an email. It took a bit to find Badger's company online. *Titanium Corp.* Once Iain found it, he stared, amazed to see the group photo of the men of steel, standing with their arms around each other. Their prosthetics were obvious, but the bonds were just as evident. With that, he grabbed the contact email and quickly sent Badger a message.

Looking at the picture on the main page, he knew at least three of the other men too. Iain's heart ached as he realized how much he missed that camaraderie, that sense of belonging, that knowing that you weren't alone in this world. That's how he felt right now, kind of adrift.

Even though he had a lot of physical support here, they wouldn't be there for his tomorrows. They wouldn't be the people who helped him make the shift from this end of his rehab to the next stage in his life. He'd come here with such high hopes of a new beginning, a chance to get his right leg to do so much more than it was doing. His back, even though strong, obviously couldn't handle the long truck ride and had set him back by days if not weeks. He felt tired, and he didn't know why, but it was more at a soul level.

He chose the wheelchair and wheeled his way to the cafeteria. He wasn't even hungry, and now he was worried about Shane's words. He headed for the coffee first and, with a hot mug, wheeled himself onto the deck. He sat here quietly, all alone, trying to figure out what was wrong with his world. He sat out in the sun, pondering life, hating this slump, but realizing that, instead of looking for new hope, he needed to look in a new direction. A direction that had a future.

As he sat here nursing his coffee, Dennis arrived at his back. "Hey, not eating today?"

He looked up at him, smiled, and said, "Shane warned me it could be a bit rough. Told me to eat light."

Dennis's frown was instinctive. "Maybe light," he said, "but you can't go with nothing. If your blood sugar's low, exhaustion will take over in no time. You don't want Shane thinking that you're in such poor shape that you have to quit again."

"No, I don't really want that," he said, "but I don't even know what *eating light* means anymore."

"I got you," Dennis said. "Give me a minute." He disappeared.

Iain didn't even particularly care what he brought. It would be food, and, as long as he ate half of what he normally would, he should be okay. At least he hoped so. Shane had set off a chain of events that Iain had been trying to calm down since they had talked. And yet, all Iain seemed to be concerned about right now was worrying and fussing and looking at a million different options, but none of them seemed even appealing or possibly doable.

When Dennis returned a few minutes later with a beautiful-looking bratwurst, scrambled eggs, and a piece of whole-wheat toast, he said, "This is about half of what you normally eat, so get some of this down, and then we'll plan for a better lunch for you."

"I could be sick to my stomach by lunchtime," he murmured, but he didn't believe it. He'd yet to see anything to match his expectations coming here.

Dennis nodded, and his tone turned serious when he said, "I've seen it before. I've seen guys come in exhausted and starving. They take one look at the food, and their stomach muscles heave right away. I don't know what Shane has planned for you. Just know that it's for your own good."

Iain gave a startled laugh at that. "Is it really for my own good?"

"Sometimes the methodology seems a bit rough or confusing," Dennis said. He placed both palms on the table and leaned forward to look at Iain. "But Shane is one of the best. If he sees something he can do to help you improve, then listen to him. He'll get you there."

"And I'm wondering if there's anywhere to get to," Iain said. "I've had no progress since I arrived. The last surgeon said this is as good as the right leg will get. Maybe I'm wasting everybody's time by being here. I should just go to town, rent a place, and find a way to do something with my days and to learn to live with my life as it is."

"Screw that," Dennis said. "That's a defeatist attitude. You just got here. I already heard that you were having a couple tough weeks because of your trip here. And now that you're here, don't give up. See what Shane has got to say first."

"Well, it sounds like you're in my corner," he said with a half smile.

"I'm in everybody's corner," Dennis said, "but especially the underdog. I want every one of you to get up and walk out of here to live happy, cheerful lives," he said emphatically. "And I've seen enough here to know what can happen. I know you're probably thinking that you'll be the one case that it doesn't happen to. I swear to God, I've seen time and time again the same attitude, the same thought process for almost every person who came through those front doors.

"You're also a big man, and you know that that leg won't handle you too much longer, no matter what the surgeons have done. You'll have to strengthen it. And Shane is the one to help make it stronger. Shane'll make it work and will support you. And he'll make sure that that back of yours is capable of handling everything that's still to come. You're young, and you could have some fifty more years," he said. "You want a body that can cradle you, can support you, and can work with you," he said. "So, whatever Shane says, you do it." He smacked the table and turned and walked away.

Realizing he'd been told off in a subtle way and not really understanding how or why, Iain dug into his eggs and bratwurst and smiled. They were, as always, very tasty. His stomach was happy to get some food. He stopped with that, finished off his coffee, then slowly made his way back to his room. There, he changed into his shorts and a muscle shirt and headed to his meeting with Shane.

As he wheeled into the room, Shane looked at the wheelchair in approval. "Glad you brought that today," he said. "You'll be grateful for it when we're done."

"You'll hurt me that much?" he joked. Iain wasn't exactly sure what today was supposed to bring. Of course, with everybody warning him, he could feel his own defenses and maybe a little bit of fear rising up. Like he had said to Robin, nobody liked to be in pain.

"It's not what I'll do to you," Shane said. "It's what you'll do to you."

He frowned at him.

Shane gave him a quick grin. "I promise I haven't killed anybody yet."

"And there's always the first," Iain announced. He rolled closer, parked the wheelchair against the wall, and said, "What are we doing?"

"Floorwork," he said. "I want to see what kind of stretching we can get out of that leg."

Still seated, he lifted his right leg and said, "How will we start?"

Shane looked at him in surprise, then shook his head and said, "No, we'll start with the leg missing the foot."

"And why would you want to start there?" he asked in surprise.

"Because it's been pulling more of its own weight than you'd expect and because the other one is so badly injured. The surgeries have helped, but you have a long road of recovery to get that right leg to pull its own weight. In the meantime, the left leg is the one hurting."

Iain stared at Shane in surprise.

Shane smiled and said, "Trust me. Let's start on that one, and then we'll get to the one that's just recovering post-op." And that's what they did.

Iain didn't think he could stretch, considering he only had 75 percent of that leg. He had the knee joint, but then the stump was about four inches down, and that was it. He'd hoped that having a stump would allow him to get a prosthetic, but, so far, that hadn't happened. And all because they were waiting to see what the right leg would do. It had to support all his weight. If only he wasn't such a big guy …

"Okay, let's get started," Shane said, and he put him through the paces. It seemed minor until twenty minutes later, when Shane took the exercises to another level.

By that time, Iain felt sweat flowing freely off his body. He gasped when he finally reached a break in his exercises and asked, "So, are we done for the day?"

Shane looked at him in surprise and said, "We won't be done until noon. Unless, of course, your body needs to shut down for a while?" Shane lifted an eyebrow, as if assessing Iain's condition and his willingness to do what was needed.

"Will this help me?" Iain asked. He was stretched out on the ground, supporting his weight on his elbows, as they had been working on the abductor muscles on the outside of his thigh.

Shane smiled, nodded, and said, "You don't understand the intricacies of what we're doing, but it's very important that you get your balance tuned up. With your balance back, you can regain your strength. Then we can get you walking normally on a prosthetic."

"I would love to get a prosthetic." But he hesitantly added, "They kept saying it would depend on my good leg."

"Honestly, your *good* leg is the one that'll get the prosthetic," Shane reassured him. "The bad leg is the one that we have to build up from surgery, and that's where we'll start now."

Iain frowned at him in shock. He stared down at his right leg and winced. "I don't think I'll like the next hour."

"I'm sorry," Shane said, "but I can guarantee that you won't like it one bit."

Chapter 6

ROBIN HADN'T SEEN Iain for a couple days. She went out of her way to check his room, but, so far, the door had always been closed. She changed up her breakfast and lunchtime hours, hoping to catch sight of him, but still nothing. Finally, on Friday morning, she asked Dennis if he'd seen him.

Dennis gave a solemn nod. "Shane started putting him through the heavy paces on Wednesday," he said. "He's not in very good shape."

Her eyebrows shot up. "Well, I guess that's good," she said slowly.

He looked at her tray and said, "What do you want for breakfast?"

"Yogurt and fruit," she said with a smile. "Maybe a little extra yogurt on the side."

"Or I could make you a parfait," he said in a teasing voice.

She smiled and nodded. "And I'm not saying no to that. You do make the best." And right in front of her, he layered fresh fruit, granola, cream, and plain yogurt until she had a beautiful concoction set before her. He handed it to her, and she carried it over to the coffee station. She poured herself a cup and stepped out into the sunshine.

She couldn't stop thinking about how Iain was surviving. He'd been afraid that what he had was what he would be stuck with, that his hope of a new beginning was useless, and that it wouldn't happen. Did he still feel that way? She glanced around, sitting in such a way that she could watch everybody come and go. But still saw no sign of him. She finished her breakfast, refilled her coffee, and headed to work. She and Stan had no shortage of appointments today, and she was kept busy right up to lunch. She was almost ready to miss lunch when Stan stopped in, looked at her, and said, "I don't even have the energy to go upstairs and grab food. How are you doing?"

"Same," she said.

He nodded, looked over at their receptionist at the front desk, and asked, "Annette, how are you doing?"

She looked at him, smiled, and said, "Why don't I run get food for both of you? What do you want?"

"What's on tap today?" Stan countered.

She picked up the phone and quickly called upstairs. Robin had to admit it was a huge boon to have food right now, right there, hot and ready.

"Something Spanish," she said with a shrug.

"That's fine," Stan said. "Get us two of everything."

Annette laughed. "How about I see what I can get on one tray."

"Or take the trolley," Robin suggested.

Annette looked at her in surprise, then nodded. "You know what? That'd probably be the best idea. Maybe I'll grab myself something too." The trolley was a teacart made out of stainless steel. She moved it to the elevator and disappeared from sight.

Stan and Robin looked around the front room, which was empty for once.

Robin said, "I feel like I shouldn't dare mention the fact that we're caught up because we'll immediately have a dozen vehicles pulling in the parking lot."

He laughed. "Isn't that the truth. And it's not even a surgery day."

"Thank heavens," she said. "Of course it's way worse when we're booked like this, and then we have emergencies coming in as well." She noted how tired Stan looked. "Are you sleeping okay?"

"Not last night," he said. "Don't know what was wrong, but I was walking around outside at midnight."

"I have done that a time or two," she admitted.

"How are you and Iain getting along?"

Her eyebrows shot up.

He shrugged and said, "I've seen you spending a fair bit of time with him."

"Not this week," she said with a shrug. "Apparently Shane started putting him through the paces, and Iain's been noticeably absent for the last half of the week."

"Well, it is Friday," he said. "If you wanted to spend some time with him this weekend, I'm sure that could happen."

"If he's in any shape," she said with a nod. "Maybe even just to get out to the pasture and lie down and sunbathe would be nice."

"Says you," he said. "I'll sleep. Besides, we'll have patients all weekend, so I'll be back and forth checking in on them."

"Right, we've got what? One dog and one cat for the weekend?"

"And then the regulars," he said. "That's why we have got to solve the Hoppers problem."

"Iain did say that he was pretty handy with a hammer and nails."

"If he were a little bit further down his healing road," Stan said, "I'd probably get him to come take a look, offer some suggestions on what we could do. What does Hoppers actually need?"

"Basically a covered outdoor run and a way to get back inside," she said. She walked over to the nearest window and studied the many dog runs they had. "Why can't we convert one of these to accommodate him?"

"There's an idea," he said, standing next to her. "Even if we just made him a smaller one off to the side."

They stepped outside and walked around to where dog runs were. They weren't huge, but they were large enough that dogs could stretch their legs, run back and forth, and somebody could throw a ball for them.

As they stood at the fourth one, she nodded and said, "We could even put a little doorway through here and make him a separate run." She studied the exterior of the building and then sighed. "But that'll mean giving him access through this big foundation wall."

Stan stepped to the side and said, "Well, what about using this nearby door instead? We could inset a bunny door in this side door and put another little small fence around here, cutting into the dog run, but redirecting to the side piece here, and then Hoppers can come and go as he wants to."

The two of them discussed it until they heard a shout from inside. They headed back in to see Annette pushing the trolley, fully laden. "Oh, that looks so good," Robin said. She looked around and said, "Why don't we just eat out here in the sitting room?" They sat around a small coffee table, with Annette joining them for their lunch break, and ate large plates of wraps filled with rice with raisins and curry spices.

"I don't know what this is," Robin mumbled with her mouth full, "but it's divine."

"I didn't even ask," Annette said. "I was so busy trying to get some of everything for you guys that I wasn't too bothered about getting the names of the dishes."

"If I care enough," Robin said, "I can always ask Dennis myself."

"True," Annette said with a smile. Only as they were almost done did Annette add, "And, by the way, I saw Iain up there."

Robin froze, looked over at Annette, and asked, "Really? Do you know who he is?"

She nodded. "I figured you two were friends. He was up there, and I just happened to notice," she said with a casual shrug.

Robin sat back, wondering if both Stan and Annette saw their friendship as something more. She frowned.

"Don't bother arguing," Stan said. "We can see the sparks."

"Not a whole lot anybody can do about sparks in his condition or mine," she said with a laugh. "And hardly *sparks*. More like, gentle interest."

"This is a place for friendships," Annette said quietly. "It's a place where any connection that's built here isn't built on the physical looks but built on gaining new strength, as people go from strength to strength."

"That's very insightful," Robin said. She laid down her fork, sat back, and rubbed her tummy. "That was great."

"It really was," Stan said, as he worked on finishing the

last bit on his plate.

Robin contemplated Annette's words because she was right. This wasn't a place where physical attraction was first and foremost. It was all about seeing the soul and the character residing inside the pain and also seeing the growth of the survivor in the patient's eyes. Not the physical body but the mental body, the emotional body, and how well people dealt with life. "I think Iain will have a few tough weeks," she said to Annette.

"He looked pretty wiped out right now," she said, "but he was glancing around, as if searching for somebody." And she let her words hang in the air.

Robin frowned.

"You may want to take the dishes up yourself," Annette said. "Not that I guarantee he'll still be there by now."

"Not likely," she said. "It's Friday. I don't know what his afternoon schedule looks like."

Annette nodded. "Probably like ours, which will be hellish." She pointed to the parking lot where three vehicles were pulling in at the same time.

Stan groaned, put the last bite in his mouth, snagged his coffee, and said, "I'll be in my office."

Robin laughed and said, "My coffee is gone. I'll return the dishes and grab another cup while I'm there." And, without giving Annette a chance to say anything and ignoring her smug smile, Robin grabbed the trolley and pushed it out of the lobby and the reception area. The last thing they needed was for clients to come in with patients and see food everywhere. She quickly closed the elevator door and zipped up to the cafeteria level. There, she pushed the trolley and headed toward Dennis.

Dennis smiled, took one look at the trolley, and said, "That's what I like to see. Empty plates."

"It was fabulous," she said. She quickly unloaded the trolley and grabbed more coffee. Then she caught sight of gooey melted chocolate chip cookies. She sighed and said, "I'll get fat here."

"I think that's a complaint everybody has," a man said behind her. She spun and saw Iain standing on his crutches, looking like he could collapse. Instinctively her hands moved out to his in an offer of support.

"Oh my," she said. "You look like you're done for."

"That bad, huh?" He squeezed her fingers and gave her a crooked grin.

"I've got about five minutes, if you want to talk," she whispered.

He shook his head slowly. "Honestly I'm not done yet. I have some more work to do at the pool, and then I have appointments this afternoon."

From his tone of voice, she could tell they weren't appointments he looked forward to. "I'm sorry," she said. "I'm around most of the weekend though, if you want to visit."

"That would be great," he said with a smile.

She looked at the clock on the wall behind him and realized that she didn't have five minutes at all. "Look. I'm really behind downstairs," she said. "How about I check in with you over the weekend? Maybe we can sit and have coffee or something." A smile flashed on his face, and it looked genuine. Tired and worn out but genuine.

He nodded. "If my door is shut, don't wake me though," he said with a half grin. "I might sleep through to Monday."

"And, if you do," she said warmly, "then you needed to."

With that, she dashed off, barely avoiding spilling her coffee on the trolley as she headed downstairs. But, as she bolted in, ready to tackle the afternoon's worth of work, she had a smile on her face. A knowing grin on Annette's face as Robin blasted past told her that her friend had taken notice too.

GETTING TO THE pool was agonizing. Iain didn't know why the hell Shane had been hiding all this from him through the first three weeks, and yet maybe Shane had been right to take it easy on Iain those initial weeks so the swelling in his back and both his legs went down. But getting to the pool today had almost maxed his abilities. He'd changed to the wheelchair because absolutely no way could he manage crutches.

Once downstairs, he pulled to the side of the pool, locked the wheelchair, reached out a hand for the railing that would lead to the steps into the water, and slowly stood on his weak leg. Reaching for the second bar, he hopped closer. And then, with one final push, he jumped into the water.

As soon as the cool waves caused by his exuberance closed over his head, he felt some of the stress sliding off his shoulders. He didn't even want to surface. He wanted to stay under and float in a space where he didn't have to worry about his body not supporting him. A space where he didn't have to worry about his build being too much for his leg, where his oversized body—that he'd always taken so much pride in—was now going against him. A place where he could just relax and be free. But eventually he had to surface, and he did so slowly, releasing the air in his lungs and taking a deep breath of more. When he opened his eyes, Shane stood there with a frown on his face.

"That frown doesn't make me feel good," Iain muttered.

"You're done for the day," he said. "Here I was hoping

to get a few laps out of you, but you're too tired."

At that, Iain gave him a flat stare and said, "I can do at least two." And he started off with a front crawl. He still couldn't stop the rotation though, something that he knew would improve his strokes and would take away his exhaustion faster than anything because swimming was something he could get into a rhythm, and it didn't tire him.

He could go for miles, but, with only one whole leg, he found himself constantly rotating at the hip level. He focused on keeping his body straight and his legs moving from the thigh, not the foot. Realizing that that was where the mistake was, he slowed down his strokes and moved steadily forward. He came to the far wall, flipped, kicked off, then turned and headed back toward Shane. But he didn't stop there. He did another flip turn and headed back, finding it easier as his body loosened up a bit more.

After another eight laps, he came to a slowdown and stopped in front of Shane. "It's much easier if I remember to kick from the hip joint," Iain said.

Shane crouched in front of him. "I think that's one of the biggest lessons for anybody in this situation. You have to maintain your center of gravity and remember where your baseline is. Every set of joints is important all the way up, but you have to make sure that the spine and the hip joint are squared off to the rest of you and then stay that way."

"It's like relearning how to walk all over again," Iain said. "Now that I'm in the pool, I'm having to relearn how to swim."

"That's exactly what it is," he said. "I know it sounds funny, but, even if you just lost toes or half a foot, you would have a similar adjustment. It wouldn't be quite so large and exasperating, but you would still have to make an adjustment."

"Now what?" he asked. "I did ten laps. That's not a whole lot, but I am feeling a bit better."

"And you're looking a bit better," Shane said. "We'll do some stretches to finish off."

"Well, what stretches are to you," Iain said, "is a full-body workout to other people."

"And that's quite possible but hardly my concern though. I don't worry about other people. Let's worry about you."

"How do you separate the two?" he asked. He didn't know if he was delaying the stretches coming up—as the new muscles had to be gently teased into cooperating, when they didn't have any intention of doing so. It was like they tacked cement on or a steel bar from each muscle point to the insertion point.

"Partly it's my job," Shane said. "Partly it's experience. And partly I don't separate them. I draw from one experience to the other. The same as you need to draw from your old experience to now."

"I thought it'd be easier if I forgot all that beforehand."

"Sure," he said. "I want you to forget about the ten years in the navy before your accident, but I want you to remember way back to childhood, when you were still learning to do things. Where you had to learn to walk. Where you had to learn to bend over and touch your toes, and when you couldn't do it. All because the back of your legs weren't limber enough and your back didn't bend enough. And how it felt to actually stretch out all those muscles and get there."

"The thought of touching my toes ..." He shook his head. "That seems a long way away."

"It's not," Shane said. "Let's get started."

Chapter 7

W HEN ROBIN WOKE up Saturday morning, she laid in bed, tired and worn out. She'd been up to help Stan in the night, the two of them unavoidably coming in to check on a patient they were each worried about, only to find that both the dog and the cat weren't doing well. They'd stayed for a couple hours, until they were sure that their patients were improving. And then, they both crashed again.

Now she was lying in her bed on a Saturday, staring out and groaning. Stan would work a half day but another vet tech, one who came in to help when they got too busy, was here so that Robin had the full weekend off. But having the full weekend off when you lived beside the vet clinic didn't really mean you were *off*-off.

She often went in and checked on the animals kept there. Hoppers always needed to come outside; the horses and the llama needed grain and to be fed. And, even though that wasn't her job, she couldn't help feeling like maybe she should check outside to make sure it was being done.

As she sat up in bed and swung her legs to the floor, she groaned again. "If this is how I feel after a bad night, I can't imagine how Iain or the others feel." She stepped into a hot shower and realized that was a big problem, almost an impasse between them.

It's not that she couldn't understand, but it was outside her experience to fully comprehend. And she had to let him have the full experience of what he was going through and also honor that, without criticizing or in any way making it look like she could understand—because how could she? She could empathize and be grateful that she wasn't experiencing what he was, but absolutely she had no way to contemplate his situation to the same level which he was going through, day after day after day.

She'd been physically healthy all her life. She had worked with animals in difficulties and with major problems, but she couldn't do a whole lot to help any animal or any person without being an empathetic person. Yet that wasn't the same thing as being somebody who could say that she fully understood, had her own experience going through something the same, and could truly sympathize. Sympathy was fine and good, yes, in some situations, but that was the last thing she wanted to give Iain.

As she checked her watch after her shower, she realized she'd already missed the breakfast hour. But then that was okay because the last thing she wanted was food. What she really wanted was to go for a long walk out in the sunshine. She quickly braided her hair into a plait down her back, put on shorts, a decent walking shoe, and a T-shirt. Then she grabbed her phone and headed out to the animals. She had a bottle of water with her, and she'd do coffee and food when she got back.

She started off at the pasture with the animals, giving greetings and handfuls of grain to the horses and to the lovely llama that had joined them. Even the little filly was doing so much better, and she was definitely not the little-filly size that she had been before. She was growing every day. Her temperament was beautiful too, and she had an absolutely lovely blond mane.

Robin stood a moment, brushing the animals gently, just enjoying being with them. Finally saying goodbye, she headed off down the pasture where several acres of open land were. It could be more than that; she had no idea what an acre looked like down on the ground, and she wasn't sure what property belonged to the Hathaway House. She knew Dani did a lot of riding, in the mornings especially, and seemed to stay on the property and yet kept going for hours, so Robin didn't exactly know what property lines there were.

This morning she was just looking for something like an hour's walk. As she walked along the pastures and came up on the far side of a fence and walked all the way around, back to where she had started, she realized that that had already taken her the better part of an hour. She came up to the front parking lot and then walked to the veterinarian parking lot and went back to her own apartment.

Stepping inside, she thought about putting on coffee and then decided that maybe she'd go to the cafeteria and grab one instead. Inside, she was hoping that maybe her path would cross with Iain. Something was so very wonderful about him. She'd met a lot of the other men here, but they didn't have the same effect on her that Iain did. Maybe that was good. He was definitely the most interesting male she'd met in a long time.

As she walked inside, the cafeteria was empty, and all the trays clean and shiny, waiting for the lunch rush. She walked over to the coffee service, poured herself a cup, plus snagged a bottle of juice, then headed out to the deck. As she sat down, a voice hailed her. She turned to see Shane. She gave him a smile. "How are you doing?"

"I'm doing great," he said. "How are you settling in? It's been a couple months now, hasn't it?"

"Almost, yeah," she said. "And you?"

"Years and years and years," he said with a big laugh.

"Well, it seems like you're getting the job done," she said.

"How do you figure?" he asked with a questioning look in his eye.

"This place is such a success, and you are a huge part of that." She smiled. "A certain comfort is in that though," she said. She lifted her cup, blew at the hot brew, and added, "Not the least of which is you've had so many years of Dennis's cooking."

"I have, indeed," Shane said, patting his belly. "And eight years of trying to combat the extra waistline."

She burst out laughing. "I think that's a common complaint here."

He grinned. "So, how are you and Iain doing?"

She slowly lowered her cup and leaned forward. "Does everybody think something's going on between us?"

"Well, I personally notice things like that," he said. "And I know that Iain is often searching anytime he's out in the public spaces, as if looking to catch sight of someone."

"Might not be me," she warned.

"Might not be," Shane said cheerfully, "but I bet it is."

She could feel some heat flush her cheeks. She shrugged self-consciously and said, "Well, I must admit I hope he's looking for me," she said. "He's an interesting man."

"He is. He is also struggling in some ways."

"Why is that?"

"I don't think he thought it would be as hard as it is."

"I think he figured he had done as much improvement

as he could," she said. "This was kind of a last-ditch effort to go beyond what the surgeons had said. And then, when nothing happened in the first two to three weeks here, it's like he gave up. He was getting ready to walk away, giving up his bed for someone else who really needed it. With that thought, he had to start thinking about having a different life."

"I heard something like that from him," Shane said. "Only it's not that cut-and-dry. And he's a long way away from seeing his optimum self yet. And that's good."

"I'm glad to hear that," she said seriously. "We do a lot of very deep talking," she said with a half smile. "It's interesting getting to know who he is on the inside."

"It's one of the reasons I love my job," Shane said, "because the real person only shows up when trouble moves into their lives."

She thought about that for a long moment, then sat back and realized he was right. "You must have seen some incredible people throughout your years here."

"I have, indeed," he said. "It's been a joy and an honor to help these people."

"Do you have any concerns about Iain?"

He shook his head. "Not really," he said. "I think, as long as he's striving and still driving for something better than what he has, he'll be fine. We'll end up in trouble only if he gives up."

She frowned at that. "And is there any reason he would give up?"

"He'll come to a point in time where his body can't be improved anymore," Shane said. "When the muscles are as strong as they'll get, without expending more time and effort into building them up. Meaning, more energy than he has available."

She had to work her way through that convoluted explanation and then understood. "So, really there's a point where he'll max out his potential. Even here."

"Yes. To know if he's happy with where he's at then is hard to say."

"I know he really wants to get a prosthetic on that leg so the one that had all the surgery is strong enough to support him."

"And that may or may not come to pass," Shane said. "I know he'll try it no matter what we say, but that doesn't mean he'll like the end result."

"Right," she said. "And I guess that makes sense, even though it's sad to hear."

"It doesn't have to be sad," he said. "The thing to remember is that life is all about finding where you're at and going forward with what you have. There's a certain comfort in having hard rules to follow."

"If you say so," she said. "It seems very odd though."

"No," he said. "It's a good thing."

"Maybe." But she seemed doubtful at first. "I know what he really wants is to walk on his own two feet."

"We'll do our best to get him there," Shane said. "But it's not just about building up. It's also about letting go. It's releasing the stiffness from the muscles as well as the stiffness from his needs and wants. As much as this is a physical process, it's a mental one as well. That can be the hardest part." And, with that, he got up and walked away.

She sat here for a long moment, thinking about their conversation. She had never really considered that psychological part of the equation, but it matched up to what she could see in other people around her. Even with her brother

Keith. Only she hadn't really put two and two together. Because she dealt with animals, she didn't have to explain what was going on to the animal itself. She couldn't ask the animal to stretch and to do what it needed to do. They almost instinctively did it anyway.

She had seen some horrific injuries where, when she saw the animal next, they were completely comfortable with that. And, in some cases, they'd healed better than before. The human body was just as marvelous, but the human mind had the ability to stop or to start the healing process. She wondered if Iain understood that too.

When another voice called to her from the doorway, she shifted to see Iain standing there on crutches, a surprised look on his face.

She got up and walked her empty coffee cup to the sideboard for dirty dishes, then headed toward Iain. "Hey," she said. "How are you doing? I expected you to sleep all weekend."

"No," he said. "Not something I was intentionally trying to do. I felt like it, but I haven't even eaten yet." He glanced at Dennis, who was wandering around in the back. "But it looks like we still have an hour until lunch."

She nodded. "Do you need food though? Because I'm sure Dennis can get you something."

Iain laughed. "No, that's fine," he said. "I was just stretching out by walking up and down the hallway a bit. My shoulders are still pretty stiff."

"You can go for a swim in the pool," she suggested.

He studied her in surprise, then said, "Join me?"

She frowned, then nodded. "Sure. Why not?" she said. "It's a beautiful day out, and we still have at least an hour until we can eat."

"Did you not eat?"

She smiled, shook her head, and said, "No, I didn't. I went for a walk instead."

"Good," he said. "I'll meet you down at the pool in ten?"

She nodded and said, "Ten it is."

And they split at the doorway. She headed back to her apartment and quickly changed. She grabbed a cover-up and then a big towel and headed up to the pool deck. Self-conscious but grateful she was here first, she tossed off her towel and her cover-up, and dove in with a nice, clean breaking motion into the water. And as soon as she broke the surface, she kicked out strongly and did several laps.

When she slowed down, she noted somebody in the pool stroked out strongly beside her. She smiled and made one more lap with him, then waited at the pool steps for him. And finally Iain stopped his laps, looked at her, and said, "You're right. This was a good idea."

"It's a great way to loosen up muscles," she said. "And I find it helps me to loosen up my thoughts."

That startled a laugh out of him. "Interesting way to look at life again," he said. "I really like that about you."

She smiled and said, "I like that about you too."

IAIN HADN'T REALLY expected her to come to the pool with him, yet having her here beside him felt natural. Water was his element, where he didn't need both legs to stand; and he was as much a fish as any good swimmer was, so he could hold his own. He dove into the water, then came up several times, just loving the feeling of being free. "My muscles do feel a lot better."

"Good," she said. "I'll do a few more laps, so I can work up a bit of an appetite."

"I highly doubt that's an issue," he said. "Especially if you haven't even eaten anything and already did a long walk."

"No, maybe not," she said, "but I don't get enough exercise as it is. Plus I find that I get fairly stressed in my job too, since I worry about all the animals that come through the clinic. So this is a great way to unwind."

"Well, it's not that I need to unwind," he said, "but I do need to stretch."

"How are you finding Shane to work with?"

Iain looked surprised at her question, then glanced around to see if anybody was close enough to hear them. "I think he knows his stuff," he said. "I'm not sure I always understand his instructions though."

"I hear you on that," she said, "particularly if it's cryptic."

"It's often cryptic with him. Some of the instructions are dead straight with their wording. *Lift your arm, lift this way, move this direction,*" he said with a laugh, "but a lot of it isn't clear from Shane. A lot of it is much harder to sort out."

"You can always ask him for added clarity."

"I could," he said. "But sometimes it's almost like the confusion or the lack of clarity is part of the challenge, and I'm supposed to figure it out myself. As if, by figuring it out, I'll gain an extra reward in there for having done so." He shook his head. "Listen to me," he said. "I'm daft."

At that, she burst out laughing. "I'll race you." Without giving him a chance to respond, she started toward the far side.

He immediately dove in after her, his right arm and his

left arm finding that same steady rhythm that he used to be so good at. And, by focusing on keeping his hips level and flat, he plowed right ahead of her. When she finally got to the far side, he was already there, waiting.

She laughed. "You might not be able to walk fast," she said, "but you swim like a dolphin."

"I do," he said. "It was one of the reasons I was absolutely ecstatic to find out a pool was here."

"Have you recommended this place to any of your friends yet?" She stroked out slowly, heading to the shallow end with the steps.

He looked at her in surprise and then slowly shook his head, following after her. "You know what? I haven't. But I should."

"If you think it's helping you, then you should," she said. She nodded to the far wall. "I'll do another lap." But this time, she laid on her back and just floated her way to the far end.

He floated gently beside her. "I didn't even think about it," he said. "I met a couple guys at the other hospital. They were kind of stuck, figured that this was their life."

"Kind of like you, huh?"

He looked at her in surprise, then nodded slowly. "Yeah, exactly like me. They had the same mind-set."

"Makes you wonder if you didn't have that mind-set because everybody around you also had that mind-set. And the same for them. If they don't know that there's another way to look at life and if they don't see any progress, then maybe they won't know to expect that either."

"Huh," he said. "I may have to say something to them."

"And a place like this always is interested in helping as many people as they can," she said. "I don't even know that

IAIN

they have any beds available as my own brother is on the waiting list, but if your friends need a place ... get them on too."

"Well, I definitely think a couple guys might benefit from being here," he said. "Jaden is one. Lance is another."

"Tell me about them?" They had reached the far wall to the pool again, and they both hung on, kicking with their feet to stay afloat.

"They were teammates in a mission that went bad. A roadside bomb hit them. Jaden got badly hurt, his right leg damaged, then burned, and their vehicle overturned and landed on his right shoulder. His thigh bone took a lot of shrapnel, so he has more steel pins in that leg than bones. So he's got a leg, but it's pretty useless," he said. He gave a clipped nod. "Shane might very well do something about that."

"It's possible. And what about Lance?"

"Lance got shrapnel damage too I believe, but most of his injuries are structural, more so than external. He took several hits, clipped a lip off one of the vertebrae, took off the top head of his hip bone, and his ribs are just a mess."

"But he's in a VA hospital?"

Iain nodded. "One of his ankles was smashed, and he can walk, but badly."

"Sounds like maybe Shane or somebody else here could do a lot for him as well."

"I haven't even told him how I'm doing," he said.

"And that, I think, is because you thought this new beginning, this stage of life, was what you would have to live with," she said. "So, you didn't see that you had anything to tell them."

"But I was wrong," he said slowly. "As much as I hate to

admit it, Shane's work and knowledge of his field is amazing—and, no, I'm not really seeing any change yet—but, if it doesn't happen, it won't be from Shane's lack of effort. And maybe that's why I'm holding back because I'm not seeing the progress yet."

"And how much are you holding yourself back?"

"What do you mean?" he asked, his forearms on the edge of the pool to hold him up, his tone sharp. "I'd never do something like that."

Chapter 8

HEARING THE HARSHNESS in his tone, Robin realized she was on delicate ground. "Sometimes I think that we don't always know how much we're holding ourselves back," she said slowly, swimming toward the pool ladder in the shallow end with the steps. He splashed beside her. He was willing to be mollified, but, at the same time, she could sense that he didn't really want to broach this. "Remember some of the heavy conversations we've had?"

"Sure," he said. "Sometimes they stick in my brain and just won't get out."

"Right. So, if your body is unyielding, maybe look for a place in your mind where your mind is unyielding."

His eyebrows shot up.

She shrugged. "I know I've had to do the same for myself," she said. "At one point in time, I wanted to be a vet. But I didn't want to be a vet just to be a vet. I wanted to be a vet because I felt that other people would then respect me more."

"How does that have anything to do with it?"

"Because I'd *be* someone," she said quietly. "But I had to realize that I had to be somebody inside before I could be somebody outside, at least according to somebody else."

He blinked. And then he nodded slowly. "I see what you're trying to say," he said, "but that's hardly my case."

"No, and it doesn't really seem to fit what I was trying to say either," she said. "I guess it's more a case of understanding who we are inside and realizing that what we believe about ourselves and what we believe about our progress and our own mental state affects who and what we are on the outside."

"I've said that a time or two myself," he agreed, his good mood apparently restored.

Yet somewhere along the line he hadn't got the message. She didn't really want to try again because it was just nice and friendly to be on the same page, but she could sense that something inside needed to be pried out for him to take a closer look at. "Well, I'm sure Shane has a lot to say about it too."

Iain nodded. "But, like I said, sometimes his instructions are a little convoluted."

"You mean, a little obscure?" she said with a bright smile. "Like you have to dig deep to understand what he's saying?"

Again, that sharp look came her way, and he nodded. "Something like that, yeah." He took a deep breath and said, "I think I'll get changed and then grab some food. I'm quite tired again."

"I'm sorry," she said immediately. "Was this swimming too much?"

"I don't think so," he said. "I think it was an accumulation of things over the long week."

As she watched from the pool, he made his way awkwardly to the wheelchair before he sat down with relief. "Do you want to meet at lunch?" she asked. When he hesitated, she felt her heart wrench slightly. And then she backed up immediately and said, "Actually, no, I might have a nap myself."

"Good idea," he said a little jovially, almost too happily. "I'll have a shower, and then I'll see. We have a two-hour window for eating."

"Have a good rest," she called out. And she made her way slowly to the steps in the shallow end, as she watched him leave. Leaving the pool with a heavy sigh, she grabbed her towel and sat down in the sun, despondent all of a sudden.

She shouldn't have brought it up. It was for Shane to do. Or the psychologist. Or another specialist she didn't know about. But she definitely felt a sense of Iain being locked on the inside, whether he knew it or not. And that lock had to open up and free him ever-so-slightly in order for him to see the progress that he sought.

Groaning, she realized she wasn't likely to see very much of him at all this weekend now. Somehow she'd just changed everything between them. And not in a good way. She grabbed her towel and quickly dried her hair, then wiped down her body and headed back to her apartment. She didn't even want to go in for lunch now.

Instead, she considered getting *away*-away, taking a drive into town, picking up a few things that she needed, maybe having lunch at a restaurant in town too. Just taking a complete break from here. A change of location was supposed to be good for the health of the body and the mind. And it would stop her from looking around every corner to see if Iain was there. Now that he hadn't even mentioned lunch, she knew that was a dead deal too.

At her place, she quickly dressed into casual clothing to head into town, then grabbed her purse and hopped into her vehicle and took the long drive out of the property. She needed a real break. Especially today.

INSTEAD OF GETTING dressed and heading down for food, he collapsed onto his bed, a little more worn out than he expected. Not from being physically tired. His mood was the flattest of all. Her words had struck a chord, as if she knew something he didn't, as if she'd heard something he hadn't, and as if she was trying to get him to see something he needed to see that other people saw, but he couldn't.

And, if one thing was guaranteed to piss him off, others talking behind his back would do it.

Or to think that other people knew something that he should know, but they were leaving it for him to figure out. One of his old girlfriends had been like that. His buddies had all known that she was having an affair, and they'd waited for him to figure it out. Nobody, not one of them, had nudged him in that direction to say, *Hey, take a closer look at what's going on here.*

He'd been so angry at the end of that relationship that he'd lost his friends at the same time. No, he hadn't really lost them. He'd walked away from them and realized they weren't exactly what he wanted in a friend. He knew it was the bro thing to do with some guys. To either tell all or tell nothing. And all of his bros—apparently—had been of the *tell nothing* variety. This just brought all that back up again too. And it sucked. Who needed that crap?

Now that he was collapsed on his bed, he had a two-hour window before he needed to get food. Otherwise he would have to wait again. And he hadn't had breakfast either. He closed his eyes, willing his body to relax and to drop off for a short nap. Yet, every time he closed his eyes, he saw Robin.

He should text her and see if she was willing to meet him for lunch after all. Or not. Maybe it would be better to figure out her words first. Sometimes one had to go it alone, and just no other way would make it happen. And then he remembered Bruce and how long it had been since he'd contacted Iain. Or Iain had contacted him. So Iain quickly grabbed his phone and sent his buddy a text, checking in to see how he was.

Bruce answered almost right away. **Hey, we extended our stay once again, so we just got back two days ago. How are you?**

Good, Iain typed with a smile as he responded. **Working hard. How was your trip? Successful?**

That's great. And yeah we're giving us a second chance. Had like another honeymoon after we talked things out. And you? Making progress?

That was great news on Bruce's relationship. Yet Bruce had asked that same question that Iain hated so much, and he didn't even know what to say. He tossed down his phone, punched his pillow, and closed his eyes. He willed sleep to take him under so he didn't have to answer. And, when his cell buzzed again, he bet it would be Bruce again. Iain ignored it. At least for the moment, he needed to just be alone and to figure this out for himself.

Chapter 9

R OBIN KEPT GLANCING at the purchases she'd made a couple days ago. She was getting ready for work, but her gaze kept falling on the bag with the two journals in it. She didn't know why, but something about them had caught her eye. She's been in the dollar store, amazed that items of such quality were at such a cheap price. It had been almost like fate calling to her. She wanted something like this for herself to work through some of her own issues, realizing that it had been a long time since she'd had a relationship. Also noting that she was still, although she didn't mean to, looking at every man and judging him. Until Iain.

After meeting him, talking to him, she found that things in her life had focused in on this time, on this person, and she realized that she needed to be the best that she could be too. And that was likely way too New Age–sounding for anyone. She groaned and finished brushing her hair, braiding it up nicely and then walked over to pull both journals out of the bag. They were nice and simple, almost masculine looking, but had enough of a feminine touch to make her smile. She left one on the table and reached for the matching fountain pens that she had bought too.

"This is way too quirky," she muttered. *"His and hers,* when there isn't even a him and a her yet is a little bit pushy."

But she tucked the journal into her scrubs pocket, grabbed a fountain pen, and stuffed it into her other pocket. Then she headed into work. Sometimes, in life, one had to take a chance. She may have already pushed it too far with Iain that last time they were together in the pool, but she realized that was just part and parcel of this journey. If he wasn't for her, then fine. If she wasn't for him, well, maybe not so fine. But still, it's something that she would live with. At least she hoped she could.

She worked through her morning, kept busy with a steady stream of clients and animals, from clipping toenails to changing the tomcat's way, to stitching up another cat that had gotten into a scrap, and then a dog with a boil to be lanced. By the time she was done, she called out to Stan and said, "I'm heading to lunch."

"I'll leave here in another ten minutes or so," he said, distracted. "I've got a bunch of paperwork I need to finish up."

"That's because you're the boss," she said, laughing.

"Don't remind me," he groaned.

Still smiling, she headed upstairs to the cafeteria area. She had both the journal and the pen in her pockets still. And she was still of two minds as to whether she should give it to Iain or not. She didn't want to push him or to make him feel uncomfortable, and she was likely to do both.

In the cafeteria, she took a long look around. So many people were here that it was hard to see if Iain was around or not. She walked over, got into line, and, when she got up to Dennis, she asked him, "Have you seen Iain yet?"

He was busy serving people ahead of her, but he glanced back, frowned, then shook his head. "You know what? I don't think I have." She nodded and grabbed a large salad, but he shook his head and handed her a plate with a rack of ribs.

She nodded with joy. "I'll never say no to your ribs."

"You better not," he said. "You'll make me overhaul all my recipes again."

At that, she laughed joyously. "You have the best recipes."

"Me and Grandma," he said with a nod. "We're forever trying to outdo each other."

"Keep it up," somebody said behind her. "Because we're the ones getting the benefit of it."

Dennis's big grin flashed. "Yeah, that's why I do it."

Robin moved down and grabbed a cup of coffee and a glass of water and then sat outside in the shade. She'd been craving this heat, and now it was too hot for her. She sat in her corner up against the wall and ate quietly, loving the food, especially the ribs. When she was done, she sat back and sipped her water, looking at her cold coffee. "I should remember to not get the coffee at the same time," she muttered.

Dennis had been working his way through the tables, cleaning up dishes, when he heard her and said, "I'll get you a fresh cup."

"You don't have to serve me," she said, pushing her chair back to stand up.

"But if I don't serve you," he said with a smile, "I'll be serving somebody else. And there's nothing wrong with serving you, so let me do this."

She frowned at him. "Don't you have help to clear all this?"

His grin widened. "But it's not about having help," he said. "I enjoy this. I enjoy having the time and the opportunity to talk to everybody. Collecting a few dishes won't hurt me. Not only that but it also keeps me humble." And, with that, he took off.

She sat back down, wondering, because he did have a great attitude to life, and they could all learn something about that from him. When he returned with a fresh cup of coffee, she murmured, "Thanks."

He looked at her quizzically. "Something on your mind?"

"Just contemplating the convoluted way that we look at life."

"Ah," he said. "Those kinds of questions."

"Do you ever get hung up on them?"

"I try not to," he said. "*Hung up* is not an easy way to live. You've got to keep things flowing. Otherwise you're stuck, and you can't move forward. And we're never stuck for the reason we think we are."

"I've heard that phrase used regarding anger," she said. "Like we're never angry for the reason we think we are, but I've never really understood that. I guess what you're really saying is, we have to dig deeper to find the true reasons for our actions."

He grinned and nodded. "Something like that." Then he took off again.

She sat here, wondering what her reasons were for buying the journals. She really just wanted to give Iain an outlet that, if he didn't want to talk to her, and he didn't want to talk to his psychologist, Iain could hopefully work out his own problems himself. And, with that, she stood, her coffee cup in her hand, and headed toward his room. When she knocked on the door, she got no answer. But the door itself didn't appear to be quite latched because it pushed open ever-so-slightly. She pushed it open a little bit wider and called out, "Iain, are you there?"

Still no answer. She poked her head around the door, but his bed was empty. She walked in, placed the journal and the pen on his bed, and then walked back out again. He wouldn't necessarily know it was from her, but she could always send him a message later. On that thought, she frowned, walked back over, picked up the pen, and on the first page wrote a simple note, saying, *This might help you work your way through things.* And walked out. She hated to admit it, but, as she left, her footsteps increased in speed so that she was almost running. No *almost* to it. She *was* running away.

WHEN HE GOT back from his session with Shane, he found a little leather-bound book and a pen on his bed. He looked at it as he slowly stripped off his hot and sweaty clothing. He wanted a shower and then to head out for some food. It had been a rough morning and an even rougher weekend. He couldn't help but feel like he was pushing Robin away, and that made no sense to him because he really wanted to be friends with her and potentially see if they had more than that between them.

Of all the women he'd met in his life, she was the only one who had shown any interest in who he was now. And that meant everything to him. To create a relationship in a place like this meant seeing each other with all the ugly bits and pieces showing. And also a lot could be said about a woman who could like who he was now. And maybe, if he was lucky, even fall in love with who he was right now.

It had to be a good thing because she'd be seeing him for who he truly was, instead of the image he may have projected before. And no doubt he was a very different person now than before. He'd still been a good man regardless, but he'd been cocky and sure of life, sure of what he was doing. At least he tried hard to project that image. Whereas now he'd had his feet knocked out from under him. Literally.

After his shower, he made his way back to his bed with his crutches, a towel wrapped around his hips and a second one in his hands to dry off his hair. He sat down on the side of the bed, groaning with the effort.

No doubt something was going on inside him because he could feel himself resisting Shane, resisting everything he was pushing Iain forward to.

Whether it was Iain's belief this was all a waste of time, he didn't know. He was dealing with so much pain, and he was at this point in time where it didn't seem like there was any progress, so why bother? And yet Shane was so encouraging and seemed so cheerful and happy about Iain's work that it's almost like a disconnect existed between Shane and Iain. Or at least between him and the reality of his body.

Iain didn't see any change, didn't see putting his body through all this for no change whatsoever, whereas Shane said he definitely saw an improvement. Iain couldn't see it, and he was so caught up in the pain and the torture that he was going through on a daily basis right now that it was hard to see anything optimistic. He wanted to believe Shane, but how was Iain supposed to do that?

He picked up the notebook, then opened the front cover and read the note. His eyebrows shot up. "Well, you definitely bought this for me," he murmured. He looked at the fountain pen and smiled at the old-fashioned tool. It brought back memories of school days where he'd taken a calligraphy course for an easy elective class, something that he'd really enjoyed at the time. But he wasn't much of a writer, so he hadn't really found a whole lot of purpose in it.

Putting the two gifts on his bed, he dressed slowly and grabbed his wheelchair, knowing that, in his mind, it was a cop-out, but everybody else would say, *You have to save your energy for another day.* Then he headed down for his lunch. As soon as he got into line, Dennis was there.

"Robin was looking for you earlier," Dennis said. "She has already gone back to work now though."

"I had a rough morning," Iain admitted. He looked at the food and sighed. "It all looks so good. But I don't have too much strength or energy to eat."

"You can always have one plate now, and, if you need more, you can come back," he said. "What can I get you?"

Today was Chinese day because he saw noodles and stir-fry and ribs maybe, but how did that work? Still, he went for the ribs and a big plate of stir-fry.

Dennis nodded with a big grin. "Now I approve of these choices," he said. "They might seem like they don't go together, but you've got something for the soul and something for the body here."

Iain looked at him in surprise. "I kind of like the way you separated those."

"Separated and yet joined together," Dennis said. He handed him the full plate. "You need a hand?"

"No," Iain said. "I'll be fine." And moving slower than normal, he headed his wheelchair over to the closest empty table. There, he put down his plate and dug in. He was halfway through the vegetables when he realized he'd left the ribs on the plate for later. His body did need the nutrition.

Dennis arrived soon afterward with a large glass of water and a glass of milk. "I don't think you're getting too much calcium these days," he said. "So you can get that down."

"Not a problem," he said. "I do like my milk. And I guess, if I'm not eating yogurt or cheese, milk is the easiest way to calcium, isn't it?"

"Any reason you don't like cheese or yogurt?"

"I like them both," he said. "I just don't tend to eat very much of them."

"You might want to think about changing that," he said. "I get that you're building muscle and nerves and trying to regain your strength, but your bones also have taken a huge beating."

"Well, I don't have a problem drinking milk," he said. He picked it up and had a big gulp. He really loved the taste as it slipped down his throat.

"We can add one to your meal every time now," Dennis said.

"That would be good," he said, and Dennis disappeared at that. Iain finished off his vegetables and tucked into his ribs. By the time he was done, he pushed his plate back ever-so-slightly and just relaxed. The drive had been to get here before the lunch hour closed, and, now that he'd accomplished that, he could feel the fatigue setting in. Particularly with a full belly.

He had appointments this afternoon—not with Shane, thank God—but with one of the doctors and maybe his psychologist? That would never be an appointment he looked forward to. But still, it was something he couldn't get out of. He slowly made his way back to his room, picked up the notebook, smiled, and realized he hadn't had a chance to say thank-you but tucked it into the pocket on the side of his wheelchair along with the pen. Then he grabbed his iPad and checked his schedule. With that on his lap, he headed toward the office where he was expected.

As he wheeled in, Dr. Broker looked up, smiled, and said, "How is Iain today?"

"Tired, sore, partially wondering why I'm still here," he said.

The doctor looked at him in surprise; then he glanced down at his paper file and flipped through a few pages and said, "Tell me about it."

Just like a dam had been broken, Iain explained how he'd come for this new beginning, and yet, when there was no progress and still wasn't any progress, he now realized that he needed to make peace with what he had and move on from there. So, it felt like he needed to cut short his time at Hathaway House.

"And yet everybody else seems to think you're making great progress," the doctor said, sitting back and playing with the pen in his hand.

Iain's eyes studied the pen as it twirled around and around.

"But *I'm* not seeing the progress," he said quietly.

"What are you seeing?"

"Somebody who needs to face the reality of his situation," he said. "Realize that this is it. I need to accept what I am and go on from here."

"And what are you?"

And this was just one of the reasons why Iain hated coming to these visits. The constant questions, the constant searching, the constant looking for answers and realizing that the answers he had were not necessarily the same answers everybody else had. "A disabled man who needs to find a way to lead a fulfilling life."

"Okay," the doctor said. "And what do you say about everybody else having seen progress?"

"All I see is pain," he said. "Every session with Shane hurts."

"He can ease it back," the doctor said quietly. "We don't want you in so much pain that it becomes a problem."

"It's not," he said, "but it does feel very much like I don't need to work that hard."

"So, if it's not hurting too bad, and you're still attending all his sessions, and he's seeing progress, what do you think the problem is? Or is it a case of you can't see what's right in front of you?"

Iain snorted at that. "That's quite possible," he said. "Do we ever?"

The doctor smiled. "Sometimes we don't see very clearly at all," he said. "It's interesting that I have such positive reports from everybody but you."

"I don't know about that," he said. "I did have somebody mention that maybe I had a bit of an inflexible attitude."

At that, the doctor's eyebrows rose, and the corner of his mouth twitched. "And do you think so?"

"I didn't think so," he said, "but maybe. Maybe I just had it locked in my head that the surgery would be the be-all and end-all and put me back on my feet. When I realized that it would only partially put me back on my feet and that both my legs were still weak and that I was still suffering, then I just locked down on that."

"What will you do to ease that?"

He just gave him a flat stare. "I have no idea."

The doctor nodded slowly. "Do you have a journal?"

He stared at him in surprise. "Somebody just gave me a notebook and a pen to do something along those lines."

"Maybe instead of judging yourself, just open up your mind and open up to a page and see what comes up? See how you feel about your whole situation. See if you really feel like this. See if this is a blockage or if this is something you're trying to avoid."

He frowned. "What could I possibly be trying to avoid by doing better?"

"Success," the doctor said bluntly. "So many people sabotage their own world in order to avoid becoming a success. Success is scary."

"Success would be to get my body back," Iain said harshly. "How is it I could possibly be afraid of that?"

The doctor looked him straight in the eye and said, "And that's what I want you to tell me when you come back here next week." With that, his phone rang on the desk. He picked it up and answered it.

Iain didn't even hear the conversation. He slowly wheeled himself back out and headed to his room. That was just another one of the reasons he hated these conversations. Nothing was ever clear; nothing was ever laid out. He was very much a person who, if he was told two plus two made four, then it made four.

But this kind of mental crap just seemed like an endless gamut of right and wrong answers, and it was a minefield. He didn't want to walk a minefield anymore; he wanted to know that what he was doing was right and correct and would lead exactly where he wanted it to. The trouble was, he no longer knew where that was.

Before he came here, he'd been all about making that last surgery a success. And when it hadn't been, he'd come here thinking that *this* would be the answer. But he quickly realized it wasn't the answer either. This is just who he was, where he was, and what he had to get used to. So, what the hell did the doctor mean?

Confused, irritated, and frustrated, Iain made his way to his room and realized that, with all the appointments he had had this afternoon, it was already four o'clock. He wanted desperately to have a swim, but he was edgy and didn't want to be around people.

By the time he made his way to the bed, he crashed and stared at the window. Was he afraid of success? Was being a failure more comfortable? What a horrible thought. What did being a failure mean? In a place like this, he got a lot of attention, he got a lot of help, he got a lot of assistance, and he got a lot of service from others. Was he such a poor human being that he was more concerned about receiving attention than doing things on his own?

He was used to being severely independent. What had happened to that? And was it success or really the fear of failure again? Because what if he was a success and then failed at that too? When he heard the words in his mind, he winced. He slowly picked up the journal, looked at it, groaned, then reached for the pen and started writing.

Chapter 10

S EVERAL DAYS LATER, when she kept looking out for Iain but never saw him, Robin realized just what an omega-size problem she had with him. A part of her felt lost without him here, without seeing him on a regular basis, without even just touching base and moving along that pathway of friendship and knowing that they were both together and caring about each other. No doubt she cared about him. She cared about his recovery. She cared about the life that he was leading, whether it was messed up right now or not.

By the following Friday, she was once again looking at her weekend and wondering if she should go into town and spend a day there as a break. At two o'clock in the afternoon after a particularly rough day, she'd come up to grab five minutes and a cup of coffee and a bite to eat. She had missed lunch. Dennis, when he'd seen her, had shaken his head and *tsk*ed, then had brought her a huge sandwich. It was lovely. Every vegetable she could possibly imagine being slapped between two slices of bread. Protein was in there too. She thought it was ham or maybe roast beef but also peppers and onions and lettuce and tomatoes and cucumbers and pickles, and it just went on. She smiled as she munched her way through it. It was a sandwich to make her soul smile.

When Dennis appeared a few minutes later, holding a pot of tea in his hand to deliver to a table beside her, she looked at the tea in surprise. "I never thought of having a pot of tea here."

He looked at her. "I've got lots of little pots," he said. "Any time you want a pot of tea here or to take to your office or back home, you just let me know."

"I hate to disturb you."

"Ah, ah, ah," he said. "None of that. We already went over that once. If you want something when I'm not here, the cupboard underneath the coffeepot has a few teapots just for that purpose."

She smiled, nodded, and said, "Fine, maybe I'll take a pot back with me."

"You do that," he said.

And just like that, he was gone again.

She wondered if she could do the job that he did and still have the same attitude. It was a job that offered so much pleasure to so many people, and yet much of the world looked down on it. They'd say he was just bussing tables or whatever derogatory term that people could slap on him at the time. And yet something was almost spiritual about what he did. She didn't even mean it in a necessarily religious way but didn't know how else to describe it.

It's as if he passed out joy and advice freely, and everybody felt better that they had seen him that day. Kind of like the way she felt when she saw Iain. The trouble was now, she hadn't seen him in days, not since she'd given him the journal. She had received no response from him, no acknowledgment, nothing. He hadn't sought her out nor had he found a way to thank her over the phone, if he even knew how to find her. But then he could have called the veterinarian clinic at any time.

Depressed, she finished off her sandwich, pushed her

chair back, and stood. She carried the dirty dishes to the waiting trolley and headed down the back stairs to see the horse called Appie and the llama named Lovely. Both of them raced over to visit. She scratched the big horse and the beautiful little llama, enjoying the chance to connect with them.

When she looked across the hill, she could see one of the men lying in the tall grass. He was beside Hoppers. *Hoppers was free?* She frowned as she watched, but the rabbit didn't appear to be bothered about going anywhere. A lot of fresh green grass surrounded him, and he was nibbling and nudging his way over each blade. Stan must have let Hoppers go outside with this man in order for Hoppers to be here, and that surprised her too. Stan didn't do that lightly. She wandered closer and then recognized Iain.

He looked at her, smiled, and said, "There you are."

She reached out a hand, palm up, and said, "I've been here all along."

"Nope," he said, an odd note to his tone. "I came down to find you, but you weren't there."

"Ah," she said. "I missed lunch, so I went to grab a bite of something to get through the afternoon."

"I bet Dennis didn't let you get away with that without making you something special, did he?"

She laughed. "Absolutely not. Our Dennis is so very special."

"He cares," Iain said simply. "I've come to understand that that's all it is. He cares. He comes from the heart."

She sat down beside him, watching as Hoppers meandered another few inches over. "Stan let you bring Hoppers out?"

"I think he asked me to bring him out specifically," Iain

said drily. "Apparently you're still looking for a pen for this guy."

"We'd love to leave him loose, but he's just as likely to end up on the road and get hit by a car than anything."

"He's pretty big for a predator to take on, which would be the normal danger we'd expect of a rabbit."

"Yep, but anything big enough that could take him down would get several good meals out of him," she admitted.

He just grinned, reached down, and gently rubbed Hoppers's back. Hoppers didn't seem to mind in the least. "I never had a rabbit as a pet," he said. "Never really considered it."

"And would you now?"

"I'm not so sure," he said. "But he's definitely peaceful to be around. Again, kind of like Dennis. They come from joy."

She loved that. "I hope you wrote that down in your journal."

"What, that Hoppers comes from joy?" he asked, laughing.

"I think that we should strive to come from joy," she said quietly. "If I end up learning that lesson before I die, I'll consider this life one well-lived."

"Hadn't thought about that," he said. He looked over at Lovely and Appie, the llama and the horse wandering toward them and said, "They all do though, don't they?"

"They do. They're full of forgiveness. They're full of joy. They're full of just being who they are," she said. "I have to admit, I'm jealous."

"Why? What part of you isn't good enough?" he asked with a sideways look.

"The insecure, scared-to-brave-the-whole-new-world me," she said. She hopped to her feet and dusted the dirt off her butt. "As much as I'd like to stay here and talk, I'm expected to work this afternoon."

"I took the afternoon off," he said. "I just thought maybe you'd meet me at the pool at say four o'clock or whenever you're done."

She hesitated, looked at him, looked at the pool, and then nodded. "It's a date." And she disappeared back inside.

IAIN WATCHED HER go, a smile playing on his lips. Hardly a date but, hey, he'd take what kind of a date facsimile this could be anyway. He should have thanked her for the journal but hadn't. He'd have to remember to do so when she came back out. He was feeling kind of odd and spacey himself.

Once he'd started writing in the journal, it seemed like he couldn't stop. Now he'd covered pages and pages. He didn't know if that was good or bad, but it was something that he seemed unable to change. Finally he got up, his thoughts heavy, and looked down at Hoppers. Iain was wondering what to do about the rabbit, when Stan called out to him. He looked over, and Stan walked toward him. "I'll bring him back to his hutch."

"It seems like such a shame," he said. "It's a perfect pasture for him."

"I know, but he's not exactly house-trained, and he won't stay close by without a fence of some kind. And we don't want to put him in with the horses either."

"Right. Gotta keep him safe," he said. He watched as Stan crouched and picked up Hoppers. Hoppers made absolutely no effort to get away and instead cuddled into Stan's neck. Iain grinned. "You're really blessed to be doing the work you do."

"I am," he said. "I think that's one of the joys of being in this world. We get to make choices. I'm happy to say I made a good choice." With that, he headed back inside.

And that left Iain wondering if everybody in this place was full of those heavy New Age comments. Because of all the choices he'd made, he'd been absolutely ecstatic with his. To go into the navy and making it into the SEALs had been his best day. But now? Now he had a whole pile of new choices. None of which he felt qualified for. Or none involved where his joy of being in this world was, like Stan talked about. And that brought Iain back around to the doctor's question about whether Iain was afraid of being a success.

Maybe the question really was if he was afraid of being a failure.

Slowly, his heart heavy, he made his way back to his room on his crutches, and, as soon as he sat on his bed, he reached for the journal and started writing again. And again, the words just flowed. Some of it didn't make any sense and didn't seem to matter as his hand flew across the page. He realized he would run out of pages before too many days had gone by. He made a concerted effort to write neater, smaller, only to give it up because it seemed to impinge on his ability to let the words flow. The deluge was everything from his childhood to the problems he'd had in the navy to waking up in the hospital. None of it was very important alone— barring the event leading to the hospital—but all of it mattered.

He shrugged. "That makes no sense."

But it did because individually they weren't big for the most part, but, when the memories were added in the mix, they became one much bigger issue. Because of what he was doing right now. He was trying to figure out just what he wanted to do with his life, something that he hadn't had to do ever because he had always wanted to join the navy. And now he was no longer in active service but had money to go back to school, if he wanted to, and the world was wide open to him. And yet Iain had no idea what to do. And he realized that really what was going on—maybe for the first time in his lifetime—was fear of making the wrong choice, which he was pretty darn sure was really his fear of being a failure again.

Somehow, in that crooked, twisted mind of his, he'd decided that the accident had been his fault, ending up where he was—which was also his fault—and not having a foot. His fault too. He shouldn't have taken that damn route. If he'd gone the other way, none of this would have happened.

He'd come here *not* planning to be a failure, but he hadn't planned to be a success either.

And somehow that seemed important. He searched Google for *planning to be a success* and *not planning to be a success* and found many videos and blogs on it. He picked up his laptop, sat down, and listened to some of the recordings. Several touched him and highlighted his situation.

So much of it was about goal setting. His goal had been to get here to Hathaway House and to leave that old persona behind. Which he had done. But then he'd been in a state of existing, adjusting to what this life was all about here. He'd thought he'd been adjusting to life as it was physically now and would carry on. And Shane had kind of blown that because, according to Shane, there had been a ton of progress.

If there was this ton of progress, then Iain had to adjust again and do what? He would have to adapt. He stared out the window of his room, wondering why adapting and seeing progress would hurt. And he was pretty sure it was because he was afraid. Afraid that he'd still be this person who had to adjust and to adapt to whatever he had.

Maybe the bar would be up that tiny little bit, but it wouldn't be enough to make a difference. He wouldn't ever be whole.

He took a slow deep breath as that realization hit him. Because, of course, he would *never* be whole again. He'd lost a part of himself. He'd lost part of his leg, and somehow losing a piece of his physical body had meant that he'd lost a whole chunk of his emotional body too. Part of his soul. And that was wrong. Because, although that physical piece was missing, there was no reason that the rest of his person couldn't go on as being deemed whole and happy. But somehow he got sucked into believing that, because he was missing a foot and part of his shin, all of him was missing something. He hadn't planned to be a success—which meant "whole" in his mind—and, therefore, he was a failure because he had failed to plan for being a success, even without his foot.

With his head shaking, he looked at the clock and realized it was four. He really didn't want to go down to the pool now though. His mind was too busy churning on everything rolling through it. But he also knew that he felt a sense of grounding when he was around Robin. A sense of calmness and peace surrounded her, and, right now, with this hurricane going on in his heart and his mind, he really needed those things.

Slowly and carefully, he got dressed in his loaned swim trunks, grabbed a towel, and then moved himself to the wheelchair and headed to the pool to meet up with her. He just hoped that they could avoid too many heavy conversations. His heart was already struggling. And it shouldn't be that way. When he got to the pool, he found her already there, sitting on the edge, leaning back on her hands, facing the sun. She was just resting, her eyes closed, enjoying being done with a hard day's work, facing the weekend, and ready to spend some time with him. And he realized that, once again, he hadn't been planning to succeed with her either. He'd just been putting in time, hoping that maybe something would happen. But he hadn't taken any concrete steps to actually see that it did happen.

He sighed and slipped quietly into the water, then swam toward her.

She didn't even open her eyes when she asked, "Hey, how you doing?"

"How did you know it was me?"

"I recognized the heavy sigh," she said with a bubbling laugh, opening her eyes.

He looked at her in surprise.

She smiled, nodded, and said, "You're going through some heavy-duty stuff these days. Heavy sighs are part of that."

"So, when I solve some of these big issues, do they stop?"

"I think so," she said, cocking her head to the side. "I actually think they do."

He grinned. "Are you ready to do some swimming, or are you're just going to sit there like a sunny mermaid?"

Chapter 11

"**I** NEED TO do some swimming," Robin said. "I get so little exercise these days." She slipped into the water beside him, and together they started doing laps. As a Friday after work went, this one was pretty peaceful. She'd had a long, hard day, but she was looking forward to the weekend. Iain appeared to be working his way through some stuff, and that was always good. She didn't want to push, and she certainly didn't want to open up the topic, but he appeared to be almost incapable of relaxing. "Maybe we should just lie in the sun and rest for a bit," she said.

He gave her a distracted look and then nodded. "That sounds good." They made their way up poolside, and she watched as he sat on the edge and grabbed his towel, then dried off his good leg and used the ladder to hop up. Then he used the railing to cross the few steps to one of the loungers.

"Would it help if I brought the wheelchair closer?"

He looked at it, then shrugged and said, "I can get it later."

She studied its location and said, "I'll move it, just in case." She unlocked the bottom of the wheels and brought it back over, then parked it beside him and crashed on the lounger beside him.

"Does it bother you?"

She tried hard to figure out what the question really meant because she wasn't sure what he was asking. She looked at him and said, "The wheelchair?"

"That I have a disability."

She smiled, loving the fact that he didn't say he was disabled. "We all have a disability," she said. "Sometimes it's physical, and everybody can see it, and sometimes it's internal, and nobody can see it. But none of us are perfect. We're all dealing with something."

He looked at her in surprise and laughed. "I hadn't seen it from that point of view," he said. "And lately it seems like all I do is think about some pretty heavy-duty issues."

"We all do," she said. "Or at least I do. There are definitely good things and bad things in life right now."

"Did you buy yourself a journal too? And thank you for that, by the way."

"You're welcome," she said with a pleased smile. "I was really surprised when I found them."

"I haven't used a fountain pen since I was in high school," he said.

"I never used one before," she said. "It's taking a bit to get used to."

"I'm enjoying it."

"I am too," she said, "but I tend to leave blotches."

He laughed at that. "Me too, but whatever."

"So it's helping?"

"I don't know if it's helping or not," he admitted, "but I'm certainly filling the pages."

"Good," she said. "Then it's helping."

"Maybe, the words sound like the ranting and raving of a crazy mind," he said with a laugh.

"It still helps to get it out," she said. She shifted under

the sun and closed her eyes. "I don't want to sleep out here because that sun will turn me to a fried crisp very quickly, but I am tired." Just then she yawned.

"Go to sleep," he said. "I'll wake you in ten minutes."

She thought about it, nodded, and said, "Okay, but make sure it's not any longer than that."

"No," he said. "I'll even set my watch for you."

She shifted, laid her head down, and let the sun take her under. At least she thought she was under. It seemed like two minutes and not ten minutes when he leaned across and patted her hand gently. She opened her eyes to find him right there, close to her, and she smiled. "Has it been ten minutes already?"

"It has, Sleeping Beauty," he said, his voice thick with emotions.

Something electric passed between the two of them. She reached out and gently stroked his cheek. "Thank you," she murmured. "I wouldn't want to get burned out here."

"Then I suggest we move our chairs so that we're in the shade now." And he drew back, breaking the moment.

The fact that the moment had even existed, that it was something now in her memory, something to smile about, something to cherish, was special all in itself. She got up, stretched, shifted the chaise longue so it sat in the shade, then looked at him and said, "Maybe we should move yours here too."

He nodded, shifted onto his good leg, and stood. This was the first she'd taken a good close-up look at his leg since his arrival here. It was all she could do to hold back her shock. But he must have noticed.

He looked at her face, looked down at his leg, and in a harsh voice said, "It's not very pretty, is it?" And he slammed himself back down onto the chair in the shade.

"It doesn't matter if anything's pretty about it or not," she said. "It's a marvel of human engineering."

Startled, he stared at her.

She looked at him with a flat expression on her face and said, "Did you expect me to be turning away in revulsion?"

He shrugged. "Yeah," he said. "I did. It's pretty ugly."

"I'm not so superficial," she said quietly. "A lot in life is ugly, but it doesn't mean that there isn't something good about it." She sat down in her chaise and studied his leg. "I mean, I just can't believe how much work they did to actually rebuild that leg for you. It must have been quite the process."

"Multiple surgeries. Some of the muscle off my buttocks, some off my back," he said. "It was kind of amazing. They took a little bit from my amputated foot and shin as well."

She studied both, seeing multiple scars. "It's still amazing," she said. "The fact is, that leg is functional, and it's definitely bigger than when I first saw you."

He looked at her, looked at his leg, and said, "Yeah?"

"Yeah," she said. "Did they take any measurements when you first arrived?"

He frowned, thought about it, and then slowly nodded. "I think they did. I just don't remember what the numbers were."

"Should be in your file somewhere, I'd think," she said. "They do that. They take measurements and weights to see how some of their patients handle surgeries and whether they're building up and getting stronger. And when the bone's involved, of course, the bone regrows around the damaged area. But with muscles, it's not quite the same process."

"No," he said. "And I'm getting more adjusted to the look of the leg."

"You should," she said. "Not only is it your leg and it's the one you've got and have been blessed to have, but it also looks more like a human leg now than a chicken leg." Her voice was cheerful, and she couldn't stop herself from bursting into laughter.

IAIN SETTLED BACK and studied her. "And that's what I meant earlier. Does it bother you?"

"No, it doesn't bother me," she said. "Except that I see the ingenuity of the human condition. I see the miracles of modern medicine. And I see the incredible courage of the human spirit. Don't ever be ashamed of that."

She stared directly into his eyes. "Hold your head high and ignore anybody who criticizes you. They haven't been through the wars, like you have. They don't have any right to the inner wounds and to the war wounds that you have. Wear them as badges of honor," she said. "And tell anyone else who makes a negative comment to stuff it."

He burst out laughing at that. "Out in the real world, I'd spend my entire day doing that some days."

She grinned. "I guess that's true. I just don't know why people have to be so mean. And why these mean people have time for that kind of crap."

"Exactly," he said with a laugh. "I certainly don't. I'm too busy trying to rebuild a life."

"Good," she said. "I'm really glad to hear that."

Chapter 12

S EVERAL DAYS LATER, with both of them slowly spending a bit more time together, she was sitting down alone for breakfast when Shane approached. She looked up, smiled, and said, "Hey, how is the boss?"

"Hardly the boss," he said, pulling out the chair and sitting down with a cup of coffee.

He looked tired. She frowned. "Are you spending too much time on your patients and forgetting to look after yourself?"

He looked up, then smiled, and said, "Well, I wouldn't have thought so, but it has been known to happen a time or two."

"Absolutely," she said. "How is Iain doing?"

"I was going to ask you that," he said in a teasing voice. "Seems like you two are really hitting it off."

"Maybe," she said. "I know he's got some issues, and I would like to see him get a little further down that path."

"Does his issue bother you?"

She shook her head and smiled. "No, but I don't want to hold him back either. I don't want him to be stopping short or shortchanging himself because I'm here." Shane stared at her in surprise, and she shrugged. "Just something I've been wondering about."

"Sounds like you need to shut off that part of your

brain," he said.

"Maybe," she said, "but he doesn't see his progress. I did ask if you guys had taken any measurements. And he said yes, but he didn't remember them. I told him to ask you about them. Or, at least if I didn't, he should." She laughed. "We get into such deep conversations that sometimes I forget what's been said."

"It's a good idea though," he said. "I was planning on taking more in the next few days anyway."

"Good," she said. "It might help him see that progress better."

He nodded. "What about you? You staying around now that you've been on the job what, four or five months?"

"I love it here," she said with a smile, "but it's not been quite three months, yet it seems like I've always been here."

He leaned forward and said, "And what if he leaves?"

She winced. "Right," she said. "That's not such a happy thought."

"Yet that's what we want for him."

She nodded slowly. "I guess it depends on what he ends up doing for himself."

"Exactly. And where," he said with a smile. He looked up and nodded toward the doorway. "Speaking of which, there he is."

She twisted, saw him, lifted a hand, and waved. "I guess those future discussions are something that might need to be discussed sooner than later."

"Something is there between you. It might help both of you if you could get a few of those details worked out."

She laughed. "Doesn't mean any of the details are ready to be worked out," she said.

"Maybe, but getting some of that stuff out of your head

will help you to not worry so much."

"Me or him?"

Shane stood as Iain approached. Shane looked at her with an insightful gaze and said, "How about for both of you?" And then he smiled at Iain and said, "Hey, Iain, how you doing?"

"Well, it's Tuesday. I made it through Monday," he said. "So, maybe we're doing okay."

"Maybe," Shane said. "We'll take a bunch of measurements here this Friday and see how your progress is doing."

Iain nodded. "That's a good idea," he said. "Maybe then I can see something tangible."

"Ah," Shane said with a smile. "Here I thought they were very tangible. But you're looking for data, aren't you?"

Iain shrugged. "Maybe," he said. "I hadn't realized how much I was looking for proof."

"Another very interesting and valid point," Shane said. "I'll see you later today." And he took off.

Iain sat down slowly, then put his crutches to the side.

She looked at the crutches and smiled and said, "You must be feeling better today."

"Tuesdays are often rough," he said. "After the weekend, Shane gets ahold of me on Monday and doesn't let go. On Tuesdays then, I tend to pay for it, but yesterday wasn't too bad."

"I think, like everything," she said, "it takes six weeks to get used to any routine. I'd sign up for a yoga course, and, for the first six weeks, that instructor would twist my body into a pretzel and force it into all kinds of movements, and I'd pay for it in pain for weeks. Then, all of a sudden, around six weeks, it'd be like my body would automatically form that pretzel without being forced into it, and I wouldn't have the pain afterward."

He chuckled. "Same for any new gym routine too," he admitted. "So maybe I'm finally adjusting to being here."

"How long has it been?"

"A couple months," he said easily. "But let's not forget I set myself back at the very beginning."

"Yes, you did," she said. "Doesn't matter though. There's no back. There's no right. There's no wrong. You're where you're at right now, and it sounds like maybe there is some progress."

"Maybe," he said. "Mentally as well. Thank you for that journal. I know I thanked you once, but I didn't really realize at the time how much it has helped. But it has."

"Good," she said. "I've barely taken the time to write in mine."

"I was wondering if you can get me a second one."

She stared at him in surprise, but, with a pleased smile, she nodded. "Absolutely. When do you need it?"

He shrugged. "I'm probably fine for the rest of this week."

That startled a laugh out of her. "That must be an interesting read."

"Nobody will read it," he said. "I plan to rip out all the pages and tear it apart afterward, maybe in a fire ceremony."

"I've heard that has helped a lot of people too," she said.

"It still feels a bit stupid though."

"It's not about feeling stupid. Remember?"

"I know," he said. "It's about doing what needs to be done. Getting my thoughts on paper."

"Exactly." She smiled and said, "Now I have to head to work."

"And I'll go get breakfast," he said with a laugh.

And that's the last she saw of him for a couple days. She did manage to get into town midweek and returned to the dollar store, but the same journal wasn't there anymore. Frowning, she headed to several other stores, but she wasn't impressed with those journals at all. She went to a discount store. As she wandered through, she asked one of the clerks. She took her to a large stationary section. There, she found two black journals. They weren't necessarily the same quality or the same type, and they were certainly double the price she'd paid last time, but she bought one for him.

As she headed back to Hathaway House, she put it on the seat beside her and drove all the way to her apartment. There, she grabbed Iain's newest journal and headed out for dinner, but she saw no sign of him. Frowning, she worried about that, but she ate her dinner and then headed down the hallway to his room.

When she knocked on his door, he called out, "Come in."

She opened the door and poked her head around. "Hey. You up for some company?"

He groaned. "I should be, but I'm pretty tired today."

She held out the journal and said, "I just wanted to give you this."

His face lit up. "Thanks," he said.

"It's the only color I could find," she said.

"Color doesn't matter," he said. "Now that I'm into this groove, I feel like I need to just keep pouring everything out."

"Understood," she said. And, with a smile, she turned and walked to the doorway. She stopped though and asked, "Did you get any dinner?"

He shook his head. "Honestly, I'm too tired."

"How about I pick you up something and bring it back?" He hesitated, and she shook her head. "Remember? I'm just being of service, like Dennis. It's not the same as having to ask for help."

"Hardly," he said, "but, … if you could find me something simple, … not too much though."

She nodded and headed back down, then snagged Dennis and told him that Iain was laid up in bed and asked if Dennis could put a plate together for Iain. And before long, she had a full tray. She was afraid it might be too much food, but he didn't have to eat it all, if that was the case. She made her way back and had left the door open so she could nudge it with her foot, then she headed inside and placed the tray down.

"You asleep?" she asked him softly. As his chest rose and fell, she realized he really had crashed on her. She went to lift the covers and realized he was holding the first journal open with his pen. She took the pen from his fingers, placed it down nearby, picked up the journal, and went to close it but caught sight of her name.

She warred with herself to not read it and then read one line that had been underlined, and it said, *Future uncertain*. Frowning, she quickly closed his journal, put it down on the table, pulled the covers up over his shoulders, and left. She closed the door behind her, wondering just what was going on in that mind of his. She really wanted to read his journal but knew that wasn't fair or right. It was intrusive and would probably just confuse the matter because, like he said, it had been ramblings, words that needed to get out of his head. But that mention of her was hard to let go of.

She headed back to her apartment, confused and more than a little worried about just what their future was.

IAIN WOKE THE next morning to see a tray of food sitting beside him and remembered asking her to get him something. "Crap," he said. He was covered in a blanket too, which meant that she'd returned with the food, covered him up, put his journal and pen to the side, and left him here. He sighed and shifted his body, wondering at just how tired he really was. He'd made all sorts of progress last night as he had sifted through some of his feelings of insecurity and failure from his childhood.

They weren't even big issues, but they were momentous enough for him to remember, and he'd worked hard at releasing them and forgiving everybody involved, including himself. Now he just felt fairly emotionally overwrought. He got up and managed a hot shower. And, by the time he was dressed, he was feeling fine but emotionally tired. He made his way to and in his wheelchair and headed to breakfast.

As soon as he saw him, Dennis asked how was dinner.

He shook his head. "I'm sorry," he said. "I was asleep when Robin brought it back."

Dennis nodded. "I'll collect the tray later," he said. "Sleep is always the best answer."

Iain realized he should have brought it back with him. "And I was obviously too tired this morning to think about bringing the tray back myself," he said. "I'm sorry. I could have saved you a trip."

"Have to get my exercise somehow," Dennis said with a big smile. With that, he served up breakfast and carried it over to the deck to eat. By the time Iain was done and made it to his first appointment, Shane was sitting at the computer, waiting for him.

"We'll run through a bunch of tests and do a progress report," Shane said. "It's been eight weeks since you've been here, so it's perfect timing." He quickly took a bunch of measurements from Iain's legs, waist, hips, and had him stand. Then he took a bunch of photographs, the same ones that he had done as part of his initial intake analysis and then, when he sat him down, Shane said, "So let's go through some of these."

"Is there anything to go through?" Iain asked.

"There definitely is," Shane said. "Take a look." And there in the file were his stats.

Iain realized that his thigh—his chicken thigh—had gained three and a half inches in bulk around the top of the thigh and a good two inches around the base of it. He stared at that data in shock. He looked down at his leg and said, "You know what? Robin did say something about my thigh looking a lot better now, but I hadn't seen it."

"Well, this'll help," Shane said. And he brought up two pictures side by side on the monitor.

Iain stopped, stared, sucked his breath back, and went, "Wow."

"Now you look me in the eye and tell me," Shane said, "when you look at these two pictures of your thigh—when you first arrived and your thigh now, today—has there been any progress?"

Something inside had broken free, something needing to crack and to collapse around him, releasing something he didn't quite understand. But he could feel hope. He could feel a sense of life and a sense of something inside himself bursting free as he stared at those images. He smiled a huge grateful smile, a beaming smile. "I don't know how you did it," he said, "but that's not just progress. That's incredible progress." Shane lifted a high five, and Iain slapped it hard and said, "Whoa, can we repeat that?"

"I fully intend to," Shane said. "I think it's important that you take a look at this." And he opened another folder he had on his desk, then held up two pictures. One was a mangled-up leg, and one was a healthy, strong leg.

"And whose are those?"

"Another patient who was here about six months ago," he said. "This was his before, and this was his after photo."

Iain stared at them, and he could feel tears in his eyes. "Why didn't you show me that when I first arrived?"

"Because it was too far in the future for you to fully grasp," he said. "But now that you can see this much progress in your own body, I can make sure that you get this as your end result."

And, for that, Iain would give anything. "If you can do that," he said, "you're a miracle worker."

Shane grinned. "Not me," he said. "*You*. I don't do this. *You* do this."

Chapter 13

MAYBE ROBIN HAD picked up something from Iain's mood, but it seemed like her life was off today too. When Dani called her into her office at the end of the day, Robin was surprised and worried. As she walked in, she sat down with a hard *thump*. "Problems?"

Dani looked up at her in surprise and then laughed. "I'm so sorry," she said. "No, there's absolutely no problem." She shook her head. "I keep forgetting that I'm the boss, and often people get nervous when I ask to speak with them."

"Especially when we've had such a hard week downstairs," Robin explained. "Stan is beside himself with all the paperwork."

Immediately Dani frowned. "Does he need help down there?"

"I don't think so. We've got one of the gals on holiday, and she handles most of the bookkeeping."

Dani rolled her eyes. "We all need holidays, but covering for people off on holidays can be a real pain."

"So, is there a reason why you called me up?"

She laughed. "There is. I wanted to ask you a personal question." She hesitated and looked at the door. "You mind shutting the door, please?"

Robin hopped up, closed the door, sat back down again, and said, "Does this have something to do with Iain?"

Dani's eyebrows rose. "Direct. I like that," she said. "Yes, it does."

"I hope it's okay that we formed a friendship," Robin said anxiously. "I never honestly gave it a thought."

"It absolutely is okay," Dani said reassuringly. "The only time I intervene is if I can see that it's slowing down or completely stopping one of the patient's healing. As long as everything is moving forward, then I don't have any objection."

"Is there a problem with Iain?"

"No," she said. "I think he's had a breakthrough."

"Well, that would be wonderful," Robin said emphatically. "And I think it's long overdue."

Dani's eyebrows rose. "Tell me more."

Then, suddenly realizing that she was talking about Iain behind his back, Robin sank into her chair and said, "I'd rather not. It feels odd."

"Understood," Dani said. "As much as I'd like to know what you know, I do respect that you don't want to talk about him. I just wondered how serious it was on your part."

"I don't know," Robin said. "We haven't got that far, but I really like him."

"Good," Dani said. "According to Shane, you seem to be a strong motivator for Iain."

"And I guess that's a good thing, providing we're all on the same page."

"Exactly," Dani said with half a smile. "Which is why I'm asking how serious it is on your part. I'd hate to see him have a setback anywhere in the next six weeks while we sort out how far he can actually go."

"But neither do I want to be something that I'm not in order to keep his progress going," Robin said slowly. "So I guess it's a good thing that I really like the man, huh?"

Dani burst into a bright and light laughter, filling the room and spreading beyond. Robin had spent a fair bit of time with Dani since she'd arrived here but never really on a one-to-one basis. People were always around Dani. Robin really liked the woman and loved her heart. "I'll tell you one of the odd things about Iain was we get into these really philosophical questions," she said. "Or maybe more like New Age healing kind of questions. I bought him some journals to write in."

"I saw those," Dani said in surprise. "I wondered where he'd gotten them. Of course everybody is allowed to have stuff like that, but often I offer journals for people, if they need them."

"Well, the first one," Robin said, "I just picked up at the dollar store, and he filled that one fairly quickly, which really surprised me. So then I got him a second one."

"It's a lovely gift," Dani said warmly. "It's not just the gift itself but it's the opening up of a doorway that allows somebody to help heal his own problems."

"I thought it might help him. Me too. In a way, I'm used to being alone, and I find that sometimes interacting with somebody on a personal level makes me feel awkward," she tried to explain.

"A long time since your last relationship?"

"Yes, certainly. A few months before I came here," she said. "And definitely a relationship that wasn't healthy. So I was grateful for a chance to leave and to get a start fresh."

"As long as starting fresh isn't ..." And then her voice fell away.

Robin nodded. "As long as starting fresh isn't trying to hide, you mean?"

Dani nodded with relief in her eyes. "Yes," she said. "Then I realized how personal I was being, and it wasn't my job to poke at you."

At that, Robin started to chuckle. "Versus poking at the patients here?"

"Exactly," Dani said. "You're not one of the patients coming here to grow and to learn."

"But I don't see how anybody can't grow and learn while here," she said. "Just so much healing is going on around us that it's almost impossible to stay unaffected."

"Exactly," she said. "But, in an odd way, sometimes you can become dulled to it because there's just so much of it. We see the same thing over and over again. Yet it's always different. It always has a different face, always has a bit of a different twist, as it's individualized per patient. But you become almost accepting that it's happening, and then you become blasé about it."

"Maybe for you," Robin said. "I haven't been here that long or had the same interactions that you have had. I deal with the animals downstairs, and it often amazes me just how much healing they accomplish all on their own, without any of this head stuff. Whereas we humans make life so difficult and so complicated. If we could get out of our own heads, our bodies know exactly what to do."

Dani stopped, stared at her for a long moment, and then nodded. "I agree completely," she said. "It's one of the reasons I love my horses, and I love the freedom of when they can just run and go for miles. Sometimes I used to do that to get away from my problems and my troubles, whereas the horses didn't seem to have that same issue. They just ran because it was beautiful to run, and it felt good. It was freeing, and they loved the sensation. I loved it too, but, for me, it was more—at the time—a case of needing to get away. Now I ride because I'm in the same space as the horses. I love the freedom it offers me and just the sense of enjoying the wind in my face and their muscles underneath my legs." She gave her a smile.

"Iain misses horses," she said abruptly.

Dani stopped, looked at her, and then gave a clipped nod. "I think I remember something about that from when he first arrived." She shuffled papers on her desk. "We could also talk to him about doing some horse therapy."

"I think he would absolutely love anything that would get him back to horses, even if it just means going out for a couple hours."

"Has someone told him that he's allowed to be down there at the stables or in the outlying pastures?" Dani asked with a frown.

"I'm not sure," Robin said. "I think it would be a wonderful gift for him."

"Maybe I'll go talk to him now," Dani said. "I've got a bunch of other horses coming in. They're traveling through the countryside and needed a place to unload to give the horses a rest from the long trip."

"Well, that will be nice. Are they friends of yours?" she asked curiously.

"Yes, they are," she said. "I've got twelve gooseneck trailers coming in, hauling up to forty-eight show horses."

Robin's jaw dropped.

Dani laughed. "There'll be quite a few horses to see, if you're around this weekend," she said. "Obviously we need to be extra careful. The horses are allowed to have their own space, but I'll be moving all our animals over at least one or two pastures." At this, she looked out her window, as if she hadn't decided exactly what she would do yet. "But I think maybe, if Iain's around, we can get him down, at least in the wheelchair, where he can visit with the horses a little bit."

"I'm sure he'd love that. I caught him out with Hoppers on the lawn here not too long ago," she said with a laugh. "He just wanted to see Hoppers out of his cage and running free for a bit."

"And, whether he knows it or not, that's synonymous with how he feels himself," Dani said with a smile. "Thanks for reminding me about his love of horses. I'll see if I can come up with something."

"I don't know if he's seen any of the progress that we all see yet," Robin said, "but if he has, maybe as a reward?"

"Interesting," Dani said. "Rewards are something that we try not to hand out because we think every day showing up for the rehab deserves a reward, and, therefore, very quickly they almost become meaningless. But maybe as a treat."

"Same diff," she said. "Not quite, I know, but it does effectively address what I was hoping for."

"Let me see if I can swing this so soon," she said. "It'll be a busy weekend, so I don't know if I can make anything happen at this point."

"Not necessary either," Robin said, standing up. "Just nice to know that maybe he can make some time for himself down there."

IAIN HAD TO admit he was feeling incredibly emboldened and hopeful after his Friday afternoon session with Shane. He'd gone looking for Robin to share the good news. She had been super-excited, even though she had already seen his progress that day by the pool. They'd had dinner together, and then he'd kind of crashed, his energy cycling downward, and she'd left him at his room soon afterward. Now, it was Saturday morning, and he heard sounds of large vehicles pulling in. It surprised him, and he got up and got dressed, then made his way out in his wheelchair onto the deck of the cafeteria and watched as several huge horse trailers came in.

Dennis came up to his side. "Dani is up to it again," he said with a big smile. He handed Iain a cup of coffee. "You'll need this."

"What's going on?" he asked.

"A large group of show horses are moving across the state," he said. "Dani offered a couple pastures today and tonight, for the horses to get out of the trailers. They can only travel so many hours before they need to be let out again."

"Wow," Iain said. And in a nice and orderly fashion, all of the big trucks and trailers pulled up beside each other.

Dani was already there, talking to the drivers, and she was opening up pastures. And before long, at least forty horses were unloaded and moved into the fields. Two were pastures, several cross-fenced, and the horses immediately took to the grass, which was pretty high, some eating, and some kicking it up, dancing to be out of the trailers.

He stared in amazement. "Dani's heart is really big, isn't it?"

"The biggest," he said. "Anytime she can help others, she does, particularly when it comes to animals."

"I wish I could be down there," he said.

"I don't know if the actual trucks will stay around. I imagine some will head into town. This is for the horses and not so much for the people," Dennis said with a laugh. "At least I haven't been given any instructions that I'll have an extra thirty-six-odd people today."

A note of worry was present in his voice, and Iain looked up at him and laughed. "Would it matter to you if you did?"

Dennis thought about it, shrugged, and said, "Nah, we always have leftovers anyways."

Iain nodded. "That's what I expected," he said. "It seems like there's always lots of food at your table."

The two men continued to watch the horses, and, sure enough, several of the vehicles filled up with people and disconnected from the trailers and headed back out of the parking lots again. Some were staying, and it looked like four people were hanging around to keep an eye on the animals. Which, considering the amount of horse flesh out there, made a lot of sense. And yet, for all Iain could see, a lot more than four were needed to mind some forty horses.

At one point in time, he saw Dani looking up in his direction. He waved to her, and she waved enthusiastically back. Within about ten minutes, she marched toward him, standing under the deck. "Do you want to come see them?" she asked, her face alight with joy and excitement.

He hesitated. "Do you think the wheelchair will spook them? I don't have my crutches with me."

"Nah," she said. "These guys have been flown all over the world. They're used to all kinds of travel, including scooters and wheelchairs."

He nodded. "I'll head down the elevator and come out the bottom."

"I'll walk with you," she said and met him soon afterward. "Have you had any experience with horses?"

"Lots," he said, "when I was younger. I haven't ridden

since my accident."

"Well, you might go for a ride today, if you want," she said. "I probably have to give Shane a call first though."

"Well, how about you don't call Shane," he said, "and you let me go for the ride anyway?"

She stared at him for a long moment. "How's your back?"

"The back is pretty good. The leg is much better," he said, and he shared the results from Shane's progress report.

"Now that," she said in delight, "is awesome."

"I know," he said. "That's what I was thinking. So, horseback riding would be lovely."

As they walked outside, Robin walked toward them. She was laughing. "Dani, when you said horses were coming, I didn't realize you meant *horses* were coming. I know you said how many but that didn't compute until I actually saw them altogether."

Iain looked at her and said, "Did Dani tell you?"

"Only that she'd offered up pasture for horses to have a spot to run around after being transported," she said. They walked up to one of the gates and just stood and stared at the horses, beautiful chestnuts and palominos and every color under the sun as they moved through the pasture. Some were running; some were kicking up their heels, happy to be out; and some were immediately head down in the grass, and even two were lying down.

"Aren't they beautiful?" Robin said.

"Do you know how to ride?" Dani asked.

Robin shook her head. "City girl all my life," she said. "No opportunity. This was a rich kid's sport."

"Or a poor kid's sport," Dani said, laughing. "I used to ride because I mucked out the stalls, and that was my job."

"I hear you," she said. "We didn't even have horse barns around."

"Interesting." They moved along the pasture with several horses coming over to talk to them, and two of the men came over, shaking hands with Dani.

"You've got a hell of a setup here, Dani," Wesley said.

She nodded. "It's been a long haul to get here, but I'm sure you can understand the joy to be in this position now."

"Absolutely," he said. He looked over at Iain and reached out to shake his hand. "I'm Wesley," he said. "Six of these horses are mine."

"I'm Iain," he said. "One of Dani's current residents upstairs."

"I'm Robin, one of the vet techs who works at the vet clinic downstairs."

The men turned to look at the main building and nodded. "We've heard Dani's done incredible things here."

"Well, I can attest to that," Iain said quietly. "I just had a progress report yesterday, and I'm amazed."

"That's what we like to hear," he said. "I got a nephew who's in bum shape, just returned from Afghanistan. They thought he would come back in a pine box, but he's still kicking."

"When he's ready," Dani said quietly, "send me his name and file, and we'll see if we can get him in."

The man's face worked up with emotion, and he nodded. "Thanks," he said. "I don't know what it costs, but it's not a price any of us have a problem paying if it gets the boy back on his feet."

"Exactly why I do what I do and why our donations are so important," she said. "Because unfortunately a heavy cost is involved in doing this, but it's fairly amazing when you think about just what we can do. And how far these kids and men," she said, with a nod toward Iain, "come. That leg of his was pretty much useless, but he has done very well now."

Just then Stan came out to join them, looking a little bit rough.

"Stan, you haven't had your coffee yet," Dani said with a smile.

"Sure haven't," he said. "But I wouldn't miss a chance to see this many horses all at once." He reached out and shook hands with the two men, then introduced himself as the vet for Hathaway House's animal clinic.

The men nodded and one said, "You've got a great reputation here too."

"Well, if I do," he said, "it's based on a lot of hard work and a lot of heart."

"That it is," one of the men said. "Anybody who works with animals has got to have a lot of heart."

Stan looked at Iain and said, "You have experience with horses, don't you?"

"Yeah," he said, "but not since my accident."

"I'm pretty sure Midnight would let you go for a ride, if you want to give it a try."

"I'd love to," he said, "but what I don't want to do is set back my own healing."

Dani nodded, pulled out her phone, stepped away a few steps, and made a call. Stan stepped forward and said, "I've got a western saddle around here," he said. "I doubt you do English, do you?"

Iain chuckled. "No, my experience is cowboy style," he said. "Give me a western saddle or even bareback." But then, he thought about it and said, "Or maybe not bareback at this point. But, man, I'd love to get back to riding."

"Bareback is hard on the butt," Stan complained. "I can ride well enough," he said, "but horses like this, well, they're just so superb," he murmured in delight as they all stared out at the massive pastures thriving with the visiting horses. Even Appie and Lovely, Midnight and the others, like Molly, had walked over to visit with the new arrivals.

One of the two men looked over and asked, "Is that a llama?"

"She is," Stan said. "She was a rescue and came with Appie the Appaloosa. The two of them have been together since they were born."

"Got to love that," the man said. "I've got a goat at home that won't be separated from my dog. I used to take the dog everywhere but that also meant I had to take the goat. So I leave them both at home now." He shook his head. "The bonds that animals make is just amazing."

"That it is," Stan said. "That it is."

Dani came back a few minutes later and said, "I just talked to Shane, and he says, if you'll just walk the horse on the field—no trotting, no jogging, no galloping—he's all for you getting on the back of a horse."

Iain looked up at her, hope in his eyes, and said, "Seriously?" He looked over at Stan and back at Dani and said, "But do you have a western saddle that might fit?"

"Absolutely," she said. She put her fingers in her mouth and turned toward Midnight and let out a sharp whistle. Midnight's head and ears came up, and he came galloping across the pasture toward her. All the men watched as she walked to the gate and opened it up. Midnight immediately walked out, and she brought him to where Iain was.

"You don't need to put lead on him?"

"No. He knows exactly where he belongs," she said with

a laugh. "Give me about ten minutes, and I'll have him dressed up." She walked with him back to the barn on the side of the pastures at the back. And, while they watched, she threw on a blanket, tossed up a saddle, and put a bridle on his head. With a bit in his mouth, she carefully draped the reins over his back and then walked with Midnight at her side, joining them once more. "The only thing that I don't know," she said, "is how to get you up there."

"Depends on the stirrup length," he said. "And I might manage to get up from a fence post." He stood up on his one leg and said, "I wish I had my crutches right now."

"I'll go get them," Robin said, and she disappeared.

"If I can help, let me know," one of the two men said, stepping forward.

Iain looked at him. He was big enough. He was about his height. "If you can give me a hand to get over to that fence," he said, "I think I can hop up a couple slats and just slide over onto Midnight's back." And, with a stranger's arm around his back, Iain managed to make his way to the fence. There, he climbed up to the top by hopping. Dani led Midnight to him. And, grabbing the pommel, he slid over to the horse's back and sat astride Midnight. The horse shifted ever-so-slightly under his weight, and he put his good leg into the stirrup and then chuckled. "This must be your saddle, Dani. Look at the stirrups."

She laughed because his stump was almost the right size for her stirrups. She walked around and quickly lowered the other stirrup and said, "That's about all I can do on this saddle. I guess I need to find a half dozen more for patients, don't I?"

"This is your horse though," he said. And with a gentle *click* and a nudge of his knee, Midnight shifted forward slightly, but waited for Dani to return. Dani walked to the pasture she'd come out of and opened the gate.

She had a second halter in her hand. "Am I riding your saddle?"

"Yep," she said. She called out to a different horse, and the mare came walking over.

He said, "That one looks like I should be on her, just in case."

"Nope," she said. She tossed the halter up and around, put the bit into the horse's mouth, and, with a smooth movement, hopped onto the back of the mare's withers. At the nudge of her knee, she said, "Let's go for a walk." With Stan and everyone else standing behind at the closed gate, she led Midnight up and around the pasture at a gentle walk.

Iain walked carefully, waiting to see if his hips jarred his back. When he realized the pain was not hitting him every time the horse walked, he settled in. As he settled in, the horse's gait also smoothed out.

"Good," she said. "Midnight is doing just fine. How are you?"

"Well, he's doing fine because I've now calmed down," he said with a pleased smile. "This is truly a gift. I never thought in my best days that I'd ever get on the back of a horse again."

"Well, I sure don't want you out here working and roping calves," she said. "But, as a horse lover, I can certainly relate to it being something you strive to get back to."

"And how," he said. He turned his face up to the sun. "Just even knowing that I'm out here ..."

"I know," she said. "I completely understand."

And he could hear the catch in her voice and knew that she really did. They were out for an hour, and he could feel his back muscles twitching. He looked at her and said, "As much as I don't want to stop …"

"I was about to suggest we go back. Shane said no more than an hour anyway."

"And that was probably a tad too long anyway," he said. "But I don't care. This was truly a momentous day, and I thank you so much for the honor." He leaned forward and gently rubbed Midnight on his big neck, threading his fingers through the silky black mane. "This is your personal horse, isn't he?"

"Yes," she said. "He and I have been together since he was a colt."

"And he's blessed," Iain said. "We don't always have friendships like this."

"No, but you have a friend who drove you from the VA hospital to here. And he did it against his better judgment, and he did it because it's what you wanted to do," she said quietly. "So I wonder if you realize just how hard that was for him."

And then he remembered how he hadn't texted Bruce back. He groaned. "I seem to have forgotten so many things that are really important in life lately," he said.

She chuckled. "You know what? You're not alone in that. It's something that happens on a regular basis to a lot of men here. I don't know why, but it's like, as they move forward in one aspect of their life—and in this case it's the focus on your healing or strengthening your body and getting your movement back—so much else falls by the wayside. I have found that, no matter who the people, they tend to be very forgiving because they know that what you're doing here is super important and takes extreme focus."

"But who said that kind of focus," he said, "meant dropping everything else? Bruce was my best friend for so long, and I haven't yet told him about my progress."

"Well, I have my cell phone," she said. "Do you want me to take a couple pictures?"

He grinned. "I so do." And, with that, as they walked, she took several photographs of him on Midnight. By the time they made it back to the gathered crowd, Midnight backed up to the side of the fence. It was all Iain could do to swing his partial leg over the fence and step onto the railing as he swung his right leg over. He managed to hop down and stand against the fence, but his good leg was trembling. He had a four-foot climb to get back to where the wheelchair was parked. He knew he really needed to make it, but, boy, it looked a hell of a long way away.

Wesley stepped up and said, "I'm here to help."

Iain looked up at him, smiled, and said, "And I'll accept that help. Thank you."

And, with that, the other man gently assisted Iain up the short distance, until he could sit back down in the wheelchair. When he collapsed, he groaned and said, "I so wanted to do that with crutches, but …"

"One of the things I've learned in life," Wesley said, "is you got to take everything one bite at a time. You can't eat a massive smorgasbord at once, but you can take one bite, enjoy it, and then have another bite and enjoy it. This is a journey, and, for you, it's likely to be the only journey you ever need to have in this direction. So, I get that you want to reach the end as fast as possible, but don't forget to take the journey in small bites and to enjoy each and every one."

Chapter 14

TEARS WERE IN Robin's eyes, and she kept wiping them back. But she reached down and gripped Iain's shoulder from behind him. Almost without thinking, he reached up and laced his fingers with hers, and the two just hung on to each other. She was overwhelmed with emotions. The joy on his face when she'd seen him out there on the horse, seeing his body hold him and giving him that moment of joy, she knew that this was just a starting point to even more emotional and joy-filled moments. The fact that he'd gotten on a horse and had made it an hour out there was absolutely phenomenal.

And she knew that, no matter what else he tried to do now, he'd do just fine. He was a special man. He'd gone through so much, and here she was, the one who was not doing as well. And she didn't have any valid reason not to. And she was desperate for him to do well, and, at the same time, she also knew that it could mean he'd move on and move past her. She gripped his fingers even harder, and, when she tried to release his hand, he wouldn't let her go. She smiled and said, "I don't know about you, but I haven't had breakfast."

He looked up at her, then smiled and said, "No, I haven't either."

And, with that, the crowd started to disperse. He'd been

so happy and so proud, as if he'd finally succeeded at something. She walked beside him, her hand still on his shoulder, even as he needed both his hands to push his wheelchair toward the elevator. She could feel the stress in his back with each shove forward. "You know that I could push you," she said hesitantly.

"No. Carry the crutches," he said. "We'll go back to my room and put those away and then head for lunch, if that's okay with you."

"Definitely okay with me," she said. Stan had gone somewhere. She presumed he was still talking with the others, but she knew Iain needed to go relax. "Unless you need to lie down."

"I'll have a nap this afternoon," he said, "but I want to eat out on the deck and watch the horses."

"That we can do." They made their way to his room, where she put away his crutches, and then, walking back at his side, headed over to the cafeteria. A noisy crowd was in the center of it. She looked at him and said, "Do you want me to get food for both of us, while you claim a table out in the sun?"

He hesitated.

She looked at him and said, "There's no need to not accept help again."

"I seem to be bad at that," he said. Then he nodded. "If you wouldn't mind," he said. "We will have to compete for a table out on the deck."

"Go," she said. "Get us one, and I'll come join you in a few minutes." She watched as he headed out, completely okay to do that, and realized just how far he'd come. As she got into line, she grabbed two trays. Dennis was once again at the forefront, serving and talking to everybody as they came by.

He looked at her, smiled, and said, "I saw Iain on the horse."

"Did you see him?" she said with a beaming smile. "That was one happy man."

"And he should be," Dennis said. "He's a good guy." He looked at the food and said, "But I bet he's really hungry now, isn't he?"

"Hungry and very tired," she said. "Not that he'll admit to the last part though."

At that, Dennis chuckled. "No, of course he won't," he said. "That would make life too easy. Men are complex."

"Nah," she said teasingly. "Women are complex. Men are simple."

He beamed a grin at her. "You could be right," he said. "Men just want the basic needs."

"What's that?" she asked. "Beer, ribs, and football?" Several of the men around her cracked grins. Dennis waved a finger at her admonishingly.

She laughed and said, "Good food. He definitely needs good food."

"Well, I've got all kinds of it here today. What would you like?"

She quickly made choices for both of them, with Dennis loading up their plates, and knew she couldn't carry both trays if she loaded them too heavily. So, she put one by the coffee area, carried one out, and then came back and got the other one. By the time she was done, they were both sitting on one side together, the table pushed up against the railing so they could see as much as they could. Iain ate slowly, but his gaze was on the horses.

"I think an awful lot could be done with horses, don't

you?" she asked him.

"Some friends of mine back in New Mexico," he said, "they formed a new company to help veterans get employed, to find a second career, even to build suitable housing for returning vets. I sent one of them an email a while ago, wondering what all their operation did. I haven't even checked to see if he has responded yet."

"And then what?"

"Then," he said. "I was wondering about setting up something like what they have done—but here."

She looked at him in surprise, but something warm and caring wrapped around her heart like a hug. "So, you're thinking about staying close?"

He looked at her, smiled, and said, "That's where you are, isn't it?"

She nodded slowly. "Yes," she said. "That is definitely where I am."

"In that case," he said, "yes, I'm looking at staying somewhere close. We still have a ways to go on this journey of ours, but I'm sure not ready to call it quits." Just then, shouts of laughter came from behind him, interrupting their conversation. He looked at her, smiled, and said, "Eat. We'll talk later."

"Sounds good," she said. And they proceeded to dig into lunch, but her heart was full, and her soul was happy.

IAIN SHOULDN'T HAVE said anything about his plans because he really didn't have any plans; it was more a vague dream. But he'd been emboldened by the horseback ride. He looked at her and said, "It might not work out."

"What might not work out?"

"If I do decide to do something like that."

"It's an idea," she said in surprise. "Ideas are just that. I hope something like that does happen for you. I think you would find a great deal of personal satisfaction in helping others get established."

He nodded slowly. "That's what I was thinking. I know these guys in New Mexico. They've done so much good for other people. I was just thinking it might be nice to do something like that myself."

"So, work toward it," she said. "You're probably not capable of doing it all yet, but that doesn't mean in a few months you won't be."

"After today," he said, "it does feel like I've made some major strides. I'm not there yet, but I'm getting there."

"Is there anything else that you want to work toward?"

"Unless I wake up tomorrow morning," he said jokingly, "and I think this is a terrible idea."

She looked at him steadily. "And, if it is a terrible idea," she said, "maybe what you need to do is look at why you suddenly feel that way. Because it sure doesn't sound like a terrible idea to me."

"Maybe," he said. "Maybe I'll spend some time with that journal and dig a little deeper."

She gave him a fat smile. "You do that."

"And you," he challenged. "What about your journal?"

"I haven't even started," she admitted.

"Well, while I work in mine, you do something for yourself," he said with a smile. "It'd be nice if we both move forward together."

"It would, wouldn't it?" she said. "I need to work on a couple things definitely, so maybe I should."

"No," he said. "Not *maybe*. We've made a lot of progress together. Let's keep that up."

She smiled, then nodded and said, "I can work with that."

"Good," he said. "Now, I hate to ask, but how do you feel about getting us some coffee?"

She chuckled. "I can do that too."

Chapter 15

ROBIN WAS HAPPY that, for the next few weeks, it seemed like there was steady progress. At least on his part. She tried to open that journal because it had been her idea after all. But, every time she did, that blank page just stared back at her, daring her to mark it up. If she really wanted this relationship with Iain to work, she knew she had garbage she should let go of. Everybody did, right?

She could feel the frustration building inside her. She didn't know what she was supposed to do about it and went through the day's motions with a smile plastered on her face. But inside, she held this knowing worry that just maybe, maybe Iain was better off to go forward and to leave her because she hadn't done her work. Maybe she didn't have any pressing work to do, but it just meant that he was that much more progressive about his life, and she felt like she needed to at least have something to offer of herself.

The days were busy and packed with animals coming and going, and, at the end of Wednesday, when she collapsed on her back on the grass outside the vet clinic, propped up on her elbows, and just stared at the pastures and the horses, it seemed like the weekend with the show horses was a long time ago. It had only been two days long, yet still one of the major events that Iain talked about. And she was so happy for him. At the same time though, it left her feeling empty on the inside. She groaned out loud.

"That doesn't sound very positive," Dani's cheerful voice broke through her reverie.

Robin sat up slowly and looked at her. "It's been a rough couple days," she admitted.

Dani nodded. "I hear you. It's been busy upstairs too."

"Still," she said, "what you did for Iain was huge."

"And yet you appear bothered, like something is not quite right," Dani said. She slipped the halter off Midnight, plunked the saddle down on the ground in such a way that it seemed to rest upon air, and walked over closer. "Everything okay between the two of you?"

"Yes," Robin said. "It's just that I feel like he's doing so much and making progress in leaps and bounds ..."

"And you feel like you're supposed to be doing something to keep up with him?"

She shrugged. "When you put it that way, it sounds stupid."

"It is stupid," Dani said. "It's not a competition."

"I know that," she said. "I don't feel competitive. That feels wrong. But it also feels like I should be doing some prep work myself."

Dani looked at her for a long moment. "Where's this coming from?"

"Inside," Robin said instantly. "It was my idea to buy the journals. I thought that maybe I had some issues to work on."

"Remember that you can only work on things when you're ready to work on them," Dani said slowly. "No good can come from pushing something like that."

"But what if I don't quite get there?" she asked. "Or are we back to the fact that things have to happen in the right time?"

"What makes you think anything's broken inside?" Dani asked. She squatted in front of Robin. "You seem well-adjusted. You're healthy. You haven't been tossing yourself at every man who comes by. You've picked somebody stable and steady and who has a wonderful spirit," she said warmly. "Why is it you feel like you need to be working on you?"

"Because everybody has something to work on," she said.

"I get that," Dani said. "We all have issues. We all have childhood traumas. We all have resentments, and we all feel guilty for something. But again, those aren't things that you can just pull out and say, *Today I'll deal with this.* A trigger usually happens, that sets off something, and then you grab it and say, *Okay, now that you've shown me the light, I'm dealing with it.*"

"And in the meantime?"

"Maybe you should be asking yourself why you feel like you need to do this."

"You're right. I need to be doing something for myself."

"Or what?" Dani asked, still prodding.

She took a deep breath and said, "Or I'm not as good as him."

Dani's eyebrows shot up. "So, it's not a case of being in a competition but suffering a judgment?"

"No," Robin said, shaking her head. Then she stopped and said, "Well, kind of." Confusion filtered through her. "I don't know what I'm saying," she cried out.

"And that's the issue facing you right now," Dani said. "Forget about all your history. What you need to work out is why you feel that you need to be working on you in order to catch up to or to be as good as Iain."

And, with that, she grabbed her saddle and walked toward the barn, leaving Robin sitting in the grass, staring out at the pastures all around her. Is that what this was all about? Because, in her logical mind, she knew that was garbage. But, inside her heart of hearts, she did wonder if maybe, maybe she wasn't as good as him. She wasn't applying herself as hard or as effectively as he was. He hadn't seen any progress and figured there wasn't any to have, and then, all of a sudden, he'd come up with all kinds of progress. Would it be the same for her? And why is it that she felt like she needed to have that same kind of progress? She hadn't been through anywhere near the trauma he had.

Confused and wearing herself out emotionally, she got up and slowly walked to her apartment. She had a shower to help relieve some of the stress still settling on her shoulders, and, rather than going out and grabbing food, she grabbed her journal and sat outside in her small rear patio. She opened a bottle of sparkling water and sat in the shade and wrote down some of the words that Dani had said. As she started, her pen picked up and moved faster and faster and faster. By the time she finally drained her brain of whatever rolled around in there, she had to shake her hand out from cramping.

But inside, she was elated. Because *this* was what she had wanted. She had had her breakthrough. However, some-where in her stream of consciousness rambling was the *something underneath* that consequently had to be worked on. She glanced through her writing, hoping to read whatev-er were the important parts, hoping she could still decipher her own writing done so fast and so sloppily.

The main question was, *Why did she feel not good enough?*

Granted, her ex made her feel less than, but even now, not a full year later, she already knew that their relationship was not healthy, was not right, was not good for either of them. So she felt like she had a handle on that event. Yet the same thing was coming up now with Iain. Why did she think she was not good enough for him? Why this recurring judgment?

Robin had previously thought something in her present situation was the trigger, which trigger issue Dani had brought up earlier today.

It wasn't Robin's present situation at issue at all. It was her past. Her response just kept recurring, like with her ex, like now with Iain. That was her underlying problem that she needed to address right now. Because she knew one thing for sure. Iain would be quite unhappy if he thought his breakthroughs and recent successes were the trigger to finding where her current problem issue lay.

But the fact of the matter was, she had been working on the exact same issue inside her that Iain had been dealing with here at Hathaway House: feeling the pressure to succeed, seeing others' successes, and not having some of it and yet wanting it.

Instead, for Robin, a whole other issue lay beyond that had to be reopened and dealt with.

As she stared at the words on the page, she realized how absolutely incredibly stupid it all was. Iain would be angry to think that she was feeling less than him because he'd finally started to make progress. To Iain, there was no downside to his recent successes. He would be hurt to hear that from her. *From her*, who was standing beside him in so many ways, but … wasn't really happy for him? Even she ached when she thought that.

But she knew that wasn't the truth. She didn't want to derail him, and she sure didn't want to disappoint him. She had to fix this. *Now.*

Right now.

And, in fact, it was almost conceited, arrogant of herself. He'd been through so much and had survived and done so well, something that she knew she couldn't have done even half as well as he had. And she'd been sympathetic and wanting him to get that same breakthrough. So was this all talk and no real heartfelt sentiment?

Then, as soon as he made major strides at really healing himself, she had immediately felt less than him. She shook her head, wondering where all this came from. Then she had reached back, far back into her life, pinpointing a couple times in her childhood where a judgment, then a grief—or was it vice versa?—had overwhelmed her senses.

She found it in her rambling writings. *Like when her mother had passed away. Like when her brother had been kicked out of the house at sixteen, leaving Robin alone with her father and his new wife.*

At the time, Robin's grief had warred with her anger and her judgment and had left Robin feeling like *Robin* wasn't important enough for her mother to stick around. It made no sense. Not to the adult and grown-up Robin. Her mother didn't choose to die. Her mother didn't choose to leave Robin and Keith. Yet her mother's death felt that way to Robin back then as a child—and maybe to an extent still did. How sad was that?

Her brother and father had never got along, and she knew Keith had been just as devastated when their mother had passed away. Her father had turned to alcohol to handle his sorrows, then to a much younger woman, much to her and Keith's disgust. She had tried so hard to stay in Keith's life, refusing to let him go too, even when she knew that he had nothing to do with the rest of the family.

Then, when Keith had joined the military, she'd moved out of her father's house into Keith's place. Maybe to be closer to him. And that helped distance her from the rough homelife of her father's new family, where she was not accepted once more, where she didn't belong either. And it was hard to look back to all those long-ago years and realize how much of that little girl still remained inside Robin and how much these memories triggered her right now because she'd felt *less than good enough* way back then and still felt the same way right now.

It was all so stupid.

She sighed, leaned back, and said, "I wonder if we ever grow up fully." Because really, she wasn't sure that there was any such thing. It's like people took steps forward and then fell back into old childhood patterns. She was thinking she was doing okay but had a few things to deal with, and look at what popped out.

But now she felt more at peace inside. She wasn't done yet, but she was getting there.

She let out a big sigh. This wasn't about Iain. She had never been jealous of his successes. Not in any way. She just wanted to be the best Robin she could be for a worthy man who was giving his all to be the best Iain he could be. He deserved no less. And she now knew that she was plenty good enough for him. She smiled as the tears gathered.

This was the tough part, facing down her demons. The rest is easier. Just look at Iain. She wiped away her tears, but her smile remained.

She put down the journal, threw back the last of her sparkling water, and walked out for dinner. And realized it was almost the end of the dinner hour. She shook her head in surprise and quickened her pace.

As soon as she got to the cafeteria, Dennis raised his eyebrows. "And here I thought you'd be with Iain."

"I was delayed," she explained. She looked at the little bit of food left. Most people had eaten and were now sitting and talking. "Wow," she said. "Did all those horse people from the weekend come back here and clean us out?"

"Not sure what's going on," he said, "but a lot of people were here today."

"I hadn't even realized what time it was," she said. "I've just been so busy." She looked at the food in front of her and said, "Oh my, was it fish and chips today?"

"Well, the chips are looking a little less than perfect right now," he said, "but this is a fresh batch of fish."

She immediately held out her plate and said, "Any coleslaw to go with that?"

He smiled and gave her a big dollop of it. "What else?"

She shook her head. "This might be enough." She walked to the side, dumped vinegar all over her fish, picked up a fork and knife, and headed out to the shade. She wanted to be alone today. She wanted to be away from everyone. She could feel eyes on her, and she didn't know if it was Iain or Dani or someone else. But, for the first time, she understood the need to be alone and the need to just exist without having to give an explanation of what had gone on. It was amazing just what silence of the mind could do. It felt right. By the time she had eaten her fish and coleslaw, she pushed her plate back to the side. It was good, but she'd had enough.

Almost immediately Dennis was there, and he scooped up the empty plate and asked, "More?"

She shook her head. "No, that was wonderful." Then she

looked at his hand and asked, "What is that?"

"Pineapple cheesecake," he said with a fat smile, and he put it down in front of her.

She stared at it, looked at him, and said, "What if I'm dieting?"

"It's a small piece, but I can take it away if you want," he said. Almost instantly the plate disappeared.

"No, no, no," she protested. He chuckled and put it back down, and he disappeared instead. She stared at the dessert, wondering how he could have known that cheesecake was one of her favorites. When he returned a few minutes later with a small china teapot and a cup, she realized just how much he noticed about people. She said, "You'll make me cry."

"No," he said. "No crying. I've already had a lot of that. But if you want a hug …"

Immediately she bounced to her feet, and he reached out and gave her a gentle hug.

"Don't know what's bothering you today," he said, "but tomorrow is a whole new day."

She smiled, feeling the tears in the corner of her eyes, and she nodded. "It is indeed," she said. "And I hadn't realized just how much I need that tomorrow to come."

"It'll all be okay," he said. "I hope it's not anything wrong with you and Iain?"

She shook her head. "As far as I know, it isn't," she said. "Just some other stupid stuff."

"It's always stupid stuff," he said. "When you break it all apart and take a look at the little bits and pieces, you'd be surprised at just how much stupid stuff it really is."

Seated again, she realized how innocent-sounding and yet how very important Dennis's words were because all this in her mind had built up to something *huge*, and yet it really wasn't. Even feeling that *hugeness*, what she heard from Dennis was something about how she could break it down into smaller bites and deal with it. And she was grateful, not for his intervention, but for his final words to help her put some of this to rest.

When she poured her cup of tea, a shadow fell across her face. She didn't even have to look up to know. "There you are," she said in a teasing voice.

"I wondered if you wanted to be alone," he said quietly.

"I did," she said with a nod. "So, thank you for that. But I'm okay now." He looked at her with worry on his face. She smiled, seeing the gentle giant for who he was. A man, as Dani had said, with a good heart. "Just some troubling thoughts."

"Anything I can help with?"

"No," she said with a shake. "Just a few things I needed to work out for myself."

"And you're good?"

"I'm good," she said. "Look what Dennis brought me."

He stared down on the cheesecake, then looked over at Dennis. "How come you got cheesecake?" he protested, his voice ever-so-slightly louder.

"Well, if you ask him nicely, he might bring you a piece."

"Nah," he said. "I think he saves the best pieces for the girls."

"That's such a sexist remark," she said, chuckling.

"But you know it's true," he said. Yet his grin was wide and infectious.

She smiled at him. "I really am grateful that you came here to Hathaway House."

He stared at her in astonishment, and his smile fell away. He reached across and grabbed her hand. "That's the nicest thing anybody has said to me," he said, his gaze focused on her.

She squeezed his fingers, then dug her fork into the cheesecake, held it up, and said, "You want the first bite?"

He looked at it, looked at her regretfully, then shook his head and said, "No, it's yours. Go ahead."

"But the thing about me is," she said, "I can see a treat like this and realize that two people can enjoy it." And so, she held the first bite out once more. Obediently he opened his mouth, and she popped it in. He closed his eyes, and a happy sigh escaped.

"I do love cheesecake," he muttered.

She chuckled, and they shared the small piece between them, like a special treat. When it was gone, she put the plate off to the side, fork on top, and slowly drew her tea closer. They were still holding hands, something that she really enjoyed. She looked at his thumb, seeing the calluses of a working man's hand versus hers, which were usually kept in very good repair, except for scratches from various animals. She hated to wear gloves, and she always felt that the animals needed the skin-to-skin contact to help calm them down.

"So, what was causing you all that trouble?"

"Just realizing," she said, "that it's okay for somebody to do really well and for the other one to do not so well and then have the roles reversed. It's okay to be jealous for a little bit, and it's okay to acknowledge that jealousy was really something else and then to step past it." She looked at him and smiled. "See? Big thoughts."

He squeezed her fingers and slowly slid his hand away. "You know something? That's one of the things that I was thinking about. Not the same thing, but I heard from Badger."

Her eyebrows rose. "What did he have to say?" She leaned in eagerly.

"He thought that setting up a center like he had done was a perfect idea," he said slowly. "He even had a couple suggestions of who to contact here locally and also contacts about possible grant money." He looked at her a little dazed. "I really didn't expect that."

"And yet I think that's what Badger does, isn't it? And if he can help you help a dozen others, then his job has just multiplied with even greater benefits."

He smiled, nodded, and said, "It's still early yet though. I need months more here."

"And I'm glad to share this time with you while you are here," she said, "because you'll get what you need to fully heal and because I really enjoy having dinner together."

"So, maybe dinner on a long-term basis?"

She looked up at him and could feel a flush rising on her cheeks. "I'm game," she said, tilting her head. "What about you?"

"There's a lot about life that I could face alone, but I would much prefer to have someone at my side. Someone who's *you*."

"Knowing that you can face it alone," she said, with a knowing smile, "allows you the freedom to not have to."

"Exactly," he said. "I'm not 100 percent by any means."

"You're right," she said. "You're more than 100 percent. You had been knocked back about 30 percent, then picked yourself up, and moved forward at such a fast pace to exceed 100 percent. So I know you're well past where you were when you first came in here."

He looked at her, smiled, lifted her fingers, and kissed the tips. "That's one way of looking at it. I think you're biased though."

"It's the best way to look at it," she said. "I couldn't care less about your legs, the one missing a foot or the one that's being strengthened right now. I know your history comes with baggage, and apparently mine does too." And she chuckled. "It's all about tomorrow and every other tomorrow ahead of us."

"I do have some friends in town," he said. "I think I mentioned Bruce to you."

"Yes, and?"

"He's coming by for a visit next weekend," he said. "I'd really like you to meet him. I've told him so much about you."

"You did call him back?"

"I did, and I sent him the pictures that Dani had taken. At that point in time, Bruce wouldn't take any more no-talking from me," he said, laughing. "He knows me too well. I'm starting to feel whole again. I think that's what all this means. I'm starting to feel balanced and grounded, with a real future before me."

"As long as that future," she said, "involves me in some way, then I'm perfectly okay for that to happen."

"I was hoping you'd say that," he said gently. "And, if you were any closer," he said, "I'd attempt to kiss you, but we do have a table between us."

Instantly she got up and walked around the table to sit in his lap.

He burst out laughing at her spontaneity.

She chuckled, leaned over, and whispered, "Did you mean it?"

"Oh, I meant it," he said. "Will you be part of my future? Will you be part of my life? You're already part of my heart, and my soul already knows where you belong."

She nodded and smiled, then gently stroked his lips and said, "My soul knows too."

He reached up, and she leaned down. And when their lips aligned, it was like a promise coming true. When she lifted her head, she heard cheers from everybody around them. She looked out in astonishment, the whole cafeteria full of people listening and watching them. She reached up to clap a hand to her red cheeks, but Dennis just chuckled. He came over with a huge piece of cheesecake for both of them to share in the celebration and said, "That's what we like to see. Happy endings."

Epilogue

JADEN HANCOCK STARED at the email from his buddy. He typed in a quick response. **Is this for real, or are you just full of crap?** He sent it back just as fast. He watched and waited until he got a reply. Iain had been at Hathaway House for several months now. Jaden had heard a few intermittent responses but nothing major, until this one where Iain said he was a new man, and his life was great. If there was any way Jaden could make it happen, he should be coming to Hathaway House too. But, instead of an email coming in, his phone buzzed. He stared at it in surprise and said, "Iain, is that you?"

"It is," said the boisterous voice of his old friend. "And, no, I'm not full of shit. I've done a tremendous amount of growth and improvement here. Coming to Hathaway House was the best thing I could have done."

"Just because it was good for you doesn't mean I should do it," Jaden said cautiously. "I don't travel well."

"Then don't take a truck, like I did," Iain urged immediately. "You know how I felt about that. It was the worst mistake ever. It put me back weeks."

"Well, I don't have a whole lot of choice," he said. "I'm not sure exactly how I would get there, but just traveling alone would probably kill my back."

"And I also know that you think this is as far as you can

go and that you've already adapted and that you've already moved on, so why bother? I'm here to tell you that you can go a whole lot further physically."

"Says you," Jaden scoffed.

"Absolutely, I say so. I've got a call in to Lance too because I think both of you in particular could do well here."

"Maybe. But just the thought of having new medical staff and of starting all over again, trying to explain the problems, the difficulties, and the pain …"

"I get it," Iain said. "I really do. I just don't want you to shortchange what could be much improved on a physical level. I'll send you some photos here in a minute. Of course they're not terribly pretty, but they show the progress on my leg. And it exceeds the progress we were told to expect."

"Sure, but you had surgery. You've had lots of improvements. You're as good as you'll get."

"No, that's the mentality from where you're at," Iain said quietly. "I'm at a much further place."

"So, does that mean you're done with rehab now?"

"No, not quite," Iain said, "but I can see the end in sight."

"You certainly sound different," Jaden said with a frown. His buddy really did sound good, healthy, happy. He sounded like he was a completely new person. "What brought that about?"

"A lot of things," Iain admitted. "A partner for one. My physical health back for another. My future. All of those things are dead important."

"Did you land a partner?" Jaden sagged in his wheelchair in a daze. "I thought you figured that would never happen?"

"And I figured wrong," Iain said firmly. "Along with my mind-set, I needed to shift a lot. And sometimes, when you're stuck in the same place, you just don't see how different some other place can be."

"It's not so bad here."

"You want to stay there?"

"No," Jaden said, looking around. "It's pretty crowded, and it's starting to look like we're all the same."

"So come here," Iain urged. "Try something different."

"How different?" Jaden asked. He stared down at his hands and wondered what happened to the big, stalwart, and strapping young man he'd been, up for any new adventure possible. Ever since he'd been injured, his world had coalesced into this little tiny circle around him.

In a way, it was how he liked it. It was safe. The thought of moving to a new state, moving to a whole new medical team where he'd have to be reinterviewed and reexamined and poked and prodded all over again was enough to make the bile rise up the back of his throat and to give an instinctive and immediate *no* to the plan. But he also knew that Iain had been in a very similar position as Jaden. And, if Iain had had progress, what were the chances of progress for Jaden?

Then he shook his head. No, there wouldn't be any because this was definitely a case of there was no more progress available for Jaden. He'd already become as good as he could get. He wouldn't get any better, even if here—or there—a little bit longer.

While he listened, Iain talked about the food and the pool and the people and the animals. Jaden was more than a little shocked. When he finally put down the phone at the end of their conversation, Jaden stared out the window. He was sitting in a large lounge, and about twelve of them were watching a football game on TV. All of their wheelchairs were lined up, like geriatric patients. People had gotten into the same mind-set here, and that's what he understood now that Iain had seen for himself in places like this.

Jaden had become part of the norm, and that norm became his reality, and anything else looked scary and different and impossible to achieve. He wheeled himself back ever-so-slightly, trying to distance himself a little bit, to see just what was possible.

When his phone buzzed again, he looked down to see images of Iain's leg—the original leg, which he'd certainly seen right after his buddy's surgery. That hamburger blue-black and red gross-looking thing was supposed to be a leg, and then several more photos popped up, showing the improvements. Jaden stared in surprise. Of course his own leg would heal naturally anyway, and it would look a whole lot better with time, even if he stayed here. But when he got to the next picture of Iain's leg, where it showed a strong and fit, heavily muscled leg, followed then by the picture of Iain himself standing on a prosthetic, with no wheelchair or crutches, and a beautiful woman at his side, Jaden's heart lurched.

Crap, he badly wanted something like that for himself. His one good leg was okay. As for his other leg, the doctors had managed to save it, but it was a facsimile of the hamburger that Iain had started with. But just to think that maybe Jaden wouldn't need crutches or a wheelchair down the road? That would be incredible.

He stared at the wheelchair in the first picture of Iain's leg for a long moment. And then, with determination, Jaden headed back to his room. Somewhere had to be an application online or a phone number that he could call and see about getting in that same center. He sent his buddy a text.

Put in a good word for me, he said. **If there's a space, I really want my name on that next available bed.**

It's as good as done came back the instant response. **Now, phone them, and then send in your application with whatever medical crap they need. You won't regret it. I can promise you that.**

This concludes Books 7–9 of Hathaway House.

Read about Jaden: Hathaway House, Book 10

Hathaway House: Jaden (Book #10)

Welcome to Hathaway House. Rehab Center. Safe Haven. Second chance at life and love.

Jaden Hancock knows that things could be a lot worse. He still has two arms and two legs, even if one of his legs is so badly damaged it's virtually useless. And it's not that he isn't willing to work toward recovery—it's just hard to see the lack of progress even after weeks of therapy. While he knows that he needs to accept the current state of his body, that acceptance feels like giving up. And he's not prepared to do that.

Brianna Kole crossed the country to get away from her old life. As the newest member of the staff at Hathaway House, she's polite but not overly friendly. The last thing she wants is to get attached and to risk getting hurt again. But, in spite of her reservations, she and Jaden gravitate to each other as the two newcomers to the facility. After that, it isn't long before Brianna's questioning her feelings … and his.

Find Book 10 here!

To find out more visit Dale Mayer's website.

https://geni.us/DMJadenUniversal

Author's Note

Thank you for reading Hathaway House, Books 7–9! If you enjoyed the books, please take a moment and leave a short review.

Dear reader,

I love to hear from readers, and you can contact me at my website: www.dalemayer.com or at my Facebook author page. To be informed of new releases and special offers, sign up for my newsletter or follow me on BookBub. And if you are interested in joining Dale Mayer's Reader Group, here is the Facebook sign up page.
http://geni.us/DaleMayerFBGroup

Cheers,
Dale Mayer

About the Author

Dale Mayer is a *USA Today* best-selling author, best known for her SEALs military romances, her Psychic Visions series, and her Lovely Lethal Garden cozy series. Her contemporary romances are raw and full of passion and emotion (Broken But ... Mending, Hathaway House series). Her thrillers will keep you guessing (Kate Morgan, By Death series), and her romantic comedies will keep you giggling (*It's a Dog's Life*, a stand-alone novella; and the Broken Protocols series, starring Charming Marvin, the cat).

Dale honors the stories that come to her—and some of them are crazy, break all the rules and cross multiple genres!

To go with her fiction, she also writes nonfiction in many different fields, with books available on résumé writing, companion gardening, and the US mortgage system. All her books are available in print and ebook format.

Connect with Dale Mayer Online

Dale's Website – www.dalemayer.com

Twitter – @DaleMayer

Facebook Page – geni.us/DaleMayerFBFanPage

Facebook Group – geni.us/DaleMayerFBGroup

BookBub – geni.us/DaleMayerBookbub

Instagram – geni.us/DaleMayerInstagram

Goodreads – geni.us/DaleMayerGoodreads

Newsletter – geni.us/DaleNews

Also by Dale Mayer

Published Adult Books:

Hathaway House
Aaron, Book 1
Brock, Book 2
Cole, Book 3
Denton, Book 4
Elliot, Book 5
Finn, Book 6
Gregory, Book 7
Heath, Book 8
Iain, Book 9
Jaden, Book 10
Keith, Book 11
Lance, Book 12
Melissa, Book 13
Nash, Book 14
Hathaway House, Books 1–3
Hathaway House, Books 4–6
Hathaway House, Books 7–9

The K9 Files
Ethan, Book 1
Pierce, Book 2
Zane, Book 3
Blaze, Book 4
Lucas, Book 5

Into the Abyss
Seeds of Malice
Eye of the Falcon
Itsy-Bitsy Spider
Unmasked
Deep Beneath
From the Ashes
Stroke of Death
Ice Maiden
Psychic Visions Books 1–3
Psychic Visions Books 4–6
Psychic Visions Books 7–9

By Death Series
Touched by Death
Haunted by Death
Chilled by Death
By Death Books 1–3

Broken Protocols – Romantic Comedy Series
Cat's Meow
Cat's Pajamas
Cat's Cradle
Cat's Claus
Broken Protocols 1-4

Broken and... Mending
Skin
Scars
Scales (of Justice)
Broken but… Mending 1-3

Glory

Genesis

Tori

Celeste

Glory Trilogy

Biker Blues

Morgan: Biker Blues, Volume 1

Cash: Biker Blues, Volume 2

SEALs of Honor

Mason: SEALs of Honor, Book 1

Hawk: SEALs of Honor, Book 2

Dane: SEALs of Honor, Book 3

Swede: SEALs of Honor, Book 4

Shadow: SEALs of Honor, Book 5

Cooper: SEALs of Honor, Book 6

Markus: SEALs of Honor, Book 7

Evan: SEALs of Honor, Book 8

Mason's Wish: SEALs of Honor, Book 9

Chase: SEALs of Honor, Book 10

Brett: SEALs of Honor, Book 11

Devlin: SEALs of Honor, Book 12

Easton: SEALs of Honor, Book 13

Ryder: SEALs of Honor, Book 14

Macklin: SEALs of Honor, Book 15

Corey: SEALs of Honor, Book 16

Warrick: SEALs of Honor, Book 17

Tanner: SEALs of Honor, Book 18

Jackson: SEALs of Honor, Book 19

Kanen: SEALs of Honor, Book 20

Nelson: SEALs of Honor, Book 21

Taylor: SEALs of Honor, Book 22

Colton: SEALs of Honor, Book 23
Troy: SEALs of Honor, Book 24
Axel: SEALs of Honor, Book 25
SEALs of Honor, Books 1–3
SEALs of Honor, Books 4–6
SEALs of Honor, Books 7–10
SEALs of Honor, Books 11–13
SEALs of Honor, Books 14–16
SEALs of Honor, Books 17–19
SEALs of Honor, Books 20–22

Heroes for Hire
Levi's Legend: Heroes for Hire, Book 1
Stone's Surrender: Heroes for Hire, Book 2
Merk's Mistake: Heroes for Hire, Book 3
Rhodes's Reward: Heroes for Hire, Book 4
Flynn's Firecracker: Heroes for Hire, Book 5
Logan's Light: Heroes for Hire, Book 6
Harrison's Heart: Heroes for Hire, Book 7
Saul's Sweetheart: Heroes for Hire, Book 8
Dakota's Delight: Heroes for Hire, Book 9
Michael's Mercy (Part of Sleeper SEAL Series)
Tyson's Treasure: Heroes for Hire, Book 10
Jace's Jewel: Heroes for Hire, Book 11
Rory's Rose: Heroes for Hire, Book 12
Brandon's Bliss: Heroes for Hire, Book 13
Liam's Lily: Heroes for Hire, Book 14
North's Nikki: Heroes for Hire, Book 15
Anders's Angel: Heroes for Hire, Book 16
Reyes's Raina: Heroes for Hire, Book 17
Dezi's Diamond: Heroes for Hire, Book 18
Vince's Vixen: Heroes for Hire, Book 19

SEALs of Steel

The Mavericks

Lennox, Book 10
Gavin, Book 11
Shane, Book 12

Bullard's Battle Series
Ryland's Reach, Book 1
Cain's Cross, Book 2
Eton's Escape, Book 3
Garret's Gambit, Book 4
Kano's Keep, Book 5
Fallon's Flaw, Book 6
Quinn's Quest, Book 7
Bullard's Beauty, Book 8

Collections
Dare to Be You...
Dare to Love...
Dare to be Strong...
RomanceX3

Standalone Novellas
It's a Dog's Life
Riana's Revenge
Second Chances

Published Young Adult Books:

Family Blood Ties Series
Vampire in Denial
Vampire in Distress
Vampire in Design
Vampire in Deceit
Vampire in Defiance

Vampire in Conflict
Vampire in Chaos
Vampire in Crisis
Vampire in Control
Vampire in Charge
Family Blood Ties Set 1–3
Family Blood Ties Set 1–5
Family Blood Ties Set 4–6
Family Blood Ties Set 7–9
Sian's Solution, A Family Blood Ties Series Prequel
    Novelette

Design series
Dangerous Designs
Deadly Designs
Darkest Designs
Design Series Trilogy

Standalone
In Cassie's Corner
Gem Stone (a Gemma Stone Mystery)
Time Thieves

Published Non-Fiction Books:

Career Essentials
Career Essentials: The Résumé
Career Essentials: The Cover Letter
Career Essentials: The Interview
Career Essentials: 3 in 1